CITY OF DAY

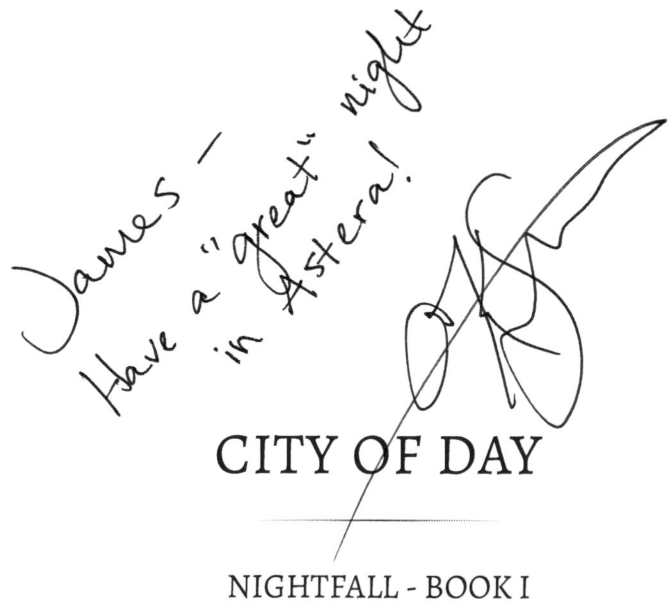

CITY OF DAY

NIGHTFALL - BOOK I

OCTOBER K SANTERELLI

Cover Design by Justin Glanville

To Tutu.
Now everyone knows you exist.

And to Mr. Todd from 2nd and 3rd grade.
You're the reason I love words.

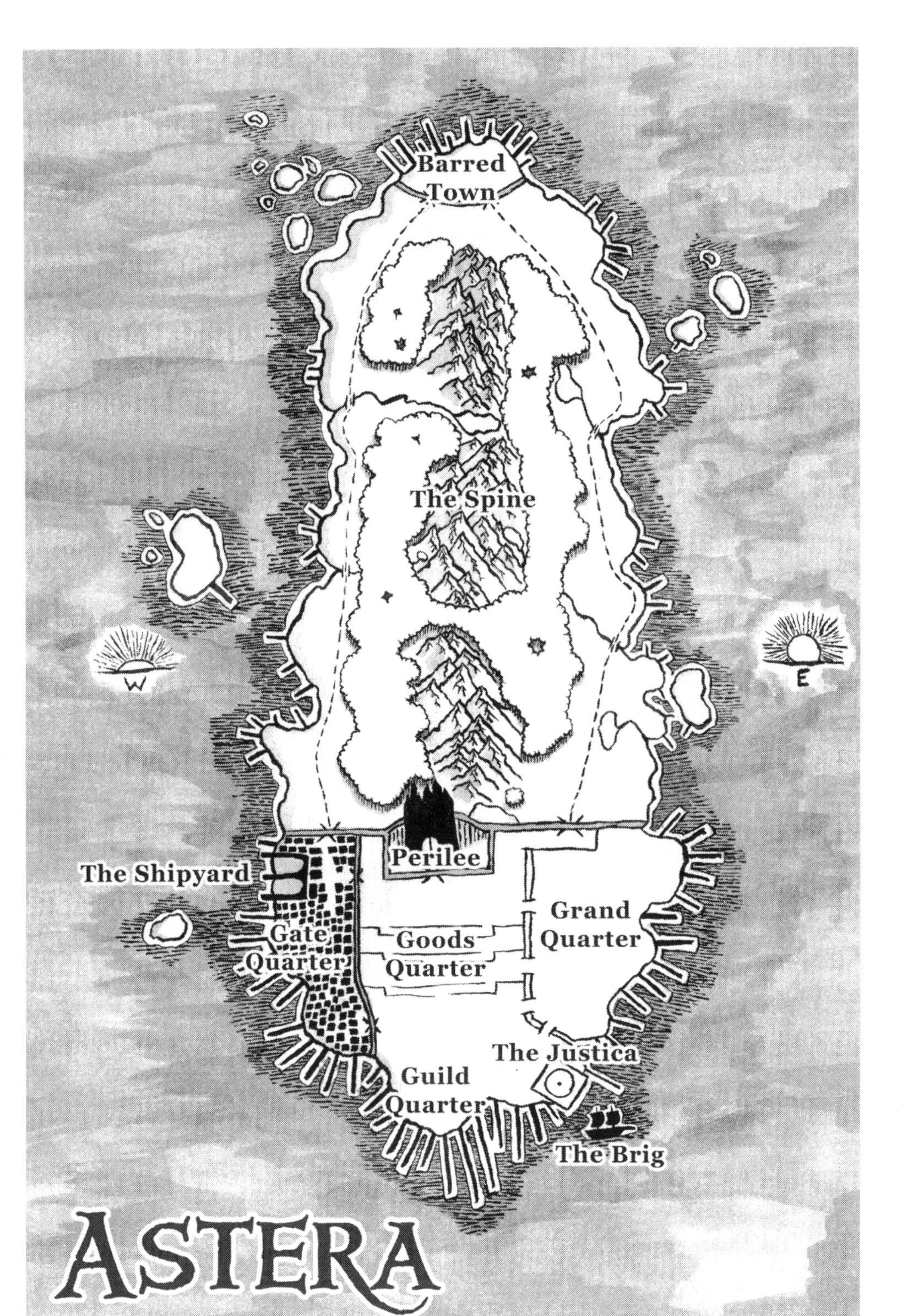
Barred Town
The Spine
W
E
Perilee
The Shipyard
Grand Quarter
Gate Quarter
Goods Quarter
The Justica
Guild Quarter
The Brig
ASTERA

1

I'm going to miss the damn boat!

Thislen knew it was true. Still, he ran down the cobbled street as fast as his feet could carry him. His cloak snapped like a banner in his wake. His breath sawed in and out of his lungs. The smell of his own sweat filled the air and glued his shirt to his back. The thunder of his pulse in his ears muffled everything around him. It sounded like a war drum, insisting that he match its pace. *Run faster, boy, or face the peril to come,* it whispered. The stabbing stitch in his side argued with his heart, begging him to slow down with every throb. He didn't dare listen. A tangled knot of dread in the pit of his stomach spurred him forward. To give up now meant death.

The dead are coming.

The city was empty and silent. The only sound was that of his passage echoing off the stones of every dark house and shuttered shop. The occupants were already gone, safely stowed away on their ships.

Too many mistakes today, and all of them leading up to this. Why did you try to steal that damn pie? He berated himself. His failed attempt to steal the hot, flakey meat pie that had smelled so wonderfully of gravy and fat had attracted the shopkeep's attention. Of course, the man then called for the City Guard. Thislen had been forced to run inland through the warren of Astera's streets to avoid them—and he still hadn't eaten. He tried to steal an apple next and was spotted again. A whole day lost and not a single coin in his pocket or morsel to eat. If he hadn't tried to steal the fruit, he wouldn't have had to hide in the cemetery to avoid the Guard. If he hadn't hidden in the cemetery, he wouldn't have seen his father's grave.

His father's final resting place had been too long neglected, tucked away in a weed-choked corner of the graveyard. Thislen hadn't stopped by in moons. He knew it was foolish to sit down and pull the ivy from the headstone. He knew he shouldn't have used the knife from his boot to dig dirt out of the epitaph. He knew he shouldn't have sat down at all! The sun had already been sinking. It had been too late in the afternoon, and he was too tired and too hungry.

Thislen had fallen asleep. When he jerked awake to the last tolling of the bells from the Justica down by the water's edge, he *knew*. The sun hung too low in the sky. It was going to be impossible to get to the docks in time.

It was a mistake already made.

"Idiot!" Thislen spat as he tore around another corner. It didn't help. He had already lost too much time. Astera's streets were a maze under the best of circumstances, let alone when you were running for your life. *What the hells was I thinking?*

The scent of the sea always filled the air of the tiny island kingdom, but it grew rank with rotted fish and the sour smell of algae-slick wood as he neared the docks. The discordant clang of a ship's bell rang somewhere just out of sight - a final call to any left on land. His heart rose in his chest, and he put on a burst of speed.

Maybe I can make it after all! With any luck, his ancestors were looking out for him.

Thislen rounded a corner so quickly his feet slid out from under him, sending him careening into a shop's wooden sign with a clatter. He fell. Hard. His elbow throbbed as he rolled back to his feet and turned toward the docks, struggling free of the tangle of his cloak only to discover he was too late.

He had missed the damn boat.

Docks, piers, and quays were built along every inch of the city's shoreline, broad fingers of wood and stone stretching into the sea as if they, too, wanted to escape the island of Astera and the city that shared its name. Each was capable of holding several large ships at berth. Each stood utterly empty, their occupants floating just off-shore with their sails lowered and lashed for the night—except one.

The last ship anywhere near land pulled free of the pier's end. Its half-furled sails snapped as they caught the breeze, moving sluggishly into the open water. Even if he ran as quick as lightning struck, Thislen would not make it to the ship before it left the docks behind. He had no hope of swimming after it, either. Being caught in the water after the sun set was far, far worse than being caught on land. What lay beneath the waves at night would drown you slowly. At least the shore promised a quick death.

Thislen stood frozen between the buildings, chilled to the bone by more than the evening's cool air. The wind whipped past, wrapping his cloak around him as if it sought to comfort him in his final moments. He stared blankly at his last safe haven as it drifted toward the fleet of ships bobbing at anchor in the waters around the city.

There's no reaching any of them now.

He turned to the looming buildings of Astera, craning his head back to study the castle set into the side of the mountain above, his hood falling away from his face. The great spires of the keep caught the last rays of the fading sun with a flash. They glinted and gleamed even as darkness drew its shadows close, like a fish trying to elude a net for as long as possible.

Time is running out. The thought spurred Thislen to action. He paced, pushing a hand through his short, dark hair. Equally dark eyes scanned the cobblestoned street as his mind raced. The thief paused again, looking up at the distant walls of the castle. They called it *Perilee,* the pearl. The treasure of the island. Thislen glared at it as if it had brought this upon him out of some malevolence.

He plucked anxiously at the collar of his cloak and the front of his dark gray shirt, the sweat of his exertions prickling against his skin as it chilled. His heart felt cold beneath his ribs. It hadn't slowed its thunderous pace one bit.

I am not dying here. I have to find a way off this damn rock! More important, Thislen had to do it without touching the water. He didn't have a boat. *This is impossible! It isn't like I could* make *a—*

The shipyard! The shipyard in the Gate Quarter. Every floating vessel on the island was built there, from the flat-bottomed river scows the miners used to the three-masted ships for long sea journeys. If Thislen had any hope of finding something that would float until dawn, that was where he needed to go.

He ran through the streets once more, coursing like a hound on the hunt. A glance over his shoulder as he left the shore behind showed the sun sinking into the sea, a dome of burning orange behind the naked forest of silhouetted ships.

The streets themselves were quiet. The houses leaned in, dark and unfeeling as he passed, the glimmer of fading light flashing in their windows. The faint creak of a sign above a door and the skitter of parchment across the stones seemed to whisper about him as he passed, mourning him in hushed tones. Shadows were the only things gathering in the streets of Astera to watch him as daylight vanished. No one lit lanterns in a city no one slept in.

His boots slapped against the cobbles as he navigated the never-ending warren of streets and alleyways in the Guild Quarter. He could taste copper on his tongue, and he felt the stitch in his side twist itself into a knot. *It isn't far,* he assured himself, *just a few more streets to the wall.*

Time stretched on, twilight hanging in the air, so a moment felt like an age. Thislen faltered, foot catching on a cobblestone. Part of him considered giving up and letting himself fall, a flash of bone-deep exhaustion—but he wasn't ready to die. He caught himself, scrambled to his feet, and ran on, ignoring the sting in his hands.

The broader streets with their well-loved shops and small, orderly gardens ended abruptly at the wall that separated the capital city's Gate Quarter from the rest. Its smooth sides

loomed head and shoulders above the nearest buildings. Heavy metal doors were set into its base at regular intervals. Lucky for Thislen, they had never been closed in his lifetime, and they stood open.

The breeze off the sea grew cooler as the shadow of the wall swallowed him. For a moment, he feared he had run out of time. Thislen flew through the short stone tunnel and into the narrower streets of the Gate Quarter. A weight lifted off his shoulders as he ran into the fading gold of twilight.

Here, the worn buildings leaned precariously over the paths below, looming monoliths with empty eyes. There were no gardens. The signs above the shops were weathered and faded; many bore no letters. Rubbish piled high in the bins in the narrow alleyways, smelling of sweat and rot and tar. Some of the cobbles were missing from the streets. Others lay crumbled and cracked. It forced Thislen to slow his pace or risk stumbling or falling again or twisting an ankle.

He picked his way along as deftly as a dancer. His breath scraped its way out of lungs that felt full of glass and cotton, every exhale bringing with it the sharp tang of blood. *It isn't far,* he repeated over and over. *Don't. Stop.*

The buildings fell away on either side, and Thislen slid to a stop moments before tumbling off the wooden walkway surrounding the shipyard. Inlets of smooth stone stood here with broad platforms encircling them for the shipwrights. Skeletal wooden monoliths stood in the furthest two spaces, half-finished ships bound for different islands than this one. Their curved rib beams reached towards the heavens, drawing Thislen's attention to the first stars dotting the evening sky above.

If I can see the stars, there is precious little time left. Night was falling. He tore his gaze from the sky and set off as quickly as he could manage on the wooden walkways, made slick in some places by the sea.

Thislen groped for the ring that hung around his neck on a leather cord, safely hidden beneath his shirt. Its weight was comforting, its shape and feel as familiar as his own limbs. Wordlessly, he sent a prayer up to his ancestors. *Please, if you can hear me—get me off this damn island! I'll do anything, anything you want!*

Perhaps his visit to his father's grave paid off, for almost as soon as he finished the thought, he spotted the rowboat. A wordless cry left his lips as he ran to it. Two oars and no visible holes. It was half-painted, which meant that it *must* be water worthy! He hauled it off its perch.

Thislen was slight, even if he had a man's height, and he realized quickly that his battle had just begun. He struggled along the dock with all the strength he could muster, the scrape of wood on wood echoing off the stone nearby. It was awkward to grasp, and he didn't dare stop to change his grip or wipe the sweat from his brow. Water slapped louder and louder against the wooden posts of the walkway. He was nearly there! If he could just drag it far enough—!

He turned to see how much further there was to go, blinking rapidly to clear his eyes. Suddenly there came a rattle, a thud, and the boat lifted. The scraping stopped. The thief almost fell backward with the sudden loss of the weight, jerking around to see what had happened.

Another young man stood there, a year or two older than Thislen. He hefted the other end of the rowboat with an expression equal parts sheepish and concerned, though his brown eyes were wide enough to see the white all around. His clothing was made of velvet and silk, embroidered at the collar and the cuffs and tailored to fit him like a glove.

A nobleman, Thislen realized, the thought flat and sour. *He must have had the same idea as me.*

The sweat that drenched the nobleman's dark brow stuck strands of black curls to his forehead and dripped in beads from others, silent proof of how far and fast he must have run to reach the Gate Quarter from the

Grand Quarter on the opposite side of the city. He held tension in his shoulders, uncertainty in the tilt of his head. His voice was strained as he spoke. "It's getting dark, and I've missed my boat. Perhaps we could share?"

No. The thought was quick, instinctive. The nobility of Astera couldn't be trusted. All of them were vipers, power-hungry enough to stay in this hellhole of a kingdom just for the chance to step on those below them. Yet even if he didn't want to share, the alternative wasn't something he would wish on anyone—even his worst enemies. Reluctantly, Thislen nodded. "Let's just get it in the water," he managed, "we're running out of time."

"My name is Percivan." The nobleman panted as they struggled to move the boat down a set of worn wooden steps that creaked and groaned alarmingly beneath their weight.

Thislen felt that thread of connection winding toward him like a noose. *First, he'll spend all night thanking me, then he'll want to assuage his gratitude with coin and favors. Pah! I don't need that sort of attention.* On the heels of that thought, however, came the flutter of hope. *Or he can give us the writ we need to get out of here. There's no reason he couldn't.* Except once the danger had passed, would any deal they made still hold? Thislen grit his teeth and said nothing, saving his breath for navigating the way down onto the stone and toward the water.

"My name—" Percivan began again.

"Thislen," he said shortly. That invisible thread tangled around him. *What have you done?*

Relief hit Thislen like a blow as he stepped into the shallows, even before they lowered the boat. The sea swirled around their ankles, urging them to hurry, to get out on the water. Moments. They had only moments left to climb into the boat and get off the island.

Thislen climbed in first while the nobleman held the stern, then turned to offer Percivan his hand.

As his fingers stretched toward the other young man, the last of the light vanished. A bitter wind moaned through the streets. The air plummeted to frigid temperatures around them. Thislen breathed out a single cloud of air that curled away in the sudden chill. He watched it vanish with a strange, languid detachment. His mind felt miles away from his body, paralyzed.

It's too late, he realized. His gaze met Percivan's.

"The Vaim," the noble whispered, eyes wide.

As if speaking their name had summoned them, the shadows between the buildings darkened and swelled, drawing Thislen's gaze to the city's edge. Bulbous black mounds broke into horribly twisted shapes that lurched out of the gloom. It took each figure several twitching, disjointed steps to stand upright, as if they had to remember how to exist within their bodies. They carried their arms at strange angles, and their heads cocked to one side like hounds scenting the wind despite their lack of noses. One by one, they stretched their arms up toward the night sky. Every time one broke free of the shadows, another bulge rose to follow. They boiled out of nowhere like ants, quicker than Thislen imagined they would, only to stand still amongst the crowd of their fellows.

He stopped breathing. He *couldn't* breathe. He didn't dare. He couldn't remember how to move at all. He wasn't sure he wanted to, as if such bravery might draw the attention of the spirits. His heart felt like it had gone still in his chest, his spine cold beneath his skin.

One of the horrors snapped its gaze toward the pair of them. Its face was a dark hole but for the dull red coals of its eyes, fixed in a rictus of anger. A low moan began somewhere. If he hadn't been staring directly at the Vaim, Thislen might have assumed it was the wind whistling between the buildings. He could see the others turn in answer to that first Vaim's call, and the sound swelled as each new set of eyes fixed upon them. The first of the ghosts lurched forward, unfurling fingers that were too long and sharp.

The sudden feeling of a hand around his jerked Thislen from his stunned reverie. He looked down at Percivan. The noble's fingers dug into the skin of his wrist. His eyes were bulging, lips pressed together in a tight line. There was no time. They had *no more time*. Thislen pulled.

One boot. The nobleman got one boot off the rock of the island and onto the edge of the rowboat before the first creature reached them. Thislen saw the shadow of it slow as it came up behind Percivan and embraced him like a lover, with one hand resting against his neck and the other wrapped close around his chest. The nobleman dropped a hand to cover the spirit's, their fingers interlocking for just a moment. He shouted hoarsely, his grip tightening around Thislen's wrist until it hurt.

He could do nothing but watch as Percivan's eyes widened, as the specter's fingers sank through the flesh of his chest. Black blood bloomed across his tunic and spilled over his hand. "Find Soren, he—" he gasped desperately before the Vaim tightened its grip on his throat, piercing the skin. His words were cut off with a sickening wet rasp.

Blood fountained free as the creature withdrew, taking a single step backward to observe its prey. More Vaim surged toward them. Percivan gurgled and coughed, falling backward into the waiting arms of the abrupt crowd of dark and lurching monsters. His grip weakened.

Thislen refused to let go. "Hold on, Percivan!" he shouted, voice cracking. He pulled as hard as he could to get the near-stranger onto the boat, unwilling to leave him with the grasping nightmares even if he were dying, even if Thislen couldn't save him. A harsh shout tore from his throat as he fought with the monsters in a gruesome tug-of-war.

The Vaim only then seemed to realize his existence. Dark hands shot from the crowd toward him, baleful red eyes fixed on a new and living prize. They swarmed over and past Percivan with his ashen face and steady, desperate gaze.

Thislen was plunged into a sea of shadows, reaching for him, grasping at him. The Vaim pulled at his cloak, snatched at his pants, and seized his hair. He swung his free arm wildly at the shadows, shouting in alarm. The rowboat wobbled beneath him.

Percivan's hand slipped from Thislen's grasp. As the dying man fell back into the tangle of spirits, his lips parted in faint surprise. He vanished in a swirl of dark arms as Thislen lunged forward to try and grab him again.

Long, dark fingers caught at Thislen's wrist, holding him fast. Where they touched his skin, it felt like being plunged into ice water. The cold spread up his arm, seeping beneath his skin and slowing the pulse in his wrist. The ghost's smoky shell felt smooth as cool satin against him. He could feel a second pulse, not his own, thrum between them.

Even as he realized that heartbeat belonged to the Vaim, the monster pulled him forward with a sharp tug. He caught his balance with a boot planted against the stern of the rowboat, but a lance of pain shot through his shoulder. He looked down to find himself pierced by one of the long talon fingers of the creature. Had he fallen any further, it would have gone through his heart. As it was, it hurt. Ancestors, it *hurt*! It felt like ice upon the surface and fire beneath his skin. The pain of it spread through his body with every beat of his heart, searing through his veins like a poison. He shouted again and jerked away, flinging himself backward.

It was enough.

Thislen's wrist slipped out of the Vaim's grasp, and he fell into the bow of the rowboat with a thud and a splash, droplets of cold water hitting his face in a spray. His heart pounded so loudly he could hardly hear over it. The lapping water, the fading groans of the shades, the creak of the wood around him—all of it sounded muffled. He gasped for air and clutched his shoulder, steeling himself for the final blow he knew would come.

The pain began to fade as warm blood flowed over his fingers. His shirt clung to his skin, sticky and uncomfortable. The fire in his veins was spreading, dissipating. Belatedly, Thislen realized the blow wasn't coming. The rowboat drifted a few feet away from the shore, carried by his fall. The Vaim weren't following. He pressed down on the hole in his shoulder with a hiss, huddling in the bow. Hot dark blood ran over his hand, gleaming black in the night's gloom. A stab of pain shot down his arm—proof that he was alive. Slowly, he levered himself upright.

The Vaim were a writhing mass of dark twitching limbs and sullen red eyes. The boat floated languidly away from the shore, caught in the retreating tide. He had made it off the island. Relief washed over him, leaving him lightheaded. He slumped back against the wood of the hull.

Percivan's body was a dark lump in the shallows, abandoned by the specters now that the young man no longer breathed. The nightmarish creatures continued to lurch along the water's edge like hounds that had treed a fox, waiting for him to return to land. He was close enough they could see him, and they were loath to give up their prey. A new sound began to rise beneath the slap of water against the boat and the mournful whistle of the breeze. One by one, the spirits stilled. The noise grew louder and louder.

The Vaim were whispering, whispering—whispering words he could not hear.

HE WASN'T certain when he fell asleep, huddled in a haphazard heap in the bow of the boat. When he woke, it was to the clamorous chorus of bells from the ships out at sea, a hundred of them heralding the coming dawn with their own cacophonous birdsong. Thislen untangled himself from his cloak, moving stiffly to stretch out cramped legs and a crick in his neck. He rubbed grit from the corners of his eyes. It felt as if he hadn't slept at all. A chill had settled bone-deep beneath his skin, but his shoulder burned. He could feel the edges of the wound throb in time with his heartbeat. Thislen avoided looking at it, turning instead to the city.

Dawn's light broke over the horizon. Astera's buildings were outlined in pale yellow and blue. The three mountains that served as the Spine of the island stretched away to Thislen's left, shedding the coat of darkness for the rich and mottled green of pines and aspens topped with pristine white snow. Only the nearest mountain bore the visible mark of human hands with Perilee set into the side of it that faced the city. Astera's outermost wall ran from the cliff face the castle had been built against down to the shore, ending in the sea beyond the shipyard.

The growing light revealed the sprawling terraces of the merchant's Goods Quarter below the castle. The stout white stone buildings with their brightly painted shutters vanished from view only behind the Gate Quarter's wall. The looming buildings he fled through the night before were now revealed for the ramshackle shacks they were, propped against one another like tired, sagging drunkards.

Behind him in the sea, the ships unfurled their sails one by one to return to shore. They had gone out only far enough to make space for one another, and in the morning light they drifted home like so many ducks upon a pond's surface. A few of them rang their bells as they passed, signaling their intentions. People emerged slowly from below-decks to begin their days, tiny figures lining the railings to watch the city approach. Sailors stood in the rigging, waving at companions they knew and shouting their hellos as they brought the residents of the island back to shore now that it was safe.

Safe. Thislen scoffed quietly at the thought as he turned to dig the oars from the bottom of the boat. Astera hadn't been safe for hundreds of years—not since the Vaim had first appeared. Countless lives had been lost to the creatures in the first fortnight, a tale whispered only in pools of golden lamplight, safely aboard ships and far from the dark and grasping hands. Countless more had been lost since, and still the island was not abandoned.

If you listened to the merchants, it was because of Astera's economy. Thriving trade in jewels found only in the Spine's mountain depths and lustrous blue pearls found only in the shallows kept trade on the island. The best shipwrights in the world were Asteran as well. Some kingdoms would freight wood across the ocean *and* pay a hefty sum for the work—all to call an Asteran ship their own. Others would buy a carpenter or a whole team of them outright, paying handsome prices to lure them to their countries. The shops of the Goods Quarter were filled with neat little stores that all professed themselves the best in the world—with no worldly experience to contradict them. They traded and bartered with visiting traders and made their coin off their guests and fellows and the rich. The craftsmen of the Guild Quarter worked hard to be better at their work than the one before, believing that such effort would lift the entire island. No, the merchants and traders and craftsmen of this small kingdom had found a way to live with the Vaim, blind to them, rather than leave.

Fools. The lot of them.

The wealthy were a different breed altogether. Anyone with power on the island chose to stay purely to wield that power over the less fortunate. The Vaim that sprang to life every night hardly affected *them*—they had their own ships, their own docks, their own massive estates. The rowboat system that served as ferries from one end of the island to the other didn't put a dent in their pockets the way it did for the less fortunate. Travel was easier, living was easier, and there was always a ready source of labor. The desperate took pennies on the day for the pleasure of working in the homes of Astera's nobility, all for the chance to be crammed into their own little cabins on the large ships.

It's disgusting, how they keep gardeners and maids. After all, people hardly lived in their houses. Balls were thrown on a ship the wealthy had built for just that purpose, in a stateroom lined with windows and safely off shore. Their clothes were on their ships, they ate their supper on their ships. The great decorated houses of the Grand Quarter were little more than shells to have luncheon in. Massive bedchambers needed dusting and airing, but no one ever used them. Large corridors needed sweeping and high ceilings needed checked for cobwebs, but they were all empty more often than not. Still, it kept dozens of people from the boats of the Gate Quarter.

Boats which even now were coming in around him. Thislen's arm ached and sent lances of pain to his fingertips if he moved it too much, making it difficult to row. With only one oar, he started the arduous process of getting back to the island.

The poor had no choice. Astera was an entire kingdom all to itself, an island that was long and narrow like an eel. It only had two proper towns and a few dozen fishing and farming villages, all along the shoreline and within safe reach of boats. Many of the fishermen and farmers lived on houseboats, fully outfitted with everything they needed. The poor in the cities could not do the same. The massive ships of the Gate Quarter were strung with layer after layer of hammocks. There was nowhere to keep personal belongings, nor any privacy. A few City Guard were assigned to each ship to pace back and forth as people slept and keep the illusion of safety intact, but the reality was that the poor of

Astera were crammed together like so many fish in a barrel. Accidents happened, and worse.

Those oldest and most decrepit of ships were important, however—important to maintaining the illusion. Anyone on the island would be given berth on a Gate Quarter ship without paying. It kept them away from the Vaim, after all. It was better than death. The Vaim served only to help the Ruling Council keep their flock docile. After all, they were *safe*.

I won't be like the rest of these people. I won't live my entire life around the whims of monsters. Thislen thought fiercely as he paddled. It was the one thought to which he had always clung, and the one that would get him to shore now. A little more stealing, and he could afford passage on a ship away from this place forever.

I'll get a writ of passage. I can climb on the next merchant ship and be gone. It took a lifetime for most people to earn enough gold for a writ. Then you'd have to spend another six months booking passage on a trader ship off shore. There were no dedicated passenger ships, not that Thislen had ever seen. No one came to Astera for pleasure—and he wasn't the only one who wanted to leave.

Thislen had lived his life in the Gate Quarter, full of its abandoned houses and ramshackle shops. All the jobs that no one else wanted were moved there, and all the precarious tenements were used only as storage for a change of clothes and a carefully hidden bit of coin. He had watched people stealing from one another his entire life, all trying to earn enough to move to the Goods or Guild Quarter, or to escape the island entirely. Both cost about the same—too much.

Thislen wanted to escape. *I'm tired of Perilee looming over my shoulder all the time. I want to start a new life, damn it!*

A life where he didn't have to duck and hide every time he heard the clatter of a carriage. A life where he could sleep in a bed on land! A life where he *had* a life. Was that so much to ask?

The first of the ships pulled into the docks with sailors leaping onto the wooden walkways to tie them fast. One slid home nearby. Most people in the city worked near their assigned ships, which meant the likelihood of shipwrights arriving at the yard soon was high. Loathe to be questioned about what happened or who he was, Thislen redoubled his efforts. He was glad the tide hadn't carried him too far from shore.

By the time the hull scraped against the stone, he felt exhausted again. His arms were quivering with fatigue. *That's not a good sign. Damn it!* He thought. He jumped out of the rowboat, the sea splashing around his boots. It was frigid after the long night, and the shock of it pulled some of the fog away from his mind. A quick haul had the rowboat safely berthed. The shipwrights would come and find nothing amiss. Nothing except...

Reluctantly, Thislen turned his gaze to Percivan's body, still slumped on the stone in the shallows with his eyes glassed over. *Dark,* he noted, *like mine.* Thislen shuddered. *That was too close a call.* A moment longer and he, too, would have gone from a living, breathing person to a corpse in the water. The image of dark, fountaining blood flashed before his eyes, followed by the stunned moment of quiet surprise on Percivan's face when he had let go of the nobleman's hand. He felt the chill settle deeper within his chest. His stomach churned.

There was nothing that you could do, he scolded himself. If only he believed it. *This is for the best. At least now there are no nobles trying to thank you. You told him your* name! *Don't make the same mistake again.*

Thislen knelt to close Percivan's eyes, bowing his head briefly. "May your spirit find your ancestors among the stars." he whispered. It wasn't last rites, but the thief hoped it might bring the noble's spirit peace.

"Find Soren, he's—!"

Thislen jerked to his feet, looking at Percivan's silent, unmoving body in the water. Of course, he hadn't spoken. He was dead. *I'm imagining things.*

Voices grew louder upon the docks and within the city, the hum of life returning to the streets. No one had appeared at the shipyard yet, but that didn't mean that he could linger. He did not want to be discovered here. That would lead to too many questions he didn't want to answer. He didn't want to be tied to the body of a dead noble. No one would care that he, a common thief, had tried to help. They wouldn't believe his story; they'd say he had abandoned Percivan to the Vaim. Even if they did believe him, he might still have to face an inquiry by the Ruling Council. The risk of being exposed was too high. Thislen and Percivan's shouting might have been heard, echoing over the water in the still night air, carried across a sea as smooth as glass. Some of the ships might have been close enough.

Thislen imagined a throng of curious people threading their way through the city, eager to find the latest victim and spread the latest story. So long as it hadn't happened to them or theirs, it would be fair game. The first death in three years at the hands of the Vaim—it would be the talk of the town!

He did not want to be part of that story.

"Find Soren!" Percivan said.

No! Thislen thought instinctively. He hadn't asked to grant the dying wish of a stranger. He hadn't asked to get involved. All he wanted was to get off the island.

But you let go of his hand.

That wasn't enough to sway him. Resolutely, Thislen turned away to face the city, pulling his hood over his head and wrapping himself in his cloak to hide the dark stain of his wound.

Like the ghosts, he vanished with the dawn's light.

2

Daylight gleamed off the spires of Perilee above Astera, a proud sentinel watching over the bustling residents below despite its lack of royal presence. It had been a few hours since the dawn had come, and the city's residents had debarked. With morning well and truly underway, the streets were bursting with life.

In the Grand Quarter, servants ran to fetch the carriages that would carry their noble and wealthy patrons to their homes and work and meetings. The wealthy merchants and esteemed nobility of the city donned their finery and wandered the decks of their elegant ships on promenades while they waited. Their household staffs had been fed and diligently worked in gardens, kitchens, and grand corridors. The Ruling Council's horse-drawn hansoms set out from their estates to carry them away to the Council Chambers in the castle. Three hundred years had passed since the coup, but still they sat before the empty throne to discuss the business of the day.

In the Guild Quarter, craftsmen called out to and worked alongside one another in a clangorous symphony. Tanners used wide wooden spoons as large as oars to stir hides in foul-smelling vats. Weavers shouted over the clatter and clack of shuttle and loom in their workshops. Carpenters with cloth tied over their faces bent over half-finished tables and chairs and decorative pieces, surrounded by a cloud of sawdust that would coat their clothes for the rest of the day. Import merchants unloaded their wares for the City Guard's inspection before anything could be taken to the next Quarter to be sold. Their freighters and the craftsmen's journeymen and apprentices were even now preparing to ferry those wares over to the terraces of the Goods Quarter.

The Goods Quarter sat below Perilee, the castle at the heart of the city. There, cobblers and tailors worked in shops that stood side by side, with window displays bursting with bright colors. Goldsmiths had shops every few streets where they fashioned the fine blue pearls into even finer jewelry and cut and set the gemstones from the Spine's deep mines. Bakeries filled the air with the scents of bread and sweet pastries cooling on windowsills in the small back gardens, where hungry fingers could not find them. Eateries opened their doors and set out benches for the breakfast rush.

In the Gate Quarter, the only district with a wall around its boundary, a different story unfolded. A ripple of rumor spread through the seedy taverns and the leaning tenement buildings. The discovery of Percivan's body raced from the shipyard like wildfire. The poorest of Astera's residents whispered to one another as they passed in the streets on their way to jobs in laundry houses and brothels, in tiny resale shops and second-hand merchantries. The ashmen and the binmen carried the news to those passing by on their way to jobs in other Quarters.

Just ahead of that wave of rumor, Thislen stumbled through the streets with his eyes fixed on the distant spires of the castle. His hand was pressed to his shoulder as he walked. It no longer throbbed dully but burned like a fire. Every beat of his heart sent heat through his body, and every brief moment of stillness left him cold as ice. He was clammy, strands of black hair clinging to his forehead beneath the hood of his cloak. His vision narrowed to a pinpoint as the world spun around him, forcing him to freeze and just breathe. In. Out. It was the only thing that still seemed easy.

When his vision returned, it was strange and sluggish. Everything turned slowly when he craned his head from side to side as he staggered up the terraced steps of the Goods Quarter on his single-minded trek toward Perilee.

The castle's great towers glinted and gleamed like a jewel for the rest of the city, keeping a careful watch over its people, but not for Thislen. To him, every twinkle of the glass in the spires above was more like a flash of lightning in a dark storm cloud, trying to warn him away. *Beware the past that awaits you here...*

Still, he struggled along the city streets, drawn to the one place on the island he most fervently wished to avoid.

The streets of the Goods Quarter began to hum around him. People were opening their shops and unshuttering their windows. Workers from the Gate Quarter called their hellos as they reported for their day's tasks. Neighbors passed news to one another from windows across alleyways and streets while they cooked their breakfasts. People passing on the street stopped in eddies of calm conversation, only to break away and continue to their destinations. Wooden stalls lifted their awnings and began selling fresh warm food for breakfast and luncheon, passing tales along with every warm roll.

"Did you hear?" A manservant asked as he picked up his master's shoes from the cobbler.

"Hear what?" A woman asked.

Thislen reeled to a stop in an alleyway, huddling against the wall to catch his breath.

"They found a body. The Vaim got to someone again. A noble this time, by the sound of it. City Guard is investigating."

"Investigating a Vaim attack? That's unusual. Why?"

"Apparently, they think there was a witness!"

Thislen felt his stomach churn, and a chill settled between his shoulder blades that raised the hairs on the back of his neck. He couldn't tell if it was nerves or his illness. Perhaps it was both.

"A witness?" The woman asked as she handed over the soft cloth bag that held the shoes.

"There was a rowboat with blood on it and boot prints leading out of the water. They've dried by now, but the Guard said they were there. Led right into town."

This time, Thislen knew it was nerves. He felt that thread of connection swell into a noose. *Curse that damn Percivan. Why the hells did he miss his boat!?*

Find Soren, he—!

Thislen looked up sharply, meeting Percivan's dark-eyed gaze across the street. He shuddered, bending over to retch up a mouthful of bile onto the cobblestones of the shadowed alley. When he looked up, Percivan was gone. His head fell back against the stone wall of the shop, and he stared at Perilee's spires just over the rooftops. His body ached to drag itself to the castle, but his strength was waning. If he could just make it to the gates, he'd...

He'd what?

A light winked off one of those high spires as if someone were watching him. Thislen felt well and truly trapped. *I was so close to leaving. Curse me for a soft-hearted fool,* he berated himself. He could turn around. He could still get away.

"Here now! Move along, you! What's the matter with you? Are you drunk?" The cobbler woman waved a handkerchief at him, lip curled and her nose plugged with her fingers.

Slowly, he lurched into the streets once more, threading his way between people dressed in the bright colors that Asterans favored. Yellows, blues, pinks, and reds bled into greens, browns, azures, and rusts. Many people in the Goods Quarter, the second wealthiest in the city, had embroidery on their cuffs and collars that caught at Thislen's wandering attentions. Flashes of dainty flowers and curling vines spiraled into swirling shapes and delicate scrollwork. The world was spinning and melting together like wax—nothing felt truly real.

I'm not going to make it much farther.

Thislen's knees seemed made of jelly, buckling with every step, leaving him wobbling and uncertain whether he could take another. His head felt full of wool, and his eyes slid in and out of focus. A ringing began in his ears, growing so loud that everyone's voices sounded far away. He couldn't find Soren *or* get off the island, not unless he mended first.

At Perilee, a voice whispered in his ear.

Bile coated the back of his throat, threatening to make him vomit again. He stopped in the middle of the street, closing his eyes and breathing deeply of the salt-sweet air. *I'm going mad.*

"I say, are you alright there?" A woman's voice asked him, deep and soft like a quilted blanket.

"Healer?" He begged, the word a gasp.

"Just around the corner, dear. It's right across from my flower shop. Olen's place. A good man, Olen Ominir. Come on, then. Lean here on my arm. My name is Evelie, and it's nice to meet you. What's your name?"

Another thread curled through the air and threatened to ensnare him, to tether him to the people he wanted never to know and never to be known by. Another person who would ask questions, who would remember that he existed. He wasn't supposed to exist. He wasn't supposed to be noticed. *Lie. Run. Say nothing!* he thought.

He chose the last, staying silent as he fought another overwhelming wave of nausea. He was going to fall, he knew, any second now.

Evelie's hand came up under his arm to guide him closer, and he reluctantly leaned upon her. He told himself he had no choice. She was warm, her grip strong and gentle in equal measure.

Thislen opened his eyes, and her face swam into view. The woman had brown hair the color of polished wood, mixed with white and gray from age. Lines from many years of smiling had etched delicate folds into the skin around her eyes, which were green as tree leaves and brimming with concern even as she gave him an encouraging smile. A basket filled with fruit, bread, and cheese hung over one arm, and now she bore Thislen upon the other.

"Let's get you to Olen," she said, warm and encouraging.

Was my mother like this?

Where had that thought come from? His mother was difficult to think about. Thislen pushed her from his mind.

Evelie towed him along through the steady stream of people, stopping now and then when he squeezed her arm. Thislen kept his eyes closed, forced to trust this stranger to take him to safety because every step brought a fresh wave of nausea. She led him to a small courtyard off the broad street, lined with five little shops. A bright and bustling inn stood at the head of the dead end, with a small stable and a pleasure garden fenced off from the rest. They would have a set of rooms on a ship cordoned off to rent, and more inside. From the smell of hearty stew and hops, their common room was of good quality and undoubtedly drew many loyal patrons.

The florist's shop burst with color on one side, standing shoulder to shoulder with an equally bright tailor's shop. Across the way was a potter's, and the quiet and unobtrusive front of the apothecary.

There was quite a crowd here. People made their way into or out of the inn for their breakfast. The tailor was putting out a mannequin dressed in a bright, layered gown. The potter was adjusting a sign denoting a sale on his wares. Outside the flower shop, a young man tended to customers from a table with vases of bright blooms. The florist had Evelie's wavy brown hair and bright green eyes. He waved at her as she gave Thislen a moment to breathe. She waved in return before leading her temporary charge toward the quiet apothecary opposite.

It was a pool of calm amongst the crowds. The sign above the door read 'Ominir Apothecary' in neat, fresh letters. A bubbling cup denoting medicine had been painted on one side, and the green leaf of healing on the other.

We made it, Thislen thought, sagging against the wall as Evelie slipped out from beneath his arm to open the door unhindered. While her back was turned, Thislen hastily pulled the ring on its leather cord from around his neck. Her arm came around him again even as he slipped his one treasure safely into his pocket. *Better that it isn't seen.*

Thislen tripped over the stoop, and they both stumbled through the open door. The inside of the building was blessedly dim, cool, and calm. Shelves lined the walls of the front half of the small shop. Jars and paper satchels marched along the shelves with small paper labels pinned to the wood beneath them. A counter divided the space, and worktables filled the back half in a comfortable, cluttered contrast to the neat order near the door. The air was full of the scents of flowers and herbs that hung in various states of drying from the dark heavy beams of the ceiling. A few glass-sided lanterns added light to the space, though more poured in from the shop's front window and a door in the back, propped open with a simple stone, the room beyond a riot of greenery in a glass-walled garden.

It was there that two figures stood. A young woman leaned against the doorframe, dressed in bright blues and yellows, with her honey-brown hair pulled away from her face by a scarf and her arms folded across her chest. The second figure stood in the glass room beyond her, a watering can in his hand. He was a large man with broad shoulders and a craggy face, mostly hidden beneath his beard. A mane of wild red hair sprouted from his head, gone gray at the temples. His clothes were mixed of rusts, yellows, and oranges like a flame, painted all the brighter in the morning light through the bubbled panes of the greenhouse.

"Good morning, Olen, Mila—I think this young man could use a bit of help," Evelie called to the pair as she and Thislen found their feet again. There was a tightness to her voice that belied her calm smile.

Thislen pulled away from Evelie as the pair turned towards them, blinking in hopes that the spots would disappear from his vision. He saw the bright blue eyes of the red-headed man beneath thick brows like caterpillars as Olen turned to them. He watched the brows jump upwards as they took in his appearance.

I must look as awful as I feel, he realized. It felt as if he were watching the scene unfold from underwater. Everything was slow, rippling strangely at the edges. Part of him wondered if any of this was real. Had he collapsed in the street somewhere? Was he dying?

Olen stepped toward them, pushing the watering can into the woman's arms. As she turned, Thislen realized Mila was not as young as he had thought. She was around his age, just slight and small. Her eyes were the same bright and penetrating blue as her father's.

As Thislen stared at her, the edges of his vision darkened. His ears were ringing again, the sound growing louder and louder. Blackness crept across his eyes, and his knees gave out at last.

Everything flew upward abruptly—no! He was falling! As Thislen collapsed, he saw Mila's eyes widen and heard her gasp. One hand uncurled from around the watering can, reaching for him. Then, darkness swallowed him whole.

THE FIRST THING he heard was the muffled echo of voices as if someone were shouting at him from above a pool of water as he floated in comfortable, painless darkness. Nothing could truly reach him here. It was calm. Still. Peaceful.

Come, a voice whispered, *sink deeper.*

Wait—!

Thislen jerked awake to find himself on one of the worktables, the clatter of things being moved still hanging in the air. Three people bustled around him. Heads, faces, and hands flashed in his field of vision too quickly for him to make sense of any of them. His shirt was being pulled off, his cloak's clasp wrestled free. His arm burned as it was moved, stabbing pain racing through his chest and down to the end of his fingertips. An involuntary ragged gasp escaped him.

"Ancestors, look at it!" The young woman was saying. *Mila.*

"Mila, get hot water." The large man ordered, words clipped and solemn and firm. His voice was as steady as a stone and deep as a spring. "Careful, Evelie, careful there."

"Hurts—!" Thislen tried to say. He felt his lips move, but no one heard him. His face twisted into a grimace, teeth bared and clenched.

Evelie dropped his clothes to one side. She hovered above him, pushing his damp hair back from his forehead. Her eyes tracked Olen as the healer bustled back and forth. He pulled a rolled leather case from a shelf and unrolled it, deftly selecting a small array of tools.

"I didn't realize he was hurt. Just feverish, I thought. Like the one last month who ate that bad meat." Evelie said. The tightness in her voice was much more noticeable now than before, accompanied by the slightest waver.

"We'll do everything we can to fix this." Olen turned back to them, something glittering in his hand. The short paring knife caught a glimmer of light from the window that ran up the length of the blade, twinkling merrily at the tip.

Thislen's stomach churned. *Why does he need a knife?* The thought felt loud as it fluttered through his head and got stuck in his heart, making it beat faster still. His shoulder throbbed again, the pain of it radiating up the side of his neck and down his arm. A groan filled his ears, haggard and agonized. It took him a moment to realize it was him making the sound.

A kettle whistled somewhere, the shrill screech cutting through the fog of pain and pulling his feverish gaze away from Olen for a moment. Stairs led up from the back of the shop to a second level, tucked out of sight of the storefront. That must have been where Mila had gone.

His head lolled as he looked for her there, only to catch sight of his injured shoulder for the first time. The puncture was swollen around the edges, puckering as it swelled. It was covered with a mottled black and rust of dried and clotted blood, but the skin visible beneath it was bright red or an angry, bruised purple. New blood welled brightly where cloth had been pulled away, and scabs had cracked from movement. Thin black veins spiderwebbed away from the wound in every direction. It was as malevolent as the Vaim themselves. Thislen's breath caught.

I'm going to die.

Olen appeared, pressing down on his arm to hold it in place. "Evelie, hold his shoulders." The apothecary said firmly.

No, no, wait! Don't cut me! "No—!" Thislen gasped, trying to sit up.

Evelie was there at Olen's command, leaning down on Thislen's chest with all her weight. His fever made him as weak as a stalk of grass. He couldn't writhe free. His feet kicked and scuffed at the tabletop beneath him, rattling things he couldn't see. He let out an alarmed shout.

Footsteps pattered quickly down the stairs where he couldn't see. Evelie grunted as she caught at his wrist, holding him still. The knife was lifted, winking in the light. It dropped.

Pressure, then pain. It bloomed out along his arm and across his chest and up his neck into his face, a tingling agony like being bitten all over by fire ants. Blood rushed free, the feel of it sticky and thick on his skin. His head swirled like it had when he was young and spun round and round in circles until he fell over. He thought he would be sick again, and he might have if there had been anything left in his stomach. Thislen watched as bright red blood and something black and thick like oil flowed out of the wound and over his skin, landing on the wooden table with a patter like raindrops.

His vision narrowed to a tunnel of black with a pinpoint of red light at the end for several seconds. An overwhelming wave of nausea rolled over him, but he couldn't tell if he had thrown up or not. All he could taste was bile. Voices spoke somewhere above him, beside him, around him. They echoed as if whoever was speaking was standing in a cave, and he was outside. They swirled and floated in a strange way so he couldn't tell where they came from. His own breathing was loud and hoarse in his ears, nearly drowning them all out.

Something hot poured over his shoulder, hotter than his own blood. The pain began to ebb. Slowly, his vision swam back into focus.

He was staring into big green eyes. Evelie's face broke out into a sudden brilliant smile. Her hand was cupping his cheek, warm and comforting. Her thumb ran gently over his clammy skin. "There you are. Welcome back," she said softly.

Hands were on his arm and shoulder from above, and he could just barely see the bright yellow sleeve of Mila's shirt. Turning his head would have dislodged Evelie's calloused hand, and he didn't know if he had the strength to do so. *Or if I want to.* Was this what it was like to be soothed and comforted? His shoulder throbbed in time with his heart, but he could also feel quick bits of pressure and small prickles of pain.

"He...he *cut* me," Thislen said at last. His tongue was thick and unwieldy, making the words come out slurred and fumbling. The room spun slowly behind the florist's head. His stomach churned. His head felt like it might float away with the slightest puff of air, like the seeds of a wishing flower.

"I had to clear whatever infection that was out of your blood," Olen said, not unkindly, from somewhere near the stabbing thorns of pain in Thislen's shoulder.

"I've never seen an infection that looked like *that*," Mila said lowly.

"Hush, Mila."

"But Father—" she tried to say.

"Not right now. Let's tend to our patient first, yes?" Olen interrupted. There was a stern edge beneath his bright and cheery tone.

Tension hung in the air for several moments like a cloud, prickling with the energy before a storm. The hands on his shoulder didn't stop working for even a moment. Thislen watched Evelie looking between the pair, her kind smile wavering.

"Perhaps I'll fetch some cool water and a cloth for his fever." The florist offered, giving him one more kind smile before vanishing from view.

Thislen looked out over the apothecary's shelves to the shop window, watching in a detached fog as flickering glimpses of people passed by. His eyes grew heavier and heavier each time they closed. His head felt like a great stone. Everything drifted further and further away. Thislen let himself relax, slumping to the table and closing his eyes. The relief was instantaneous.

"It will need more stitches, won't it?" came the low and melodic voice of Mila. *It reminds me of a stream running over stones,* Thislen thought.

"I think I'll need another needle, too. Where are they?" Olen asked.

"I'll clean one." The pressure of hands on his arms and shoulder disappeared, making him aware that it had been there in the first place. Thislen could hear Mila's footsteps and the crinkle of a paper packet.

"I'm just going to check the back of his shoulder," Olen said. Action matched words as Thislen was rolled slightly onto one side. It hurt like he was being stabbed again as the shoulder moved, conjuring a flash of the angry visage of the Vaim—but he was only shifted just enough by the large, steady hands for his healer to get a good look.

A soft grunt sounded. "All the way through. Not by much, though. Few stitches ought to close it up. Lucky young man. This isn't that far from his heart. Luckier still that it missed anything important."

"What happened, do you think?" Mila asked in a hushed murmur.

"Not in front of the patient," Olen said firmly. "We've *talked* about this, Mila."

"He's asleep, or fainted again."

He was lowered back onto the table. Thislen didn't bother opening his eyes or even so much as twitching a finger. Whatever reserves of strength remained to him were being used simply to listen, and he could feel even those draining quickly. His head was growing lighter and lighter.

"Well," Olen conceded, "the closest I can come to this sort of wound is a rapier tipped with poison."

"The closest you can come? Here." There was a rustle of fabric.

"There's something not quite right about it. I've never seen..." Olen trailed off. He was calm, but there was a thoughtful weight to each word. Maybe the puzzle of the wound bothered the man.

Thislen considered telling the healer what had happened—and thought better of it nearly at once.

I want no ties to Percivan, he told himself firmly, *and besides, how would he react to someone having survived the Vaim? Having touched one, been attacked by one, and lived? No one survives the Vaim! It would be a tale worth retelling, and that's not the sort of attention I want.*

Olen could call for the City Guard. He could run to tell the town criers. He could have Thislen arrested for hiding his involvement with Percivan until now. Best case, he would merely gossip, and the rumor would spread and spread until someone *else* came hunting for him. Whatever choice the man would make, Thislen was too weak to escape at the moment. No, it was far too risky.

Something bit into the flesh of his shoulder once more, and the prickles of pain welled sharper now than they had been. He had been in a fog before, but now each stab of the needle as the wound was stitched shut felt larger in the inflamed edges of the puncture. Thislen groaned, head lolling on the hard wood of the table.

"Hold him steady, Mila."

Weight pressed on his chest and arm again, warm and firm. The pain grew, as did a ringing in his ears. His stomach contorted inside of him, roiling with nausea. Each breath felt like it would come back up with bile, though none came. He couldn't take it anymore!

Thislen followed the darkness behind his eyelids down into a place of blessed peace.

Come deeper...

3

The third time Thislen awoke in the Ominir Apothecary, it was to find himself bathed in dazzling sunlight. The warmth of it was the first thing he noticed, sinking into his chilled skin. He opened his eyes slowly, the light blinding him for several moments before it resolved into the shapes of the shop's back door and the glass room beyond, a hothouse bursting with verdant plants on shelves and hooks to take advantage of every sunlit surface. It smelled of loam and damp earth and the sharp scent of herbs. Dust motes danced a lazy gavotte in the silence that lay thick over everything, like the soft, worn blanket draped over his chest.

Thislen was tucked into a cot against the back wall of the shop. A few worktables had been moved against the walls nearby to make room for him. His head was cushioned on a feather pillow, but the mattress was simple straw. Nonetheless, it felt like a luxury. His own bed in the tiny gable room of the Gate Quarter was made of nothing but heaped blankets and spare clothes shoved into a bag to serve as a pillow.

When was the last time I had a proper sleep? He wondered.

Thislen's shoulder was numb, and his fingertips tingled like they were asleep. The wound had been swathed in clean strips of undyed cloth, soft against his skin. Most of the work they had done was hidden beneath the open collar of the oversized white shirt they had given him, its laces unthreaded to make it easier to reach what they needed to while keeping him clothed. It was a small kindness, but one he felt most keenly atop the rest.

Thislen felt his heart leap a few paces ahead when he didn't feel the weight of his ring on his chest. Slowly, he eased his hand down to his pocket. His trousers, at least, were still his own. The ring, his one treasure, was safe where he had left it.

His head felt firmly attached to his shoulders once more, no longer ready to float away like the fluff of a dandelion. He could tell without moving, however, that he was weak. He felt like a wrung-out dishcloth. It would take more energy than he had left within him to even lift his head, let alone walk out of the apothecary and once more disappear into the streets of Astera. *Looks like I haven't got a choice but to stay here and mend—even if it is a risk.*

Stay safe, Thislen, stay hidden. His father's last words drifted through his mind. He had lived by those words since his father had failed to return to him almost a decade past.

What would he say to me now? Thislen couldn't decide. He hadn't known his father well enough to tell.

A soft *clunk* drew his attention away from the brilliant sunlight he basked in, dislodging a barely dampened cloth from his forehead. He laboriously pulled the fabric away, staring at it for a moment before his gaze was drawn to Mila beyond.

She stood at a worktable near the foot of the cot, her back turned to him. Deftly, she pulled dried herbs from above her head and fresh herbs from cuttings strewn across the table, mixing them with a bit of flour and water in a small wooden bowl. When the concoction had turned to a paste, she rolled pinches of the substance between her fingers until they formed little pellets, then set them on a platter to dry. So immersed was she in her work, she had yet to notice that Thislen was awake.

"...Mila, right?" Thislen's voice was a croak, rough and slurred. He grimaced at the sound.

She jumped, bowl clattering under her hands though she caught it before any mishap. After setting everything aright, she turned to him with wide eyes and a growing smile. "You're awake!" She said, "And about time, too. I was beginning to worry."

Mila paused, waiting for him to say something. Thislen cleared his throat after a moment, but he was silent. The young apothecary's cheery expression faltered, but she caught herself before it fell. She stepped over, taking the cloth from his hand to dip into a bowl of water. She wrung it out, folded it, and lay it on his forehead once again.

"You must still feel a bit unwell. Your fever hasn't broken yet. Would you like some broth? We haven't got any bread yet, but we will. My father's gone with Evelie to the market to do the shopping." She put the back of her hand against his cheek, then touched two fingers to the pulse in the side of his neck.

Thislen felt an urge to pull away from her touch. Mila's fingers were warm and calloused but not rough. *Don't be stupid. She's just checking your health. If you draw away, she'll notice.* It didn't stop his skin from tingling like it was covered with spiders. She pulled away only a moment before it became too much.

"Well, your pulse is stronger. That's a good sign. So! Broth?" She clapped her hands together, that sunny smile forming on her face once more.

He nodded. Mila spun with a swirl of skirts and made her way up the staircase tucked at the back of the shop to what was presumably a kitchen above. He could hear the squeak and gurgle of a pump, followed by the splash and slosh of water.

Left alone in the silence, Thislen felt safe enough to start the laborious process of propping himself up. His shoulder ached and throbbed, but it did not pain him as much as it had before. With his arm cradled to his chest, he managed to sit up and twist enough to adjust the pillow. By the time he was reclined against it, his head resting on the wall and the blanket again pulled over his chest, his sweaty hair stuck to his forehead and his whole body trembled. Any thought of trying to run away was thoroughly squashed as Thislen closed his eyes, hoping the world would stop spinning.

I'm useless. Weaker than a piece of wet parchment.

With his eyes closed, it felt as though he were on one of Astera's ships, rocking back and forth. He fought the urge to retch. *How am I going to get down to the shore? What time is it?*

The world stilled around him once more. Thislen opened his eyes again. A man had appeared in the window of the apothecary, broad in the shoulders and tall. A second glance showed he was perhaps only a few years older than Thislen's own twenty summers and another young nobleman like Percivan.

If Thislen were any judge, this noble hadn't missed a meal in his life. There was a healthy glow to his pale, perfect skin. His smile was pristine and white. The man wore a green tunic edged with gold and blue, tailored closely to fit his strong figure. The nobleman was adjusting his perfectly coiffed golden curls with the help of his reflection in the window, unaware of his audience—or perhaps uncaring.

When he had finished preening, the young noble entered the shop. The bell above the door let out a merry tinkling call. He wore loose trousers tucked into his boots, the latest fashion trend to arrive in Astera from overseas. The boots had golden buttons running up the side, polished so that they gleamed even in the dim light of the store. Each step the man took clicked faintly in the near silence.

Thislen wrinkled his nose in the cot, remaining still. *Another nobleman, and this one with the attitude of the worst of them. Just my luck, isn't it?* he thought. This new noble had none of Percivan's modesty or humility. He wore his status like a shield and a banner all at once. His chest was out, his chin was high, and there was a slight smirk on his lips even when he thought no one was looking. His nose was so high in the air that Thislen could see right up his nostrils from where he lay.

The guest noticed his observer at last, the smile fading from his features. His brow furrowed ever so slightly. "And who are you?" came the vaguely irritated question.

Thislen hated him already.

"Patient," he grunted.

The man waited, perhaps expecting more. When nothing followed, he sneered and crossed to the counter, folding his arms to lean upon the barrier. "I could have guessed that much, you simpleton. You're swathed in bandages, and you look like death. Whatever ails you, it isn't...catching, is it?" His nose wrinkled as if he smelled something foul. His lip curled up. Thislen half expected him to produce a handkerchief to cover his face.

"Horribly," Thislen answered flatly.

The noble recoiled, eyes widening in shock. Mila came sweeping down the stairs a moment later, a large clay mug in her hands and a bright smile on her features, oblivious to the guest in her shop.

"Here we are! This should be easier to manage than a bowl and a spoon for the moment. Hopefully, it will tide you over until my father gets back with that bread." Her cheer was palpable and infectious. She swept in like a ray of sunlight, like a tickle of fresh air. Without even realizing the room had been full of tension, she cut it away to nothing. Thislen was touched by her thoughtfulness—for a moment.

Do not get attached, damn it. As soon as you can, you're leaving, he warned himself.

He took the mug from her hand, and she whirled to return to work. At the sight of the nobleman, she stilled so suddenly it was as if she had turned into a painting. The tension was back in the air, heavy and smothering like a blanket. Thislen noticed at once, sipping silently at the warm, salty broth.

Mila didn't even breathe for one heartbeat. Two. Three. Abruptly, she inhaled a little gasp, her smile returning. "Oh! Lord Bestant!"

Thislen knew that name. The Bestants were one of the Ruling Council families—exactly who he had hoped to avoid. He remained very, very still, forcing himself to breathe normally. Here was his number one enemy made flesh.

His brows drew in as he glanced at Mila. Her words still burst with cheer, but there was a strain behind them now, as if she were forcing it. It didn't sound like *her.* His thief's instincts had him on full alert now. Well...as alert as he could be.

"Are you here for your mother's medicine? You're a little early, you know. You weren't due until tomorrow." She didn't seem to notice Lord Bestant's expression of distaste nor the way he was staring at her patient.

Or she's ignoring it, Thislen realized. His gaze slid smoothly between the two.

"I was just at Castle Perilee for a meeting of the Council," he informed her, taking a generous, blatant step back from the counter. He relaxed as he put distance between himself and Thislen, gracing Mila with a smug, dazzling smile. "It was dreadful business today, very important work. I'm not sure if you'd heard...Percivan Coppermund died last night."

The cloth against Thislen's forehead felt suddenly as cold as ice. A shiver ran down his back. The broth in his mug sloshed as his hand twitched, threatening to spill over the rim. He brought it quickly to his mouth, disguising his sudden discomfort with the gesture. The salt-brine taste of the broth was clearing the fog from his head and soothing the new knots in his stomach, the warmth of it beating back his unease.

Percivan Coppermund. *Now you know his name.*

What could he do with it? Find the family? Tell them that he had tried? They'd clap him in irons and have him shipped off to the Brig in no time. However, that name *could* help him figure out who Soren was. It had to be someone Percivan Coppermund *knew,* after all.

If I were going to look for Soren, that would be useful. But I'm not.

The hairs on the back of his neck stood up. It felt as if someone were looming just at Thislen's shoulder. He ignored it, afraid of what he might see.

Mila moved to the worktable, checking the little paste-pills she had made with gentle squeezes of her fingertips. "We heard about it a short time ago. Father went with Evelie to get more news at the markets. We're expecting them back soon."

"What will you give me in exchange for the news right now?" Lord Bestant asked, smile widening in a way that reminded Thislen of a bear trap. He stepped forward, planting his hands on the countertop and leaning toward the young apothecary.

She stepped away as if she hadn't noticed his advance. Her head tipped to one side, honey blonde hair swinging as she sorted through a series of paper cones neatly labeled and lined up on a shelf. "Will your order do? Lucky for you, I finished it last night." Her voice was light and almost vapid, but Thislen could feel the edge of tension beneath her words.

Thislen watched Mila like a hawk with a faint furrow in his brow, waiting for her hands to tremor or her smile to falter; for something to give her away. Her cheery demeanor didn't sit quite right on her shoulders anymore.

"You would give me that for my gold, and we both know it to be true. Come on, Mila," Lord Bestant's voice dropped to a cheery wheedle as he folded his arms to lean all the further over the barrier between them. "Let me have something more. Why not let me invite you to my ship for dinner this evening, hm? A nice wine, some pheasant in a cream sauce, and then a private rowboat back to your own ship?"

She glanced at Thislen, who raised his mug to his lips as he quickly looked away. He was doing his best to look as uninterested in their conversation as possible while eavesdropping on every word.

Mila turned back to Lord Bestant, lowering her voice to a harsh whisper that dripped with fluttering unease. "Absolutely not! I couldn't possibly. My father would never allow it. It would ruin my prospects! We are an old-fashioned family, my Lord. I won't stay on anyone else's ship or in anyone else's cabin until I am married. That's the final word on the matter. Four gold coins." She slapped the paper cone of medicine onto the counter, the crack of it sharp as it cut through the air.

Lord Bestant's lips dropped into a sullen pout for a moment, then went smooth as he straightened back up to his full height. "Then marry me."

Mila gave a shrill little laugh, hand flying to her mouth a moment afterward. Her shoulders were taut, drawn up near her ears as she shrank into herself for a moment, blue eyes wide. She stepped away from the nobleman, suddenly bustling as she opened the large book the shop used as a register. She flipped through the pages with quick, jerky movements. "You cannot marry me; I'm a commoner. I don't like you mocking me about it, either."

"My father passed away last year, remember? There's no one left alive who can stop me from marrying whoever I want. I sit on one of the highest seats of the Ruling Council. Mila, if it matters to you so much, I can just *give* your father a title. We can make him an Earl somewhere, perhaps of the little farm outside the walls that helps supply your shop." Lord Bestant's hand shot out, catching Mila's wrist as she reached for her quill. She froze. "So, marry me. Marry me, Mila Ominir."

"Lord Bestant—"

"Don't give me any more excuses, Mila. Don't Lord me, don't dither. Give me a straight answer. Am I going to court you and ensure your life is full of every luxury you might wish for, or not?" His grip slid to her hand. Slow as a spider reeling in a fly, he drew her hand to his lips, placing a soft kiss upon her knuckles. He let go.

Mila drew her hand back hastily, holding it tight to her chest as if his attentions had burned it. Lord Bestant didn't notice. He drew out a coin purse and counted out four gold pieces, setting each one on the counter with a sharp *click*, one after the other. *Click. Click. Click. Click.*

"Have your answer prepared for me when I return. Speak to your father. Tell him everything. I'm certain that he'll approve." The nobleman picked up the little paper packet of medicine from the end of the counter and sauntered out the door. The bell rang cheerily as he left, then faded to silence.

The tension in the room was so heavy Thislen felt he might be crushed beneath it. So, he slurped his broth as loudly as he could. Mila jumped, whirling to stare at him.

Just as I thought. She forgot I was even here! He wasn't sure if he was relieved by that discovery or a bit hurt.

"Oh! I hadn't meant for you to have to sit through that," she said in a rush, fanning her face with a hand. Her cheeks were red, and her eyes glittered. He thought for a moment that she might cry, but the shine in her eyes was not sadness.

He lowered his mug, brows lifting slowly. "You're angry."

She waved her hands rapidly, turning away again to scoop the coins into the cash box beneath the counter and scribble down the sale. "It's complicated. You wouldn't understand."

And you shouldn't ask, damn it, he told himself, *don't you get involved.*

"Wouldn't understand what? That he makes you uncomfortable? Anyone with eyes would be able to see that. Anyone besides him, and the only reason he can't see it is because his head is so far up his own—"

"Don't!" Mila said sharply, nearly diving across the shop to clap her hands over his mouth. She drew them back just as quickly, as if scalded. "Oh, I didn't hurt you, did I?"

Thislen stared for a moment, dark eyes wide. He could feel the lingering warmth of her skin fading from his cheeks. "What was that for?" He sputtered.

"Sometimes he comes back after a few moments, claiming he forgot something or other. You could get sent to the gaol for saying things like that where a Council member can hear."

The thief scoffed. "I'm not afraid of the Council," he lied, "they can't do anything to me. Why don't you just tell him that you don't want to marry him?"

She stood beside the cot, gaze fixed on the door and the shop's front window, keeping careful watch while she spoke. "He brought a lot of business here when his mother fell ill a few years back. One by one, he started to bring his wealthy friends here. When word got around that the Ruling Council chose *our* apothecary almost exclusively, more people started coming than before. He could ruin us just as easily as he made us. He would do it in a heartbeat if I made him angry enough. You don't know him."

I don't need to. They're all the same.

"You're right; I don't," Thislen agreed, resting the half-empty mug of broth on his lap. "Tell me about him. This Lord..." He trailed off. The nobleman's name had already slipped out of his mind. Not that it mattered much. Thislen had no intention of ever meeting the man again. "He seems to have a lot in common with a horse's backside."

Mila's eyes widened with a gasp, though she then dissolved into a nervous laugh. She sank to sit on the end of the thief's cot. "He...He wasn't always that way, you know. His father died last year, and he's never been the same. He used to be polite enough, coming by to get his order and then leaving again."

"For his mother, right?" Thislen asked, gaze wandering along the bundles of herbs hung from the ceiling.

"She's prone to the most terrible headaches. My father, Olen, you met him earlier? He made a special recipe just for her. It's the only thing that helps. Lord Bestant was always kind enough, and grateful to us, and ready with a compliment or witticism. He was still as smug and pretentious as he is now, but…"

Thislen took a swallow of his broth, waiting patiently for her to continue. Mila had her hands clasped tight together on her lap. She was still staring intently at the front of the shop, but her posture had relaxed slightly.

"But?" He prompted, sensing a door in the walls she carefully hid behind smiles and busywork. Even as the word left his lips, he kicked himself for it. *What does it even matter? Why did you ask? You don't care.*

Do you?

Mila dusted off her hands, arranging her skirts delicately over her knees. She was used to having something to do with her hands, Thislen assumed. "Well, Father told me that after the late Lord Bestant passed, the next time he came for his mother's medicines, Lord Bestant was… haggard. He had dark circles beneath his eyes. Dark as the depths of the sea, Father said. He said Lord Bestant asked him a lot of questions." Her brow furrowed in a soft frown. She fiddled with a lock of her hair.

Don't ask anymore. Don't say a word, damn it. Don't you dare.

"What sort of questions?" He asked in spite of himself.

Damn it! What is wrong with me?

"Questions about our shop. Questions about my family. He started coming around often, sometimes just to speak with me. He brought more and more of his friends for even the slightest ailments. Ever since then, he's been strange. More intense, perhaps. The past few visits, though, they've gotten…" She trailed off, struggling to find the right word.

"Suggestive?" He offered quietly.

There was a pause before she nodded, followed by a heavy sigh as she tucked a loose tendril of her hair behind her ear. She clasped her hands together on her lap once more. "I don't want to marry him," she confessed. "I don't want to marry anyone. I've never even wanted to court."

A strange pit formed in Thislen's stomach, and his chest swelled at the same time. It was a foreign feeling. He couldn't identify it. They sat together in stillness and silence. Mila never looked away from the front of the shop. Thislen swallowed the last of his broth and offered her the mug. She tore her gaze away from the window to take it, smiling gently.

Impulsively, Thislen reached out and put his hand on her shoulder. That was when he realized what he was feeling in a sudden flash of clarity. *Protective? Do I actually want to help her? What is wrong with me? She's facing a member of the Ruling Council!*

She smiled, putting her hand over his for a moment. He pulled away.

What could it hurt? I could help one person in my lifetime, just one *besides myself.*

"My name is Thislen."

Mila set the mug on the work table before moving the cloth from his forehead and feeling it with the back of her hand. Her smile had returned with the offer of his name, wider and brighter than before. "Well, Thislen," she said as she dampened the cloth once more, "now that you've eaten, you ought to try and get some more sleep." She rose, pressing gently on his uninjured shoulder before turning away to her work.

The thief eased himself back down beneath the covers. For a time, he watched her go through the motions of creating medicines and salves and tinctures. Mila moved like a breeze, every motion flowing into the next step with endless grace.

Thislen's limbs grew heavy. His eyelids sank despite his best efforts to remain awake and watchful. Eventually, he let them close.

Instead, he listened. Thislen drank up the chorus of little clinks and clunks made by wood and metal. The delicate chime of glass against itself. The scrape of stones as mortar and pestle ground up herbs. He breathed in the spiced air of the apothecary, the sharp scent of something tickling his nose. Heavier and heavier he felt, like he was becoming a part of the cot beneath him.

Slowly, reality faded away. Thislen slept.

"Come," a stranger's voice encouraged, "come to me. I will help you. I finally found you. Come."

"Who are you?" Thislen asked. He knew where he was, though only barely. He was in Astera, where Evelie had discovered him earlier that day. Evelie was nowhere in sight. No one was. The streets were empty, the sky a strange slate gray that hid the time.

The voice came again from the spires of Perilee. "Come," it breathed.

"No!" Thislen said. He closed his eyes.

Crackling. The dull roar of some great beast. The beating of sudden heat against his skin. Thislen opened his eyes to chaos and fire. Flames! Fire! Burning heat roiled through the air and made it shimmer and waver.

Distant screams filled the air. Windows shattered as flames leapt out of the buildings nearest to him. Thislen shied away, arms raised as sparks flew toward his face. Closer and closer the screams crept, growing louder and more desperate. They were shrill and hoarse and never-ending, raising the flesh on his arms and chilling him to the core.

"Find Soren, he—"

Thislen recognized Percivan's voice and the dismayed shout that followed. That shout sounded over and over, again and again and again. Thick black smoke filled the sky, hiding the stars from view. He whirled to look down the terraces of the city toward the sea.

What wasn't smoke was licking flame and leaping shadow and the soot-stained monoliths of buildings. Down in the water, along the burning docks, the ships were all in flames. They were trapped. Everyone on the island was trapped.

People were everywhere suddenly, pushing him as they ran past in sheer terror. Thislen was jostled in every direction, surrounded by their screams and their faces frozen in masks of dread, each one vanishing a few steps later. Dead bodies littered the ground, dark huddled shapes scattered all around him. He stumbled over one, looking down to find it had no face. No eyes. Nothing.

Thislen tried to throw himself backward with a hoarse shout of his own, but a tremendous pressure fell upon his back. It was the massive weight of a shadow looming over him, heavy and foreboding. Slowly, he turned his head to the great spires of Perilee behind him, drawing closer and closer despite the fact he wasn't moving.

"Save us!" Voices screamed.

"Help!"

"No!"

"Someone, please!"

Thislen couldn't breathe beneath the force of Perilee's shadow, couldn't move. He was as trapped as the rest of the island. "No," he gasped.

Fire exploded from the castle towers, glass arcing through the air in a glittering cloud. It hung suspended for a moment, then began to plummet in a deadly hail. It rained down around Thislen. He flung his arms protectively over his head.

The screams were getting louder and louder until he couldn't hear anything else. A wall crumbled nearby. The city and the castle were beginning to collapse in great gouts of smoke and leaping tongues of flame.

"No, no, *stop it!" Thislen shouted, pressing his hands over his ears.*

A building fell toward him, swallowing him in ash and darkness.

Thislen woke with a gasp, grasping the wrist of the hand above his face before he realized he was even moving. Mila dropped the cool washcloth as she was caught, eyes wide despite a small smile. "Easy now. It's me, Thislen." she said soothingly.

Thislen blinked several times, very still and quiet. His heart, pounding in his chest, began to calm. He let go of her wrist and sagged back onto the bed. "Hello," he croaked.

How is it that I feel worse than before?

"Hello. You were having a bad dream." Mila explained, picking up the cloth and returning to the task of gently dabbing at his neck and cheeks and forehead.

He groaned, eyes closing. "It seemed so real. Everything…everything was on fire. Everything."

The calm and resonant voice of Olen Ominir sounded nearby, and his jovial red-bearded face appeared a moment later. "Thislen, my dear guest, you are the only one remotely close to being on fire at the moment."

"Fevers can make dreams more real, and wilder," Mila said.

"And yours is getting worse," Olen added. "Don't you worry, though. I think it might be the last push for your body. Those black veins are almost gone."

Thislen lifted a hand to his shoulder, touching the bandages gingerly despite the small shock of pain. *They must have changed them,* he realized. He was glad his ring was tucked into his pocket, safely out of sight. The fact he hadn't even stirred while they tended to him told him that he was worse off than he thought. His brow furrowed. It *bothered* him, being so weak and helpless. What if they had—

What, what if they had what? *Healed you more? That's exactly what they did. Idiot.* He lectured himself. He had very little option but to trust himself to them, at least until he had his strength back. There was no use acting feral.

"Mila, why don't you go and get him another serving of that broth and some of the bread?" Olen suggested.

"We haven't any heated."

"Go and heat it."

"But Father, I already banked the fire after luncheon!" Mila frowned.

Olen didn't say a word. He just turned to look at Mila. After a long moment of staring at one another, Mila sighed and headed up the stairs to the second level.

"You know, I have to ask, my boy," Olen said expansively as he pulled the low wooden stool closer to the edge of the cot, "what happened to your shoulder?"

Thislen felt his hands go cold, and his eyes narrowed for a moment. *Safest, probably to tell the truth—at least in part.* "I fell," he admitted.

"Fell?" Olen echoed, "On to something?" He leaned forward, fingers steepled beneath his chin.

The apothecary was blatantly intrigued by the puzzle of Thislen's wound. He felt his heartbeat pick up inside his chest. "Yes, on my way to my ship last night. I live in Gate Quarter." He hoped that would be enough explanation. After all, the Gate Quarter had no reputation for cleanliness. It was rife with the potential for illness and infection. The poor of Astera were all crammed into the smallest Quarter on the island, their streets a sign of overpopulation, and if the streets were bad, then the ships were worse. They were often packed full with people sleeping in great open cabins, stacked in hammocks one above the other as tight as fish in a barrel, or huddled anywhere there was space on the floor. Illness traveled quickly in such conditions, and cleanliness was nearly impossible.

It was a miracle the poor had ships at all, really. Even if they *were* old leaky tubs.

"I figured you were from the Gate Quarter when I saw your scar," Olen said carefully.

Thislen's eyes widened, and he started to push himself upright despite the way it made everything spin and tilt around him. His elbow buckled. He felt nauseated, stomach churning angrily and bile rising in his throat. His head felt too heavy for his neck once it had left the pillow.

Olen leaned forward quickly, getting an arm around Thislen's shoulders as he collapsed backward, easing him down again. "Here now, hey! It's alright. It's fine, *you're* fine. Rest, don't worry." The large man soothed.

Thislen's ears rang. He quietly brought his hand up to trace over the scar in question. It was simple, small, and tucked up underneath his right collarbone. The marks were made on a simple system, tallying up transgressions. The first time you were caught stealing, they cut a single diagonal line. The second time, they cut in the opposite direction, making an 'x' of the two marks about three fingers wide. If you were unlucky enough to be caught a third time, you were at the mercy of the Asteran courts. Often, they settled for cutting off a hand or two, depending on how much you stole. Sometimes, however, the Ruling Council wanted examples made of the poor and desperate, and things were worse. They could send you to your death, sentence you to working in the deepest mines, or banish you from the island entirely.

Thislen—and other thieves and frauds and cheats and smugglers—were all just lucky that the laws made when the Vaim first appeared still held. For that matter, so were the people in the Gate Quarter. More than three hundred years ago, the Vaim had emerged in the wake of the plague. A great massacre happened. Hundreds of people died. No one knew what the spirits wanted apart from death—and the Asteran Royal family had done nothing. The Ruling Council staged a coup and rescued the populace, or so the story went. *That* Ruling Council had wanted what was best for the island and ordered ships built, and the docks and piers. They had written laws to protect the rights of the Asteran people.

None of them cared *now*, of course. The power had gone to their heads within a generation or two. The laws still held, tenuous as gossamer down, because they had become *tradition*. They were just a part of how things were. Asterans did not much like change, and that was the only thing protecting them anymore. It was the only reason thieves like Thislen weren't just left on the island when the sun set.

Thislen had two marks, forming the single 'x'. He had been caught before—twice. "I swear, I haven't stolen anything except food." He gasped as the ringing in his ears subsided and his stomach settled. He floundered weakly in the sudden tangle of blankets beneath the hands gently holding him down. "I haven't done anything! Don't send me to the gaol!"

"It's alright! I'm not going to say or do anything that might harm you. You have my word," Olen assured.

Mila hurried back downstairs at his outburst, setting a thick slice of bread and another mug of broth aside to lean over Thislen. She untangled the covers and adjusted his pillow, frowning at her father. "What did you do? You're frightening him."

Thislen sagged back, giving up his feeble and exhausting fight. "I was just trying to eat."

Mila leaned over him, dabbing a cool cloth to his cheeks and neck with a small smile. "It's alright. You haven't stolen anything from us. People will do what they must to survive when they haven't got a coin to their name."

Her father let out a soft laugh. "No doubt that's why Evelie brought you here. My father and my father's father and *his* father's father all swore long ago that we would treat anyone who needed it, anyone who came to us for help. Payment be damned. Evelie must have guessed you had very little coin, if any. We can work out a small trade for the service if you wish it, but we're happy to help."

I'm not a charity case, he thought as he lay cradled in the pillows. Thislen studied his rescuers. The world had stopped spinning behind them, but the churning in the pit of his stomach hadn't abated at all. He felt it twitch and slide around like he had swallowed an eel as he took in their quietly concerned faces. They were having a silent conversation through expressions alone, about *him* if the subtle nods were anything to go by.

Knock it off, Thislen. You're leaving as soon as you're well, and there's nothing for it. It's what's safest for everyone.

Perhaps he could stay long enough to pay them for their help, as Olen had suggested, however. Repayment was a good reason to stay, and Thislen knew just what he wanted to do.

I'm going to help Mila. No one in this city has as much experience with avoiding the eye of the Ruling Council as I do. A little bit of advice to her, and we'll be done.

And he wouldn't allow himself to give any more than that. Once she knew how to be safe, and Thislen was well, he would disappear again and become just another thief within Astera's crowds.

"Are you hungry?" Mila asked, turning to fetch the food she'd prepared, "Here's that bread I promised you."

"And it's getting late," Olen sighed, "another day flown. You might want to stay awake. I asked Ivan to help carry you down to our ship for the evening. He ought to be along soon."

"To your ship? For the night?" He turned to look at the glass panes of the greenhouse, the door to which still stood open beside him.

The light of day was just now beginning to fade. Where it touched the plants, it created pools of shadow that made Thislen shudder. He half expected the darkness to bulge into shadowy fingers and glowing red eyes. A few hours remained until sunset, but the day was marching inexorably toward its end. He had spent an entire day amongst strangers.

When was the last time I did that? When I was eight?

When his father had left him at the inn, clutching the ring that was too big to fit and shouting for him to come back. He shook the thought from his head as Olen patted his arm, then stood.

"That's what you do when the sun sets on Astera, my boy. You leave it."

That's just how it is, he heard a hundred different voices say.

"Who is Ivan?" Thislen asked belatedly.

"You know, you might like him. Young man, around yours and Mila's age. He's Evelie's son, and a florist like her."

Mila shook her head with a smile as she headed back toward the stairs that led to the kitchen. "He's big as a horse, and he loves to tease. We grew up together. I'll go and bank the fire again, Father."

"I'm going to go get the litter, and then Ivan. At least try and finish another mug of broth, Thislen, and we'll get on our way before the crowds get too big, eh?" Olen stretched as he crossed the shop, waving a hand through the air. "Don't worry, lad, we'll be with you every step of the way!"

Thislen stared numbly after the apothecary as the door to the shop swung closed. *Every step of the way? That's what I'm afraid of.*

4

The evening exodus from the city of Astera was a nightmare. Thislen was keenly aware of the flip-flopping of his stomach and how lightheaded he was because of how the litter swayed and lurched with every step that Olen and Ivan took. The broth and bit of bread he had managed to eat threatened to reappear with every jostling step. The sky above them rocked and swirled. Any additional queasiness he felt came from the saccharine closeness of Evelie, Olen, and their children. Mila and Ivan were bickering playfully with one another, chattering like squirrels in the parks of the Grand Quarter. Olen and Evelie doted on one another in the way of old friends, finishing one another's sentences more often than not.

It can't get any worse than this, Thislen thought as he watched them fuss over one another while he clung to the litter. His grip was weak on the wooden frame, but it tightened as the wood creaked near his head. *Please, Ancestors, don't let it break. Don't let them drop me on my head!*

Then it got worse. Evelie smiled back at him, slowing her pace to fall into step beside him. She patted his hand where it clutched at the thin wooden pole. "It must all seem a little overwhelming, hm? I've seen you watching us." She said lowly, as if Olen just above his head wouldn't hear.

Thislen grimaced, concentrating on breathing in and out and *not* throwing up over the side of his own swaying version of the hells.

The matronly florist appeared to take his silence and his twisted expression as embarrassment. She patted his hand again with a soft, sad smile. "Have you not got a family of your own, dear?"

If I say no, is she going to try and convince me to stay? Thislen wouldn't put it past her. It seemed just the sort of thing the all-too-helpful Evelie might try. Once more, he said nothing.

"You know, I was pregnant with my Ivan at the same time as Olen's wife, Mari, was pregnant with Mila. Both of us lost the love of our life when the fever swept through the city. You might be too young to remember it, now that I think about it. Mila and Ivan were still in swaddling clothes."

Olen leaned forward enough for Thislen to look up at him, the sky swinging wildly behind his mane of red hair. "I did everything I could to help save Mari and Haran. That's how Evelie and I started talking. When they passed, we grew very close. She helped nurse Mila for me, and we took it in turns to watch them while they grew. Raised the both of them together."

"And now look at them!" Evelie said warmly, hands fluttering at Ivan on the other end of the litter and Mila walking beside him. "All grown up, or nearly so. Practically family, you two." She gave Olen's shoulder a fond little smack with the back of her hand.

He laughed, leaning back. "Ah, but when they were younger! They were absolutely wild, terrorizing the whole street. Do you remember, Evelie? That time when—"

I don't want to know their histories! Thislen thought, trying to tune the conversation out. He didn't want to remember them or their tales when he was gone. It would only make everything harder. Thislen knew he was leaving—as soon as he could.

He squeezed his eyes shut as they started down a sloping cobbled street that formed a ramp between two of the terraces of the Goods Quarter. More and more people were joining them the nearer they got to the docks. It was early enough in the evening that it was only a languid trickle of people, their chatter rising like the babble of a brook on either side.

Every night, the people of Astera followed the same paths. Houses didn't exist outside of the Grand Quarter. Every sheltered space on the island was dedicated to a purpose. In the Goods Quarter, everything was a shop or store, usually with a kitchen on the level above so that breakfasts, luncheons, and dinners could be made. In the Guild Quarter, those spaces were workshops. Only in the Gate Quarter and the Grand Quarter were rooms or buildings left idle. For the wealthy and noble elite, their homes were sprawling estates dedicated to idle pleasures. They still had beds in grand rooms dedicated to sleeping, or so the stories went. They alone were rich enough to afford to have galleys built into their ships, to eat their suppers long after the sun had set.

The Gate Quarter held crumbling ruins of residences, abandoned so long ago that no one remembered what living in them was like. The poorest of Astera's residents headed directly to their jobs and then back to their ships with whatever meager fare their pennies could buy.

Travelers were herded along by innkeepers, following after their keeper like so many sheep in a flock. They stood out, looking around at the crowd they found themselves in and carrying their things. Most travelers chose to remain on the ships after their first night, once the innkeep showed them the small block of cabins they had purchased. There were no inns in the Gate Quarter, however. No one had to pay to be packed onto those ships. Most people visiting the kingdom paid *not* to.

The night before, Thislen had faced the Vaim and barely escaped with his life, racing to the water ahead of the sinking sun. Today he had more time than he needed, and was being carried down toward the ships with some to spare. No one around them was in any sort of rush or hurry. They all ambled peacefully down toward the water.

So why does this feel far more dangerous than before?

He opened his eyes again when the ground leveled out. Mila was walking backward just ahead of the litter, her hands tucked behind her back and her smile broad and bright as she listened to Ivan.

"So, he said he wanted me to give him a bouquet of daisies *and* roses for his wife. It actually looked quite good in the end. I convinced him to add a couple dark green ferns. That's what really made it." Ivan said. His voice was as low and warm as Evelie's, and that wasn't all he shared with his mother. They had the same brown hair and green eyes. Ivan was taller, though, his shoulders broad and muscled. He looked nothing like what Thislen expected a florist should, though Ivan's smile was bright enough to grow plants on its own.

He ought to be a soldier, but instead he's as gentle as a lamb. Thislen didn't like him. He was almost too trusting, the way Olen and Evelie, and even Mila were. *What sort of lives have they led to turn out like this?* Charmed lives, no doubt. Wealthy enough to be comfortable but not rich enough to be of any note. *They don't really care about me.*

Would lying to himself make it easier to leave?

Evelie patted the thief on the hand again, and he debated letting go of the side of the litter. A sudden lurch decided him against it. "Don't you worry, Thislen. We're nearly to the ship now." She assured, mistaking his grimace for one of pain.

I don't want you to touch me, he thought. It made his skin come alive in a way he didn't trust himself to handle. It made him want to stay, to trust, to talk. It was like a hunger in the pit of his stomach, one he hadn't noticed until someone began to feed him, an ache he had learned to live with long ago.

"Anyway, what about you?" Ivan asked, drawing Thislen's attention, "I saw Bestant stop in earlier."

"Oh!" Mila's steps faltered. She turned around to walk normally, hands clasped in front of her chest. "Nothing much happened, really."

Thislen couldn't help but snort. Mila turned a silent glare back at him. He met her gaze, steady and unmoving. It was somewhat difficult to do while being swung from side to side. She was the first to look away.

"Nothing much?" Ivan pressed.

"He came for his mother's dose a day early is all. He was already at Perilee."

"Oh."

"Well, Evelie and I had quite an adventure today; I think that more than makes up for Lord Bestant!" Olen interjected cheerily, changing the subject. His gaze, however, was fixed on Thislen from above. "We were on our way to the market, you see..."

They passed from the last of the terraces to the gentler slopes of the Guild Quarter's streets while Olen recounted the tale of a fishmonger whose cart blocked the road and an aged woman who berated him. The five of them were a slightly slower eddy in the rising tide of people making their way toward the docks, the litter hampering their movement. The crowds parted for them and around them without a word needing to be said, but it did not make Ivan and Olen move any faster. A bubble of space accompanied them, as did stares and glances.

Thislen felt like a bug beneath a glass dome. He saw raised brows, concerned frowns, hands touched to hearts. He wondered how piteous he looked as he was carried along that strangers were sparing any thought for his condition. The thicker the throng around them grew, the more he felt like shouting at anyone who murmured soft well wishes or cast him sad looks.

Don't do it, don't draw any more attention to yourself than this, he lectured himself, sinking further and further into the confines of the litter. He hoped they would see him and forget him. He hoped none of them would ever think of him again. Thislen tried closing his eyes, but every time he did, his heart would race, and he'd imagine the crowd drawing closer and closer. He didn't trust them. He couldn't. So, Thislen kept his eyes open.

The babble around them had grown to a chittering chorus. People called their hellos and passed along their news as they walked. Couples came together after finishing their work. Friends ran up to their fellows, adding their loud voices to the excited hullabaloo. Children laughed and dashed between people's legs, never far from their parents but never slowing. Some few bid friends a farewell and walked away down different streets along the shorefront as they came to the piers at last. The crowd was now thick enough that swirls of bright clothing and flashes of smiling faces passed quickly on either side, making Thislen's unease only grow.

"Are we nearly there?" He gasped at last, unable to stand another second.

"Yes, we are. Our ship's that first one there, nearest the shore." Olen assured.

The sinking sun painted everything in oranges and blacks, reveling in its twilight. The hulking shape of the ships on either side of the docks were black monoliths with gilt gold accents, all tricks caused by the fading light. Each vessel was one of the many arranged on the spokes of the docks and piers and quays that snaked away from the island at the water's edge, a floating home away from home for the evening. Those from the Goods Quarter had ships nearer to the shore to compensate for their living inland. Those from the Guild Quarter were berthed further out, making everyone's commute to their evening berths roughly the same. The parade of ships left and returned in the same order every day, with the vessels further out departing first and returning last. It was much more desirable to move up from the Gate Quarter to any of the others, to buy precious time each day.

And space! Thislen had most often spent his nights crammed tight into the packed bunks that lined the battered ships of the Gate Quarter, where anyone without coin was at least granted a patch of deck to sleep on. The ships of the Goods and Guild Quarters were far less crowded, and he found himself looking forward to sleep without the stale scents of sour ale and rank sweat in the air, or an elbow in his back, or a knee in his face.

Olen and Evelie owned shops mere streets away from the castle, near the heart of the Goods Quarter. Those shops nearest Perilee and the great market square before its main gate had ships that docked right up against the shore. Such coveted spots were passed down from generation to generation—or bought at great expense. They were some of the first to come home each morning and nearly the last to leave each night.

The gangplanks onto the great ships were sturdy wooden walkways with ropes threaded through metal posts to serve as handrails. True to his word, Olen turned around and began backing up the gangplank of the very first ship.

As the apothecary tilted the litter to carry it up the wooden pathway with its meager protection from falling off either side, Thislen clutched anxiously at the frame. The water between the ship and the dock sloshed and slapped against wood and stone as if it were angry to be contained this way and eager to make others feel its wrath. He tried very hard not to think about trying to swim with his injured shoulder and weak, feverish body if he were to fall in. Ivan followed after the healer, holding his own end of the littler higher to keep Thislen relatively balanced.

When he caught his passenger staring down at him with wide eyes and a furrowed brow, pale as a sheet, Ivan gave an easy and reassuring smile. "Don't worry; we'll get you settled on the deck for a bell or two. Best place to eat supper is in the sea air on a fine night. After that, we can take you below-decks to get some rest."

"A fine idea, Ivan," Olen said smoothly, interrupting the cutting reply Thislen thought to make. "Feed a fever, they say."

The apothecary headed for the ship's prow once they made the deck, ignoring Thislen's quiet, pleading look.

"It's starve a fever, feed a cold," Mila called as she trailed after them.

"Is that the saying?" Olen asked, "But you oughtn't starve *any* illness!"

"I agree. A bite or two never hurt anybody." Evelie said firmly as if that settled the entire matter.

Thislen sagged back in the litter with a sigh. He wasn't getting any rest, it seemed, until he ate again.

Unlike ships used exclusively for sea travel, the decks of Asteran home vessels were lined with benches, and the masts were often strung with low-slung awnings to provide shelter from inclement weather. There were worn rugs here and there, tarred to the decks on the corners to keep them from falling overboard in a storm. It gave the impression of some strange, great chamber open to the skies. Neighbors and friends would gather to talk and share their suppers on clear nights. Some people started games of cards or dice. Women would often sit together, going over skeins of yarn or bits of thread to trade back and forth.

The prow of this particular ship had a pair of benches that dovetailed into one another against the ship's side up in the bow, making a perfect corner to prop Thislen up in. It was well sheltered from the breeze off the sea by the railing. With the pillow from the litter behind his head and the blanket they had wrapped him in draped across his lap, he found himself relatively comfortable. The litter was tucked beneath the seats, much to his relief.

If I get the chance to break that thing into pieces, I will. He vowed.

Once his patient was settled, and Evelie had satisfied herself with fussing, Olen offered her his arm and the two of them set off across the deck to find supper. Mila settled beside Thislen, careful not to lean into him and press his injured shoulder into the wood on the other side.

Much to Thislen's discomfort, Ivan chose to sit near his feet and face them both, pinning a corner of the blanket beneath him. "Budge up; you're on the blanket," he said shortly.

"Oh, sorry," Ivan said, carefully tucking it beneath Thislen's foot instead.

Why did you say anything? he asked himself. *That could have turned into a fight. Are you losing your mind?* Maybe the fever was driving him mad.

"Alright, Mila," Ivan said, looking across the deck to track the back of Olen's head. "What aren't you telling me? What is it you're trying to hide from your father?"

Thislen's brows rose. *So, he can see right through her, too.* He glanced sideways at Mila.

"Don't look at me like that!" She admonished them both, unfolding a shawl to wrap around her shoulders with a frown on her face. "I just don't know how to start the conversation. What if we don't see this the same way?"

Thislen grimaced. *If her father wants her to marry Lord Bestant, there's nothing more she can do.* The archaic laws of the island kingdom said she was nothing more than her father's property, and if he wished her to marry, she'd have to. *Unless she runs away or marries someone else first.* If she had no other suitors except Lord Bestant, either option would be difficult at best.

"See what the same way?" Ivan asked.

Mila took in a deep breath. "Well," she began with a sigh, "you know that Lord Bestant came to visit earlier today, right?"

"Right," Ivan said, leaning forward.

She quickly relayed the whole of her encounter with Lord Bestant inside the apothecary, brushing off what Thislen had seen as clear discomfort around the matter. In fact, she left her emotions out of the retelling entirely. Despite her best efforts to remove her personal opinions on the matter, however, Ivan's sunny smile had vanished by the end of the tale.

Ships further along the docks had begun to pull in their gangplanks and unfurl their sails to start the short journey into the open water around Astera. The sky was painted with purples and oranges that bled into one another, touched here and there with scudding gray clouds. Thislen looked at the distant spires of Perilee above, watching them wink and glitter in the fading light. This time last night, he'd woken up afraid he'd never see another sunset.

Mila stared down at her lap, fussing quietly with her skirts and giving her brother in all but name time to think.

Ivan, too, stared off into the distance. His gaze slid over the harbor, watching the most distant ships drift away from the island while he mulled over his thoughts. "I really don't know if there *is* a good way to tell Olen, Mila," he said at last.

"There isn't," Thislen said, voice flat and hoarse in his ears, "especially because she doesn't want to marry him."

"And how would *you* know? You only met her today," Ivan said. There was a hint of a frown on his features and a quiet edge to his words.

Thislen's brows rose. *Maybe he's starting to feel the same way about me as I feel about him. Like oil and water.*

Mila huffed and smacked Ivan's knee. "Don't go puffing your chest out over this. I told him, that's how he knows. He was there when it happened. It isn't like I could have hidden it from him."

"But you were going to hide it from me?" Ivan asked slowly, brows drawing in as he gave Mila a reproachful look. There was a strange note of hurt in his voice.

Jealousy? Thislen wondered. What call was there for Ivan to be jealous of someone Mila had just met?

He was distracted by a familiar pair of shapes heading toward them from across the deck. "Best figure out how you're going to have this conversation quickly. Your parents are coming," Thislen pointed out, dropping his head back to rest against the pillow behind him and closing his eyes.

Are people always this exhausting?

MILA WATCHED Thislen sag against the wood of the ship, eyes closed in his ashen face, and wondered briefly if she had upset him somehow. *That might make him worse in the long run.* There was a crease at the bridge of his nose that never entirely went away. Was it pain, or was it her and the problem she had unceremoniously dumped into his lap earlier that very day?

She pulled her shawl tighter around her shoulders, automatically pushing herself to smile as she turned to watch Olen and Evelie return, their arms laden with supper. They had brought a large round of bread and soft cheese to spread over it, and mugs of warm broth for everyone to share. For dessert, there were three apples, rich and crimson and sweet. They passed their foraged findings around and arranged themselves in the small, comfortable corner of the prow. As they settled, sailors came by to light the glass-walled lanterns strung in the rigging and hung from the awnings above, bathing them all in a warm golden glow.

There was a clatter of wood on wood and the sharp, loud clang of a bell as the ropes were cast off and their ship eased itself away from the island, one of the last to seek open waters. The breeze off the sea grew sharper and colder as they left the relative shelter of the shoreline behind.

I should have picked a thicker shawl; it's going to get cold tonight. She was sheltered, however, by Olen on one side and Thislen on the other, the pair of them serving to break the wind and keep her warm. She knew she would survive.

Mila was pleased to see Thislen take the bread and cheese she offered, taking a bite despite his apparent fatigue. She was only her father's apprentice, still, and she could have kicked herself for thinking of starving the young man. After that first bite, Thislen ate like a man who hadn't seen food in a fortnight. He consumed it all with gusto, tearing into the bread with bared teeth and devouring half an apple in short order. He didn't slow down again until his second slice had vanished, and then he leaned back and nursed his mug of broth.

Of course you feed a fever; he needs all the strength he can get, she thought, taking in the high spots of color that tinged his cheeks. His eyes were almost too bright. She didn't even have to touch her hand to his forehead to know his fever was back in earnest.

The food will help, she soothed herself. *Goodness, but he was ravenous!*

There was some quiet chatter as they passed things back and forth, but for the most part everyone was silent as they ate, leaving Mila a short amount of time to gather her thoughts. Her heart quailed at the thought of discussing this with her father, wondering if his support was truly as unconditional as she hoped. Silently, she tried to navigate the different outcomes of the conversation in her head, settling at last on telling him in the privacy of their cabin at the end of the evening. *That will work well, I think. I want him to react honestly.*

Ivan cleared his throat after the last of the apples had been sliced and eaten, drawing everyone's attention. "So! Mila has something to tell you," he announced to their parents, shattering the comfortable silence of those filling their stomachs.

Oh, I could just strangle *him right now!* She thought, glaring daggers at Ivan while heat rose in her cheeks. Much to her dismay, there was a prickle in the corners of her eyes and a lump in her throat. She hoped her glare on the florist could curdle milk, though she knew that with her rounded cheeks and button nose, she was anything but intimidating. She fumbled as she set down her mug. When had her hands gone cold?

Olen turned a warm and curious look upon his daughter, his great fuzzy brows drawn upwards, wrinkling his forehead. His smile crinkled the corners of his eyes. Evelie's expectant expression was much the same, even as she smacked at Ivan's knee in silent reproach for putting Mila on the spot.

What will they say? Mila felt her heart flutter in her throat. With a deep breath that didn't seem to lift the pressure off her chest, she recounted what had happened with Lord Bestant one last time.

Evelie's reaction as she told the tale was much what she had expected. The matronly florist brought the back of her hand to her lips, eyes growing wider and wider as Mila spoke. Her father's features, however, grew grim and dark like a storm cloud. His thick brows knit together in an uncustomary frown.

"And that's when he asked me to marry him," Mila finished helplessly.

Evelie gasped loudly, hands fluttering. "He proposed! Oh, *our* Mila, a nobleman's wife! Lord *Bestant's* wife! My goodness, what a turn of fate! I think he could be a nicer boy, perhaps, but still!" She fanned herself, smiling giddily.

Just as I feared, Mila thought, heart sinking in her chest.

"He wants you to, what? Marry him and raise a brood of children to be as spoiled and entitled as he is?" Olen blustered, harrumphing mightily. "Has he no respect for what you want to do? You tend to those in need! That's important work!"

If Mila knew anything, it was that she was expected to pick up her family's mantle and continue their legacy. She was expected to marry *someone,* she knew, and have children who could do what her ancestors had done for as long as anyone could remember. The Ominir line had served as menders to the residents of Astera for generations.

I know it's important *work, too, work that's sorely needed—but no one ever asked me if doing it or passing it on was all that I wanted to do!*

She wasn't certain she wanted to stay in the shop for the rest of her life. She'd never lose the skills of an apothecary, but what if she wanted to do that work somewhere else? For as long as she knew about the inequality on the island, she had wanted to go down to Gate Quarter and help mend anyone there who needed it, but her father insisted they remain in their shop and only take those who came to them.

"I just don't want to give up on my own path to try and fit into someone else's expectations," she said pointedly, meeting her father's gaze.

Oh, she had fallen into the role easily enough from a young age. It was just her and her father most days. When he had asked her to sweep the floor or help him dust or rearrange the shelves, she had. She loved watering and tending to the plants in the greenhouse. Lessons on their uses and how to turn them into salves, potions, tisanes, and more followed soon after. Before she knew it, she had become an apprentice apothecary.

The only problem was that Olen never asked her if that was what she wanted. In fact, no one had ever really asked her *anything* until Lord Bestant, and his question wasn't meant to be answered with a 'no, thank you.' His proposal was more a formality than anything else, a courtesy extended for propriety's sake. He expected he would get what he wanted.

But why does he want me?

For as long as she could remember, Mila had felt like something was *waiting* for her somewhere. Just around the next street corner, or tucked up on a shelf. She didn't know when it would find her, but it would. Maybe it *was* Lord Bestant she was waiting for.

"He's assuming quite a lot, isn't he?" Olen continued to grouse. "You're not the sort who could sit idle and fuss over pretty dresses. What are you going to do? Fritter your time away walking through gardens or embroidering pretty cushions or some such nonsense? I don't know what the wealthy kept women of the nobility even do!" He banged a hand onto the bench between them, rattling the mugs.

When did he stop listening to me? She thought with a soft sigh. Recently she had begun to feel that no matter how much she loved her father, he'd be hurt and betrayed if she did even one thing differently than he had planned.

Mila turned to gather the mugs and tuck them somewhere safe from her father's quiet fuming, only to catch Thislen's fever-bright eyes staring at her. The strange, wan young man had eyes so dark a brown they were nearly black. They bored into her, through her, and beyond. She had the strangest feeling that *he* knew what she wasn't saying, that *he* saw so much more of her than anyone else.

Perhaps he sees more than he should, she mused, wondering for a moment if she ought to be afraid.

Ivan leaned forward, putting a hand on her knee. She tore her gaze away from her patient to meet his earnest green eyes. "But you don't want to marry him at all, right? That's what you said," he asked intently.

Another expectation, one I just can't meet. Her heart broke in her chest. It stung, knowing she was going to lose Ivan as a brother someday in the future. She couldn't remember when she had realized Ivan wanted to love her more deeply than that. Evelie and Olen would both be thrilled if Ivan ever crossed that invisible line and asked to court her, but Mila was profoundly glad he had not. Yet.

Mila had been *raised* with Ivan, grown up watching him skin his knees or cry over trampled flowers on the road. She knew him too well. If they married, nothing in her life would ever change. There might be a silent and unspoken wish for them to join their families, but once they did...

Mila would be expected to produce children. *I have no interest in that sort of thing. I don't want to get married at all! No one asked me if I ever wanted to get married in the first place!* She felt as if the air itself were conspiring against her for a moment as it refused to enter her lungs. At last, she sucked in a small breath, putting her hand over Ivan's and giving him a small smile that felt as brittle as spun glass.

"I don't want to marry *anyone*," she said as gently as possible, hoping beyond hope that he might understand.

When his shoulders relaxed and a great smile wreathed his face, she knew he hadn't. His relief was so palpable that there was no way he could have understood that she included him in that decision. Her fingers curled tightly into the folds of her shawl as he pulled his hand away. A pit formed in her stomach as she realized this was something she would have to deal with, bluntly and soon.

"Well, if you're *absolutely certain* you wish to reject his proposal, we'll need to figure out how to do so without being seen as rude," Evelie fussed, patting Mila's knee reassuringly, mistaking the tension in the young woman for nervousness of a different sort.

"Well, if that's all." Olen chuckled, leaning back against the balustrade. "Easily done. I'll just refuse on your behalf."

"With what excuses, father?" Mila said, unable to keep the edge of exasperation from her voice.

Ivan snapped his fingers. "I know. A noble like him will lose all interest when a better match comes along."

"So, we just have to keep them from getting engaged until then!" Evelie chimed in.

"How?" Ivan asked.

"We can send Mila away for a little while until he's betrothed to someone else," Olen said reluctantly. "I'll miss you terribly, my dear, but it's probably safest."

Her heart swelled within her chest, lifting her up with it. She straightened where she sat, catching her father's hand and clasping it in both of her own in sudden eagerness. "I could go to our farm outside the walls! The one that supplies our shop? I can even keep working out there!"

Yes, going *somewhere is what I've been waiting for! Let me go somewhere where green things thrive and grow!*

"He's going to look there," Thislen said quietly somewhere near her elbow. It was the first he had spoken since they started the deliberations. She had nearly forgotten he was there.

"What?" Olen asked, "How could you know?"

"He knew about the farm. He said he could make you an Earl of the land there if it would make Mila want to marry him."

Her heart sank again. *He's right, of course.* She sagged back against the ship's wooden side.

"Well, he doesn't know that much about Ivan and me, does he?" Evelie asked suddenly. "The flower farm we work with is a bit further across the island and on the other side of the Spine. On the eastern half of the island instead of the west." She traced a finger through the air like a small map. "Why doesn't Mila go and work there for a season or two? When we know it's safe for her to return, it will be easy enough to send for her."

Olen's thick brows drew together sharply, and he combed his fingers through his wild beard. Mila knew when her father was agitated. *He doesn't like the idea of me being somewhere he'll have no excuse to go and visit—but that's the point!* Wasn't it?

"I don't know," he grumbled, the words sour and flat.

Mila leaned forward, catching his eye. "Father," she pleaded, "let me go. I don't want to risk the shop, and I don't want to risk my own future. Please, let me do this." She held out her hands.

His gaze grew more intent, staring deeper, searching her face. His frown darkened, the wrinkles of his face deepening in the space of a single heartbeat. His expression relaxed abruptly into something resigned and quietly, subtly hurt.

Does he know that I might never come back? She wondered with a pang.

His own hands wrapped around hers, large and warm and familiar. "As you wish, Mila. I love you. I want you to be happy, no matter where you are."

Her heart sank and the bottom of her stomach fell away. Some part of him *did* know! *I can't help that I ache for something to be different every day, for something new to happen!* She didn't even know if she would like this choice in the end. All she knew was that she was burning with the chance to *try*.

"Don't worry, father. I'll be back before you know it," she said as brightly as she could manage. She wasn't certain it was the truth, but the reassurance was needed—for both of them.

He smiled at her, wrapping a heavy arm around her shoulders in a warm and comforting embrace. "That brat has a lot to answer for, going forward. Do you hear me, my Lord?" He raised his voice, calling out over the water. Everyone jumped as the anchor rattled just below them, the clanking of the heavy chain telling the ship's residents that they had found their berth for the night.

Mila laughed, leaning into her father. Evelie and Ivan joined her. The tension in the air dissolved into something warm and soothing, like a blanket. Thislen was the only one who was still, silent, and solemn. His dark eyes observed them curiously like he wasn't sure how to speak to them or be one of them. She felt her father's whiskers tangle with her hair as he gave her a kiss on the head.

"Ah, my beautiful daughter. I'm going to miss you terribly." Olen lamented. "Ancestors curse Lord Soren Bestant."

Thislen jerked suddenly beside her, flying upright to lean around her side. His eyes were fixed intently on Olen, face pale and clammy. A grimace had twisted his features. "What did you say? Who?" he asked harshly.

Mila faltered with her hands upraised toward the thief. She had sat up abruptly, worried he had perhaps injured his shoulder or was afflicted with some other malady, until he spoke. Her alarm bled into confusion, heart pounding in her chest. She glanced at her family, eyes wide, relieved to find similar expressions of befuddlement on their faces.

Maybe it's his fever making him a bit strange, she decided.

"Lord Bestant," Mila began, "you remember him, yes? From earlier today?"

"His name, though—his name is Soren?" Thislen asked, gaze locked on Mila.

There was something about the intensity with which he asked that frightened her. She drew back, arms wrapped around herself as a sudden chill settled around her. All she could do to answer was nod.

He sagged suddenly back against the bow. A distressed cry left Mila's lips as she leaned forward, fingers at his neck to take his pulse. It beat as rapidly as her own, though it was weak.

Bitter was the lament that left his lips, spoken too lowly for anyone but her to hear. "*Find Soren,* ha."

His eyes fluttered and he went limp. Her breath caught in her chest for a moment, eyes wide with fear until he breathed.

Lord Soren Bestant's very name had made Thislen faint.

"Find Soren, he's—"

"Find Soren!"

"Soren!"

"Curse Lord Soren Bestant!"

Voices echoed in Thislen's head, distant and fast fading.

What happened? The last thing he remembered was Mila's face hovering nervously above him, and then nothing but twisted dreams of fire and ash.

Thislen was tangled in a cocoon of blankets, rocking gently from side to side on something soft. His clothes and the covers around him were drenched with sweat, clinging to his limbs in a sticky, uncomfortable mess. His head felt stuffed full of sheep's wool, and his eyelids too heavy to lift. With great effort, he wrested them open enough to stare at the wood-paneled wall a hand's breadth away from the tip of his nose.

Cabin, he realized sluggishly. He was below-decks, tucked into a bunk in a cabin. Slowly, he fought his way free of the confines of his covers and rolled over.

It was a small room, plain and nearly empty—but blissfully private. His bunk was set higher in the wall. It was narrow, just wide enough for one person to sleep comfortably. A small curtain had been strung across its mouth to offer some meager semblance of privacy if the occupant wished.

Carefully, he levered himself to the edge to take in the rest of the space. His shoulder gave a soft pang at the motion.

Below him was a bunk wide enough for two to sleep abreast, jutting out from the wall to fill the rest of the cabin. He could barely make out Mila in the slim glow of the crescent moon outside the single porthole. Soft gurgling snores from the shadows beside her spoke to Olen being beneath him, tucked out of sight against the bunk's wall.

Built into the wall beside the bunks and just beside the door to the small cabin was a wardrobe. An unlit lantern swung from a hook in the ceiling, its glass catching the faint silver light now and then, close enough that Thislen could reach out and touch it had he wished to.

He didn't remember coming down here. It was disorienting, waking up somewhere he hadn't gone to on his own two feet. Where was the stairway up to the deck? If he had to escape, how would he know where to go?

Escape what? To where? He asked himself, trying to wrest his mind back from the fog that had enveloped it.

Curse Lord Soren Bestant!

"Find Soren!"

He sat up abruptly, hunching to avoid hitting his head on the ceiling and staring down at his trembling hands. The voices weren't part of the fever if his had broken.

The dead can't get angry with you if you don't do what they want, he thought, *and it isn't my fault that I let go! He slipped! It wasn't my fault!* He bore no guilt in Percivan's fate. He had *tried*!

"Find Soren!"

Percivan's last choked words haunted him anyway. They echoed in his head loudly enough that he worried the dead nobleman would be standing in the corridor outside the cabin if he dared to open the door.

His heart was pounding in his chest, and blood roared in his ears. He couldn't avoid the desperate dark eyes of the nobleman in the shadows behind his eyelids. Guilt rose from his gut, threatening to choke him, to smother the breath from his lungs as it filled up too much of his chest. A shudder wracked him from head to toe. He gasped.

He sobbed. Thislen muffled the sounds with his hands over his mouth, but tears fell unbidden, unwanted, and unstoppable.

What do you want from me? I never asked for this, any of it! He shouted at the darkness in his mind.

"Thislen?"

Mila's voice was soft in the gloom, pulling him out of the spiral his thoughts had been trapped in. It gave him something to focus on. He wiped roughly at his eyes and swallowed his feelings for now.

Mila sat up slowly, unbound hair tumbling over her shoulder, silver and black in the moonlight.

"What?" Thislen said, hoping it sounded flat and disinterested instead of sullen. He plucked the damp fabric of his shirt away from his skin. The sweat prickled and itched as it dried.

"Are you alright? You gave us quite a scare, fainting like that." She admonished gently, lifting a hand to rest on the wooden lip of the top bunk. The pale light through the porthole painted her skin an unearthly blue. He had an urge to touch her, to reassure her the way she did for him, perhaps. Or perhaps he was still afraid, and wanted the contact to prove that something was real.

Don't, he whispered to himself.

"I was just…I was asked to find someone named Soren." Thislen said slowly.

"Asked to? And you think Lord Soren Bestant is the one you're looking for?" A soft frown turned down the corners of her lips. "I suppose it's not a very common name, is it?"

"The person who asked me to look for him would be part of the same circles. Wealthy, privileged, that sort. I wasn't sure I was going to do it," Thislen admitted quietly, feeling the shadows of the cabin drawing closer.

"And now?"

"Now I guess I am," he said slowly. He knew it was true even as he said it, the overwhelming rush of voices in his head dying down as he accepted Percivan's last request in the depths of his mind. There was nothing else he could have done, he realized. If he tried to walk away from this, Percivan's ghost would haunt him for the rest of his days.

"Why are you looking for him?"

Thislen hesitated. "I don't know," he said at last.

The admission hung in the silence between them for some time. Slowly, Thislen lay back down in the bunk, wrestling the blankets into some semblance of order. Once he had stilled, he traced his fingers over the bandages encasing his shoulder, then dropped his hand to his pocket. He could feel the familiar shape of the ring. He pressed the band against his leg through the cloth, the weight of it a comfort.

"I don't understand," Mila whispered at last. "How do you not know why you're looking for him?"

"Go to sleep, Mila." He sighed.

"But Thislen—"

"I can't explain it right now. Not yet." Slowly, he rolled to face her, his hand on the sheet mere inches away from hers. She didn't press him. He watched her shadowed features range from confusion to curiosity to something quietly baffled. Eventually, they faded into resignation. Her insatiable need to know things about him had not been satisfied, but it had been controlled—for now.

That settles it, he thought to himself, heartened by her patience. Her silent acceptance and understanding cemented a decision he hadn't realized he had made earlier that evening on the prow of the ship.

Someone has to help her, and I know the Ruling Council best—better than anyone else on this island.

Mila Ominir was leaving the city. Not many people traveled in Astera, despite it taking only a few days to ride across. Thislen had done it, hunting for opportunities to earn the coin he needed to get *off* the island. Merchants did it, and some miners and fishermen. There was a small ferry system of men and women with rowboats who would deliver people around the island for the right— expensive—price, but they charged much for their safe travel option. Otherwise, there were only two roads: the West Road and the East Road.

No one traveled for pleasure here. It just wasn't done. The residents of Astera never seemed to question the why of it. One of the groups that most rarely traveled was the Ruling Council. They viewed their duties as too important, their own wants and needs as paramount. Evelie and Olen were right—if they made it hard enough to find Mila, Lord Soren Bestant would give up. After all, Mila was just a shopgirl.

When he had silently agreed to do a service to pay for his healing, he hadn't imagined it would involve crossing the entire kingdom, even if that kingdom was very small. If she could respect his boundaries despite her gnawing curiosity, however, he felt safe offering her something in return. Even if Mila Ominir was his only tie to Lord Soren Bestant, Thislen knew she would be safer *away*. He knew far too much about the Ruling Council to trust them.

"I can't promise that I'll tell you, Mila. Maybe ever. But I can promise you something else."

She tipped her head to one side, waiting. Slowly, hesitantly, Thislen put his hand over own.

"I can help you get out of the city. I can help you get away from him."

5

Thislen woke with the clangor of the ship's bells at dawn as the vessel began to make its way back to shore, the thin morning light painting the cabin in pale yellow. His fever had broken in the night, and the few hours more he had slept did wonders. While still weak and wobbly, he discovered he could move under his own power. He would not have to rely on Ivan and Olen and their rickety stretcher to carry him around!

Please, Ancestors, make it so I will never have to ride on a litter again, he wished fervently as he left the confines of below-decks for the open sea air. Their ship was one of the first to drift into port. It looked like a strange sort of invasion in his eyes, watching so many vessels close in on the small island kingdom and its quiet, empty streets.

They met up with Evelie and Ivan on the deck, and once the gang-plank had been lowered, they set off through the streets of the city. Thislen was still the center of the strange group, leaning upon Olen or Evelie or a reluctant Ivan in turns as they made their slow, laborious journey to the small courtyard and its assorted shops. He stubbornly refused to stop and rest, which would only slow them down further.

Besides, being one face in a crowd like this makes it safer to speak.

"I can help Mila get out of the city. I can help her cross the island." He said with a slight wheeze, winded by his exertions. "This is the best way I can think of to pay you back for your kindnesses. I don't know much, but I do know how to travel quickly and quietly."

Ivan frowned, passing Thislen off to Evelie with a shrug and a roll of his shoulder. "I'm not so sure we should trust Mila's safe passage to someone we don't know. You're a stranger. I'll take her."

And badger her with your feelings, no doubt, Thislen thought sourly. He took a deep breath, counseling himself to have patience with those less experienced in running and hiding. "If anyone sees you leaving together, they'll tell anyone who asks. If you two are tied together, she might not be safe on your flower farm."

Mila swatted lightly at Ivan's arm. "Besides that, Thislen knows a lot more about travel. Look at the clothes he arrived in! I've never seen garments so travel-stained on anyone but a merchant. I trust him well enough to walk along a road. You know how long it *should* take me to get to the farm, and how long it should take a letter to come back. If you haven't heard from me by then, you can put out a call with the City Guard."

Thislen paled, blood draining from his face so quickly that he felt lightheaded. He missed a step and stumbled. Olen caught his arm, giving him a kind smile and gilding Evelie to slow her pace.

"Well," the apothecary said, looking his daughter over, "we can spend some time putting your affairs in order and getting some provisions, yes?"

"Write no letters, tell no one you are leaving who doesn't already know," Thislen interjected quickly. "You can do that once you are safely away, but not before."

"Isn't that a little paranoid?" Ivan asked, his voice crisp as he stopped in front of Thislen.

Thislen nearly ran into him, brow furrowing as he shuffled a few extra steps around the florist. "Why don't you ask Mila what she'd prefer? Mila, would you rather be a little paranoid now and end up safe, or would you like to take your chances?"

Ivan fixed a glare on him, but Thislen had his hands full with making it up a short stairway between terraces and hardly noticed. Mila, however, seemed surprised at the question and took it at face value. She fussed with a lock of hair while she considered.

"Well," Mila said at last, "I don't know how Bestant will react when he finds out I'd rather leave than marry him. He's always been kind enough, but it's never felt..."

"Real?" Thislen asked.

"Exactly. It's always felt like looking at a house from the outside. You can't tell what's behind the doors. I think it might be better to feel a little silly once I'm safe in the countryside."

Ivan pulled Mila ahead to talk, the pair of them waiting at a corner just ahead for the slower trio behind them.

"You had best keep her safe," Evelie said, her gaze on the young woman ahead. "She's as dear to me as if she were my own."

"Thislen, my boy, as much as I like you," Olen began quietly, "if my daughter does not write me a letter and if you do not bring that letter to me yourself, you will have far bigger problems than the City Guard." He patted Thislen's hand on his arm.

Thislen wrinkled his nose, watching his feet as they walked. With each new threat, he felt more and more as if he had painted a target on his back. Regret swelled in the pit of his stomach. He argued with himself with every laborious step.

I can still change my mind. Lord Soren Bestant will be furious when he finds out his bride-to-be has disappeared into thin air.

The lord would no doubt start asking questions of all those who had seen her in the days before her disappearance, putting him squarely before the Ruling Council he had spent his life avoiding—*if* Soren remembered him as the patient in the shop.

Or the City Guard could find him and arrest him on Olen's behalf and drag him up before the courts. Three of the High Court judges also had seats on the Ruling Council.

It all boils down to there being a chance, however small, that I will wind up squarely within the sights of the damn nobility. More of a chance than there would be if I just walked away now, Thislen thought grimly. Yet another thought was louder than the rest.

I can't leave Mila to face an enemy she doesn't really know.

Mila whirled to greet them as they caught up, skirts flashing in shades of greens. She put her hands on her hips and lifted her chin. "We can do this." She sounded so confident, so certain.

Thislen felt the tension melt out of his shoulders in the wake of her sunny assurance, at least a little. "We'll get you there within two days, and the letter back here on the fourth day. Today will be for packing and provisions. Do me a favor, though."

"What is it?" She asked.

"Try not to act like anything different is happening."

She laughed. "Thislen, what do you think I'm going to do? Lean out the windows and waft my handkerchief in the air, blowing goodbye kisses to all and sundry?"

He tried to imagine it for a moment only to snort, a small smile curving across his usually solemn features at the ridiculous image it conjured. "Bit out of character for you," he admitted.

"Exactly." She fell into step beside him, taking over for a smiling Olen as his support. "I'll do my packing today at the shop while my father works—"

"Oh, will I?" Olen asked, amused.

"You will. Ivan, you'll go shopping for provisions."

"I don't want to," Ivan said with a growl.

"Don't you worry, Mila," Evelie said from Mila's other side. "I'll put him in charge of the shop while I go get the food for you, my dear."

"Perfect! You're wonderful, Evelie. And you—" Mila turned to Thislen.

"Don't tell me to rest." He cut her off quickly, straightening as much as he could. "I'll sit on the cot while I mend my clothes, and they need washing as well. This evening, there's something I need to take care of before we leave."

"What is it?"

"I have to get something. From home," Thislen said carefully. "We can be gone tomorrow, first thing in the morning."

"Tomorrow," Mila echoed slowly.

Thislen knew how she felt. Realizing how close something was always made the plan entirely too real. He was more familiar with that reaction than he liked to admit. It always felt like the bottom of his stomach had dropped away, and a cool prickle of air touched between his shoulder blades—and yet he didn't want to wait to face the unknown.

Am I really doing this? Am I really going to help her? What the hells has gotten into me? Perhaps the Vaim's toxins hadn't all been bled away. Perhaps this was some strange sort of side effect.

Or maybe I'm just starting to care. Father always said I would.

No, he told himself sternly, *no, she's just my only tie to Soren Bestant. I have to get to know him. I have to find out what Percivan wanted me to do. On the road, I'll have time to ask her anything I want.*

If he could discharge that debt, the haunting voice in his head would leave him alone.

"So soon," Olen hung his great shaggy head with a sigh.

Evelie sniffled, bringing a kerchief to her mouth. Mila passed Thislen back to her father before falling back to loop her arm through the matronly florist's. The two of them slowed their steps, murmuring between one another, heads close together. Their expressions were solemn, their hands clasped.

Thislen watched them fall away with a soft frown. *I guess they need a moment,* he thought. He felt a slight pang beneath his ribs. *Stop that.* He shoved the fleeting feeling down inside. *I don't care. This is just payment. That's* all.

"If Soren Bestant retaliates at all, we'll need to know," Thislen said to the grizzled apothecary beside him. "I can stop by now and then for a fortnight after I return. Pass word along if it's needed." It was easier to think of plans than try and sort through that pang in his chest. "That will settle our debts, right?"

"We have no debts. However, if you help my daughter, you will never owe me another coin as long as you live," Olen promised. "But if any harm befalls Mila under your watch, you would do best to avoid me for the rest of your days. I will spend every coin in my pockets to hunt you down and make you answer for her fate."

"Olen!" Ivan said, aghast, stopping in the middle of the street. "I've never heard you threaten someone before."

Once more, Thislen and Olen nearly ran into the florist, forced to shuffle around him to keep going. Olen's gaze was fixed on his patient, who met the look after they had started down the street once more.

"Believe me, sir, you have my word. I'll do what I can to protect her."

"Good. Good lad."

When Mila and Evelie caught up with them, neither had dry eyes. The entire group fell into a melancholy silence, leaving Thislen awkwardly adrift in their company. He didn't quite understand the weight in the air.

This is what families worry about, I guess. She'll be coming back as soon as he gets married. It should only take a year. Three at most. He's of marrying age and powerful; it won't take long.

Still, he couldn't help but think of his own father. *There's always a chance you'll never see someone you love again once they leave.*

"Go with the innkeeper, Thislen. Here, take this. Keep it with you. Always, you understand?" His father pressed the ring on its cord into his hand. "I'll get it back from you in just a few hours, right? On the boat."

"But father—" Thislen started, clutching the leather cord in one hand and his small pack in the other, the innkeeper standing just behind him.

"No buts. Be brave. I promise you, I'll be right back. Stay safe, Thislen. Stay hidden." His father thumbed at his nose, working a smile from the young boy—

and then he was leaving, his back turned as he left the inn's yard and vanished into the crowds.

"Father? Wait, come back! Come back, please!" Little Thislen had shouted and shouted.

He had said he would be back. Even if his father had meant it, it wasn't always true. They didn't always make it. Thislen turned to study Mila, watching her dry her eyes on a corner of her shawl and straighten her shoulders.

When she says it, is she lying?

The rest of the trip back to the shop was made in silence. Once they arrived, everyone buried themselves in their tasks with single-minded attention.

Ivan hurried over to open the flower shop, undoing the shutters and opening the door. He vanished inside.

Evelie followed him but reappeared in short order with a massive basket over her arm and a shawl tied around her shoulders. She waved at Thislen as she strolled back into the crowds.

Olen unlocked the apothecary and stepped inside, gesturing for Thislen and Mila to follow. Once they were inside, he opened the greenhouse door and set to his morning tasks of tending to the plants.

Mila vanished up the stairs. Thislen could hear the soft thuds and rummaging noises, and her booted feet as she crossed the boards above his head over and over again while she packed her most important belongings for her journey.

For his part, Thislen settled back in his cot, propped up and resting while he stitched closed the hole in his shirt caused by the Vaim's talon. He found and mended a few other small tears with quick, neat stitches. He had taken care of his own patches and darning since his father vanished, taught by the innkeeper he had been left with. Thislen found it soothing. The needle flickered in and out of the fabric like a minnow in the depths of a canal, and the thread pulled the fabric together behind it in a perfect line. This he could manage. This he could control.

This he could fix.

From his vantage on the cot, he could just see the flower shop across the way. Ivan had set out a table and was putting displays of flowers and vases on it. He kept glancing at the apothecary, his expression bleak as a storm cloud. Ivan was pulled back to his work by a man who appeared at his elbow, gesturing at the florist's wares.

Good, he needs to avoid getting ahead of himself. Ivan wouldn't mean to, but he could ruin this entire plan.

When his mending was finished, Thislen settled in for a nap to regain what strength he could. He wanted to be at his best for his plans later.

It was a fitful sleep. He had spent many years honing his ability to wake up at the slightest noise or provocation for his own safety. On the crowded ships of the Gate Quarter, some few enterprising youths were always trying to rifle through the pockets of a heavy sleeper. Now that sheer exhaustion wasn't pulling Thislen down to dreamless depths, he found himself stirring at every chime of the Ominir Apothecary's front bell.

He woke a few hours before sunset with renewed vigor. The first thing he saw was his clothes on a clothesline strung up in the vented greenhouse behind the shop. They were meticulously scrubbed clean of their dark stains and swung gently in a tickle of air. Thislen rubbed the last of the sleep from the corners of his eyes, turning to the shop.

Olen and Mila were both at work. Olen was in the front of the shop with a dry cloth, dusting off the shelves and sorting through the medicines, paper packets, and dried herbs. Mila was hard at work mixing herbs into hot water, a tendril of hair that had escaped from the scarf she used to tie it back coiling down in front of her face. Neither of them spoke.

Thislen rolled to his feet, tucking his borrowed shirt in and slipping on his boots in relatively short order. Thus passably dressed, he ducked under the hinged part of the counter and pulled Olen aside. "Alright, it's time for me to go and take care of a few things. I won't be back tonight but look for me first thing tomorrow morning. If I'm not back by midday, send Mila on without me. You understand?"

"You're being rather dour. She's only avoiding a marriage proposal, after all, not fleeing the rule of law." Olen said. His large brows drew together sharply. "He won't even know anything until she's gone. You made sure of that."

"Because I don't trust him. I don't trust his patience. You have no reason to believe me when I say this, but I speak from experience," Thislen said grimly. "I grew up hearing about a noblewoman who tried to refuse a marriage proposal. She ran away and married someone else. She had a child. Still, once they found her?"

He trailed off, and Olen gently put a hand on his shoulder. "What happened to her?" The apothecary asked.

"...she died, in the end. They locked her away, and she died a prisoner," Thislen said quickly. It was easier that way.

"Your mother?" Olen's voice was gentle, his eyes searching.

"...yes, sir. I'm a bastard," Thislen admitted. His mother had married his father to avoid marrying another noble. A runaway lady and a simple clerk, in love. Shortly after Thislen had been born, she went to find a job of her own. A servant recognized her and reported her whereabouts, and they came for her the next day. His father had told him the story a hundred times.

"They sent personal guards, Thislen, hired hands beholden to none but the one who paid them. They grabbed her arms and dragged her into a carriage. A neighbor told me, and I ran all the way across the city to the Grand Quarter, to her big fine house."

His mother had beat at the barred windows of a room high above the ground for weeks. In the end, she had been forced to marry the Lord anyway. She hadn't said yes, his father said, though he never told Thislen how he knew that.

After her wedding, his mother had been locked in a tower in her new husband's house. She died without leaving him any children. Thislen and his father never saw Lady Elana again.

Thislen took a deep breath, pulling himself back to the present. He ran a hand down his face, hoping to scrub whatever expression he had.

Olen must have seen it anyway. He was no longer arguing, protests dead on his lips. The apothecary's brows were still drawn together, but this time in concern. He clasped Thislen's uninjured shoulder gently. "I see. I'll trust you, my boy. We'll get her to safety. Together."

Long enough to do this and only *this,* Thislen thought fiercely. He had never told this much to anyone. *This is getting dangerous.*

"I'll be back tomorrow for my things. And for Mila," he said. With the promise still hanging in the air, he slipped out of the shop. The little bell above the door chimed behind him.

The city of Astera was bustling, alive with the hum of distant voices. There were many errands to be run before the sun set, sending people bustling through the streets. Food was being purchased for suppers, the last ingredients bought here and there, or entire meals. Couriers slipped through the crowds as quick as they could with all the grace of dancers as they tried to finish their last-minute deliveries for the day with time to spare. Some people hung laundry from clotheslines in the alleyways to dry overnight, safe from the hands of thieves like him.

Thislen, with the plain shirt Olen lent him with the sleeves rolled up and the hem tucked into his dark trousers, looked like any other shop's boy in the city. He had done up the laces on the neck to hide most of his bandages. His ring was rescued from his pocket at last, too. Thislen slung the cord over his head and tucked it beneath the cloth to keep it safe from prying eyes.

This is what my life is, what it should be. He reveled in his ability to become remarkably unremarkable. It was a beautiful shield, crafted and honed over a decade, hiding him from the attentions of those he wished only to avoid. Within the space of a few steps, he was no one.

The small dead-end that held the Ominir Apothecary was only a few streets away from the Great Markets that sprawled out before the walls of Perilee. The great cobbled space was divided into three by neat rows of spreading oaks in perfectly manicured squares, and in rows beneath their branches were dozens of cloth and wood stalls. Many shops lined the edges, built into the stone buildings. It was easy there to fling open the doors and sell goods to those on the streets. The stalls and shops sold nearly everything one could desire. Furniture, art, food, clothing—and anything in between. The stalls beneath the trees were rented out by enterprising owners to foreign merchants who would bring wonders from over the water. Kingdoms such as Rava and Whitehill sent their wares by fleet from time to time, flooding the city with new trends all in one great wave.

One could always recognize the suspicious Ravan merchants. They jumped at shadows, even during the day. They were always the first to close their shops and leave for the night, too. It was generally accepted that Ravan merchants were spies. The traders from Whitehill were far friendlier and stayed longer. Whitehill was another two day's sail away from Astera than Rava, after all.

The Great Square was the largest open-air market in the entire kingdom. Not that such an accomplishment was difficult to achieve. Apart from a few scattered fishing villages along the coast, where miners and fishermen rubbed elbows during the night and went their separate ways during the day, there were only two towns on the island. Astera, located on the southern tip, was the capital and the seat of power. Anything in the kingdom worth knowing about happened in Astera. The city shared the same name as the island, after all. The other town was called Barred Town. It sat on the island's northern edge, on the far end of the Spine. It was much smaller, hardly competition for the city below the throne.

Thislen was glad for Astera's size. It was bursting with near frantic energy as people hurried to make their last purchases before stalls began to close for the evening. They milled so closely together that it was difficult to weave through the crowd. The people shuffled in lines, up one side and down another, hunting for what they needed.

Thislen joined them from a place near the castle's wall. A decorative circular pond served as a moat beneath the gate of the great keep, edged with massive stones. Its drawbridge was lowered during the day, and the great wood-and-iron gates stood open.

Royal Guardsmen in their dark blue livery stood at attention in the shade of the wall, scanning the milling crowd. No one approached the drawbridge, leaving them idle and bored, and none of them seemed to notice Thislen as he joined the throng.

What are they even guarding? Perilee is empty. He glanced through the gate at the castle's closed front doors, massive and heavy and beautifully carved.

Everyone knew the story of why. At some point, every child of Astera asked why they had to sleep on the ships at night, and every parent told the tale. Hundreds of years past, a great plague had swept over the island. The Royal Family did nothing to prevent it and ignored the plight of the island's poor in favor of throwing lavish parties. The screams of the unfortunate ill as they died drove the Vaim on the island mad, turning peaceable spirits that had always lived on the island's shores into vengeful and angry shades.

A handful of courtiers stepped in and staged a vicious coup. After three days of war in the corridors of Perilee itself, they emerged victorious. Those nobles founded the Ruling Council and took over the government of the island.

Only they didn't change anything. In fact, even though the great throne room in Perilee stood empty, the Council still met there three days out of the week to discuss business before the vacant seat of power.

It was all an illusion. Anything of true import was discussed on the great ships of the wealthy and powerful—at night. They flitted between one another's berths on little rowboats like moths drawn to the brightest lantern.

No one had ever taken up residence in the keep, nor had there ever been a royal ship to bear the ruling family off the island to safety. The Royal Guard had a boat, however. It served as their barracks at night. During the day, they still dutifully stood guard at the gates and in the corridors. Four flanked the doors of the great throne room at all times. Palace servants were still employed, paid by the Ruling Council to keep the castle dusted and swept. A small cadre of cooks had been hired to feed the servants and guardsmen during the day.

That was all there was. The stables stood empty. The smithy remained unlit. The guest wings were defunct. Perilee was there, but not there—a perfectly preserved artifact nestled in the rocks above the city. It might as well have been encased in amber for all the use it saw, a relic of a time long gone. It was just one more monument to things that no longer were, another tradition maintained for the sake of tradition.

This is how it is and how it will always be. Get used to it, he thought bitterly.

Thislen turned away from it. Just as he had in his dreams, he felt the weight of its shadow press down upon his back. Like an eel, he slipped through the crowds as he fought to ignore it.

Come, it whispered.

Thislen drifted past a clothier's stall. Under the cover of a woman's overlarge shopping basket, he was able to pinch a worn cloak off the edge of the table. Hastily, he folded it over an arm. He waited to look down at it until he was a row away.

This will do perfectly. He was pleased to discover that when it was folded, the worn hem of the cloak was tucked away, and a delicate band of embroidery around the hood's edge stood in clear sight. Though the cloth was rough, the detailing was delicate and beautifully made. Folded just so, it looked more expensive than its worth.

With this last, perfect touch, his simple disguise was complete. He slid under an arm here, twisted around a man there, and emerged from the markets into the warren of city streets once more. His steps were quick and purposeful, like a man on a mission. *That's the key to it all, now. Confidence.*

The city was arranged in its quarters: Gate, Guild, Goods, and Grand. The Grand Quarter was where the homes of the wealthy and noble were located. Money and information were the only currencies of note at play in the broad avenues there. The City Guard had been paid handsomely to run small patrols through the streets and escort those who were less desirable back to a more suitable part of the city. Anyone who didn't look like they belonged could be stopped and questioned. Those with scuffed shoes and worn clothes had to beware. Anyone found lacking a suitable answer for their presence would be turned around and sent away.

Those who persisted could find themselves detained. Thislen usually avoided the Grand Quarter at all costs. Usually.

The Goods Quarter's functional and clean cobbled streets gave way to broad, tree-lined avenues on the far side of a crystalline channel. Stone bridges spanned the water, which ran around the entirety of the Grand Quarter, with the gray-clad City Guardsmen standing watch at the far sides. They sheltered under the shade of small trees that bloomed with flowers every spring, watching everyone who passed over the narrow waterway.

As Thislen crossed, he noticed one guard's gaze fixing on him. The man's brow furrowed. His lips parted. Thislen cut off any questions that may have come by holding up the cloak folded neatly over his arm. He gave the guard a sly wink and a nod, letting him in on the little secret.

Some rich bastard is always bedding someone he shouldn't and forgetting something after. The guard's frown melted into a grin and a roll of the eyes. Thislen passed unmolested into the Grand Quarter.

The deception would buy him precious time, at least. If he could keep his expression steady and remember the way through the streets, it *could* carry him through the wealthy district without issue. If he slowed or looked lost, however, all bets were off.

The broad avenues with their shady trees were backed by modest estates at the edges of the Grand Quarter, nestled near the heart of the city. Tall houses covered in carved cornices and propped up with elegant corbels stood at proud attention in beautiful, if small, enclosed gardens. Parks lay here and there between these homes, offering various entertainments for the wealthy. One had walking paths around a small decorative pond, perfect for promenading. One was designed for riding horses—though at no faster pace than a walk. One was fairly bursting with flowers and dotted with delicate benches. Each was intended to make seeing and being seen all the easier. Wealthy young men and women flocked to the parks to stare doe-eyed after one another and decide who they wanted to woo.

Smaller estates and parks gave way to larger homes with great swaths of private gardens the further one moved away from the city center. The Bestant family, as one of the oldest and wealthiest on the island, would no doubt have their home right on the eastern shore.

Despite the fact that he felt like a knife would find its way between his shoulder blades, Thislen made no move to leave the open streets for the alleyways as he walked. On the street, he was no one of any note, just a messenger. In the alleyways, he risked being caught in those quietly off-limits areas. There were no rules against people in the alleys during the day, but the servants and binmen would no doubt recognize an outsider far more readily than their employers.

Just watch some chambermaid ask me who I'm returning it to, then raise a hue and cry when she doesn't like my answer, Thislen thought bitterly.

Still, he knew he couldn't stay on the open streets forever. The closer he got to his destination, the more suspicious the City Guard patrols would get. His story wouldn't hold up to a close inspection.

A trio of guardsmen rounded the corner, chatting quietly as they walked the streets. Thislen kept his gaze straight ahead on the corner until they passed—and then he sidestepped quickly into the alleyway between two large homes.

The narrow pathway was formed by the great walls built around the expansive properties on either side, dim with shadows as the sun sank. The warren of small corridors between each house was dedicated to those people who offended the wealthy and powerful. Binmen, ashmen, rag and bone men, charity workers, and those who tended to animal refuse—all of them used the alleyways in the early mornings and throughout the day. In the evening, they became the highway for servants returning to their family ships for their days off. This meant that Thislen had a tiny window of opportunity to use this alternate path before he risked getting caught by those homeward bound.

He moved quickly, dodging emptied bins and stepping over the odd unidentifiable heap. A left turn, then up two more rows of houses, and he came at last to a stop in the mouth of the tangle of hidden paths. *Good, no patrols.* Thislen stepped out into the sunlight once more.

Lord Soren Bestant's estate was set in a great garden with a high stone wall and large wrought iron gates to keep out the unwanted. The manor itself stood tall. Its cornices were gilded to draw the eye, glittering between flowering vines that grew up the bare patches of the walls. It looked as if it were trying to rival Perilee itself—but Perilee was older than this house could ever hope to be, and the castle had been built with more love poured into it than power.

Thislen stared at the house for several moments, gaze drifting along the highest windows while he listened to the chattering cascade of its three—*three!*—fountains in the gardens. Something fell somewhere with a clatter, and the faint voices of someone laughing and teasing someone else came from beyond a garden wall, jerking him from his reverie. He set off once more, but not toward the gate. Instead, he took one of the cobbled streets along the side of the great estate, leading to the expansive docks of Astera's elite.

Every wood and stone finger in the water held ships at berth. There were just as many vessels as there were in the other Quarters of Astera, but each was smaller and outfitted for an individual family and its live-in staff and sailors. Not a single galleon was as plain and functional as a Gate Quarter Ship, but its decorations far outshone the sociable ships of the Goods Quarter. Each ship appeared to be an attempt to appear wealthier than its neighbors. Carved mastheads were painted in bright colors and clad in gold or polished brass. The massive windows of below-deck great rooms glinted and gleamed in the fading light of day. The balustrades were waxed bright until they shone. Each ship had a name, a lineage, and a proud history, or was the latest and greatest design available. They were just as opulent as the manors and gardens in the rest of the Quarter.

And each one is worth three of the plain sloops that house hundreds of the city's residents, if not more. There's no balance to it, any of it. Thislen's lip curled up, and his nose wrinkled for a moment as he took in the splendor. *Gaudy heaps of sticks.*

The Ruling Council paid for the creation of those plain ships, using as small a portion of the taxes levied against the residents of Astera to do so as possible. When the Vaim had first appeared, people had been afraid—and the Ruling Council had been the first to begin to sleep off-shore. In the wake of the coup, when the Ruling Council was determined to do better than the Royal Family, they had promised ships for all—and thus it had come to pass.

But they still keep their own special ships all to themselves, don't they? Bare minimum for everyone else—cramped cabins for those who can afford it and stacked hammocks for the rest. Meanwhile, they sail around on party barges.

It was one of these great ships in particular that he sought. The most opulent of the ships sat closest to the shore, just behind a wrought iron gate that led off of the Bestant property, half-hidden in elegant hedges. *Well, that's as safe a guess as any.* As Thislen approached his chosen target, its name came into view.

The *Bestant Belle.*

Ha! Ancestors are on my side today, he thought with a rush.

He tucked the cloak into the belly of his shirt, flattening it as much as he could before he stepped down onto the wood of the docks. The smell of the sea was clean and crisp in the air around him, vastly cleaner than the water elsewhere along the island's shore. Sailors and merchants bustled to and fro, tending to the last of their tasks for the day.

The *Bestant Belle* was being re-provisioned. Thislen knelt quickly to grab a string of pheasants to sling over a shoulder and a great wheel of cheese to hold over the cloak in his shirt before he carried them onto the ship. He trailed in the wake of a sailor, trusting the man to believe he was one of the merchant's people—and trusting the merchants to believe he was a member of the ship's staff. Neither one would ask the other for fear of seeming rude—at least not before he was on board.

He followed the sailor down the ship's broad stairs and into a spacious corridor, then through a door into the galley itself. Though the galley was plain compared to the wainscot-clad corridor, it was well stocked and a cook was already directing two other kitchen staff in the baking of desserts to accompany dinner that evening. Thislen dumped the pheasants and cheese into the same neat pile as the sailor, who had dropped a sack of flour. The pair of them turned to leave.

"Here now, you two. Don't come back without the potatoes next; I need to cook the potatoes!" The cook called, stopping Thislen's heart in his chest for a moment.

The sailor laughed. "Alright, alright. I'll get them!"

Thislen grinned and ducked his head, playing the part of shy merchant hire as he followed the man back into the hall. It wasn't difficult to slow his pace. He paused to gape at an elegant tapestry hung on the corridor wall for a moment until the sailor vanished from view up the stairs with a knowing smile.

The bumpkin persona Thislen had adopted vanished the moment he was alone. In a flash, he leaped back down the corridor and through a different door. He turned, taking in the quiet bedroom cabin. It had a small sitting area and a curtained bunk with far too many pillows. *Must roll all over this place in a storm,* he mused. The windows set into the ship were gallery style, large and open, rather than the portholes of the working class ships.

Thislen pushed the window open and looked up, then down. *Ha, easy.* He wasted no time lowering himself down onto a decorative cornice, the smooth top of which ran all along the side of the ship. He balanced precariously on its edge. The entire galleon was covered with carvings, providing plenty of hand and footholds as he made his way toward the bow.

The *Bestant Belle's* carved masthead was a great bird of some kind, its gigantic feathered wings spread wide. Below each of those wings was a small shadowed alcove where the wood splayed out to meet and support the splayed structure on the bow. Thislen pulled the remnants of an empty bird's nest from the sheltered space and carefully wedged himself into it. Wrestling the cloak free of his shirt was difficult, but once he managed it, he bundled himself into the dark fabric, rendering himself practically invisible.

Ancestors, but I'm exhausted, he thought as he sagged against the wood. Crossing the city was taxing on the best of days, but after a fever? His shoulder ached and burned quietly in turns, protesting his use of it.

I haven't got a choice. I'm here to do this for Mila and for Percivan. I haven't the time to spare for rest and healing.

For Mila and Percivan, he told himself, but helping both of them was only to soothe his own conscience. It wasn't because he found himself growing attached to Mila. It wasn't because he felt he owed Percivan. It was purely selfish, to discharge debts real and imagined.

It doesn't matter why; what matters is that I'm here. I'm doing this. I'm helping.

There was nothing left to do now—

—but wait.

THE OMINIR APOTHECARY was quiet in the wake of Thislen's departure for some time. Mila had seen her father and the thief speak quietly for a few moments before he left, but after that? *You could hear a pin drop in here, honestly.*

Every clunk of a bowl or clatter of glass sounded so loud, but Mila didn't know what to say to fill the space between her and her father. Olen swept the front of the shop with long, slow pulls of the broom, gaze a million miles away.

I don't want to leave you, father, but I don't want to stay put either, Mila thought. Every step toward what she wanted seemed to be a step away from what she had. Adventure, new scenery, a journey—all of it finally about to happen out of nowhere! It was a dream come true! Yet it meant leaving all she knew—and who knew for how long?

When I come back, it won't feel the same. It won't be *the same.* She looked around the low ceilings hung with herbs, the neat and orderly rows of medicines and sachets on the shelves, the cluttered worktables. It was her entire life.

Tomorrow, it wouldn't be.

"I'm going to go across the way," Olen said suddenly, shattering the silence and making Mila jump, "and ask Ivan for a map to their farm. Or directions, at least." He was subdued, his ordinarily booming voice reduced to a low rumble.

"Right. I'll be here!" Mila said cheerily.

Her gaze met her father's stricken face, and her heart sank in her chest. *Oh my goodness, why did I say that?* She thought, cheeks heating.

Olen leaned the broom against the wall and left the shop, the sound of the bell fading in the air behind him.

"Alright, Mila," she said aloud, "let's just make sure everything's in order."

Mila had packed all of her belongings earlier. Now, a modest bag of clothes and a few books on plants sat neatly tucked away upstairs, right against the railing of the stairs. It was ready for tomorrow.

A second bag sat beside it, laden with food and a change of clothing that Olen thought would just fit Thislen. All it needed was the thief to carry it.

She had made tinctures for the next moon, all lined up in bottles with the date they were made neatly glued on. Mila had sorted out the dried herbs they used to make medicines, discarding any that hadn't dried right into a bucket to go into feed for animals. She had gone over the sums in the shop's register ledger for her father. Now she was pretending to organize the worktables, though they had never found a way to organize them that didn't become a mess again the next time they made something.

It is much better when I have something I can do *about my problems at last.* How many moons had it been since she had noticed Soren Bestant getting more and more forward? It had taken saying aloud to Thislen that she didn't want to marry for Mila to gather the courage to *do*...well, anything!

Mila's gaze drifted to the clothes drying in the greenhouse, then turned to the shop's window. She hoped that Thislen would appear. *If he were here, I could at least talk to him about what he has planned.*

A moment later, she groaned and ran her hands over her hair. *Silly thing, you know he won't be back until tomorrow! He said as much.*

It was impossible to focus. The sun had begun to sink toward the horizon, but the time before her journey began stretched and bent until it felt like she had to leave *now,* and yet would not leave for a year or more.

A carriage clattered into sight, drawn by a handsome bay horse and startling her out of her reverie. There was no crest on the side, merely elegant scrollwork painted gold. Two richly dressed young men climbed down from within. From their bearing alone, Mila could tell they were nobility. The coach and their rich clothing were obvious signs of wealth, but the posture of the merely wealthy was not quite so…cultured.

How snooty, she thought as they each checked their appearance in the shop window. From their age, Mila guessed they might be the sons of nobles, if not already titled themselves.

The bell above the door jangled merrily as they came inside the shop.

"Hello," she called, straightening and adjusting the colorful scarves tied around her waist. "May I help you?"

"Well, this *must* be her!" One of the young men said brightly. His face was affable and round, reminding Mila of nothing so much as a sleepy bear. His hair was dark brown, and his eyes were the same, but his skin was pale as milk in sharp contrast. He was the shorter of the two strangers, though his shoulders were broader. The smile on his face was wide and welcoming, but it didn't seem to sit quite right.

Mila felt her smile falter just a hair.

The second man said nothing at first. He stepped up to the counter and looked her over appraisingly, making Mila feel like a horse at the fair, on display in her little corral. She stepped back. The second man had red hair, freckled skin, and dark blue eyes set in his angular face. He was tall, reminding the apprentice of the lanky statues that sometimes decorated parks and gardens.

She felt small beneath his calculating gaze. *Who* are *these people?* She wished her father would come back.

"You're right; it must be. I can see why he likes her well enough. She is fair. Some cleaning up and a good tutor for etiquette, and she'll…suffice."

She felt her cheeks begin to warm, even as her hands went cold and a knot formed in the pit of her stomach. *I'm right here!* She thought angrily, but such words would never leave her lips. Mila pushed her smile back into place. "May I help you?" She repeated with the barest edge to the words.

The tall one did not move so much as float, hand drifting through the air like the ships on the water when the sea was smooth as glass. In a fluid motion, he inclined his head ever so slightly toward her and offered his hand. "My name is Avasten Barnweir, Lord Judge of the Ruling Council. This is young Master Garridan Artaith. His father is Lord Artaith of the Ruling Council. Our dear friend Soren has sent us to see you."

The chill under Mila's skin grew, creeping through her like ice. The heat faded from her cheeks as the blood drained away. *Do they know? Are they here to drag me away?* She forced her smile a bit wider. "It's always nice to be recommended to someone new. Are you here for medicine? A salve? Perhaps something for your hair or skin?" Mila asked. She turned toward the shelves to sort through the bottles and jars.

She did not take Avasten's hand.

"Perhaps I can interest you in one of our lotions? As the weather gets colder, it's important not to let your hands chap in the sea air." Her tone was bright, almost vapid, as she turned and set a jar before them.

Garridan gave an easy laugh, moving amongst the shelves. He picked up the neatly labeled bottles and paper envelopes of herbs and teas, glancing at them and setting them back down. "No, no. Not at all. You've misunderstood us, Miss Mila. He wanted us to come and meet the woman he proposed to. You can imagine our surprise when he said he had decided on a shopkeep's daughter!"

Mila was at war with herself. On one hand, she was relieved they had only come to study Soren Bestant's prize; on the other...she felt herself warm from a core of anger in her stomach. That heat spread along her limbs, racing down to her toes and fingertips and up into her cheeks. Her smile vanished.

I wish Father was here. He has a way of getting rid of people who don't intend to spend any coin. Would they listen to me if I tried to do the same?

"I'm afraid I have quite a lot of work to do before sunset, my Lords. If you haven't any need of my services, you *are* free to leave. I haven't got the time for a proper social call," she said firmly.

"Then we *must* schedule one, mustn't we?" Avasten asked easily, voice smooth and measured. His gaze never left her face.

"Sounds like a grand idea to me. What do you say, Miss Mila? Perhaps tomorrow works better for you than tonight? You can come for tea at Soren's estate." Garridan bent to study the contents of a shelf more closely.

"Tomorrow?" Avasten scoffed before Mila could answer. "Garridan, please. She needs proper clothing first; just look at her. And you cannot invite her to Soren's estate without first telling him you plan to do so. Let us do things *properly*, shall we?" He reached out, lifting the counter leaf that separated the shop from the workspace. He gestured for Mila to step out.

I don't want to. At all, Mila thought. Her ears rang faintly, and her hands had curled into fists. She dropped her gaze demurely for a moment while her mind raced. *Would it make them leave more quickly if they believed they got what they wanted? All I have to do is get rid of them now—by tomorrow morning, I'll be gone.*

She took solace in that thought, holding it close in her heart as she left the safety of the back half of the shop.

Avasten bowed, offering her his hand once more. "Miss Mila Ominir, it would be my utmost pleasure to escort you to a tailor tomorrow afternoon to procure a gown. Afterward, I should like to invite you to tea at the Barnweir estate with myself, young Master Garridan, and Lord Soren Bestant. Would you do me the great honor of accepting my invitation?"

Something in his eyes made her hesitate. It felt as though a great hunting cat lurked behind the Lord Judge's eyes, just waiting for her to try and run so that he could pounce. Even if she wanted to refuse, she worried she would become nothing more than prey in an instant. *No, it's not like a cat,* she realized. *It's like a spider, a spider in the middle of a web watching the struggling fly.*

But this spider doesn't know that the fly will be gone tomorrow. I'll be gone, *first thing.* A fact, she reminded herself, that Lord Avasten did not know. A point she had to keep repeating to herself to stay strong. *Tomorrow, tomorrow, tomorrow.*

She put her hand in his and gave a delicate curtsey. "I would be delighted. It is an honor to be asked," she said politely, hoping he would not notice how stiff the words were on her tongue.

"Now I see it," Garridan said. "Now I see why he thinks there's hope for a shop girl."

"Garridan." Avasten chided, voice flat. "Don't be rude."

He brought Mila's hand up, lips just brushing the back of her knuckles. They were cool to the touch. She stifled a shiver.

"Until the morrow, then, Miss Mila. We'll arrive just after luncheon."

"Of course."

"Put that down, Garridan. Come, we're going to be late." Avasten bent to press his lips to her knuckles. His hand left hers, and she fought the urge to wipe it off on her skirts.

Garridan set down the bottle he had been examining and tucked his hands behind his back with a cheeky grin, ambling after Avasten as the taller man swept out into the street.

Mila fled back behind the counter as the last chime of the door's bell faded, slamming the leaf down into place. She panted softly in the gathering gloom of the shop, hands trembling on the wooden surface.

They didn't want to let me say no, she realized. If they weren't willing to leave her the option of saying no to a simple tea, how would she ever be allowed to turn down Lord Soren Bestant's proposal?

Don't forget, you're not trapped here anymore. You'll be free and clear, and they won't find you. They'll never know if you were going to say yes or *no. All we have to do is wait one night.*

Mila was no longer worried about leaving her family behind for this. There were times when staying somewhere comfortable was as good as putting your own foot in a bear trap. She'd just have to hope that her father, Evelie, and Ivan understood. She *had* to leave.

Tomorrow.

THISLEN JOLTED awake to the rattle of a heavy chain somewhere nearby. A bell clanged, followed by another further out. The sailors on the deck above were calling out to one another. *Strange how quiet they are,* he mused. The men didn't squall and bark and wail at one another as they did on the other ships. Half their calls weren't words at all; they were whistles! *Must be so they don't disturb their wealthy patrons.*

One leg was carefully stretched out, then the other—and then he tucked them back up. Stiffly, Thislen pulled the cloak's hood away from his face just enough to watch what little he could see from his sheltered position, hidden beneath the carved wooden wing.

The only other ship he could see, at the next dock over from the *Bestant Belle,* was moving out to sea. Others were undoubtedly already moving across the water, drifting off to their usual nightly berths. As one of the closest ships to shore, the *Belle* was one of the last to leave—but the Grand Quarter had the art of moving the ships onto the water down to a dance.

The ship lurched beneath him, leaving Thislen's stomach behind for one sickening moment. The shore slipped quietly away. Water burbled and rippled below him, agitated by the prow. Lights already glowed in the ship's cabins, casting pools of gold onto the water. The sun was sinking out of sight behind the city, outlining it in perfect silhouette.

As the *Bestant Belle* made her berth and turned sluggishly in the water, other ships briefly came into view here and there. They rocked atop the gentle waves like so many great lanterns floating on the sea. The *Belle* and its stowaway were one of the last to settle into its customary place. The anchor rattled away into the depths just as the last light of day disappeared from the sky.

Fitting. Powerful.

Thislen shifted again. Now that the other ships were far enough away that he'd not be noticed, he stretched out both legs and slid carefully out of his hiding place to pull his cloak on and fasten it around his neck.

What I am about to do is stupid. Very, very stupid. *What the hells put this thought into my mind?* It was too late to regret his choice, however—there was nowhere else to go. The water below was dangerous.

"What the—"

Thislen looked up quickly, meeting the gaze of the sailor he had followed below-decks earlier that day. The man's eyes were wide. As he watched, the sailor's lips parted—

"No!" Thislen said in an urgent whisper. He reached up to grab the man's arm as he pointed down. He pulled.

The sailor didn't shout as he lost his balance; he gasped. He toppled over the railing and slid down the carved bird's wing without another sound. Thislen tried to hold on to the man's wrist, but he had grabbed with the wrong hand. His shoulder burned, and his hold slipped.

The sailor hit the water with a soft splash.

There was no time. Thislen hastily crammed himself back under the wing, pulling the cloak around himself to blend in with the shadows, even as the sailor surfaced below him, treading water.

No, I didn't mean to kill him! Thislen thought desperately.

The man was pale as the moon, paddling toward the side of the ship as fast as he could. Above Thislen, several more heads appeared.

"Vern!" One of them called softly, desperately. "Someone get a rope!"

No one moved. They already knew Vern was dead.

Quite suddenly, Vern the sailor yelped, vanishing *backward* under the water. He surfaced again with a panicked shout, lifting a hand toward his fellows.

The dark water around him began to glow with pairs of angry red eyes, glowering out of the deep. One dark hand stretched out of the waves, a tendril of seaweed clinging to its too-thin arm, and laced its fingers with the sailor's. Slowly, while the sailor flailed with his free arm to stay afloat, the Vaim dragged the arm back to the water. It didn't stop, pulling further down while Vern tried to keep his face above the waves.

"Why!?" he shouted desperately, gaze locked on the shadows of the ship, on Thislen.

More hands reached out, ink-dark blots against the man's sodden wet shirt. It was the only sign of them; no others breached the surface as they dragged him down. The last thing anyone saw was the empty grasping hand of the sailor as he went into the deep.

The Vaim on the shore would tear someone apart or bleed someone dry as they killed them, but it was mercifully quick compared to those in the water. Sometimes the Vaim in the ocean would toy with a person, dragging them down and letting them swim to the surface again and again until they gave up and let the Vaim take them down below the waves. Some people didn't struggle against the specters, choosing the quicker death.

Vern was one of those. Bubbles broke the surface of the waves, but nothing more.

How many have been swallowed by the sea that way, pulled beneath the water to drown amongst a sea of shadows and burning red eyes? Thislen shuddered. He buried his face in his hands, listening to the soft conversation above his head.

"We'll have to tell Lord Bestant in the morning."

"What even happened?"

"Don't do that. Don't wonder. All that matters is he's gone. I'll write a letter to his mother."

The voices moved away, still hushed, and Thislen stifled a sob. *I didn't mean to do that! I just...couldn't get discovered. I couldn't get caught.* He didn't know what he thought would happen, but it wasn't that. He considered giving up right then and there—but he had come all this way.

Quietly, Thislen strangled his sadness for now. He could feel it *later*, after he had done what he came to do. *Leaving the apothecary to come here at all may have been stupid, and it may not even pay off, but you took this chance—so you're damn well going to* use *it now.* His anger with himself didn't help, but it at least got him moving again.

Thislen eased along the thin, carved railing that ran around the edge of the ship, feeling his way along with hands and feet. His heart pounded in his chest, so loud he worried another sailor might hear him. Now was the best chance he had of going unnoticed, while the sailors were...distracted. While the occupants of the ship were settling in for the evening. While the cooks were preparing suppers. Any stray noise he might make had a chance of going unheard or dismissed.

This could be our chance. Maybe I can help one *person escape the watchful eyes of this damned Ruling Council.*

He came alongside a window, glancing carefully around the edge. It was the galley—and so was the next window along, he realized. The cook and the two helpers were bustling around, putting the final touches on an elegant dinner that smelled amazing. Meat, potatoes, something sweet and topped with expensive cinnamon from Rava.

Thislen's shoulder sent a stab of pain all the way down to his fingertips as he lowered himself to a crouch and hung off the ledge. He barely found footholds on the delicate carvings. With his hands shuffling along the thin railing he had just walked, he crept along. He didn't dare raise himself up, not until he was past that second window.

Sweat beaded on his brow. *Just a few more feet.* He huffed and puffed. *Almost there!* His shoulder burned. Suddenly, his foot slipped off of a carved mermaid's shoulder. His knee hit hard against the ship's side, and he nearly let go of the railing. He caught himself, shoulder throbbing, but he didn't fall. More importantly, he didn't make a sound. His heart raced wildly in his chest and pulsed in his throat as he pulled himself back up and continued his painstaking way down the length of the ship. Past those two windows were two darkened rooms. Thislen climbed back up onto that narrow but safer path of the top of the railing, hugging the ship's side with one hand while the other felt over his bandages.

Good, I'm fine.

Well, for now.

The rest of the harrowing journey went without incident. Thislen reached the great room at last. Huge gallery-style windows ran along the ship's stern, filling the room inside from floor to ceiling for nearly half of it. He knelt beside the outermost of those windows, feeling around in the dark for solid hand and footholds. When he was as comfortable and secure as he could get, Thislen slipped a thin fisherman's knife from his boot. He had sharpened it a thousand times or more over the years until it was barely a sliver of metal. He slipped it between the window's frame and the sill, jiggling it slowly into place.

Shapes moved in the room beyond. Thislen froze, holding his breath. When nothing approached his hidden corner of the windows, he resumed his careful work. A little lift, a pause. A quick twist and a flick—*click*! The oiled latch of the window slid free. He froze again, waiting. Nothing happened.

Thislen eased the window open just a crack.

"—coin will come from *your* purse, of course. I am not about to pay for your intended bride's gowns," someone said a voice like oil on water.

Mila?

Thislen leaned forward just a hair. He could see right over the windowsill and into the cabin.

Lord Soren Bestant was draped over a great armchair behind a carved wooden desk littered with papers, a leg slung across one of the arms. He nursed a glass of wine in one hand, glittering blue eyes fixed on the other two occupants of the room.

A tall man with red hair and blue eyes was playing a game of Hunter's Hounds with a shorter man with dark hair and eyes and a sallow complexion. They leaned over the carved grid of the wooden board. Metal pieces that gleamed gold and silver in the light littered the board. The redhead was intent, a finger pressed gently to his lips as he calculated his next move. The shorter grinned and scratched his head.

"No one asked you to invite her to tea, Avasten," Soren said with a roll of his eyes.

"I would watch your flank there, Garridan," Avasten said as the shorter male moved a piece at last.

"Oh, good! You haven't figured out my strategy yet." Garridan sounded cheerful. "You know what I don't understand, though, Soren? Why do you even *want* to marry some common shop girl? Her face is pretty enough, I suppose, and I do like the color of her hair. She'll be even prettier once she styles it, too. Maybe in a proper gown." He leaned back in his chair. "But you could marry *any* girl on the island. What about Lady Olivia?"

"I don't want to marry Olivia," Soren said, studying his wine in the light.

"I just couldn't imagine marrying a commoner. Is it to save coin on your mother's medications?"

Soren's gaze slid to Garridan in a cool, steady stare. Garridan looked away first, rubbing the back of his neck.

"Sorry," the dark-haired noble said softly.

"Idiot," Soren sounded smug. "Shows what you know. She's more important than anyone else in the kingdom."

Avasten pushed a piece onto the board, leaning back to stare at Soren. "Is she?"

Garridan frowned at the board. "What do you mean?"

Thislen leaned forward a bit more, his own thoughts echoing the question. *Mila? She's just a shopkeep's daughter. Isn't she?*

Neither Soren nor Avasten answered. Garridan's hand hovered over the pieces, but he was clearly distracted by their silence.

"You two and your secrets. Can't you just *tell* me?"

Avasten laughed softly, turning away from his silent exchange with Soren. "You'll learn soon enough. Once you take your seat on the Council."

"Once you take your seat! It's always once you take your seat! I grow weary of the waiting," the brunet said irritably.

"Do what Avasten did and murder your father, then," Soren said airily before draining his glass.

Thislen went cold.

"You did the same," Avasten murmured, watching Garridan nudge a piece into place.

His stomach roiled. He could taste bile in the back of his throat. *They murdered their fathers?*

Who are you to judge? A voice whispered inside him, *You're a murderer, too.*

"Why!?" Vern's voice echoed in his head.

Thislen pressed his forehead to the cool wood of the ship for a moment, breathing deeply. His arms and legs were beginning to cramp from holding so still. Slowly he stretched them into new positions while he listened. He couldn't leave now. He didn't know enough yet.

The breeze off the sea was cutting and cold, chilling Thislen's sweat and leaving him itchy and restless. Or was that the ghosts haunting him?

"I murdered my father for being an insufferable old relic. You murdered yours to learn what I already knew," Soren pointed out.

"Regardless of reason," Avasten said, waving a hand fluidly through the air. "Soren, if she *is* from...*that* bloodline, I approve. Most heartily, even." The redhead moved a hunter, taking one of Garridan's silver hounds off the board.

"I think you're going to have problems convincing her, though," Garridan said, rubbing his chin as he stared at the board with a frown.

"Nonsense. I have money. I can buy out most of her excuses. More important, I have power. I simply intend not to take no for an answer.

Mila Ominir is part of my plans now. If she doesn't work with me, I will simply have to take measures. If I must, I can take her to Father Theobalin."

"Theobalin! Didn't he marry my father and his second wife?" Garridan asked curiously.

"He did. He'll marry anyone, even if the woman is kicking and screaming."

Garridan laughed. "I'll bet he costs a pretty penny for that."

"He does, which brings me back to my first point," Soren smirked. "I have money. And I can promote him to a proper bishop of the Ancestors."

"I suggest you make it clear to her where she stands with you, Soren, and soon. She's willful, too much so for my liking." Another piece slid across the board. "There, I've cornered that entire lot."

"You did not," Garridan said smugly, countering and removing several pieces from the board. "Captured! Ha. How long have you been trying to court her, anyway?"

"Moons," Soren sighed. "She didn't catch on until I laid it out plainly, and then she acted like it came out of nowhere, and I was trying to ruin her virtue. Old-fashioned nonsense, really."

"Are you sure she isn't just...simple?" Garridan tossed one of the captured golden hunters up and down while Avasten stared at the board in quiet consternation.

Calculated, more like. Thislen guessed that she had masterfully deflected Soren's advances for as long as she could if her performance in the shop had been anything to go by.

Soren frowned at his empty glass, holding it up to the light and staring through it at the lantern. "It wouldn't matter if she were—I don't need her for her brains. However, she seems intelligent. Very clever, just...reluctant, perhaps. What do you suggest, then?" His gaze fell to Avasten.

The willowy redhead studied the board for several more moments in silence. He played a piece before he spoke. "Well, it was an awful shame what happened to Percivan Coppermund," he said calmly.

Thislen's grip tightened on the wood carvings, eyes widening. He lifted himself a hair higher, gaze intent on the men in the cabin. He felt a prickle of ice form between his shoulder blades.

"Find Soren, he—"

"You know what happened to him, Avasten," Garridan said. "The Vaim got him."

"Yes, I do. But we might take advantage of the situation. Did the report not mention a set of boot prints rumored to be on the ground?" Avasten met Soren's curious gaze.

Soren straightened suddenly in his seat, leaning over the desk. "Ah, yes! Awful shame," he agreed. "How dreadfully unsafe. There's a potential murderer on the loose."

I didn't murder him; I tried to save him! Thislen thought furiously.

But you killed the sailor, that voice argued.

He closed his eyes for a moment.

"The City Guard simply must conduct a cursory investigation in the city, of course. I presume it will take them a fortnight or more, at the very least." Avasten slid a piece across the board, the scrape of it loud in the otherwise quiet cabin. He had a cold, twisted grin on his features.

"You know, I think it would be remiss of me as a suitor not to send her a personal guard from my own household in these...trying times," Soren mused, lips curling up like a cat in the cream.

Garridan set a piece down with a faint furrow to his brow. "I don't know if that's warranted. We don't actually know what happened yet, after all. And I don't think we should draw any attention to ourselves over Percivan's circumstances."

So they had something to do with why Percivan was on the island?

Both of the other noblemen looked at the brunet in stunned silence. Soren's eyebrows rose so high that they vanished beneath his golden curls. Avasten's lips parted, jaw slightly slack. Neither expected Garridan to talk back to them.

"What? What do you mean?" Soren demanded.

"I mean the Vaim aren't all that frightening during the day. She'll suspect something. Who needs a guard against the ghosts when the sun is up?"

Avasten and Soren exchanged long looks.

"Just hire some toughs from the Gate Quarter instead, have them rough up the shop. I'd do it while she's at tea, and after we come up with some story to draw Olen Ominir away," Garridan continued.

Soren's brows vanished beneath his hair once more. "That's...actually not a terrible idea, Garridan," he said slowly, rising from his seat. He began to pace—toward the window.

Thislen eased slowly out of sight, grimacing as his shoulder protested the movement.

"We can arrange the toughs on the morrow. Garridan can hunt for some whilst I take your bride to the tailor's."

She's not his bride! Not yet. Not ever, I hope.

"In the meantime, I will arrange for a spy to be set on her. I want to know if my bride's reluctance has anything to do with rival suitors," Soren said.

Thislen swore softly to himself. *If they set a spy on her, they'll know when she leaves! They'll know where she goes! If they get a chance to set that spy, we'll be caught.*

He had heard enough for now, and his arm was trembling. Any longer, and he risked falling into the water. That would only get him killed and Mila caught.

Thislen left the window cracked open and began to ease back toward the ship's bow, moving slower this time. His arms and legs tingled and burned in turns as life returned to them after being held in those cramped positions for so long.

His mind raced the entire time he made his precarious way back along the side of the ship as it rocked slowly in the waves.

They had something to do with Percivan's death, or they know something about it. Think of the way they said his name. Think of why they don't want to tie themselves to his body!

"Find Soren, he—"

He what, Percivan? He killed you? Thislen silently asked as he tucked himself back into the shadowed embrace of the wooden bird's wing. Gingerly he felt over the bandages on his shoulder, massaging life back into it where he could. *Did they put him ashore themselves?*

Percivan was dead and beyond Thislen's help—but finding an answer might be enough to stop the spirit from haunting his dreams. The more pressing issue at hand was Mila.

Mila was in danger.

Thislen reluctantly pushed all thoughts of Percivan's shocked, blood-spattered face from his mind. In the shadows of the *Bestant Belle,* he plotted and schemed and supposed. He found himself burning with the need to go and *do* something.

I wish I could find Mila right away. I'd put us on a rowboat and paddle us the length of the island this very instant.

But Thislen had very effectively trapped himself by sneaking aboard the ship, and there was nothing more he could do. Not tonight.

Tomorrow, he told himself. *First thing tomorrow.*

6

Why!?" Shouted the sailor in Thislen's head. He floundered in the sea, Vaim boiling in the water around him.

"Find Soren!" Percivan shouted, his hand outstretched as he fell back into the waiting arms of a hundred angry specters.

"Stay hidden, stay safe," his father's voice whispered in his ear, but no one was there when Thislen turned.

"Come," A voice whispered. "Come."

Thislen jerked awake with a deep breath, eyes flying open. Dawn had come with a cool, clinging fog that coiled over the calm waters of the sea in delicate tendrils. He was glad he had stolen the cloak. Even swathed in the extra layer of wool, he was cold. The tip of his nose felt like ice. Autumn was well and truly on its way.

The light was pale and thin. It was sometime before dawn, but still the ship was raising anchor. The chain rattled up from the depths, eerily muted. None of the Grand Quarter's ships rang their bells, choosing instead to sail back to shore one by one in the wake of the *Bestant Belle*. They looked like so many ships in the clouds—or worse—like ghost ships —as they drifted through the fog.

The noble and wealthy occupants of the ships slept blissfully on in the silent return to the island. No cabins had lanterns lit now, though a few hung off the railings above, warning others as to her location. The *Belle* drifted across the water like a specter, creaking wood and soft whistles from the sailors the only sounds Thislen could hear. The sea today was black as obsidian and just as smooth. The fog seemed to rise up around the bow, reaching along the sides as if it wanted to hold the ship back or drag it down beneath the waves.

As the docks loomed out of the shadows of the dawn, a quiet dread settled in around Thislen. He stretched as best he could in the confines of his hiding place, then shed the cloak. It fluttered down to the water without a sound, barely rippling the sea's surface, where it was swallowed swiftly by the deep.

His limbs had stiffened horribly in the night, and his fingers were almost numb. There wasn't enough room to work life back into them. *I'm just going to have to trust that I can do it.* Thislen hoped fervently he had regained enough strength since his fever. He held his breath, waiting as the ship slowed and the gray smudge that was the shore loomed into sight. He braced against the ship's edge.

The first ray of dawn broke over the horizon behind the ship, painting the fog pink and blue. The anchor chain began to rattle as it fell. The island was safe now, as was the sea. Thislen quickly pushed himself off of the small ledge.

His stomach flipped as he fell. The frigid water swallowed him with a splash. It was deep enough that he didn't find the bottom with his feet. Hastily, he kicked for the surface. Thislen crested the water, biting back the urge to gasp, the fog swirling about him. The cold clamped over his chest like iron rungs wrapped around a barrel, and he doubted he could have breathed deeply anyway. Instead, shivering and panting shallowly, he tread water.

No shouts or alarms greeted him, and the anchor's chain stopped rattling a few pounding heartbeats later. *I did it,* he thought numbly, looking up at the side of the ship on his left.

There was no time to lose. He would freeze, or bring his fever back if he stayed in the water too long. Thislen cupped his hands, sliding them into the water as carefully as he could, pulling himself toward the shore. His shoulder burned. The salt stung as it soaked through the bandages and wormed its way to his skin.

Paddling along the ship's length felt as if it took an age, but mere minutes had passed by the time Thislen made it to the wharf and scrabbled his way into the shore. The spatter of water sloughing off of him accompanied his safe arrival onto land. Thislen flopped onto his back with a wet smack, shivering madly. He was soaked through and freezing.

The sound of wood on wood met his ears. The gangplank had been lowered from the side of the *Bestant Belle.* Servants and sailors would be ashore soon. The dawn was growing stronger, and the concealing fog would vanish with the warming light. Those thoughts drove him to his feet.

Thislen set off at a dead run into the fog on legs he could hardly feel. Each step squelched beneath him. The broad streets slipped past him, empty of patrols and servants and binmen and nobles and wealthy merchants. He couldn't slow down, however. He'd have to be swift to be out of the Grand Quarter before the City Guard was off their ships and arriving at their posts.

A soaking wet servant running away would raise questions. I can't get caught. Someone has to warn Mila. If we don't start moving right away, it'll be too late!

He wanted to stop by the small gable room he had found abandoned all that time ago, the secret space he called home. He had planned to get all of his coin to ensure none of it would be discovered when he returned from all this.

There was no time. There was *never* enough time.

Once more, as he had days before, Thislen found himself racing through the streets of Astera. This time, cold, wet clothes clung to his legs and arms and chafed against his skin. He ran slower than the last time, suffering still from the ravages of his fever. Regardless, he charged down the streets he had walked through before. He practically flew over the delicate bridge spanning the canal.

I have to find Mila. I have to help her. I have to hurry!

We have to run.

Faster! He demanded of himself. *She doesn't know how far they're willing to go. I was right! I was* right, *damn it all! She has no idea how trapped she really is. It's now or never.*

The rising murmur of distant crowds met his ears as he made it to the sprawling market before Perilee's closed gates. A few scattered people began to appear as dawn well and truly filled the city's streets with its soft blue-gold light. He slowed to a walk, shivering and gasping for air as he tried to mix amongst the milling crowds of the homeward bound.

There was no comfortable feeling of anonymity in the throng today, not with him soaked through and shivering. He wondered if his lips were a little blue, if his skin was gray. He pushed those thoughts aside as he wove through the streets of the Goods Quarter as quickly as he dared, scanning for familiar faces with every step. Evelie, Ivan, Olen, Mila—they had to be here somewhere!

Thislen made it to the shop without seeing them, shuttered and quiet. He tucked himself against the wall to wait. Very few people turned onto the quiet dead-end street, making their way to the inn.

There!

A familiar head of wild red hair rounded the corner, and Mila's honey-brown hair a moment later. The father and daughter were walking arm and arm together, both of them looking at their feet as they conversed in low voices with reserved, melancholy expressions.

"Mila! Olen!" He called as calmly as he could manage, lifting his hand in greeting.

Mila's grip tightened on her father's arm when Thislen called, her eyes wide as she looked up at him with a jolt.

She looks like a deer that heard a twig snap.

He was at her side a moment later. "We need to leave. Now," Thislen said quietly, urgently. He glanced back at the mouth of the quiet street. "Soren is sending someone to spy on you. He has a plan that will make it so you'll be under guard while he courts you. If we don't move fast, you won't make it."

Color drained rapidly from her cheeks. She stopped walking. Olen's thick eyebrows shot up toward his hair.

"How?" Mila demanded in a gasp, "How do you know?"

"I spied on them. No," Thislen said, cutting her off as her lips parted, "I can't explain how now. I'll tell you everything after we're away from here. We have to get on the road. Come *on,* Mila. We have to *go.* Trust me."

He held her gaze, willing all the truth of his words into his eyes, hoping she could read it there. To his surprise, it was Olen who moved first, crossing over to the shop and unlocking the door.

"Hurry up, you two. Get inside," he said softly. "I'll get you some ferry fare."

"We have to take the streets—a ferryman might talk." Thislen turned toward the door.

"Why are you wet?" Mila asked as they entered the dim confines of the shop.

"I went swimming," he answered. He was grateful for his race across town that kept him warm, and twice as grateful he had clothes to change into waiting for him inside. Without a word, he began to strip right there in the middle of the shop.

"Give me those clothes, my boy; I'll get them cleaned for when you come back," Olen murmured, passing Thislen a blanket.

He wrapped it around himself gratefully, bouncing in place for a moment to warm himself up. The healer took his wet things and carried them up the stairs.

"Bring down the packs!" Thislen called after him. "Mila, you're going to take the bags across the way to the flower shop. Evelie and Ivan weren't far behind you, right?"

Mila, still pale as a sheet, turned to peer out through a gap in the shop's shutters. "They aren't here yet." Her hands were clasped so tightly together that they were as white as her face.

"Have they hidden a key somewhere?" Thislen asked.

"In the dirt, at the back of the big planter by the door," Olen answered, coming downstairs with the bags. "It's wrapped in a little piece of oilcloth."

Mila began to reach for her father. Thislen's arm shot out of the blanket, catching at her wrist and turning her toward the shop door. "Your life matters more than your goodbyes. Take the bags. Go *now*."

Mila turned a glare over her shoulder at him. A growing gleam in her eyes told Thislen he had hurt her more than irritated her. *Oh well, better alive and angry at me than a prisoner.* Olen hung the packs from either of her shoulders. Staggering under her burden, Mila fled across the street to the flower shop.

Thislen didn't hesitate to go to the greenhouse and his now-dried clothes. He pulled them from the lines, shoving a leg into his trousers. "I need more bandages."

Olen had followed him. "There was no call in being so—"

"What makes you the most important family in the kingdom? Do you know?" Thislen interrupted.

Olen froze, face reddening and eyes wide. *He does. He knows.* "I don't... That's not...I'm afraid...Excuse me?" The man sputtered.

"Whatever secret you have, Olen Ominir, the Ruling Council knows."

When Olen managed to speak, his voice was hushed, his gaze drifting across the shuttered windows. "No one is supposed to know. Only my family. The tale is passed down on our deathbeds; I wrote Mila a letter ages ago just in case. Thislen, what—"

"I haven't got time to discuss this at length. I don't care how you pass it on, either. Mila doesn't know?"

Olen's shoulders drew up toward his ears. He wouldn't meet Thislen's gaze.

"Mila doesn't know." His face was hard as iron. "You need to know that your secret is the only reason your daughter was proposed to at all. *She* doesn't matter to them, just her bloodline. Soren Bestant said he'd marry her kicking and screaming. Her only chance at something better is to leave. Right now."

And they won't stop looking for her, either. Not if she's important somehow. The farm won't be far enough. If they want her as more than just a pretty face, they'll check all her connections. She'll be discovered there sooner or later.

Hells, where are we going to go?

"You can tell me all about the secret when I come back. I can try and help you sort all of this out—or we can be done when I bring you news of her safe delivery to Barred Town."

"Barred Town? But she's supposed to go to—"

"And you know that! And so does Evelie, and Ivan! You can't spill what you don't know, so I can't tell you her exact location. I'm coming back. As soon as she's settled. I swear."

"I never agreed to—"

"I haven't got the time to let you explain everything now or to convince you of this! I have to get her out of the city. Write her a letter. Ship it as far as the farm in a flower crate."

"Now see here, Thislen, I hardly know you! What makes you think I'm going to let you walk out that door and take Mila away from me?"

There isn't time to care.

Thislen stepped forward, pulled the ring from inside his shirt, and thrust it into Olen's face. "*Trust* me, if you can. I know these people. I know what they're about!"

The apothecary looked at the crest pressed into the golden band and paled. His green eyes were wide, his mouth open as he met Thislen's gaze.

"Don't chance her safety and yours on saying goodbye. I'm leaving."

Thislen knew he was being cruel. He knew his voice was harsh. Frustration bled into every word and gave them barbs.

He didn't bother to change his dressings. He pulled on his shirt and a pair of dry pants and pulled his cloak around his shoulders. Olen took the damp clothes and hastily bundled them into an oiled sack.

Thislen paused, staring at the offering. He took it slowly, dark eyes meeting green.

"Let me pack you some bandages," Olen said.

I shouldn't have shown him the ring. What was that for? What if he can't keep it secret?

Olen went behind the counter, kneeling to scour the shelves built into the back of the thing. Thislen didn't bother to wait. He reached up, muffling the shop's bell with his hand and pulling it from its hook. He set it gently on the nearest shelf before slipping silently out the door.

The open air of Astera was just now coming alive. Thislen hadn't even been in the shop for half a bell, a quarter at most. People were still arriving to homes or jobs. Shops were only just setting about the tasks to open their doors. Some people made their way down the quiet street toward the inn's common room for their breakfasts. Everyone was moving with the bustle of the start of the day.

Except for one.

Thislen did not turn his head toward the intersection, choosing instead to stretch before the shop's door for just a moment as he subtly watched the stranger on the corner. There was a twinge of pain in his shoulder at the motion and an answering stir of unease between his shoulder blades. It was a man in plain clothes, common enough for the area if not as brightly colorful as the rest of the Goods Quarter's residents. His posture was casual, leaning against the wall and looking for all the world as if he were waiting for someone, loitering about until they appeared. Except his gaze stopped too often on the shuttered window of the Ominir Apothecary.

Well, good news is that Lord Bestant couldn't afford a good *spy on short notice,* he thought wryly. The nosey nobles had gone for quick over quality. Still, the spy's presence was a problem in and of itself.

Thislen wandered away. Away from the apothecary and away from the flower shop across the street. He walked into the inn's yard and made a grand show of inhaling the heady scent of fresh bread.

"Hey!" he called at the door. "Got any rolls for a penny?"

"Aye, hot and fresh!" A girl called out, waving.

Thislen dug a coin out of his pocket to pay for the lightly sugared morning roll. He ate it slowly as he aimlessly explored the quiet corner street. Olen had appeared to pull the shutters down from the shop, capturing the spy's gaze. When the apothecary spotted Thislen, he opened his mouth to speak. Thislen gave a subtle shake of his head.

Olen paused, looking around.

Don't do that! *He'll notice! Damn it.*

They were lucky; the spy didn't seem particularly clever. The man also looked around, trying to see what the apothecary was looking for. Thislen gave a short sharp whistle, drawing Olen's attention. The thief gave a quick slicing motion with his hand.

Knock it off!

Olen's eyes widened, and he turned back to his work. His brow was furrowed, but he got the hint. He said nothing.

Thislen wandered over to the tailor's shop beside Evelie's, plucking thoughtfully at his cloak as he kept watch on the spy. He wouldn't be able to stay here long without having to go inside.

I need Ivan or Evelie. Thislen glanced at the flower shop. It was still closed. He took a deep breath.

Evelie and Ivan turned into the square, hurrying along.

"I can't believe you lost your boot, today of all days." Evelie was scolding. "That's why I say, keep your things organized!"

"Mother—" Ivan began, pausing as he saw Thislen.

"Good morning!" Thislen said brightly. "I was hoping you'd come soon. It's my aunt's birthday again. I came for those daisies like I got last time, for my mother's. Daisies, roses, and ferns. Do you remember?"

I'm a customer, Ivan. A customer!

Ivan's eyes widened.

Evelie looked just as startled as her son. "Why, This—"

"Is early, you're right, Mother!" Ivan said, cutting her off before she could finish saying Thislen's name.

"Yes, she loved them last time. Aunt Mary was fair green with envy, so I thought I'd get her the same. Do returning customers get a discount?"

Ivan forced a laugh. "Oh, you'd be surprised how often we hear that. Come inside; let's get you sorted," he said with forced cheer. He pulled a key from his pocket and went to unlock the shop.

Evelie followed after them, catching on at last. "Yes, yes! Right this way, young man! For your aunt's birthday, you said? You're a thoughtful boy." She ushered them both inside.

As he stepped through the door, Thislen chanced a glance at the corner. The lounging spy wasn't paying the slightest bit of attention to them at all. He was chewing idly on a thumbnail as he watched the apothecary and waited.

Good.

The flower shop was smaller than the apothecary. It had a tiny counter at the base of the stairs instead of the dividing counter-wall to separate a workspace from the shop front. The walls were lined with buckets and huge clay vases full of water and flowers. They perfumed the air with scents of lily and lavender and rose and jasmine. Shelves above the army of rainbow blooms held decorative vases and bright colored paper and fanciful ribbon.

There was presumably another living area above, and that must have been where Mila had gone, for the shop was empty, still, and cool.

Thislen let out a brief exhale. "One of you needs to keep opening the shop as usual."

"Thislen, dear, what is going on? What was all that play-acting outside?" Evelie demanded.

"Mila? It's us," he called toward the stairs. "Someone's already out there."

Mila came down the stairs like a silent piece of down, a shadow in the back corner of the shop. Her eyes were wide, and her face pale. "What?"

"Hey! What's the big idea? You sent Mila to break into our shop?" Ivan asked loudly.

"Will you shut up?" Thislen snapped.

"Don't you talk to him that way," Evelie said quickly, "I don't like that tone of voice. You need to explain this to me, Thislen, or I'll—"

"I can help with that," Mila said. The air was thick with tension as she stepped out from behind the counter. She had changed into her traveling clothes already. They were in muted browns and rusts, colorful but practical for the dirt of the road. Trousers were tucked under a half-skirt, and sturdy boots reached up over her calves. They looked new, or nearly so. Her hair was tied back in a bun, and she clutched at a shawl she had tied around her shoulders over a vest and shirt.

"Please do," Evelie said with a soft huff.

"Thislen went to spy on Lord Bestant last night. He heard..." She trailed off, glancing at Thislen.

She opened the door for me so they'd pay attention. Clever. He gave her a quiet, grateful nod.

"I heard them talking about marrying her kicking and screaming, about sending toughs to break into the apothecary and make her afraid so they could give her one of Bestant's personal guards. They'd say it was for protection, but—"

"They'd use the bastard to keep her trapped where he could find her!" Ivan said, heat flaring in his eyes.

"Aye, exactly," Thislen said, "They also decided to send a spy along, in case she has any rival suitors he'd need to get rid of. They weren't specific on how."

Evelie gasped, a hand flying to her mouth. "You don't mean to imply that the Ruling Council would resort to *drastic* measures, do you?"

"I wouldn't put it past them," he said grimly.

"But they're meant to take care of us." Evelie's crestfallen face tugged at Thislen's heart.

Damn all these threads. He wished he didn't care that she was upset.

"Well, she'll be gone, won't she?" Ivan asked. "We're sending her away."

Thislen turned to Mila. "It might already be too late."

Mila nodded. "You said someone's already out there?"

"Where?" Ivan peered through a crack in the shutters, craning to see the entrance to their small street.

Thislen ignored him, stepping closer to Mila. "Look, I haven't got a full plan yet. I thought we'd have more time. What I do have is this—we have to cause a distraction. We have to separate, and you'll have to meet me outside the East Gate. Meet me under the first tree within sight of the road outside the gate, you understand?"

"Thislen, you're scaring me," she whispered, her fingers curled tight in the fabric of her shawl.

"Get the packs. I'll take mine. Evelie, you open the shop, and Ivan—"

Anything else Thislen might have said was interrupted by the rattle of shells above the flower shop's door. He turned to see Ivan had vanished outside. In a flash, Thislen was across the room, peering through the same crack in the wooden shutters that the young florist had been using a moment before.

Ivan was rolling up his sleeves out front of the flower shop, his gaze fixated on the spy. He looked like an angry bull about to charge.

No, Thislen thought numbly, *there's no way he's going to...*

"Mila, the packs, now!" He barked. She pulled them out from behind the counter.

She's not ready. I'm not ready. What is he thinking, *that stupid, reckless—*

He grimaced as the pack pressed on the wound on his shoulder, but he didn't wait. "Get your pack on, run when the man is distracted, and go to Barred Town if I don't show up by noon! Understand?"

"Thislen—!" she cried, but he was already out the door.

His pack banged against his back as he jogged to catch up to Ivan. Thislen bumped into the florist pointedly. Hard. He hastily turned and caught at Ivan's shoulders after the gesture, patting him down.

"Oh, I say! Didn't see you there. Are you alright? Didn't bruise you, did I?" Thislen said loudly.

"What are you doing?" Ivan hissed, trying to shrug him off.

"Ivan, shut the hells up," Thislen hissed. "The best way you can help Mila right now is to do *exactly* as I say. Understand?"

Ivan's brow furrowed, but he gave a brief jerk of his head. *I'll take that as a nod.*

"Good. When I turn and start toward the corner, you're going to pat all of your pockets. You're going to shout thief at the top of your lungs. You're going to chase after me. I'm going to run headlong into that man, and you're going to pick him up and fuss all over him, same as I'm doing right now to you. Do you hear me?"

The entire time he spoke, Thislen was adjusting Ivan's clothes, grasping his shoulders, and thoroughly blocking his view of the spy on the corner. *Come on, you thick-headed idiot. Do it for Mila, for the affections for her that you're so awful at hiding.*

"I don't want to. I can just hit him."

"You go over there and hit that man, you will get arrested, and Mila will still get caught. Don't be stupid. Follow the plan."

"That's your plan?" The florist asked heatedly.

"It is now that you've bungled any chance I had of a better one." With that, Thislen patted Ivan's cheek and turned to walk briskly away. He didn't look back.

Two heartbeats. Three. Four. He was halfway to the spy when he heard Ivan behind him.

"Hey! Oi! Thief, that man's a thief!"

That drew the attention of everyone in the quiet street, including the spy. Thislen broke into a run, barreling toward the wall where the man was leaning. He turned his head to feign a glance over his shoulder a few steps away, then veered abruptly sideways, bracing himself.

The impact was expected, but that made it no less confusing. Arms and legs and Thislen's cloak were all wrapped around one another, flashing past his face in a disconcerting welter. He kicked and pushed, the scuffle carrying them into the middle of the street. The spy cursed and spat at him as they wrestled on the ground.

"Hey there! Leave that man alone!" Ivan shouted somewhere nearby.

Thislen rolled away and scrambled to his feet, ignoring the stinging throb in his shoulder and the gentle, sticky trickle of blood down his skin as he bolted for the streets beyond.

Now I just have to hide a few streets away and wait for Mila!

Thislen didn't make it that far. He rounded the first corner and ran smack into the gray-clad back of a member of the City Guard. He went cold all over as he bounced off the man's back.

"Oi, what's the big idea?" The guard asked, turning around.

"Thief! Did you see which way he went? I say, sir, are you alright?" Ivan called from somewhere behind him.

Oh hells.

The guard's eyes grew wide. He lunged forward at Ivan's words, and Thislen answered by flinging himself away from the man. He turned to barrel down the street in the opposite direction at a dead run.

"Stop in the name of the Council!" The guard brayed.

Thislen did not, of course, stop. He darted through the crowds like a breeze between the leaves of a tree, ducking low and turning sideways to slip around the surprised residents of Astera. He tore down an alleyway, then back out onto another street. He threw himself across a cart's path as it clattered down the street.

Thislen didn't dare look behind him, though the sound of following footsteps stopped after the cart. He kept weaving through the throngs of people and ducking down promising thoroughfares, burrowing deeper into the city. At last, he could run no more and came to a stop. Thislen hunkered between two bins in a shadowed alley, legs drawn up. The shadows of the small recess hid him from view and bought him time to breathe. Great lungfuls of air were gulped up as he sagged against the cool stones.

I could have run twice as far if I hadn't been sick. He kicked himself. It was probably better to push to his feet, to keep going. He *knew* that. Still, Thislen didn't move.

A clatter of boots sounded nearby. Four gray-liveried guardsmen ran past the mouth of the alley. Thislen jerked his head back to ensure he wasn't seen. He held his breath for several heart-pounding moments before he dared relax again.

I couldn't run another second, even if I wanted to, Thislen realized. His side had twisted into a knot. His shoulder throbbed. He could feel his lungs press against his ribs with the taste of copper on his tongue. The sky above swung slowly, not quite spinning—but threatening to.

Thislen watched the sky from his hiding place. It was a small sliver between the buildings, a slate blue expanse quickly filling with great gray clouds. The clouds were thick and full of shadows, rolling in off the sea in a towering fury. They were heavy with the promise of rain and rumbling with thunder, changing the taste of the air to something sharp and peppery.

How long was it until noontide? Where was he? How far was the East Gate?

I hope Mila made it, he thought.

MILA OMINIR CLUNG to the straps of her pack so tightly that the woven cloth bit into her skin. Her heart was thrumming in her throat like a hummingbird. She watched through the shop window with Evelie hovering at her elbow as Thislen ran into Ivan. They murmured a moment, Thislen fussing over Ivan's clothes.

What is he doing*?*

The thief turned and simply started to walk away. She breathed a sigh of relief. Surely that meant that Ivan was going to come back into the shop.

Instead, Ivan patted his pockets, making a great show of it, then pointed at Thislen's retreating back. His shout was muffled by the window, but even still she knew what he was calling.

Thief.

"Oh, oh, that *must* be it. Go, Mila! Now!" Evelie said, pulling at her arm.

For a moment, she didn't budge. Mila worried that her feet had fused to the floor, that she was rooted there, trapped, doomed to wait until every opportunity to live her own life escaped her grasp. Evelie's insistent pull dragged her slowly toward the door. One foot scuffed, then the next. As if moving each foot was the key to ending her sudden paralysis, Mila found herself stepping outside.

"Stay safe," Evelie breathed, eyes filling with tears as she gently pushed Mila away from the shop entrance.

Across the way, Mila met a pair of familiar green eyes. Olen stood in the window of the Apothecary, his gaze fixed upon her. She couldn't bring herself to uncurl her fingers from the straps of her pack to wave goodbye. *What if someone sees?*

Did he always look so old and worn? She wondered as she started toward the head of the street. His shoulders sagged. His face was as delicate and wrinkled as crumpled paper. The gray in his hair was all the more noticeable today—or perhaps it was just a trick of the light.

Mila tore her gaze away. Thislen was scuffling with the man on the corner as Mila approached, only to kick free and disappear behind the nearest buildings.

"Thief!" Ivan bawled. "Did you see which way he went? I say sir, are you alright?" The florist bent to pull the spy to his feet, turning him every which way and dusting him off, fussing outrageously.

Thislen tore past in the opposite direction, a member of the City Guard hot on his heels. Mila froze.

No! If he gets arrested—he already has two marks!

That could be a hand, or slavery in the mines!

"Took my entire coin purse. My grandmother gave it to me for my birthday when I was ten! The nerve. Can't ever get it back. And there were only pennies inside!" Ivan said.

She was so close to the spy, to being caught. Everything seemed to be moving underwater around her. All the excited chatter over the commotion was muted and distant. It echoed strangely in her ears. The bustling people with their brightly colored clothing passed like gently floating flowers on the summer breeze, drifting this way and that in the hubbub. Ivan's hands slowed, turning the spy's face away from their quiet street under the pretense of checking the swelling near an eye.

Now, Mila. Now or never.

Outwardly, she hoped, she looked calm. She walked past without looking at the florist or the spy. *My eyes will not be wide as teacup saucers,* she willed. *My cheeks will not be pale as cream.*

Mila was grateful that her steps didn't falter. She rounded the first corner, all at once feeling like she could breathe again. The world leapt to life around her.

"A real shame, isn't it? The way some people in this city think they can get away with stealing. Why, I've half a mind to follow after him myself." Ivan was saying, each word dripping with bravado. "I think I could really give him what for if the City Guard doesn't get to him first. Ha! Now, what did you say your name was, fellow?"

"I didn't!"

"Right, right. Well, some people, eh?" Ivan said brightly.

"Will you get off me!?" The spy said, exasperated.

The conversation faded behind her as she kept walking, calm as if she were just headed toward the market square for breakfast. *Thislen risked his life for me, or at least a limb.* The thought chilled her. Why? They hardly knew one another.

Yet Thislen had given her a chance at what she wanted, and she would be remiss if she didn't accept it.

In a daze, Mila drifted through the streets of the Goods Quarter. People stepped around her on either side as she moved almost mechanically ahead. Every step carried her further and further from the only home she had ever known. From her father, the woman she loved as a mother, and the boy she loved as a brother. What if she never saw them again?

You decided to do this, she reminded herself, *and there's too much at stake to change your mind now.* She straightened her shoulders and lifted her chin as she plunged into the crowds of the markets.

The light faded suddenly, and not just because she had passed beneath the branches of a great oak tree. Thick clouds had boiled to life across the sky. A roll of thunder followed their arrival, and the cutting bite of a cool autumn breeze. Summer was fading at last.

People all over the market were pushed into a sudden hurry ahead of the inevitable rain, pulling shawls and cloaks over baskets and satchels to protect their purchases. Many turned and left, walking briskly toward other errands, or home.

Home. She stopped in the middle of the path for a moment, fighting the urge to look over her shoulder. All of the townsfolk around her were carrying out the perfectly routine tasks of shopping and supplying and eating. Mila would never be able to do the same things as they did again. When she did go shopping next, it would be different. Elsewhere.

My entire life has already changed. Right now, it's different. It's gone. Her eyes began to sting. She couldn't swallow the lump in her throat.

You can't cry over something you asked for, she lectured herself, adjusting her pack, *at least not now.* She could, and she would cry—once she was safe, tucked under a tree outside the city walls and waiting for Thislen to meet her.

"It might already be too late," Thislen had said, voice low and urgent. His fingers had been curled so tight against his fists that Mila noticed the nails digging into the skin. His dark eyes had been intent, trying to convey exactly how serious her situation was. His brow had furrowed, the folds between his eyes as dark as the storm clouds above her head.

The thief had not told her everything. She knew he hadn't. He had promised that he would as soon they met up once more. She had to trust him.

Maybe this was a bad idea.

What secrets was he keeping? The young woman knew nothing about him other than what little he had revealed. Mila felt suddenly foolish for putting her trust in a stranger. What did he and his secrets have to do with her?

I'll ask him myself as soon as he catches up with me. It's about time I had some straight answers out of him. I won't go another step until he talks; just wait and see.

She shook her head, lifted her nose in the air, and began to walk once more.

What happens if he doesn't meet me at noon? She wondered as she walked around the edge of the market square, heading toward Perilee's wall. Thislen had told her that she would have to carry on alone, that she should go to Barred Town instead of the farm.

There were countless dangers in traveling through the countryside of Astera, especially if you didn't know where you were going. Farms and fishing villages made of small houseboats were scattered along the island, the only safe havens from the shadowy hands of the Vaim. If you didn't reach one of those water-borne residences tucked along the feet of the Spine, you could find yourself trapped come nightfall.

Mila had heard that farmers had space on the floors of their cabins for strangers to lay their heads most nights, and birthing stalls for their livestock below that for extra room. Most fishing hamlets had small inns that ran out of floating vessels. She had heard one was lost to a storm two months ago, from the man who delivered her father's extra herbs.

If Thislen did not appear by noontide, she would have no choice but to soldier on and hope the rough parchment map in her pocket would be enough to get her most of the way to Barred Town. She could always ignore his advice and take a ferry. That would ensure she made it across the island, even if it would cost all the coin Olen had given her. *Thislen didn't tell me to leave him behind out of callousness. It's practicality. It's for my safety.*

If I believe him.

Oh, what am I doing!?

She shook her head again, dismissing the doubt with a huff. He was paying off a debt! Thislen had no reason to harm her or lie to her. Did he?

Mila passed a delicate bridge that spanned the canal around the Grand

Quarter. The City Guards on the other side lounged beneath their trees, paying her no mind. Still, their presence was enough for her to feel cold inside and out.

Her destination was lying in the shadow of Perilee's wall. At the north-east corner of the great market was a wide street that ran along the city's outer wall. It was called the High Way, a partially raised balustrade for travelers to reach the East Gate without sullying the beautiful streets of the Grand Quarter below. The High Way was the most used road in the city. It was the shortest path to Barred Town, after all, if only by two bells by horse. The cobblestones there were oft replaced as they crumbled beneath the weight of cart after cart, meaning it was heavy with work crews of masons who pressed clay bricks from the earth they removed from the mines.

That meant the carts had to weave back and forth around workmen, causing delays that guaranteed there would always be a queue.

The important part is that there are only a few guardsmen, and they're at the gate.

The *most* important part was that it would take her further away from Lord Soren Bestant.

A roll of thunder rumbled heavily through the air. The first spritz of rain followed after, sporadic droplets that drove the current of people around her to move faster.

Mila stopped at the corner, taking a deep breath. It was mid-morning in Astera, gray, and beginning to rain in earnest. It didn't feel quite right, heading for the gate. That spark of something she had been waiting for her entire life, the rising fire she had felt on the deck of her family's ship, had fizzled and waned.

Just go, Mila. Just move! She willed herself forward. There would be plenty of time to sort out her feelings under the tree on the other side. She tipped her head back to stare at the massive stone bricks, hewn hundreds and hundreds of years ago and stacked so high, no one rightly knew how the stonemasons of old had done it. The wall had never been needed, and it did no good against the enemy that had truly invaded. Walls didn't protect anyone from the Vaim. Still, it was an impressive illusion of safety. Mila hated to leave it behind.

One step at a time. She turned to climb the gentle slope of the High Way. The wall ran along her left-hand side, looming solidly over everything and everyone below. The stone railing lined the right-hand side. Carts and horses and merchants packed the street the nearer she got to the gate, waiting in line for their turn to leave the city. A single cart-wide lane had been left open for those coming *in* to Astera. Peddlers with great heavy packs leaned against the wall to relieve their burdens. Merchants in their carts argued with their porters and hired hands. A farmer or two sat above empty carts, eager to get home after spending a night in the city.

Everyone seemed anxious to get out to the countryside and be on their way to their next destination. They clamored and chattered, shouting and conversing in turns as they waited to be called at the gate. Mila joined the throng, a lone traveler in a sea of strangers.

Her heart sank even as it raced in her chest at the realization. *I've always had someone around,* she thought. Ivan, eager to get into trouble with her or to have a new adventure. Evelie who always gave the kindest advice and made the best cup of tea. Her father, Olen, who had tended to every skinned knee and hurt feeling she ever had. Now there was no one as she faced the unknown. Her head was light as a feather, as if a good breeze could blow it from her shoulders.

The rain picked up. Mila pulled her shawl over her head, but she knew she'd soon be soaked. She was glad her pack was made of oiled leather. It would protect the few things she had inside. The flow of people out of the city was sluggish. The milling line shrank before her with all the speed of molasses. The gate's great arch grew closer and closer as Mila fought the urge to give up and go home.

There's still time. I can turn around. I can just give up.

No, no, *I can't! I don't want that life.*

Not that she knew what life she wanted instead.

Two city guards stood at either side of the gate, and one stood in the middle. The three of them took it in turns to gesture someone forward, ask a few questions, inspect the carts if they needed to, and then send their travelers onward. Some few were sent back while Mila watched. One merchant was pulled aside to the guardhouse built into the wall to have their cart searched thoroughly.

Mila's grip tightened on the straps of her pack again, the sharp bite of the cloth against her skin keeping her from panicking. *What will they ask? What will I say? I haven't got a tale for my departure.* Would that be her downfall? Would that be how she was caught?

I'm not doing anything wrong!

Why did it feel like she was?

Her heart fluttered wildly beneath her ribs, like a bird beating its wings against a cage.

"Next."

Mila found herself standing before a young guardsman. His cheeks were barely covered with peach fuzz, and he leaned on his spear like it was a walking stick and not a weapon. He looked her over quickly, dismissively, and then sighed. "Name?"

He doesn't want to be here either. "Mila. Mila Ominir."

"Where are you off to, then?"

"Visiting a cousin on a farm near Barred Town," she said brightly, bouncing once on the balls of her feet. *That will have them looking outside of the cities. Barred Town is large enough that I can disappear there. Change my name and wear different clothes...*

That was why Thislen wanted her to go there, she realized. To vanish.

If Lord Soren were to question the guards and this one happened to remember her, he would be scouring the farms outside the walls for some time before he thought to look in the city itself. She would have valuable time to hide.

Thislen would be proud that I've figured it all out. The thought made her heart swell in her chest. Mila was delighted at how easily the words had fallen off her tongue. She could lie!

"Got a few days of walking ahead of you to get that far. Couldn't get a horse?" The guard asked.

"No, sir," she said, smiling a bit. "I don't mind a bit of a walk, though. The next village is only half a day's journey, isn't it?"

"Closer. You'll get there long before nightfall if you keep a good pace. Alright, then. Next!" He waved a hand to dismiss her.

The tension bled out of her hands at once. Her shoulders relaxed, and she took the first step toward her freedom. She drew in a breath of air as the gate's great shadow fell across her shoulders. The road was still cobbled as it led away from the gate, coiling north and east over low hills that reminded her of a fallen piece of cloth. On the left, the Spine's great peaks rose above the city and the path. The massive forest carpeted the mountains, fading away in a fog and haze as the rain fell steadily.

"Just a moment, Miss Ominir."

It was a voice different from that of the guardsman who had interrogated her, a smooth and cultured voice. She felt the bulk of a man come up behind her and turned slowly. Mila came face to face with the badges and braid of an officer of the City Guard, wrapped in a half-cloak, rainwater dripping from the brim of his hat. Her eyes met his, set in a stern but kindly face.

"Excuse me?" She breathed.

"I'm afraid you are wanted for an inquiry. You'll have to come with me. Please," he said, tone polite and distant as he swept an arm toward the guard house. He didn't know who she was, she realized. He didn't know what she was wanted for. It didn't matter, either. This was the sort of man who simply did his job and did it well.

It didn't help her feel any better. A ringing started in her ears, high pitched and tinny. Voices sounded distant, like they were on the other side of her window, echoing and rattling strangely around her. She watched his lips move again, but she couldn't make out the words. "What?" She asked.

"I said, it is an order from the Ruling Council, Miss. Will you allow me to escort you to the Justica, or would you prefer cuffs in the back of a cart?"

Mila didn't look down to see, but it felt like ice was forming on her skin, delicate snowflakes of tingling cold that spread until their edges touched. The chill settled in from the crown of her head down to her toes. The only warm part of her was her heart, thrumming in her chest.

"You're saying, sir, that I haven't got a choice?"

"I'm afraid not. Your decision, please, Miss?"

Mila glanced over her shoulder at the countryside beyond the gate, at the road that stretched away from the city, gleaming and wet. The rolling foothills, the speckling of pine and aspen. She could see the first tree outside the gate in the distance, where she would have waited for Thislen until noon. The ocean was gray as iron, tipped here and there with white as the waves frothed and churned. Freedom, wild and untamed and *so close...*

She turned away from the sight, staring at the Grand Quarter below. "I'll walk, thank you."

Side by side with the Guard Captain, Mila walked back toward the heart of the city in the hazy rain.

THE RAIN HISSED down from the sky, hitting the cobblestones and windows and walls of Astera with gusto. It drummed incessantly on the bins on either side of Thislen as he pushed himself to his feet and pulled up his hood. He had waited long enough. He tucked his pack beneath his cloak to protect it some, then stepped out into the crowds.

There weren't nearly as many people as the rain picked up. Everyone he saw was either traveling with purpose or searching for somewhere warm and dry to take shelter. When he reached the Great Market Square, it was to find that most of the stalls had packed their wares away. Merchants and peddlers sat upon their crates, tucked beneath dripping awnings and watching the sky. The paths between their stalls were nearly empty. Only the most stubborn shoppers still stood against the weather.

Thislen ignored them as he made his way toward the broad ramp of the High Way along the far wall. It saved time, cutting through the market instead of circling around it. *At least the rain is good for something.*

He had waited until it was nearly noon, so far as he could tell, with the sun hidden behind the storm. It would be a close call to arrive on time, but even if he were a few moments late, he would still be able to catch up with Mila. *I hope the tree she's under is big enough to offer some shelter from this rain,* he mused. He didn't know if she had packed a cloak that could stand up to real weather.

Thislen joined the throng of carts and peddlers and merchants, all swathed in caps and cloaks, water dripping off their noses. *Well, this will take a while.*

If the rain kept up, it was likely the residents of the island kingdom would go to their ships early for fear of being late. These kinds of days were rare, where the weather hid the sun so thoroughly, but they happened from time to time. He hoped the farmers along the road had lit time candles when the clouds began to roll in. *What if we find the nearest farmhouse, only to find their boat is already out to sea?* That would bring their entire trip to an abrupt and permanent end if they were unlucky. A ferry could be convinced to come to shore—if one were docked in whatever hamlet they ended up in. Otherwise, they'd have to steal whatever would float.

Still, Thislen found himself looking forward to the trip, even if the first day promised to be soggy and uncomfortable. Once the danger had passed, once they were on the road, he would be able to breathe again. He looked forward to traipsing through the mud and sleeping in a pile of sweet-scented summer hay. *I can ask her about Soren as we go and be all the more prepared when I come back to do whatever Percivan wished for me to do.*

The line of carts and their goods moved slowly forward, and he found himself positioned right beside the great stone balustrade that overlooked the Grand Quarter below. It was a perfect vantage point for the poor and untitled masses to look upon the splendor of their betters and seethe with jealousy. The best part, of course, was that those masses couldn't sully the perfect streets.

It's a disgusting show of self-importance is what it is, he thought with a wrinkle of his nose. A raindrop landed right on the end of it and he sputtered quietly. He shook his head and turned away from the sight.

The cart in front of him rolled forward only a foot, and Thislen's brow furrowed. *I haven't got time for this.*

He wove between the lines of carts, ducking around their broad corners and patting horses on their flanks as he passed.

"Oi! What are you doing?"

"Hey, get back in line!"

Thislen ignored the odd shout or two from behind him. The merchants might be annoyed at his impatience, but he was running out of time. What if it were already noon?

Mila is waiting for me.

The gate itself was wide but barely tall enough for a covered cart to travel through. Heavy iron portcullises hung above on either side, built into the thick stone wall. Solid wooden doors on the outside of the wall stood open. Thislen could not remember a time in his lifetime when he had seen them closed.

Well, who is going to rob the ghost-city after nightfall? He thought dryly.

Three guardsmen stood in a row at the portal, asking questions and inspecting carts and wares. Everyone, including the inspectors, looked miserable and sodden—or well on their way to it. Thislen wove toward the front of the line without hesitation.

There was no warning. As he neared the gate, the door to the guard house tucked beside the gate opened, and three guards came out. They headed right for him, trying to appear casual. They didn't shout. They didn't say a word.

Thislen froze at their intent approach, then quickly ducked behind a cart, peering around the far edge.

The guards split to flank the wagon, hurrying their pace.

I'm not going to make it, he realized. He cursed under his breath, sending a silent apology into the air for Mila. *Run, Mila, run.*

With one hand, he pulled the ring from around his neck and hastily tucked it deep into his boot, inside his stocking. *I'm not getting out through this gate.* Thislen turned back toward the city. *I could go back to the apothecary and explain. Olen will understand. So long as Mila got out, that's all that matters.*

Or the West Gate! I could go down to the West Gate in the Gate Quarter and still get to Barred Town. If I hurry, I can wait for her at the gates there.

He set off quickly, glancing back only once to check whether or not the guards were still following.

They were. Thislen broke into a run, turning back—only to run face-first into someone else. The spy from out front of the Ominir Apothecary grabbed his arm. Thislen flung himself backward like he'd been scalded with hot water, but he couldn't get loose.

"Well, hello there," he said. His voice was like oil sliding across water, and there was a cold glint in his eyes and a cruel twist to his smile.

Thislen twisted his arm and pulled, but his shoulder protested with a blinding stab of pain. He fell still with a gasp, arm trembling. *I'm not giving up that easily.* Thislen grimaced, silently struggling to pry the fingers off his wrist.

Bodies slammed into him from behind, driving the air from his lungs even as they bore him to the ground. It was two of the guardsmen. The ensuing fight, if that's what it could be called, was brief. Thislen swung his free hand wildly, feeling fist and elbow connect with different targets. There were grunts of pain and muffled curses, but the third guard appeared and pinned his arm to the wet cobbles. He was wrestled onto his stomach, the captured arm twisted behind his back and held in place. The edge of a cobblestone dug painfully into his cheek. Damp soaked through the front of his shirt. Thislen slapped his free hand on the stones in frustration, growling like a wounded animal.

The spy let the guards hold him fast, squatting down where his trapped prey could see him. He patted Thislen's cheek, giving a long, sad sigh. "I can't believe I let *you* lose me my quarry. Did you think I wouldn't be able to recognize a distraction when I saw one?" He said, low enough that only Thislen could hear.

Thislen spat.

"Oh no, none of that," the spy said, covering Thislen's mouth with his hand so tight it hurt. "And don't worry. Someone else found her and picked her up on my behalf. Unfortunately, boy, my pay is at risk. I have to bring *someone* in to answer for this mess. I'm afraid today that will be you."

Thislen struggled against the weight of the guards that held him pinned. An elbow dug painfully into his back. The spy leaned back, uncovering Thislen's mouth. "Yes, this is the armed thief. He nearly murdered someone this morning."

I what?

Thislen's eyes grew huge, his heart hammering in his chest like an alarm bell. A charge of attempted murder and theft could get him killed! What was this madman thinking!? "No, I didn't!" he shouted desperately.

The guards hauled him to his feet, catching his other arm and dragging him toward the guard house.

Thislen cast wild looks at the merchants and peddlers around him. "I didn't hurt anyone! Please! Help me!"

None of the merchants nearby would look at him. None of them were calling after him anymore. Every single person there was looking at anything else but what was happening.

No one is going to help me.

"Get him to the Justica. He'll face trial for what he's done," the spy instructed.

The guards tied a rough rope around his wrists. They pulled it so tight it bit into his skin. Thislen grit his teeth against the pain. Every movement chafed and burned. They tied his feet, too, hobbling him like a horse.

The spy leaned in, ignoring Thislen's dark-eyed glare, the only armor he had against his mounting panic. "Better luck next time, little pickpocket."

Thislen was yanked away, gasping as his shoulder twisted. He felt another hot trickle of blood against his skin. The guards shoved him unceremoniously along, forcing him to quickstep to avoid falling. They continued to push him along, back toward the city proper. Even as he was forced down the High Way, however, he kept craning to stare back at the gate. His brow was furrowed. Something the spy had said was important. Something he was forgetting. Something about...

Mila.

"Someone else picked her up on my behalf."

Thislen stopped moving, his entire body going numb. Someone else had caught up to Mila before she could escape.

Mila was in danger.

The guards grabbed hold of his arms. He let them half-drag, half-carry him toward the heart of the city. It was what he deserved. All of this effort to help someone else had been an utter waste. Mila was caught. Evelie, Ivan, and Olen may never even know she hadn't made it out of Astera until it was too late; until she was married.

Thislen had failed.

7

They called it *The Brig*. Where on most ships, such a name was reserved for a row of cells at the lowest level of the vessel, this was an entire ship all its own—a massive floating carrack that served as Astera's prison. Thislen had been aboard the ship twice before for theft, kept overnight in a cell on the first level belowdecks.

The justice system of Astera was...unique, to say the least. Thislen presumed it, too, was a holdover from the time when the Ruling Council was attempting to look merciful and good. Instead of sentencing every malcontent and criminal to certain death, they had built them a ship to rot on, safely away from the rest of society.

The guards had a barracks there to keep an eye on the oft-crowded cells for minor crimes. Thieves, cheats, and smugglers were held there until the clogged lesser courts had the time to sentence them, usually in groups.

The second level down was for more serious crimes. Physical harm, fraud, forgeries, and more were housed in those cells, sometimes for days. It was also where those sentenced to longer punishments, time in the gaol, were kept four to a cell.

The lowest level was nearly always empty. Thislen's time in the cells before had not given him any answers as to who these rooms were intended for, but now he was in one. He wasn't alone, however. Someone was rustling softly in the cell beside his. He couldn't see them—three of the four walls that housed him were thick wood. The last was made of iron bars flaked red with a crust of rust.

Thislen was laying on his back on the narrow wooden shelf that served as a bunk, padded with a layer of loose straw that smelled musty and damp. He had been silent as the grave the entire time he was brought belowdecks, numb with self-loathing and disappointment. Water dripped somewhere, a constant reminder that he was below the waterline. He stared blankly at the wooden ceiling, tracing the heavy wooden beams that formed the floor above back and forth and back again. The wall at the head of the bunk had no windows. It curved inward at the base, forming the hull of the boat and making the ceiling of the cell wider than the floor.

They probably keep bad murderers down here, he decided at last, *or secrets.*

The water drip-drip-dripped away, the smell of salt and damp wood thick in the air. His cell was dry, however. The floor was plain. So were the walls. Thislen could see clearly into the cells across the narrow corridor between the bars, but they were empty. What meager light there was came from a gently swinging lantern between his cell and the next, glowing dimly on its hook. Every time the ship swayed, the light and shadows did too. Back and forth. Back and forth. Back and…

He sighed heavily. *What's going to happen to me this time? I've already got two marks. I'm young, and after my shoulder mends, I'll be strong enough. What if they send me to the mines?*

Thislen tried to imagine it. The ground swallowing him up. Being held in iron shackles around his ankles every day, trapped staring at a rock wall. The impact of a hammer against stone over and over again, rattling his hands and spraying him with dust. Two hours before sunset, he would be led out of the darkness and into the belly of a ship to wait for the next day and do it all over again.

Alright, let's hope for something better than that.

Like losing a hand. He could probably manage without both hands. They'd take his right, not knowing he preferred his left. They always took the right hand first.

Archaic. Barbaric. Not even the backwards, superstitious, close-minded Ravans leave the choice between disfigurement and slavery.

But if it worked, it worked—and the Ruling Council was always loathe to change what worked.

A soft sniffle came from the cell nearby. Thislen ignored it. Whoever it was, he wouldn't be able to help them. Just like he couldn't help Mila. *If they captured her, they probably took her right to Soren. She's somewhere far away from here.*

Neither Thislen nor his unseen companion had spoken since his arrival. He hadn't seen the other cell's occupant when they dragged him down the stairs. He had been stripped of his cloak and his pack. They had been thrown back down the way, no doubt locked up beneath the stairs. One guard searched him roughly for weapons, taking his knife from his boot—and missing Thislen's ring by a hair's breadth. He was unceremoniously shoved into the cell after the rope had been pulled off, leaving his skin burning and red, chafed to bleeding in a couple of places. The heavy barred door slammed shut behind him with a massive clang, as final as a nail in a coffin. No one had said a word to him the entire time, and neither had he.

When I get to the courts, I'll just plead as a thief. I'll beg them to spare me. I'll try to look younger and more frightened than I am. They'll treat me better that way; they'll take my hand for sure. Anything is better than a murder charge. Murderers in Astera were hung or beheaded. Or worse, fed to the Vaim. There were no second or third chances for them. Thislen wasn't sure if attempted murder came with the same finality of punishment or not, but he couldn't afford to be imprisoned while Mila was in danger, either.

They take the hand, I go to Olen, and he mends me right up, and then I just have to go to Soren Bestant's fancy mansion or ship and break Mila out.

He tucked his hands into his armpits despite his thoughts, stubbornly ignoring the chill that settled into the skin along his spine. His stomach was empty and almost hollow apart from strange flutters, like he had eaten butterflies. No matter what he told himself, he didn't want to lose his hand.

How long have I even been down here? It felt like hours, or perhaps a day. Without a window, it was impossible to tell. He had dozed when he could but woke to the same nothing as before. No one had come to feed him or his unknown companion. Thislen wondered if time had stretched and distorted, spanning out interminably and barely passing—or if he was simply not to be fed.

Wood creaked somewhere out of sight, near the staircase. The tread of heavy boots and the muffled sound of voices followed. The footsteps grew louder. Thislen sat up.

"Just down there, my Lords. The two you wanted to see," came an unfamiliar voice. *Guardsman,* Thislen guessed.

"Thank you, Captain. You are dismissed."

The second voice was familiar. Very familiar. Thislen frowned and stood, staring at the bars with his hands curled into fists, braced for the moment when Lord Soren Bestant stepped into view. He did a moment later, dressed in a sable doublet and shirt picked out with pale gold embroidery and swathed in a dark cloak. His expression was pensive, as if he had much on his mind. He didn't look at Thislen. Not yet.

Garridan stood just behind him, the swarthy young man dressed in similarly dark clothes of gray and silver.

All dressed up for their secret meetings, Thislen thought with a curl of his lip. He quickly smoothed his expression as Garridan leaned back against the bars of the cell across the way, considering him.

Thislen took the opportunity to study his enemy. When else would he have a chance to get this close? His father had told him about the Bestants, about the Artaiths. His father had told him long ago about *all* the families of the Ruling Council and what he knew of their secrets. His voice was clear as a bell in the back of Thislen's mind.

"Never, ever catch their eye. The best way for us to survive is to hide from them. We will never be strong enough to challenge them, Thislen, and I want you safe."

Thislen's brows drew together. *All I've ever done is make myself smaller to let these assholes trample over everyone. Now I'm caught anyway. I could lie, maybe. I could get out of this—but then it's right back to being alone and hiding in the shadows, waiting for the day I can run away.*

I'm tired of it.

Mila, Olen, Evelie, and even Ivan had shown him something else. Thislen didn't understand their bond, but he could *see* it, and ached for it like a man starved. If he were being honest with himself, he wanted the same.

And Soren Bestant was trying to take away any chance Thislen had of finding that peace—and he didn't even know it.

Soren tucked his hands behind his back, standing perfectly centered between the bars of the cell door, as if he were a banded picture in a frame. At last, his gaze lifted. His eyes scanned Thislen slowly from head to toe.

Thislen knew his dark hair was an unkempt mess, most likely with a piece of straw stuck in it. He knew his shirt front was dirty from lying in the street in the rain, that his knees had mud on them. He knew there was a small rust-red stain on his shoulder. His boots were spattered, his wrists were bleeding, and his eyes were hard as obsidian.

What do you see, Soren Bestant? What do you make of me?

"We meet again," Soren stated idly.

Thislen didn't bother to answer. His brow furrowed.

The blond seemed to take his stony expression as confusion. "You were at the Ominir Apothecary, yes? A patient?"

"Was I?" Thislen asked, voice flat.

A flash of fire gleamed in Soren's eye. His beautiful face twisted into a snarl for a moment before it vanished. It was so quick, Thislen wondered for a moment if he had imagined it. When Lord Soren spoke again, his voice was calm as a still pond. "Who are you, then? How do you play into all of this, hm?" A glove-clad finger trailed over the rusted bars with a soft *thrum, thrum, thrum.*

Thislen was silent. He was still.

Soren's brow furrowed in irritation yet again, and he sighed. "I hate to do this when you might be perfectly innocent, but you're not leaving me much choice. I'm used to getting answers when I ask questions."

I bet you are.

"If you refuse to answer me, there are *other* ways of getting what I want. I will have my answers, either way, it just may be more painful for you if I have to resort to...drastic measures." The nobleman gave a small, taut smile that didn't reach his eyes.

Torture. He was threatening torture. He thought Thislen was disposable, some poor person no one would miss. Thislen's lip curled up in disgust. His nails dug welts into his palms as he squeezed them into fists. How far would his captor go to get the answers he sought? As far as torture, yes—but what about death?

"This will be the last time that I ask nicely. Who are you?"

Thislen crossed the small cell to stand in front of the bars, meeting Soren's gaze. "Do you really want to know who I am? Because I know more about you and your family than you think I do." His words were crisp and fragile like autumn leaves.

Garridan's intent stare broke suddenly as the young noble stepped away, out of his line of sight. He returned a moment later with a lantern in his hand and held it aloft, looking between the pair with his brows raised. Thislen did not shy away from the bars or his quiet battle of wills with Soren Bestant.

I know. I know, even if you don't, he thought, heat in his heart and cheeks and burning in his eyes.

"So fierce a glower. If you truly know something others may not, why not inform me? Tell me why you were caught trying to leave our fair city —and through the same gate as the lovely Mila Ominir?"

Is he trying to figure out if I know her family's secret? He cursed himself silently for not asking Olen for the details when he could. *Stupid, trying to operate without all the facts!*

Thislen spat at Soren's boots.

"No words for us now, eh?" Soren smirked, smug and superior. "Could it be that you are why she's so reluctant to accept my proposal? Are you courting her, boy?"

"No, I'm not," Thislen said vehemently.

"Soren," Garridan said softly, an urgent whisper.

The blond noble held up a hand, cutting off whatever the stocky Garridan had been about to say. "You could have gone anywhere to be mended, but you chose the Ominir Apothecary. Tell me how you came to that decision, and I might see it in my heart to spare you. *If* you are not lying to me."

Thislen's gaze had left Soren's face and fixed on Garridan's, taking in the growing unease in the stocky brunet's face. "The courts spare prisoners, not the Ruling Council," Thislen said.

"Soren—" Garridan tried again.

"Not now!" Soren snapped, "I am the reason you will be charged with murder. I have the power to tell the court that it was all a dreadful mistake; we caught the wrong man. I can see you sent on your way. I can put you outside the East Gate with a satchel of coin, and you can be free by dawn."

Thislen froze, eyes widening for only a moment. *That much coin would put me over the edge. I could leave the island. I could* go—

But not without Mila. Not anymore.

He was surprised at himself, at the unspoken answer to the escape he had wanted his entire life. *No,* he had chosen. When did those small threads turn into tethers, binding him to Astera? When had he lost his steely resolve to something softer?

"Just tell me what I want to know," Soren wheedled.

"You cannot solve a problem like me with bribery. I'm not afraid of you," Thislen hissed. He realized he meant it, too. Here he was, face to face with the man who haunted him. He had done something to Percivan, he had done harm to Mila, and he had done something unforgivable to Thislen's own family years ago.

"Who are you to—" Soren's fingers curled around the bars.

Something snapped inside him. Thislen stepped forward abruptly, capturing Soren's wrists and holding him fast. "I am Thislen, son of Elena Bestant, *cousin*!"

"Soren!" Garridan shouted, wrestling the lord free from Thislen's grasp and pulling him away from the bars. Stunned silence followed, broken only by panting and the steady *drip drip drip* of the water.

It felt *good* to finally admit his tie to his mother out loud. He felt powerful. Here stood the person who had ruined the life Thislen could have had, looking as stunned as if he had been slapped, by someone they discounted as unimportant, as *nothing*.

How does it feel to be wrong? he exalted.

Soren Bestant's eyebrows were high beneath his curls, the color gone from his face as he stared at Thislen. Garridan could not meet his gaze.

"That's right, Lords. Your father ripped my mother from a loving marriage and *a son* before marrying her off, Soren. He married her off to Lord Artaith—as a second wife. You knew, you *knew* she had a child, both of you!"

Garridan looked at Thislen with a frown. "We were toddlers! And you could be lying."

"Am I? Who did your family tell? Who did Soren's family tell!?" Thislen banged his hands against the bars. "*Who else would know?*"

"Enough," Soren said abruptly. Slowly, the Lordling straightened. He adjusted his cloak and tunic and stepped back over to the bars. When he spoke again, his voice was soft. "I find that I believe you, cousin, but that still does not make you important. It doesn't make you matter." Each word dripped with venom, grit out between his teeth with hisses and spittle as his anger mounted. His fingers curled around the iron bars until the soft leather of his gloves creaked from the strain. "You will tell me what I wish to know, and your connection to Mila Ominir."

Thislen's lips curled up into a small smile. *You don't even know what you don't know, Soren.* He had spent his entire life hiding from the Ruling Court, avoiding connecting himself to them, steering clear of any potential encounters just to survive. It was too late to do so any longer. He had expected to be upset—that it would be painful. Instead, he felt as if a weight had been lifted from his shoulders. He began to laugh loudly, a deep laugh that started in his belly and boiled out of him with a maniacal edge. Thislen doubled over with it, laughing all the harder at Soren and Garridan's discomfort as they exchanged wary looks.

Abruptly, the thief's laughter stopped, and he lunged back to the door, hands wrapping around the bars just above Soren's.

The lord recoiled as their hands brushed, stumbling back a step.

"*What* did you do to Percivan Coppermund?" Thislen asked flatly. *After all,* he thought, *what is there to lose? At this point, I'm dead anyway.*

Garridan's eyes widened until they bugged out of his head, but he didn't move or speak.

"Ha!" Soren said, straightening his clothes and drawing himself up. The lantern overhead swung slowly back and forth, back and forth. "Ha. You appear from the gutters and come to us demanding answers to things we know nothing about?"

"Awful shame what happened to Percivan Coppermund," Thislen said, perfectly mirroring Avasten's sly and pointed tone from only a night before.

Garridan stiffened, eyes growing wider as Thislen's gaze slid sideways, fixing on him.

"You know what happened to him, Avasten."

Garridan choked at the echoed words of their private conversation from the *Bestant Belle*. The blood ran out of the swarthy man's face. "How did you—" he stammered.

"Enough!" Soren shouted, voice ringing off the metal bars of the cells only to be swallowed in the steady sound of water. "I owe you no answers. You will face the courts tomorrow, cousin. I will see you suffer. Do you hear me? I will end this problem now."

Thislen pressed his face up against the bars, grinning madly. "Good luck, Soren," he said in a sing-song tone. There was no point in hiding or pulling his punches any longer, nor in burying his hatred and pain under layer after layer of anonymity and caution. They knew where he was and what he looked like. They knew his name. They had him in a cell!

Tomorrow he would be charged for crimes he didn't commit, all because he knew too much. This might be his last night in the world, and all he felt was dizzy and *angry*. Fury beat through his veins like a fire.

"Do you know what Percivan said just before he died? Do you know what he told me about you?"

"You—you were there! You were the one in the rowboat?" Garridan asked.

"Shut up, Garridan. Everyone knows there was a set of boot prints."

"Do you know why he missed his boat, Soren?" Thislen sang.

Soren's hand shot through the bars for Thislen's throat. Thislen jerked out of reach. His maniacal mirth died on his lips, leaving him staring down the lords with a steady, burning gaze. He was triumphant, even imprisoned, even facing his end. He was *free* from his secrets.

Are you? his steady gaze asked.

Garridan's shoulders were hunched as he and Soren stepped away from the bars. Where the blond looked as if he were fighting for his composure, smoothing his hair and fixing his doublet, the shorter nobleman did not bother to hide his discomfort. Little Lord Artaith was frightened.

Good. Be afraid, be very afraid, for if I ever get out of here alive, I'm going to destroy you all.

MILA SAT on the narrow bunk in the gloomy shadows of the *The Brig,* her knees drawn up against her chest and her arms wrapped tight around them. She was holding her breath. Her cheeks still stung from the tears she had wiped away when she heard Lord Soren Bestant's voice nearby.

Every word was clear as crystal. She listened as Soren asked Thislen why he had come to her family's shop. *Evelie brought him to us.* She heard him ask if Thislen were courting her. *Of course not!* She thought, agreeing with Thislen silently.

How possessive is *Soren?* she wondered, heart pounding against her ribs. How dangerous had Thislen's offer of help truly been? She hadn't even realized it was him in the cell beside her until he spoke. He was trapped with her, caught up in something far more serious than she had intended. *All he wanted to do was help me.*

"I am Thislen, son of Elena Bestant, *cousin*!" Thislen roared suddenly beside her.

Her ears were ringing. She sucked in a deep breath, pressing her hands over her heart as if it would muffle the overwhelming battering of it beneath her skin. It would explain his knowledge of them, his fierce desire to avoid them, his heart-breaking wariness. Thislen was forced to be a lonely observer in a city that didn't want to see him. *He's so different from them.* If only he weren't, if only the Ruling Council were more like the injured thief who had put himself in so much danger, on accident, just to help someone who helped him.

"Do you know why he missed his boat, Soren?" Thislen sang madly, and Mila stopped breathing again.

"I'm looking for someone named Soren," Thislen had said.

For Percivan Coppermund? The noble who died by the Vaim? Thislen had more ties to Soren Bestant than she knew—and she was only one of them.

What a fool I was, believing him, trusting *him!* she thought with a rush of heat through her cheeks. A moment later, it faded. ...*he said that I needed to trust that he knew the dangers. Maybe he really does, and this* must *be why.*

Footsteps tore her from her thoughts. Her hair hung loosely around her like a curtain, and she hastily pushed it away from her face. Mila lifted her chin and forced her shoulders down, hoping her lower lip didn't wobble as she put on the bravest face she could manage. She may have been locked in a cell against her will, but she would not be cowed by it.

That's just what he wants.

Lord Soren appeared a moment later with Garridan on his heels, though Garridan was looking over his shoulder, fixated warily on Thislen just out of sight. Soren's features were artfully arranged, painted in the glow of a lantern that Garridan held aloft. He looked like an angelic being draped in the colors of sympathy and mourning, descending into this nightmare place to rescue her.

It made her blood run cold in her veins. *Don't forget, he did this,* she reminded herself, remaining where she was despite the deep urge to go to the bars and plead for her freedom. His farce had almost worked.

"Oh, Mila. Are you well?" he asked delicately, looking her over from head to toe. "They didn't hurt you, did they?"

"Well? Am I *well?*" she echoed, voice lifting several octaves at the last word.

"Mila!" Thislen cried out of sight, followed by a thud against the wall and the sound of metal smacking against flesh. His hand appeared for just a moment, twisting into view. It vanished just as quickly as Garridan leapt forward, hand outstretched.

Mila was on her feet in a heartbeat, feeling nauseated. *He didn't realize it was me, either. What if he thought I got away?* His heart must have been breaking to find out she had been captured—just as he warned her might happen.

Soren looked coolly to one side as Garridan scuffled next door with Thislen, then back to her and her cell. He studied the tiny space with a measure of regret so exaggerated it bordered on comical. His brow had furrowed, and he all but pouted. "I had worried they would treat you unkindly. It seems I was right to do so. Mila, I'm afraid you may have been led astray by that patient of yours. He's actually a dangerous criminal. A murderer. A kidnapper."

"I am not!" Thislen snarled from somewhere next door.

"Silence!" Soren snapped, features twisting into a sneer.

There was a thud and a grunt. Thislen coughed and gasped, and Mila heard something slide down the other side of the wall.

They hit him! She pressed a hand to the wood.

When she turned her wide-eyed gaze back on Soren, he had calmed himself. His face was angelic once more. "I truly hope this was all a misunderstanding, you see. I would hate for you to have to face the courts for something that could easily be resolved between you and I, right now."

He'd let me out. All I have to do is say that it was Thislen's fault. It was a way out of all of this. Blame the thief she barely knew, take Soren's hand, and walk away.

Mila very nearly fell for it. *What happens after that?* She'd have to marry him, of course, and sacrifice her freedom.

No, wait—she realized, looking up at the bars between her and Soren, *he already* took *that!*

Heat rose in her chest, and blood rushed in her ears. Her hands curled into fists and began to tremble—but not from fear. "Astray?" She hissed quietly. "A misunderstanding? They were waiting for me *by name,* Lord Bestant. Why is that?"

Soren's solemn and regretful expression vanished instantly as his eyebrows shot up toward his cherubic blond curls. His mouth worked, but he didn't say anything.

He truly doesn't know me at all! He expected me to fall right into his arms and beg him for mercy. Not today. Not any *day.* A hot coal sat in her belly, radiating warmth down to her fingertips. She slipped off the wooden bunk and stepped toward the bars, feeling as though that heat was dissipating into the air itself, making it waver and dance around her.

This time, her voice didn't shake. "You simply cannot *fathom* that I don't want to marry you, is that it?" she asked, slow and calm and seething like a pot about to boil. "You cannot imagine a world where your pretty face and your father's coin can't buy anything you'd like! I have some news for you, *Soren,*" she spat his name as she stepped even closer. "It's not the coin or title I hate; it's *you.* I was trying to get away *from you!*"

The young lord stilled, his features going entirely flat. The sudden disinterested chill in his posture sapped the heat from her ire. The shimmering waves of it around her vanished. His eyes were intent upon her and yet so cold and distant she felt he didn't see her at all. His lips pursed.

What is...

"Interesting," he said, the word clipped and brief. "Well, I had hoped that you might choose me, Mila. I've found that there needs to be a certain amount of choice at the beginning of a relationship for it to work. Your ragged little friend reminded me of that. We can discuss this again. After your trial, yes? We'll see then if your answer is the same."

With that, he reached through the bars, glove coming toward her face. Mila stepped back, hands drawn up close to her chest. Soren smirked, then walked away. The light from Garridan's lantern followed, leaving her in the dim light from above once again.

Mila no longer felt like crying, despite the sting in her eyes. She wanted to *hit* something, to fight or scream or *anything*. Anything.

She didn't. She stood there trembling with barely suppressed fury. The heavy tread of the boots faded away. As silence settled around her, the heat in her chest began to cool as quickly as it had come. Mila sank numbly onto the edge of her cell's bunk, then slumped slowly to lay on her side.

What did I just do? What is he going to do to me?

"Mila?" Thislen asked softly.

She couldn't bring herself to answer.

"Mila, are you alright? Did they hurt you?"

The steady drip of water was the only sound this far belowdecks. Thislen didn't ask again after that. She heard him slide down the wall between their cells, a hand's breadth away that might as well have been miles. In silence, the two waited for a morning they could not see coming and the summons that would follow the sun.

THE JUSTICA WAS a beautiful domed building with glittering panes of bubbled glass that glinted in the morning light. It stood head and shoulders above the houses around it, half from the Guild Quarter and half sprawling estate houses of the Grand Quarter. They were separated by the last curve of the manicured canal. Mila had only ever seen it from the Guild Quarter's streets before. There, she had often stood and admired its colossal stone facade. Nearly every inch was carved with images of people holding up successive tiers of the city's residents until they reached the throne at the top of the peaked roof. There, a great statue of King Aldan Asteran, founder of the kingdom, sat above his people. One hand bore a scepter, but she had always liked how his other hand was stretched toward the open square below the building, as if he wished to pull all of his subjects up with him.

The back of the structure was quite a different sight. Approaching in a small rowboat that jounced in the steely waves of the sea with her hands cuffed and fastened to an iron loop set in the floorboards, she had never felt so small. The carvings along the back were similar—tier after tier of people had been carved into the stone of the Justica. These people, however, were not looking up toward their king but down. Every face was twisted into a grimace in the mid-morning light, the shadows cutting them artfully into resentful, hateful masks. There was another statue of King Aldan Asteran here, his calm stone gaze directed out and away, over the ocean.

He won't help us. This is the path for those the kingdom no longer sees or loves, she thought softly, *even if they've done nothing wrong.* Her heart ached in her chest. Someone inside that building had to look down. Someone had to believe her. *I just want to go home!* Never before had she longed for her father's warm embrace so much.

It was an ages-long tradition to hold trials in the Justica, one that had never changed even in spite of the Vaim. In fact, the only change that had come to Astera's justice system had been in the wake of the formation of the Ruling Council. The laws had been eased to reassure the populace that the new oligarchy was nothing like the Crown. The Vaim had been factored into the island's gaol system, and *The Brig* had been built. Mila even remembered the little poem Olen had taught her about it when she was small.

Ruling Council, trusted, just, and fair—all innocent 'til trial bear. It was awkward, she decided now. A clunky tool to help children feel better after learning some people were sacrificed to the ghosts. Everyone had a chance.

I have a chance.

Her shoulder rubbed against Thislen's as they huddled in the belly of the dingy while two guardsmen rowed and a third sat just behind them with a hand on his sword hilt. They were being steered toward stone quays in shadowed tunnels at the back of the building. The guards hadn't said a word the entire time, sitting in stony silence. Thislen tried to speak to her when they put him in the boat and had his ear cuffed by a guard for his trouble. They hadn't spoken since.

Even with the thief by her side, she couldn't help but feel dreadfully alone. Gulls cried mournfully overhead. She watched them circle and felt as if she were adrift in the waters they rowed through, about to drown. Her wrists chafed, and an ache was settling in her shoulders. Her breaths came short and quick. She could feel herself trembling, unable to stop it. *Is it the cool breeze off the water?* She clasped her hands together, trying to still their quaking.

Beside her, Thislen looked up at the building with a calm she wished she felt. The breeze pushed his dark hair back from his face, his high cheekbones and strong brows no longer hidden behind the messy mop. His dark eyes were intent on the statue perched atop the Justica. Despite his bonds, his shoulders were relaxed, his brow smooth. She wanted to scream at him, to shake him.

How can anyone face uncertainty this way?

The morning light, thin as it was, vanished abruptly as they drifted under the stone archway and into the darkness beneath the building. The water slapped against the rough stone walls, chiseled out of the rock of the shore. Below the waterline, it was worn smooth and gleamed with dried salt. The stone ceiling of the tunnel arched over their head, plain heavy white stones that looked gray in the shadows. The rowboat bobbed to its berth at the stone jetty in the water, the thud of its impact echoing around them.

The guardsmen changed their cuffs with a rattle of chains, one and then the other. They were rough, caring little for their charges as they hauled them out onto the stone and then shoved them up a set of stairs so worn that the middles had been worn away into smooth dips.

How many hundreds of criminals walked up these steps? How many weren't criminals at all? Was she one of a hundred, a thousand? Did anyone know? Did anyone...care?

They were led into a broad room that reminded Mila of nothing so much as the great cattle faire held outside Astera's gates each summer. Farmers drove their herds into great railed pens that lined the road as far as the eye could see, and the neighbors would pool together to buy a calf or a heifer and divide the meat.

The space they were led to was neither a corridor nor a room, but somewhere in between. The gallery had low stone walls built along the sides to form pens large and small and in-between, all fitted with metal gates. Members of the City Guard in their gray tabards stood on either side of the gates and at the joints of the pen walls.

Some people had already been ferried across the water from *The Brig*. They sat or stood listlessly in the open cells, cuffs heavy around their wrists. Some were fastened to cuffs that hung on hooks in the walls or floor, but they were few and far between. There were only two exits; the great double doors set into the far end, or the dock where they had arrived.

Mila's arm was taken, and she was pulled away from Thislen. Her heart leapt into her throat, worried they would be out of each other's sight. *I don't want to be alone in this!* She struggled against the man holding her arm.

He shook her roughly. "Hey, knock that off, or I'll slap you. Stupid girl."

She stopped, feeling the prickle of a flush creep up her cheeks. She didn't want to be humiliated—not here.

Thislen and Mila were pushed into two of the smallest stone pens nearest the dock entrance. She stumbled over a pair of cuffs set in the floor before finding her feet. None of the guards followed her in. She moved quickly toward the low stone wall that separated her from the thief.

"Thisle—"

"Shut up, girl!" Her guard barked. "If you can't keep silent, we'll gag you."

So I can't even talk to him? Her heart shrank in her chest. Every ounce of her bravado from the day before was gone. Thislen met her gaze. The corners of his lips quirked up just a hair, and he gave her a solemn nod. The silent reassurance was enough to bolster her flagging courage —for now.

I wonder how I look to him. How I look to them, she wondered. She tore her gaze away to scan the guardsmen every few feet. Her clean clothes in dun colors from the day before were now rumpled and smudged with mud and dark brown wood stains in places. Hay clung to her skirt and tickled her scalp, though she had tied her hair into a tail at the nape of her neck before her they bound her hands.

Well, this won't do. Evelie'd faint if she knew I went before a judge in this state.

Despite the heavy metal cuffs around her wrists, Mila set to straightening herself out. She plucked the straw from her clothes and let it drop to the floor. She adjusted her skirts. She adjusted her shawl. She carefully felt over her hair until she thought it was clean enough.

I wonder if I have circles under my eyes. She had hardly slept at all. Her face would be pale, making the circles all the darker. *Well, there's nothing I can do about that,* she thought with a heavy sigh.

Mila sat on the stone floor and waited, fidgeting with the hem of her traveling skirt. Other people arrived, led by guardsmen past her pen and into their own holding cells. Their eyes and faces alternated between blank, angry, and scared. She understood every one of them.

Part of her was furious, a hot coal she could almost touch rolling around inside her chest. It radiated with danger, like an open flame beside a silo of wheat. Her unease was small, like a lost child. All it wanted was for her father to fix things. and a cup of Evelie's tea. The emotion she pulled around her shoulders like a cloak, however, was Thislen's blank calm. It was a sense of apathetic detachment, as if nothing around her were real. It was numb, inside and out, and kept her safe.

Don't draw attention, don't make it worse.

Mila wondered idly which of the courts would try her case. The low courts had panels of three judges who meted out the fates of first-time thieves, cheats, and drunkards who had gotten into minor scuffles. The high courts were overseen by five seated judges who decided the fates of more severe crimes. That, she decided, was the most likely. She hadn't committed any crimes, but Soren wanted to intimidate her. The only court higher than that was the Ruling Court, reserved only for crimes committed by and against the nobility.

He wants me cowed and obedient, but everything he does to push me there pushes me further away. What little respect she once held for Soren was gone.

Ugh, isn't it time yet? Waiting in this pen in the Justica was worse even than waiting in her dim, swaying cell upon *The Brig*. At least there, she knew nothing was going to happen. It was its own agony, having to wait for an unfair trial.

Even with guardsmen and prisoners all about, the room did not get particularly crowded. Other gray-clad men and women came to pull those facing charges through the far set of double doors to meet their fates. There were never more than five people to a pen at any given time, and twice she saw all five taken at once. *They must sort us somehow. What do the pens mean?*

She set herself to trying to solve the puzzle by guessing the crimes of others in the pens, but without asking someone, she had no idea if she were correct. Somewhere above, the great bells of the Justica chimed the noontide hour. They rang out over the city and reverberated through the stone in a muffled call.

The bell faded, and the gallery was suddenly full of activity. More guards poured in through the Justica doors to escort prisoners to their trials. Double as many guards went out to the docks to fetch rowboats and set to ferrying prisoners back and forth. A pair of men with braids on their uniforms stopped beside her small cell and pushed open the metal gate with a squeal of hinges.

Mila's mouth went dry all at once, and she forgot for a moment how to breathe. The bottom of her stomach vanished and a great chasm churned in her gut. Every limb felt made of lead as she pulled herself to her feet. *I'm not ready.*

One of the guardsmen swept his arm wide in a silent 'after you,' giving her a polite and disinterested smile.

Mila's head swam. She looked at Thislen with wide eyes. Her hands were trembling again; *all* of her was trembling, so badly that the chains between her cuffs rattled.

Thislen did not look away. He gave her another slow, encouraging nod. "Go," he mouthed.

She took a step. Another followed. Her knees felt like jelly, and her shivers shook deep in her chest. They flanked her on either side and led her down the penned gallery. The guards made no move to grab her or push her along, a small act of kindness that helped. Barely.

Through the great double doors they went, into a long plain corridor. More doors were set into the walls at even intervals. Guardsmen led cuffed prisoners into and out of those doors, to the courtrooms beyond. She caught only glimpses of large rooms with wooden podiums and a great many benches.

Mila was walked down the hallway, past plain door after plain door, all the way to the end. Set into the same wall as all the rest, there was a pair of carved and polished double doors. They were the only such pair in the hallway.

No.

"Where—" she began, voice wavering as she turned to the guardsmen. Her escort did not give her a chance to finish her question. One pushed the doors open, and they both grabbed her arms and shoved her unceremoniously into the room beyond. She glimpsed a tremendous vaulted ceiling painted with frescos of Asteran ancestors looking down on her as she stumbled. She barely caught herself before she could fall onto the stone floor.

The murmur of voices in the cavernous room halted abruptly, their echo fading soon after. The silence was broken only by a rustle of fabric here and there and the soft hiss of a whisper or two. She stood still as a statue, heart hammering in her chest. *I can't move. I can't. I can't do this!*

"Mila! Let go of me! *Mila*!"

Her head jerked up at the heart-wrenching cry, eyes wide and stinging with tears in an instant. She would recognize her father's voice anywhere. The room was massive, a third of it separated from the rest with a carved stone railing lined with armed guards. The gallery behind the banister held many benches and was crowded with scribes behind little writing desks and clusters of people sitting or standing with baldly curious stares.

And Olen. Olen was pressed right up against the stone railing, behind the crossed pikes of two guardsmen. His hands were clasped so tightly around the barrier that his fingers were white. He wore blacks and grays instead of his usual bright and festive colors, and his easy smile was nowhere to be seen. The lines of his face looked so much deeper! His wild red hair stuck up in the way it always did when he ran his hands through it too often with worry. Olen's grief was palpable, as if he already mourned her loss one way or another. It pulled a shadow over the entire room.

Hot tears ran down Mila's cheeks. Her hands were numb. Somehow, her father's pain made everything absolutely unbearable. She couldn't move. Her knees buckled with the sudden urge to sit right where she was and cry.

Don't you dare. Father couldn't take that.

She steeled herself, swallowing her tears and wiping her eyes as she turned to the rest of the room and her audience.

There was no doubt this was the highest court on the island: The Ruling Court. Two rows of seats formed the bowed sides of the judge's dais. Twelve men were seated behind their podium desks, swathed in white robes that symbolized the purity of truth. They wore rounded hats with tassels on the back upon their heads. At the center of the topmost dais were another three seats, the middle raised above the other two. Three more men sat there—one she recognized. In that highest, center-most seat was a familiar pale face beneath the only golden hat.

"Step forward," Lord Judge Avasten Barnweir commanded her.

The gloom in the air settled in further, weighing on her shoulders.

In the dead center of the room was a set of steps that led up to an exposed platform of plain stone. Mila walked toward it, head held high and shoulders back. *If I could spit in every one of your eyes, I would,* she thought as she met the closed, stern eyes of the judges who peered down on her. She could feel the eyes of the curious crowd boring into her back. Her heart fluttered in her throat.

The platform seemed to grow further and further away with every echoing footstep. Her passage was the only sound in the room but for the soft whisper of parchment. She willed herself not to look back, not to break down, for Ancestor's sake, not to run! Then, she was there.

Mila lifted her gaze from the stairs to the dais, then higher, to the wall behind the benches. The sunlight played through the stained glass in brilliant rainbow ribbons that brought no light inside. Candles, torches, and lanterns had to push back the shadows where nature failed. Half hidden in the shadows cast by the streaming sunlight was a statue of King Aldan Asterian. He had strong cheekbones, she realized, and heavily carved brows. He, too, was dressed in the garb of judgment. A crown sat around his own tasseled hat made of stone. His over-large gaze was fixated on the platform, and the young apothecary couldn't help but feel her knees weaken.

Is he judging me, too? Would he *believe me?*

There was only one way to find out, to get answers. Mila mounted the steps.

"She who stands before us answers to the name Mila Ominir." Avasten drawled as he leafed through a sheaf of papers.

The two judges on either side of Avasten, clad in silver hats, looked at him with some quiet surprise, but no one said anything.

"Miss Ominir, do you know why you stand before us this day?" He appeared bored by the proceedings, though every other judge's gaze was intent and focused.

"No," she said, but her voice was barely a whisper. It didn't echo off the stone like the Lord Judge's did. She cleared her throat softly, straightening her sagging shoulders. "No," she said louder, "I do not."

"Allow us to inform you. Read the charges." Avasten commanded. He still hadn't bothered to look at her.

It made her skin crawl to be so disregarded. She felt like a bug beneath the shadow of his boot.

One of the twelve lower seats of the Ruling Court picked up a piece of paper and stood behind his podium. Mila didn't know who he was.

"Mila Ominir, here to face the Ruling Court for charges of seduction and spell craft toward a member of the Ruling Council, abuse of healing powers, blackmail, and lying in an attempt to escape prosecution." The man read as if he were merely reciting his grocery list.

Her heart skipped a beat. The chains around her wrists rattled as she pulled her arms close to her chest. "Seduction? Spell craft?" she echoed, her alarm ringing through the air.

"Do you deny the charges, then?" another judge asked.

"Yes, I do," she said firmly. She grasped at the coal in her chest, pulling its heat to steel her spine. "First of all, everyone knows magic bled from the land long ago. No one can do spell craft anymore; no one can make new magic!"

"That is true," one of the judges admitted.

"Hedge witches can still perform the smallest magics, can they not?" another said.

"No, no, that's all crockery."

"Gentlemen, the spell in question was a simple spell to cause headaches. Any clever hedge witch or apothecary could do such," Avasten said.

"Cause headaches? To who?" Mila demanded.

"Lady Bestant has been suffering headaches for three years, and *remarkably*, the only apothecary in town capable of healing them is Master Olen Ominir—and you, Miss Mila."

Murmurs rose in the gallery behind her.

"That isn't true!" Olen shouted.

"Silence in the gallery! If that man can't hold his tongue, have him removed," a judge shouted.

"As to seduction," Mila interrupted loudly, silencing the entire room with a single pause. "Lord Soren Bestant asked me to marry him, and I *did not* want to do so. I wanted to *escape* his attentions. I was trying to leave the city when I was detained!" She was trembling again, ever so faintly, but this time it was not from nerves. It frightened her to find how deep that well of molten emotion ran inside her, but she would not let them lie about her this way.

I will not *be bullied by you. I am not afraid!* she thought vehemently. A lump formed in her throat and threatened to choke her. She imagined it burning away until she regained her composure. *So, I'm afraid. It won't stop me. Not anymore.*

"Even now, she tries to lie to us. No doubt she does so out of self-preservation," Avasten said imperiously from his high seat.

Mila turned her gaze upon him. "Don't lie," she said firmly.

He snorted, looking up from his papers at last and studying her like one might observe an insect they had found stuck to the bottom of their shoe. "Look at this display. She tries to convince you I am lying without an ounce of regret or remorse." He pushed himself to his feet. "Look at her, trying to convince us all that Lord Soren Bestant, the most powerful Lord in Astera, would propose to the plain bedraggled daughter of a shopkeep." He scoffed. "*Look* at her, trying to sway us with trembling hands and a loud voice. She tries to play the part of the lamb instead of the lion, but the playacting leaves something to be desired, does it not?"

There was scattered laughter from the judges. Mila's cheeks grew hot. She blinked away the sudden sting of tears, refusing to let them fall. *I will not give them the pleasure of seeing me cry anymore.*

"I don't want anything to do with Lord Bestant, and I will prove it. Banish me, since you judge me to be after him! Send me far away from him, to a place where I can never enter his presence again! Exile me from the city of Astera, and I will gladly take my sentence!" She stamped her foot upon the stone, and the sound echoed alongside her voice in the distant recesses of the painted ceiling. No one spoke while the reverberations of her words faded. The judges exchanged surprised glances.

Now they believe me. Who would ask to be banished but someone telling the truth?

Avasten lowered himself into his seat once more. His chair creaked softly as he sat, fingers curling around the edges of his podium as he looked down upon her. Once more, she was reminded strongly of the callous look of a spider in its web, waiting to consume her. The silence stretched on.

"You *dare* presume to order us about?" he asked softly, voice cold as ice and whispering around her in faint echoes.

"I should say not," the judge sitting on Avasten's left scoffed.

One of the twelve lower judges slammed his fist against the wood before him with a cacophonous echo. "She displays naught but rudeness and disdain for this court!"

Another rose to his feet. "I say we make an example of her for such impudence!"

"Flog her!"

"Lock her away for a year!"

"Cut out her tongue so she may never seduce again!"

"Sell her to a brothel; they'll teach her what true seduction is!"

Mila's ears began to ring, nearly drowning out the judges as they clamored to devise dreadful punishments to fit her fabricated crimes. Each idea that dropped from their lips was worse than the one before. All of them were based on the lies they had been fed. None of them looked at her; none of them *saw* her.

Her chest was so tight she could hardly breathe. Shallow pants of air were all she could manage. It took every ounce of her strength to remain on her feet as she stared up at Avasten. The dawning horror of her fate to come rose like bile in her throat.

Lord Judge Avasten Barnweir stared steadily back over his podium, a corner of his lip quirked ever so slightly upwards. She had been caught in his web and was at his mercy, and they both knew it. He raised his hand, and the roar of voices died at once.

"I agree with your proposal to send a firm message, Judge Tethwen. However, I also propose mercy. Her…piteous display has moved me," Avasten said, splaying the fingers of one hand over his heart.

Liar! She thought heatedly. Her fate had been sealed before she ever set foot in the court.

"Thus do I suggest to you, good sirs, a quick death for the poor seductress—or a chance to prove herself innocent. I believe a night upon the island will suit her crimes. Let the Vaim decide her fate. If she survives, this court shall swear to let her live peacefully wherever she so desires."

She stood frozen, her face a mask. She did not dare glare or cry or show a reaction to the judges. She heard Olen cry out behind her, accompanied by the clangor of weapons. Mila fought the urge to turn and look.

He can't see me like this. Not like this. It would break his heart.

"Get *back*, damn you! Come on, get out of here!" A guardsman shouted.

"Mila! My daughter, no! Wait, please!" Olen begged, his heart breaking in the words.

Mila closed her eyes, but the shouting faded with the echoing thud of the doors to the Ruling Court as they closed.

No one survives the Vaim. Their kind and merciful offer is a lie. What sort of corruption lies at the heart of my home that this can happen to me? she wondered, for the first time questioning the glittering jewel she had lived in and loved her entire life. Her hands curled into fists. *This is ridiculous. They can't kill me just for trying to avoid marriage.*

"Are there any who protest her sentence or the charges against her?" Avasten asked, dropping his gaze back to the papers on his desk.

None of the judges said a word, their attention fixated patiently upon their leader.

"Right then. Guilty or innocent?"

The judges lifted wooden paddles from their desks. One side was painted white, the color of innocence, purity, truth—the same as the robes the judges wore.

But all that faced Mila were the black sides of the paddles. Shame. Denial. Rejection. *Guilt.*

The steel within her shattered. Her knees went weak and wobbly, and she sank to the stone, staring at Avasten with wide eyes. *No, this can't be happening.*

"The court has ruled. You are hereby sentenced to one night upon the shores of Astera. Take her away." He said, expression as distant and cold and uninterested as it had ever been.

"But why!?" she shouted, voice cracking as she surged back to her feet, "Why is he so angry with me?"

At that, Avasten let out a soft laugh. He offered no answer as the guardsmen approached her, taking her arms and pulling her away. She stumbled between them, pushed this way and that, kept off-balance by their jostling. As long as it took her to reach the podium before, it took no time for them to drag her away. The doors to the Ruling Court slammed closed behind her like the lid of a coffin. Her escort propelled her down the stone corridor and back into the penned gallery.

"Mila!" Thislen shouted as he caught sight of her stunned, pale features. He lunged toward the gate to his enclosure.

"Silence, boy!" A guardsman snapped, catching him with an arm around the neck and pulling him into a headlock. "You're next, anyway."

Mila was shoved carelessly back into her pen, falling roughly onto the stones. Wide eyes fixated on Thislen as she watched him struggle and fight. It took three guards to drag him away.

THISLEN BEGAN to pace the moment Mila had been led out of his sight. Three steps one way, then three steps back. It was all the small open cell allowed. She had been pale as a sheet when she left the room, and shaking so much he had seen the tremors wrack her body. She needed him calm and strong while she was there—but now she wasn't.

Whatever is going to happen to her, to me, it's not going to be good. He didn't dare to hope for anything but the worst. The only problem was he didn't know what the worst *was*. He had never seen these small pens used at the courts before. The last time he had been here, he was held in one of the larger ones with four other men. *This does not bode well for us.*

Thislen froze for a moment. *Can I face what is to come?*

Time crept by. The guards near the gate of his holding cell watched him with their hands hovering over the clubs on their belts as if his pacing would lead him to do something stupid—like attempt an escape. The thought *was* tempting, and Thislen didn't doubt that other people had tried to do just that.

He also doubted any of them had succeeded. Not with so many guardsmen in one room and only two doors.

Every time the doors opened, his head shot up. Usually, it was just guardsmen returning without those who had been charged and led off to different rooms for punishment and release. He remembered those rooms, plain and austere. They'd cut the marks deep into his skin to ensure they would scar, then uncuffed him and let him wander off into the city, still bleeding. He pressed a hand over the 'x' cut into his chest. *He* hadn't mattered—only the claims of the merchants at their stalls. Thislen had been young then, maybe twelve.

They could sentence her to something mild and lead her off to one of those rooms, and she may not come back at all. He almost hoped that was the case. The only people who were ever brought back to this room were those whose sentences involved imprisonment or execution.

The doors at the far end of the gallery opened, and two guards came through, half-carrying Mila between them.

"Mila!" He shouted, rushing to the door of his pen to reach out to her.

The chain between his cuffs was caught by a guardsman who yanked his arms down roughly, sending a lance of pain down his arm from his injured shoulder. The man's arm swung around his neck, trapping him against the man's side. "Silence, boy! You're next, anyway."

No, I have to talk to her! All pretense of calm was gone. She looked terrified. What had they said? What had they *done*?

The gate of his pen was kicked open with a *clang,* and Thislen struggled to pull his head free of the guard that held him fast while two more flanked him. He saw Mila fall hard onto the stones of her pen and began to struggle against the hands that grabbed at him, kicking and elbowing wildly.

He was no match for his captors. They eventually wrestled him until his arms were pinned against his sides so hard it hurt. The three of them dragged him bodily from the gallery, fighting him with every step as he twisted in their grasp. "Mila!" He called again.

Mila stared at him with eyes wide as saucers, utterly stunned. She climbed slowly to her feet to keep him in sight until the doors closed and cut them off from one another yet again.

"Mila!" he roared. "What did you bastards do!?"

"Will you *shut up?*"

Thislen's head snapped to one side, followed by the rising sting of pain in his cheek. He realized belatedly a guard had slapped him. With their captive momentarily stunned, the guardsmen hauled him down the corridor at a trot. They expected him to fight. He was tempted to do so.

The smaller doors, he knew, led to the Lower Courts. The doors halfway up the long corridor led to the High Courts. That was where he expected to be dragged, what with the false charge of attempted murder heavy on his back. When the guards didn't stop, he clenched his fists in the cuffs and began to struggle once more, forcing them to slow their pace with muffled curses. A pit settled in the bottom of Thislen's stomach as they passed door after door.

"Wait," he said as they approached the last portal, a pair of heavy doubled doors, carved and polished, that he had never passed through before. "No! Wait!"

The doors were opened, and he was shoved through. He fell to the floor, and his chin hit the flagstones. It stung. There was a rising murmur of interest as he climbed to his feet. His gaze snapped toward the crowd that waited with bated breath.

They gasped, many leaning back as if they expected Thislen to lunge for them.

Somewhere outside, beyond the door, Thislen could only just hear a familiar voice shouting in the Justica's main corridor.

"Please, just let me see my daughter! Please, take me to her! Let me back in! Mila!" Olen shouted.

The crushing weight of guilt settled around Thislen like a shroud. He knew the City Guard would escort Olen out of the building. Mila would not be granted a farewell audience with her father.

There was nothing more you could have done, he tried to reassure himself.

Percivan's face flashed into his mind's eye, lips parted in shock. His eyes were wide as the life drained from them, as blood fountained from his neck.

Vern the sailor looked up at him accusingly, his outstretched hand dragged beneath the water, his last agonized question hanging in the air. *"Why?"*

There was nothing more you could have done!

He stood frozen, shoulders hunched up toward his ears and gaze dropping to the stones between his boots. The weight of his failures was heavier than chains. They threatened to drag him to the ground.

I reached out for the first time in ages—and ruined three lives.

Two more guardsmen caught him by surprise, stepping away from their posts along the viewing gallery's rail and catching him by the elbows. They hauled him toward the raised stone platform under the curious eyes of fifteen judges.

He had never been in the Ruling Court before. He didn't know anyone who had. Now he was faced directly with the solid stone gaze of King Aldan Asteran. Thislen's heart beat steadily in his chest, but too hard. Each pulse hammered like a blacksmith upon an anvil.

You can't be disappointed in me. You never expected this to happen.

Thislen tore his gaze from the stone visage of the kingdom's founder, meeting the intent and dead-eyed stare of Avasten Barnweir. He recognized the man at once, even if the Lord Judge would not recognize *him.* His stomach twisted into a knot.

All of them, the entire Ruling Council, a corrupt knot of snakes twining around one another to get whatever they want.

The guards held him in place while a length of chain was fastened to his cuffs from either side of the platform, effectively keeping him in place. Then, they vanished from his side and left him standing alone before the court.

Time to play their games. I have chips to bargain with. Do they? Thislen felt himself growing cold and calm. He allowed himself a quiet smirk.

"Your name, I have been told, is Thislen. It is not a name that has been in the court records before. Do you wish to introduce yourself properly?" Avasten asked calmly, lifting a piece of parchment.

The weight on Thislen's shoulders was heavy. He had already lost everything there was to lose. What more could they take from him? Mila was already sentenced—his behavior would not spare her whatever fate they had doled out.

Thislen's lips curled up all the further. "I do have a last name I can tie to myself. Do you really want me to tell them?"

Nothing to lose.

"Why are we listening to all of this, Avasten? First the girl, now this boy," one judge called from his seat.

There was a murmur among the gathered judges, dark and curious.

How much did Soren tell his crony? Thislen wondered. Did Avasten know his mother's name?

Lord Judge Barnweir pulled out a gold coin from his pocket, turning it in his fingers a few times. He held it slowly up to the light. Warm sun from the window made it sparkle while the redhead studied it minutely. His gaze slid sideways to Thislen, then back to his bribe. After a long and pointed moment, he pocketed it.

"The man is more than just a common thief, gentlemen. More than stealing coins has brought him to our attention."

The judges murmured.

"I believe your questions will be answered as we continue. Yes? Very well, then. Thislen faces us today for serious crimes. He is accused of being involved in the murder of Percivan Coppermund and the kidnapping of a woman of noble birth."

"I *what?*" Thislen snapped. "I had nothing to do with Percivan Coppermund's death!"

"Do be silent," Avasten said firmly, voice rising slightly, "or we will silence you."

"Isn't the point that I get to stand before the court and defend myself?" Thislen began heatedly, even as the Lord Judge lifted two fingers. "I know exactly who was involved with his death; I tried to *save* him from you and Lord S—" A guard hastened up the steps and slapped him again. This time it was a backhand that rocked the thief where he stood.

Thislen's left ear rang. He could taste copper on his tongue. He spat at the floor, then turned to face Avasten steadily. He smiled. *They were involved in his death.*

Avasten's cold and careful demeanor cracked ever so slightly. His eyebrows lifted just a hair. It was enough. Thislen knew he had gotten under the man's skin. The blow from the guard only stoked Thislen's fire.

There's nothing else to lose. You've made me dangerous.

"Remain silent," Avasten commanded. "You are charged with having led Percivan Coppermund to his demise, a charge that would be serious enough on its own. You trapped the eldest son of a noble family on Astera's shores. While the Vaim may have dealt the final blow, he was only there because of you."

Is that what happened? They told Percivan something that made him stay on the island too long? Was he only there because of them?

Avasten had revealed more than he had planned, perhaps. Thislen's smile faded anyway. A charge of murder of a noble would be met with execution. There'd be no answers to his questions if he were dead.

"Your second charge is kidnapping. The woman in question was from a powerful noble family. Her virtue was ruined by your presence. When she returned to her family, she was changed beyond reconciliation. She later died."

The judges gasped and began to chatter quietly with one another.

Thislen's brow furrowed. "I did no such thi—" The guard beside him slapped him again. He stumbled, then caught himself with a rattle of chains. His face burned. He could feel a single drop of blood run down his cheek from a fresh cut beneath his eye. Panting softly, he turned his heated gaze back to Avasten Barnweir.

"You can see, gentlemen, that he is beyond remorse for his crimes. Clearly, he is deranged. Dangerous. A rabid animal," Avasten said, spreading his hands wide.

The judges sat silent. Some few clutched at the necks of their white robes. One had his hands wrapped so tightly around the podium before him that his knuckles were white. Several had their hands over their mouths. All of them bore heavy frowns as they watched the exchange.

So, this isn't normal. Whatever game the Ruling Council is playing, this time, their lackeys aren't on the same page.

"It is most unusual not to allow a criminal to defend themselves, my Lord," one judge said quietly.

Avasten's gaze turned slowly to the man, who quailed in his seat. "You wish to offer him a chance to lie to you, to spin tales that might put him back on the streets? Two nobles are dead because of him!"

I didn't kill my mother, you sick bastard.

"Name the woman for them, Avasten!" He shouted. This time he took a blow to the gut from the guard. Thislen fell to his knees, gasping and retching.

"Do you see? We withheld the woman's name for the sake of her family's privacy, those who still mourn her passing. He wishes to spit in the face of common kindness!" Avasten insisted.

"Then we move to sentencing," one man said.

Another spoke, voice cold and stern. "His kind should not be given any chances. I call for execution!"

"I propose we sentence him to the same fate as the seductress!"

"Are there any opposed?" Avasten asked, a smirk on his lips.

Seductress? They can't mean Mila—

The tension in the room thickened, hanging over the room like a storm cloud as the silence stretched on.

"Very well," Avasten said, waving his hand. "Vote for his soul, good men."

Lord Judge Barnweir went first, lifting his wooden paddle. The black side faced outward.

One by one, the other judges added theirs. Thislen was not surprised to find that every single strip of wood was black. Judges rarely disagreed with one another when one had made up their mind. They were all corrupt, all greedy, and all too willing to let trespasses go for the unspoken promise of future favors.

Thislen spat on the ground. "Cowards!" he hissed.

"It is not we who have anything to fear. Thislen, murderer of no family and no other name, is sentenced to one night upon the shore of Astera. May the Vaim and your ancestors have mercy upon your misguided, maddened soul."

Thislen felt as if he had plunged back into the frigid ocean. He went cold from head to toe as his mind summoned the image of the dark, boiling shadows with their angry red eyes. The unforgiving specters with their twitching limbs and sibilant whispers appeared in every shadow of the room. Their faceless masks fixated on him one by one, twisted with hatred and hunger. Mila was sentenced to the same fate?

His shoulder was burning, burning—

I'm going to miss the boat.

8

Everything moved quickly and slowly at the same time. The judges rose from their seats like mountains rising from the earth, ponderous and slow and titanic. Yet the walls behind them spun and tilted wildly. The guards materialized on either side of him, their hands drifting through the air like flowers on the breeze.

Thislen went blank. He didn't see or feel when he was unfastened from the stone platform and dragged out of the Ruling Court. He did not remember the corridor or being pushed back into his pen. All he could remember seeing, detached and distant as if he watched them from above, were men and women and guardsmen moving around him for the rest of the day. They slid around him, slow and purposeful like dancers. They were almost intangible, wavering at the edges. Thislen's ears rang so loudly he couldn't hear them at all.

Mila sat on the floor of the open cell beside him, back against the low stone wall. Her expression was as blank as the carved faces on the walls of the Justica. She didn't move or try to speak, perhaps similarly numb to the world around her.

Knowing she was safe, for now, Thislen sank into that comfortable floating place where he could watch and observe without truly existing. There would be time to fear, time to think, time to plan—later.

Thislen was only pulled from that fog at the end of the day, when he and Mila were led from the building and down to the sheltered quay and its small army of rowboats. Hours had passed entirely unnoticed. The sky was overcast. Gloom gathered swiftly as the sun approached the horizon. The sea spray prickled against his skin, scattered into the air when the water dashed itself against the rocks. He leaned into Mila as they were rowed back toward *The Brig*. The water was steely gray and churned angrily around them as they made the relatively short journey to the ship. It was rarely moved from its anchorage behind the Justica.

They were led down, down, down to the bottom floor of the ship. Everything slid past Thislen's feet, as if he floated above the decks instead of trod upon them. Four guards escorted them, two to each. They said nothing until they were being shut into their cells, wrists held out to have their cuffs removed. The guard's voice echoed strangely in Thislen's ears.

"What?" he said at last.

"Got cotton in your ears or something? I was telling you lot about what tomorrow would be like. I'm not repeating myself," the guard said, key rattling as he unlocked the first cuff.

"Tomorrow?" Mila asked, her voice small and wavering.

"We're not being left on the island tonight?"

The guard sighed heavily. "No. As I *said* already, you have to be given your last rites. Tomorrow." He unlocked the second cuff and pulled them through the bars. "Get meals again, though. Always a good thing, right?"

Thislen's expression went flat as he rubbed life back into his wrists. "Food and rites. Before we die," he said flatly.

"Of course. Don't want you two to *become* one of those monsters." The guard laughed. "Besides, always a risk trying to give the last rites *after*. Sometimes the Vaim don't leave a body behind. Sometimes there's just this big, bloody mess. It's easier to perform the rites beforehand."

Thislen shuddered. He wondered if the Vaim would have torn Percivan to shreds if he hadn't been there to distract them from their prize.

"No one ever survives, do they?" Mila asked numbly. The guards tending to her pulled her cuffs free of the cell.

The guard stepped back to offer her a shrug. "No, no one's ever survived. Sorry, you two. Pretty bad spot to be in. Can't believe you kidnapped a noble lady, though, boy. Which one was she, eh?" He grinned conspiratorially.

Elena Bestant, my mother. She ran away, he thought. "Sorry, that's one secret I'll take to my grave." He said aloud, voice cold as winter's bite.

The guard laughed again, then he and his fellows disappeared. Their footsteps faded away up the stairs. Thislen and Mila were left alone.

Finally.

He moved to the corner of his cell, sticking his arm through the cold, rust-flecked bars. "Mila?" he asked softly. "Mila, are you there?"

A rustle met his ears. Her hand slipped through the bars. Her fingers were cool as they laced through his, but her palm was warmer. She gave his hand a soft squeeze. "I'm here."

For a moment, they said nothing. Thislen drank in her presence, eyes closed. Her pulse beat in her thumb beneath his fingers.

"You're being left to the Vaim?" Mila asked at last.

"Yeah. They charged you as a seductress?"

"I tried to tell them the truth, but they'd already made up their minds! Thislen, what are we going to do? You're only in this mess because of me. They're going to put us on the island. We're going...we're going to die." Her voice was thick, the last few words wavering. She sniffled.

"Look, I got into this mess on my own. I made the choice to help you. And just so you know, I'm not done yet."

A soft, tired laugh came from the other side of the wall. "You can't even help yourself. Did they really charge you with murder?"

"Two counts. And kidnapping a noblewoman," Thislen admitted with a sigh.

"Kidnapping? They don't mean me, do they?"

"No. My mother, Elena Bestant."

"I heard you talking about that a little bit yesterday. You're related to Soren? And you never told me!"

"Would you want to admit it? Besides, the Ruling Council doesn't like bastards that claim their family names. And...that's not the only secret I'm protecting."

"What's...no, you're not going to tell me, are you?"

Do I tell her? What would she think of me then?

"No," he said at last. "Not yet, at least."

She said nothing, but even still, Thislen knew what she was thinking. *If not now, when?*

"What were the two murder charges?" Mila asked softly.

"One for my mother, who died in *their* hands. And one for Percivan Coppermund."

"They accused you of—why those pompous, self-righteous, thick-headed—" she fumed, fingers tightening in his.

"Yeah, I know. But I *was* there." Thislen confessed.

"Why? Why were you there?"

"Chance. Accident. Both? I don't know. I missed my own boat, and he just…showed up behind me. We were going to share, but it was too late. Anyway, none of it matters. They got what they wanted."

"What they wanted?" She echoed.

"Me out of the way. A neatly tied bow around Percivan Coppermund so people don't ask questions. And leverage over you. Watch, Bestant will try to turn this around to make himself look like a benevolent hero. He doesn't know what I know, though," Thislen said slowly. He paused, tongue heavy as lead in his mouth and his heart racing. How much did he dare to reveal?

"What do you know?"

He took in a deep breath, holding it for a moment. "I may know how to survive on the island," he said at last. "But it might not work. I've never tried."

Mila was silent. Her grip had gone slack in his own. He tried to imagine what her face looked like. Would her green eyes be wide? Her lips parted in surprise? Would her brow be furrowed as her mind churned? Was she struggling to believe him?

Her fingers tightened again. "A way to survive the Vaim," she echoed in a wistful whisper. "What is it? Ask them nicely not to murder us? I always wondered if that would work." Despite the levity in her words, her voice wavered again.

"No. My father told me how to do it when I was young. It's just a story, just a tale." Thislen pressed his forehead against the bars, omitting the part where his father never returned to tell him if it worked. "If it's true, though, we'll be alright. I have everything we need."

"Everything hangs on the outcome of a story!" She laughed, a sharp edge to the sound.

"I managed to get off the island without using it just a few days ago, too! I survived that night. Mila, please. You have to believe me, or Bestant will win."

"A few days ago, before you came to us at the apothecary. Is that what happened to your shoulder? You were touched by the Vaim?" she asked.

He frowned slowly, rolling his shoulder and feeling the pull of the stitches and healing skin. "Yeah. It was the Vaim. I doubt there will be another rowboat waiting for us. I doubt we'll make it to the shipyard from wherever they set us down. We won't make it that way, but if we do what my father told me..."

"It might work. And if it does work, we survive," she finished.

"And if we survive, we can get *out* of here, Mila. You and I," Thislen said earnestly.

"We could go to Barred Town. We can write to my father and Evelie and Ivan! They could come and join us, even. We can live quietly, far away from the reach of the Ruling Council and Lord Soren Bestant." Her voice lifted, her hand tight around his.

"We could leave Astera forever," he added, the words heavy with finality. Once they were off the island, he could tell her everything he knew, and none of it would matter. "You just have to trust me for one night. If I'm wrong, it won't matter anyway."

Another breathless laugh left her. "Are those my only options?"

His heart sank in his chest. "Mila," he began.

"No, Thislen. You're right. I trust you enough to try. It's that or give up, right? I'm not ready for that. I'm not giving in to those bullies. Tell me what we have to do."

He opened his mouth, but the plan he had been forming died on his lips. The wood above their head cracked heavily. Both of them fell silent. Thislen's dark-eyed gaze traced the sound of boots as they passed overhead, making their way toward the staircase they couldn't see from their cells. He hastily drew his hand from hers.

Thislen was across his cell in two steps, flinging himself down on his cot. He folded his arms over his chest as he stared up at the ceiling, brow beetling into a frown. He wasn't going to give his captors the pleasure of his waiting for them to appear. There would be no bated breath here.

"Are you there, prince of street trash?" came Soren's taunting call.

Thislen let out a short bark of a laugh. "Oh, so clever. Did it take you all night to come up with? Poor Soren, can't think of anything to make fun of his cousin for but being poor," he scoffed. "Is everyone on the Ruling Council this thick, or just you?"

Thislen lifted his head to stare at the man, lip curled up in disdain.

Soren Bestant was not alone. Once more, Garridan Artaith leaned against the bars across the way, his stocky features looking like they were carved from stone as the lantern overhead swung back and forth, casting thick shadows upon his face. Beside him was the gaunt figure of Avasten Barnweir, painted mostly in darkness and no longer dressed in his opulent white robes. The Lord Judge was studying his fingernails idly.

Garridan did not look away from Thislen at all. His dark eyes glinted in the faint light, fixated on him like a housecat that had spied a mouse.

"You made the mistakes, not I," Soren said with a smug smirk. "Your own errors decided your fate. There might still be a chance f—"

"Gloat somewhere else," Thislen said abruptly, interrupting whatever clever speech Soren had concocted. He rolled over on the cot to face the wooden wall, leaving the Lords staring at his back. "I haven't got time for your nonsense."

"I am *speaking* to you!" the fair-haired Lord snapped.

"What are you going to do? Kill me twice?" Thislen asked flatly.

"Fine. You're right. I can't punish you any more than this. I *can* make sure you have the chance to die alone, though," Soren hissed, the smug superiority back in every word.

Thislen fought the urge to roll off the cot and lunge across the cell, staring intently at the boards in front of his face. He did not roll over. Not yet.

He doesn't know; he doesn't know how much she trusts me. He doesn't know that she can see right through him. Let her handle this.

Soren's footsteps moved away from Thislen's cell, but there was no answering creak of wood from Avasten and Garridan. Thislen was being watched. He wondered what they hoped to see.

Probably someone pleading for their life. They're waiting for me to crack. Well, I'm not falling for it. We'll be fine.

He hoped.

MILA RETREATED from the bars as soon as Thislen's hand left hers. She already missed the warmth of his rough fingers, tangible proof she wasn't alone in this mess. This time she heard almost every word of their conversation, clear as crystal. The only thing she didn't hear clearly, above the dripping water and the groan of the ship as a storm rolled in somewhere above decks, was a hissed and sibilant whisper.

Her heart fluttered in her chest like she had swallowed a gigantic butterfly. Her fingers curled tight around the edge of the narrow wooden bunk she sat on as she tried to imagine what he would say to her.

What can he say after all of this? What does he think will fix this?

The flutter grew until she felt laughter burbling up inside her despite a sting in her eyes and the lump in her throat.

Lord Soren Bestant appeared in front of her cell, drawing her attention. It was common for the nobleman to wear nicely embroidered doublets and tunics over shirts with yet more decoration at the cuffs and collars, but the outfit he had chosen was far different than his usual. Tonight he wore what she could only assume was his best. Every inch of his tunic was embroidered until it looked like brocade, with beads winking softly in the low light of the lantern above. It was cream and gold and soft tan all over, like a doe's skin. His shirt's collar and cuffs were adorned with fanciful velvet trim that matched, also embroidered along the edges. A handsome brooch glittered at his throat, and he wore a few rings over his fitted gloves, each set with a large pale stone. His blond hair was perfectly curled above his pristine blue eyes. The heady scent of cedarwood soap wafted off him.

His expression, however, was not the smile she was used to. He didn't preen or posture at her, either. He bore himself with a calm and solemn mask, blue eyes as cold as ice.

"Mila," he said by way of greeting.

She gave a slight nod of her head but said nothing in return. She didn't trust her voice not to waver or crack. Not yet.

"I've come to offer you one last chance. The choice of what you do with your life is your own—"

She laughed, harsh and shrill and loud. The sound was startled out of her, and it surprised them both.

"Enough!" Soren shouted, slamming his hand against the bars. "Enough. Let me speak, woman! Because the choice of living or dying *is* in your hands. Right now, in this moment."

Her laughter died like a fading breeze.

"Agree to marry me, and I will take you to my ship. Tonight. You'll eat rich food and sleep in a warm bed, and the Vaim will never take your life. You and I will wed, and then I'll let you see your father again. Regrettably, you will be under guard until I can trust you again—but you will be *alive.*"

"You would spare me? If I married you?" she echoed.

For a moment, she tried to picture it. How miserable her existence would be, cornered into a relationship she never wanted and forced to live a life she never asked for. She imagined marrying him, carrying his children, and trying to find something to live *for,* rather than just not being allowed to die.

Soren took that as interest, leaning toward the bars, a hand curling around the rusted iron. A stunning smile blossomed on his lips. "Yes! Of course I would. I will give you a life most women only dream of. You'll wear silks and velvets every day. You can eat fine food. You can read books instead of embroider. I'll even give you a stretch of garden to grow plants in. You can have a *life*, Mila. With me. Choose me."

Does he think I have forgotten how I got *here?* That pit of roiling heat in her stomach roared to life like a furnace, and she rose slowly to her feet. Her cheeks and ears grew hot, and she turned to face the bars with her hands curled into fists.

Every word she said fell from her lips like stones, solid and hard and heated. "I *had* a garden. I *had* books. I *had* my father and food I liked, and I had my *freedom*. You wish to be seen as the benevolent savior after making up *lies* about me? After sending me to stand trial? After trying to *coerce* me into marrying you? You wrap it up in pretty ribbons of wealth and safety and freedom, but you're the one who took that freedom away! You're the one who locked me in this cell!"

"You weren't listening to reason," Soren said soothingly.

Mila's voice rose. "Reason! What reason did you have to do this to me? I do not *belong* to you. What interest have I ever shown? Polite and infatuated are not the same thing—or can you not tell the difference? You boorish *pig*!" Mila flew across the cell in a single step, slamming her hands against the bars.

Soren recoiled, eyes wide and stunned.

"You had no right to come into my life *at all*. I will gladly die tomorrow rather than ever subject myself to the *torment* of your presence again! I pray to the Ancestors that I am made into a Vaim, and that one day you will suffer under my hands the way I have suffered under yours." She spat in his face.

He jerked back as if she slapped him, lifting a gloved hand to wipe the spittle away in shock. A moment later, however, he lunged for the bars. His hands curled over her own, trapping her. His face was stretched into a twisted, maddened scowl, eyes alight with fire and teeth bared mere inches from Mila's face. She shouted at him in outrage, but she didn't budge.

"You have made the wrong choice for the *last* time," he hissed.

"I have made the right choice for the thousandth time. Be gone, you lout! You cad! You piece of refuse! Be *gone*, and fear the day we meet again." She spat at him again. There was no way she could miss.

Soren leapt back, sputtering as he wiped his face clean again. "Impudent witch!" he shouted before he whirled and stormed off.

"Finished here?" Avasten asked as calmly as if he had been waiting for Soren to finish choosing something at a merchant's stall.

Mila stepped back and sank onto the edge of her bunk, hands beginning to tremble now that the confrontation had passed. She panted softly, listening to the voices of those just out of her sight.

"I told you that wouldn't work," Garridan said, though his tone was conciliatory.

"We're done here. Our problem is just as solved if her family line dies with her. Can't be helped," Soren said. There was a sharp undercurrent to his words, a furious waver that he couldn't entirely hide. His mask of placid, angelic calm had cracked.

"I'm sure we can find a way to fix this, Soren," Avasten began. "Haven't you got that cousin who..."

The voices faded as the three headed up the stairs with a creak of wood. Mila stared blankly at the wall in front of her. The heat inside her chest faded to something cool and numb. Doubt followed soon after their departure. She had a chance to get out of all of this, and she'd thrown it away.

But would it really have been a life worth living?

She knew the answer even as the thought crossed her mind. Anything was better than being a pretty bird in a gilded cage, no matter how large and beautiful. There was no such thing as freedom in a trap made out of death.

"Mila?"

Thislen's voice was like balm to a burn. Her eyes fell closed. "I'm here."

There was silence for a time. It stretched on long enough that the apothecary wondered what the strange young man with the dark hair was thinking in the cell beside her.

He led himself right into danger for me, and more than once. What have I done to deserve such unwavering courage from him?

"We can write to Olen after we're out of the city. No one can stop us from leaving at dawn. They'll all be offshore. They won't even bother looking for us. They'll think we're dead, after all. We can still do everything you had planned, Mila."

Her head tipped back against the wood as her heart sank. "If we survive tomorrow night, I think what I want might change. I'm so *furious* that this happened, that it's probably happened before! I don't think I'll ever be the same."

The silence returned, heavier than before.

If you're being honest with yourself, you don't even believe him, she thought. There was no way they were going to survive. No one had ever survived before. No one had ever walked off Astera after a night ashore. Even Thislen had admitted it was only hearsay, only a story, that he'd only survived his ordeal by getting away on a boat. Her fate was inevitable.

Tonight was her last night alive.

9

The windowless cells of the lowest deck were an agonizing torment all their own, Thislen decided. With no light to go by, time blended into a seamless nothing that stretched hours into days and moments into hours.

Thislen and Mila had spoken softly together for some time, but then Mila had been tired. He let her rest and lay on his back, staring at the ceiling of his bunk for what felt like forever before he managed to drift off.

Thislen's dreams were fitful and restless. Every time he jerked awake, it was to barely remembered darkness and the soft whispering voice in his head, pleading for him to come home. He heard the whispers of Percivan and Vern and a hundred, a thousand faceless Vaim.

Thislen didn't want to be awake, though, not with the unseen dawn coming inexorably closer. *Today might be my last day, and Mila's. I wish I could see the sun.* So he rolled over every time he woke. He tossed and turned on the hard, narrow bunk, the musty scent of damp hay heavy in the air.

The waiting went on forever. By the time he woke from another nightmare to the heavy tread of boots upon the steps, he found himself grateful even for the chance to face his own execution. At least now, something was happening. He sat up, knuckling grit from the corners of his eyes.

It was four guards, but none of them were the ones who had led them back from the Justica. Two opened his cell door without a word, standing shoulder to shoulder in front of it as if they expected him to run. Cuffs clanked in their hands.

Where would I go? Off the side of the ship? Thislen thought dryly as he stood and offered them his wrists with no resistance. One guard bent to clasp a second set of cuffs around his ankles—just above his hidden ring. Thislen accepted the fetters with a frown. The chain between the shackles was at least long enough that he could hobble along, although it was uncomfortable and the edge of the metal dug into his shins with every step. *Off the side is right—and this would put a stop to that plan right quick.*

Part of him wondered if the cuffs might be purely for humiliation. He struggled to climb every step of the narrow staircase to the upper decks. Thislen glanced back only once and saw Mila was being led from her cell in much the same state. She stumbled as she adjusted to the restraints.

Thislen stopped, instinctively turning to go and help her, but the guard behind him shoved him back around. He fell heavily, catching himself against a higher stair with his teeth gritted.

"You don't have to push me!" he snapped.

"Keep going," the guard said, uncaring.

Thislen did. Sandwiched between his guards, he was led along the broader corridor of the next deck. Few people filled these cells, many in groups of four at the end nearest the next staircase. They were all quiet, withdrawn, watching with intent and hungry eyes.

The level above was lined with cells crammed with people until there was hardly room to sit. Some wept. Many sat still and pale. Some few jeered and rattled the bars of the doors as the guardsmen walked past with their charge. The shouting only got louder as Mila was led up. Men whistled at her and called for her attention.

Thislen couldn't look back. His guardsmen had taken hold of either of his arms, stubbornly towing him along as his steps slowed.

They emerged into the open air to brilliant afternoon sunlight, much to Thislen's surprise. He thought it was later in the day, verging on twilight. He had feared he would not get to see the sun set, and instead be given his last rites as night fell and all hope of survival was lost. It was far earlier than he had thought. *Those damn cells.*

Thislen abruptly stopped on the mid-deck, tipping his head back into the warmth of the sun hanging overhead, savoring the heat that played over his skin. *If I fail again, this will be the last time I see the sun.*

His guardsmen stood on either side of him, but this time they made no move to hurry him along. It was an unexpected kindness. *A kindness for a dying man,* he realized. Thislen opened his eyes, a frown creasing his brow as he gestured them to lead on once more.

He was not led to the rowboats on their winches that ran along the sides of *The Brig*. Instead, he was escorted to doors set in the box-like cabins built atop the deck itself. Some of these, Thislen knew, were the bunks of high-ranking City Guard officers. These were the men in charge of the prisoners and the guardsmen beneath them, and the management of *The Brig*. Any other use he was not familiar with.

Mila had been led in one direction, vanishing around a corner. Thislen was ushered around the other side to a door tucked near the stern. Once more, the guardsmen no longer pushed or harried him. The bitter taste of their sudden kindness lay thick on his tongue, as did barbed words he didn't dare speak. *Goading them into mistreating me won't make any of this go away.*

They removed his cuffs and closed the door behind themselves as they left. The lock latched with a solid *clunk.* He was left alone in the small, clean cabin.

A bathing tub filled nearly half of the tight space. It was already full of water. Coils of steam curled off its surface, vanishing in the light of the three small portholes set high in the wall that flooded the cabin with light. A dressing screen and a chair stood in a corner, bolted to the floor. A set of clean, undyed clothes was folded neatly on the chair's surface.

Against the wall was a plain altar of worn wood set with a few wooden bowls and delicate glass jars and bottles. A tapestry hung on the wall behind it, black fabric picked out with pristine white thread that depicted the Asteran star—six long points on a background of spines. Thislen stepped over to touch the star quietly.

One for peace, two for prosperity, three for understanding, four for reason, five for honesty, and six for piety, he recited in his head, remembering when his father had told him what the star meant.

"It's for our Ancestors. The way forward can always be clearly seen when you look back—sometimes because you do what your Ancestors did. Sometimes because you learn from your Ancestor's failings. Peace, prosperity, understanding, reason—all of those change. Time changes, and what people need and want changes, too. Honesty and Piety flank peace," his father had said, touching the two points on either side of the topmost. "Those never change. Being honest and being connected to our Ancestors? Couldn't change it if you

wanted to. Where you came from is not negotiable. Doing better than they did? That's admirable."

Thislen sighed softly. "I wish I *could* change where I came from. It would have been easier to leave before I got into this mess." Now he might never have that chance.

Clunk. The door behind him opened again, but instead of someone clad in the City Guard's gray livery, a brown-skinned priest wrapped in the silver and white vestments of the island's clergy entered. He gave a polite bow. "Good afternoon. You may call me Brother Restan. I'm here to see to your last rites. They usually begin with a bath, if you're interested."

Thislen stared at the man. He had a round, unassuming face and tightly curled black hair sitting over bark-colored eyes. Restan had faint crow's feet at the corners of his eyes, most likely from a lifetime of polite smiles like the one he currently wore. His hands were clasped around the slim leather *Book of the Ancestors*. He didn't appear at all concerned about being shut into a small room with an accused murderer.

"Do you do this for your daily bread, then, Brother?" Thislen asked at last, lowering his hand from the tapestry.

"Send people to their graves, you mean?" Restan asked. "Very rarely. You might be surprised to learn that we don't do all that many executions. Usually, they spend time locked away here on *The Brig* or get sentenced to work in the mines. To be executed by the Vaim is rarer still. To be sure, people die to the Vaim, but it is most often an accident. Take, for example, the late young Lord Coppermund. You heard about that, yes?"

"Find Soren!" Percivan's voice echoed softly in Thislen's head.

I found him, and a fat lot of good it did me, Thislen thought bitterly back at the shade. "Yes. I have heard of him. A bath, then?" he asked curtly.

Restan did not catch the hint. "Young Lord Coppermund was one of the lucky ones. Sometimes the Vaim don't leave enough behind to perform the last rites. His body was mostly intact. A blessing for his poor parents," Restan said, turning to rap on the door gently. "But yes! A bath. We'll get one more bucket of hot water in here to make sure it's comfortable. A clean body makes room for a spirit to leave this earth freely."

Thislen moved behind the changing screen as the door opened and a guard stepped in with a bucket that steamed. The water gurgled as the man poured it into the tub. He could just make out the shapes of the two men through the wooden filigree and parchment, shadows that moved indistinctly and just out of sight. It made the hair stand up on the back of his neck. *The next time I see shadows, they will be all too real.*

Could he survive them?

Thislen stripped down to nothing. He piled his things on the floor behind the screen, pausing as he turned his ring over and over between his fingers. After a moment of hesitation, he ripped off a small tattered corner of his cloak and tied the scrap of fabric around the ring's crest. With the sigil hidden from view, he hung the ring from its leather cord around his neck. Its weight was a balm—familiar and comforting. He took stock of himself. The wound on his shoulder had scabbed over. Remarkably, it was still clean. The bruising had faded, mottling it with a sickly green, purple, and yellow pattern. The puncture was gone, cut into an 'x' by Olen to help drain the Vaim's poison before it had been stitched neatly closed. He felt over the wound gently. *What does it feel like a second time? I'm not even fully recovered from the first round. Will it kill me?*

The door thudded closed again as the guardsman left. The lock *clunk*ed back into place, leaving Thislen alone with Brother Restan. He walked out from behind the screen, paying no heed to modesty. He climbed into the tub with a slosh of hot water, sinking into it up to his neck.

In spite of himself, Thislen let his eyes fall closed with a contented sigh. Restan made no move to hurry him. The priest opened a paneled door on the altar to produce a clean cloth and a bar of soap. The priest then stood politely near the head of the tub, contemplating the six-pointed star in silence.

If I never finish this bath, will he let me stay in here forever? Thislen wondered. He knew the answer was no, but it was a darkly amusing thought none the less. How long would Brother Restan wait before having him dragged out? A few hours? A day?

Reluctantly, Thislen sat up and took the tools the priest had set on the chair beside the tub. He washed from head to toe. Even taking as much care as possible, he was done long before he was ready to be. Restan still hadn't hurried him at all.

Thislen soaked quietly in the water, eyes closed. *This may be the last peaceful moment of my life. No.* No, *I won't let it be.*

He forced himself out of the water. It streamed off him as he rose. Brother Restan offered him a soft towel, and Thislen accepted it, stepping behind the dressing screen once more.

"There are plain clothes on the chair, should you wish. Otherwise, you can wear your own things to the island," Restan explained, calm and patient as ever.

How can he be so serene? This job would drive me mad.

Since he was planning to survive the evening if he could, Thislen pulled his own clothes back on. He emerged again, drying his hair with the towel one last time. Even if it was for such a morbid reason as this, a hot bath worked wonders. Thislen felt ready to face the Vaim, more energized and awake than before.

Restan was waiting for him with an almost apologetic smile on his features, still standing beside the small altar. "You do worship your ancestors, yes?" he asked, gesturing at the star upon the wall. It was an almost needless question. It was expected that all Asterans worshiped their ancestors. Those that worshiped other gods and walked different paths *did* exist, but they were few and far between. Most of them were from other kingdoms or descended from such travelers.

"Yes," Thislen said, turning his gaze to the symbol. For a moment, he pictured his father again. The man's towering height and broad shoulders were so different from his own. He could clearly see the dark brown eyes that saw everything, studied everything, and learned everything. He never met his grandfather, nor any ancestor before that, but he heard their histories almost every night until his father vanished.

Until his father had died. Until he had died at the hands of the Vaim all those years ago.

He thought of his mother, too. He didn't remember her at all, but he remembered how his father spoke of her in hushed words to soothe his young son, describing her as kind and fierce and earnest. He said Thislen took after her in build and the fire in his eyes.

Thislen frowned at the star, fingers curling around the fabric of his shirt and closing around the ring hidden beneath them, hanging around his neck. *I have to survive this night—for more than one reason. I need to carry on for my father. For my grandfather. I need to pass on our stories. This is about more than just Mila; it's about me, too.*

His thoughts were interrupted by Brother Restan clearing his throat. "Which ancestors should you be tied with?" he asked gently

Which Ancestors died last, you mean, Thislen corrected quietly. Each generation tied themselves to the one before, and those ties stretched back generations. "My father. His name was Linden. And my mother, Elena."

"And your surname?" Restan asked. "And your own name, please."

Thislen inhaled deeply. No one knew his surname. He took a small measure of comfort from that. No one knew who he really was. It was a secret he could take with him to his grave. "My name is Thislen. I have no surname to speak aloud."

Brother Restan's dark brow furrowed, but he gave a small nod and let the matter lie. Instead, he turned to the altar and sorted through the bottles and jars that littered its surface. He poured two oils into a single shallow wooden bowl, then added powder. A quick stir turned the mixture into a white paint that smelled of earth and spices.

"It's ground clay mixed with linseed and cedarwood oils. It makes a paint that will stay on your skin until it is scrubbed away. It will bind you to the stars. When you pass, it will create a channel to speed you to the halls of your ancestors," Restan explained.

Thislen watched the priest fetch a few brushes from the cabinet beneath the altar. The man laid each one out in a perfectly neat line.

"Do you believe that, Brother Restan?" he asked suddenly, breaking the calm silence.

"Pardon?"

"Do you believe we join our ancestors in the stars when we die? That we join with them in some never-ending watch of those below?"

Restan smiled softly. "A common question from those facing their death. I believe what the books teach us. Until the line is no more, until all their children are gathered in the heavens with them, our ancestors watch. They guide us toward our fates, pulling on the blood ties that bind us all together. When all of their line has adjourned to the stars, there is no longer need to watch. Then, together with all the people we love, we rest. I believe that most sincerely."

Thislen said nothing more as the priest lifted the bowl. He knelt, and Brother Restan began his task. The paint was cool, but it quickly warmed against his skin as Restan deftly formed sigils and markings with the brushes. Once he had finished, Brother Restan kissed his palm, then lay his hand atop Thislen's head.

"May your ancestors always be able to find you. May your spirit reach those you love in one piece," he said solemnly.

May my spirit stay inside me for a thousand nights more, Thislen prayed silently, *and may our line not end with me.*

He turned to look out the nearest porthole, watching a lone cloud scud across the sky. Though the process had taken some time, there were a few hours yet until sunset.

"What happens now?" Thislen asked, the words heavy as lead as they fell from his lips.

Brother Restan stood beside him, looking out at the crystalline blue sky as well. "I can wait a little longer if you'd like. You may pray or watch the sky. Otherwise, I will tell the guards that you are ready, and you will be returned to your cell until sunset. Are you?"

"Am I what?"

"Are you ready?"

Thislen studied the single cloud, white and fluffy as sheep's wool, for several heartbeats more before he turned away. "We're done here," he decided. *There's no point in drawing it all out. No matter how kind and patient this priest is, he isn't my friend. He's not going to save me.*

I'm going to save me.

That's what truly mattered—saving himself and doing his best to save Mila Ominir as well. He still had questions for her. He needed to know more about Lord Soren Bestant, about Olen Ominir, and about the Coppermunds. There was no way to answer any of them if he were dead.

I really hope my father told the truth. I hope he was right.

This plan *had* to work.

Brother Restan rapped gently on the cabin door.

THE SUN WAS low behind the city, a fierce red globe that cast the buildings as ink-black shadows. Thislen sat beside Mila on the bench of a rowboat, hands and feet unbound as they approached the island. There was no point in tying them up this time. There was nowhere left for them to go. The water and the island both held nothing but death after dark.

Mila's features had been painted with the same white paint, though it stood out less on her fair skin than on his. Her brow, cheeks, and jawline were marked with stars and sigils tied together with small scrollwork pieces. They were beautiful, designed to make the dead look otherworldly. He touched his cheek, wondering how they looked on him. Silently, he turned from the city and the apprentice apothecary both. Thislen stared steadily at the other occupants of the small vessel.

They were accompanied by Lord Soren Bestant and the young Lord Garridan Artaith, both of whom sat behind the two City Guards who grunted softly as they hauled on the oars. A third guard sat behind Thislen and Mila, keeping careful watch.

The lords chatted quietly with one another about game strategy in

Hunters and Hounds while the little boat bobbed across the way. Their eyes kept drifting to Thislen and Mila, studying them and watching them.

If they expect us to crack, to beg or break down, they have another think coming.

Thislen met their gazes, outwardly as calm as a still pool though his heart hammered beneath his ribs. Mila had her hands clasped tight upon her lap, gaze fixed on her entwined fingers. She was still, silent, and pale. He fought the urge to reassure her. Thislen did not want the lords to gloat in their misery—to laugh or mock or try to cajole Mila to give up and marry Soren again. *I hope she doesn't offer to. I hope she remembers to trust me.*

Most important, Thislen hoped no one realized he had a plan.

His father had told him the story a long time ago of a magic that may or may not work that was tied into the ring that hung around Thislen's neck.

"In the past, the spells were woven right into the metals of these things. Magic may be all but gone these days, but spells cast centuries ago are still there, Thislen," Linden said, lowering the cord around his neck. "Remember what I told you?"

"The story about Grandfather Rowan?" Thislen asked. Eight, with wide eyes and trembling hands, he looked like a broomstick. His pant legs were too short. His cloak was too small. Now he had a golden ring around his neck, which he clutched in both hands.

"Yes. All the old families have a ring like this. Hold on to it, and you can always be safe at Perilee."

Perilee, the castle above Astera, looming even now as the sun set. It was a beacon, one that Thislen avoided his entire life. The moment he went to that castle, everyone would know who he was.

Now he had no choice.

The trip to the shore stayed silent apart from the inane gossip of the two wealthy men. It felt like bells had passed and also like no time at all. The rowboat bumped up against the wood of the dock. The guardsman in the bow jumped ashore and roughly pulled Thislen and Mila onto land before reclaiming his spot in the safety of the vessel. That meager wooden haven, small as it was, bobbed a few feet away from the dock.

Soren leaned in toward Mila, offering her a gloved hand. His calm demeanor was now creased with concern as he tried to catch her lowered gaze. "Mila, this is your very last chance. If you want, I can take you back into this rowboat *right now*. I can—"

"No," Mila interrupted him, though her voice wavered. She cleared her throat and lifted her chin. Her fingers curled tight in the folds of her brown traveling clothes. "No," she repeated, louder. "I'm alright, thanks."

Soren's brows drew in, and his lips pursed. Garridan leaned subtly away from him, looking out over the water.

"Hey, Soren," Thislen said suddenly, "let's make a deal." The lack of formality and the dripping disdain in Thislen's words did not go unnoticed if the downward twist of Soren's lips was any indication. "The next time you see me, you'll tell me what happened to Percivan Coppermund."

The ire melted off Soren's face with a scoff and a laugh. The lord waved his hand dismissively. "Is that truly your last wish? Ha! Fine, you have my word. When I see you again as a little ghost or a corpse, I will tell you anything you wish."

"Remember your words. Garridan Artaith, you are our witness." Thislen snapped his gaze to the stocky nobleman. His hands curled into fists, nails pressed into the skin of his palms. *Say it, just say it.*

Garridan shook his head. His indulgent smile was weak and tired, as if the joke were already wearing thin. "Alright, I'm witness."

Got you. Now, if his plan worked, Thislen could possibly get all of the answers he needed, offered to him on a silver platter as a dying wish.

"If that's all?" Soren asked, his gaze on Mila.

She said nothing, did nothing. Thislen could see her trembling faintly from the corner of his eye, shaking head to toe with her eyes fixed on the gently rocking rowboat. She was silent.

Soren smirked again, gesturing for the guardsmen to begin to row. As the boat pulled away, he lifted his hand in a smug farewell.

The sun was setting. There were no ships in any direction at all. There was no chance of them running quickly enough to go from here— a dock near the Justica—to the shipyard in the Gate Quarter. There was no promise of a floating vessel being there, even if they did.

It left them only one chance. Their only hope was Thislen. He had sworn to his father that he would never do what he was about to do—not unless it was an absolute emergency.

I think this counts.

With no hesitation, Thislen grabbed Mila's hand and began to run, towing her into the city. The sun was going down.

There was no more time.

10

Thislen tore through the streets of Astera as quickly as Mila could go. Her hand in his was clammy and slick, and he held tight so she wouldn't slip from his grasp. The last thing he wanted was to leave her behind. He lagged a bit to accommodate her pace. *I wonder if she knows. I wonder if that worries her.*

Thislen tightened his grip to silently reassure her, but he did not look back. They ran through the empty streets toward the Goods Quarter and its tiers that rose above them on the hillside. They ran up toward the Great Markets near the Ominir Apothecary. They ran toward Perilee.

The castle's spires gleamed, beckoning them closer with their winking glass. They whispered softly of safety in the solid mountain hold. *Come,* the voice said in Thislen's ear, elated and eager, *closer, just a bit closer...*

They made it to the wide sweeping ramps of the Goods Quarter before the sun vanished behind them. The shadows at the feet of the buildings began to sway. Thislen didn't hesitate. He wove up narrow stairways and through slender side streets choked with darkness, ignoring the way a shadow squished beneath his foot as he tore past. Flashes of signs and colorful shop window displays half-hidden by shutters flickered past in a dizzying array. The fading odor of bread, stews, and spices still hung in the air, not yet settled into the quiet scent of nightfall. The smell of stone and shade rose in the air around them, rich and earthy and silent as the spirits.

A shadow in the lee of a shop bulged outward, swelling until the protrusion of darkness sprouted arms and legs that dragged themselves free with a groan as they passed. Thislen glanced back as the creature's oddly jointed limbs twitched and spasmed against the cobbles. The spirit rose to its feet. Red eyes bloomed to life in its face as it waited, almost serene. Thislen turned quickly away.

Mila's nails dug into Thislen's hand as they darted around the corner of a building, a Vaim looming into a solid being before them. She let out a choked, desperate sound. Another followed, rising from the shadow of a food stall. Two more rose behind that. Faster and faster they started to come, darkness itself splitting into twos and threes as the city streets filled with a throng of monsters. Thislen didn't spare a single breath to reassure her. He could taste the bitter tang of copper in the back of his throat. Every ounce of his being would be necessary to guide them to safety. Besides, what was there to say?

Sorry if I get you killed? Thislen thought. *Ancestors,* please *don't let me get her killed.*

His foot caught, and he stumbled. Thislen wouldn't have fallen—if Mila had not crashed into his back. The pair went down in a tangle of arms and legs with a yelp and a shout.

We're dead.

Thislen elbowed Mila off his back, ignoring the ache in his shoulder as he pushed himself to his hands and knees, head bowed and braced. He could see the shadowy forms of Vaim around them, hear their sibilant whispers on the breeze. Mila lay beside him on the stones, her hands over her head, sobbing.

I can't save her. I failed again.

The whispers around them grew louder. The Vaim pressed closer. He waited for their shadowy hands to fall upon his skin, to pierce him through like fire. Something barely brushed his hair. The end of his cloak stirred. He squeezed his eyes shut.

Nothing happened. A sign's metal hinges squeaked somewhere nearby as it swung in the sluggish breeze. The Vaim were close around them, their long talon fingers reaching out—to *toy* with them. Thislen opened his eyes to find them caressing the air near his cheeks, near his hair, near his shoulder. His wound burned as he remembered how those talons felt.

"Mila," he said, voice barely above a whisper. The Vaim did not stop their silent, looming observations. "Mila," he repeated.

She remained huddled on the ground, arms over her head.

"Mila, they're not…moving."

Her head shot up, face pale as parchment, and she stared into the specters' angry red eyes. She screamed, backing into Thislen, clutching his arm so hard her nails cut into his skin.

He winced but said nothing as he wrapped an arm around her shoulders, still watching them. The sea of shadowy figures shifted around them, moving closer, pressing in—but there was a distinct bubble of space around the pair that the creatures reached into but never quite breached.

"What…what are they doing?" Mila asked breathlessly at last. Her cheeks gleamed in the light of the rising moon from her tears.

"Nothing." Awe colored the word.

They sat frozen, listening to the inaudible whispers hiss through the air around them. Thislen thought he could almost make out the words, straining to hear what the ghosts had to say.

Mila was the first to push herself to her feet. The Vaim drew back, withdrawing their hands as if the air around her scalded them. Thislen rose as well, taking her hand in his. It was cold.

The spirits didn't move.

What. The absolute. Hells. Thislen thought, heat rising slowly in his chest. "You lot almost killed me a few days past, but now we're fine? Now you aren't going to touch me, eh?" he shouted at them.

"Thislen!" Mila hissed, turning to slap her hand over his mouth.

The Vaim around them drew nearer, then back again, surging more like water than like men. Their gazes never wavered.

Heart pounding beneath his ribs, Thislen pried Mila's hand from his lips. She was close enough that she stood on his toes, but she hadn't noticed. They were still untouched, the only living souls in Astera.

"What do we do?" Mila asked softly.

"…we should stick with the plan."

"Which was?"

That's right, I hadn't told her. Now I don't have to. Do I?

He took her hand again and stepped toward the Vaim. They parted before him, hands outstretched. Though he felt cold from head to toe, Thislen stepped forward again, and again after that. The Vaim's hands came close, *so* close to touching him—but they pulled away every time. They hovered over his shoulders, his chest, and his face like the branches of some kind of nightmare forest.

Mila followed him, pressed close to his side, holding on to him for dear life.

They walked through the streets. With every step, Thislen expected the sea of angry red-eyed ghosts to close upon them, dragging them to the beyond. He felt as if every breath was getting stuck in his throat. *Waiting,* he lamented, *waiting really* is *the worst of punishments.* Waiting for an end that never came was as much of a nightmare as a swift death would have been. Perhaps worse.

They stepped out of the warren of streets and into the Great Marketplace before the gates of Perilee. The shuttered stalls rose above a sea of hunchbacked shadows. One by one, pinpricks of fiery red turned toward them. The whispers grew, as did the breeze. The sad flutter and flap of fabric awnings filled the air. A loose shutter somewhere rattled with the sound of wood on stone.

Thislen didn't recall coming to a stop, but he had. He stood side by side with Mila in the open, on a patch of bare cobbles. The whispering spirits had begun to roam slowly around them, kept at bay by…something.

Is it magic? Is it because they already stabbed me once? Is it…my ancestors?

He glanced up at the sky, peppered now with stars. With a shake of his head, Thislen pushed such notions from his mind. *My ancestors can't help me with ties of blood, and it's bad luck to question good fortune.*

"Maybe they believe we're truly innocent," Mila said abruptly, startling him.

"What?"

"The court said that if the Vaim found us innocent, they'd leave us alone. We didn't do what we were accused of!"

Thislen eyed the Vaim. The air grew heavy and chill around them. His breath came from his lips as a cloud of steam. "I don't think that's it," He murmured. The Vaim were waiting. He could feel it.

But for what?

The castle's gates were just visible over the market's stalls, so close and so impossibly far away. "Let's go to the High Way. If they aren't going to touch us, we can walk to Barred Town and blend in, and this will all be behind us," Thislen said abruptly.

My secrets can wait.

"What about the story your father told you?" Mila glanced at him, her hair escaping the tail it had been tied into to fall in coils around her face.

"My father told me that those of old and noble birth are tied into the magic used to build Perilee."

"Old magic? You want to trust magic from before the Vaim to still be working all this time later? That was your plan?" Mila asked, voice rising with each question.

"What was *your* plan?" Thislen snapped.

"How did your father even know about that? How did he think it would work?"

"My mother told him. I've got Bestant blood in me. It should do the trick."

Mila let out a frustrated huff, her gaze on the distant castle gate. "I don't think I can move another step now that we're safe."

"I can." Thislen squeezed her hand gently, barely a flex of his fingers. He didn't look back at her; he only started forward again.

Mila resisted for a moment, then stumbled after him. "Don't leave me behind," she whispered.

"I won't."

The dull red coals of the Vaim's sunken eyes snapped to follow their movement as they passed. The whispers grew to a chorus that teased at the edge of Thislen's mind, never quite distinctive enough to make out the words. They lurched around them with slow, jerking steps. Dark claws curled around the corners, followed by looming faces as they wove their way slowly between the stalls. Twitching, spasming shapes fluttered in every shadow and trailed along in their wake. Too-long fingers stretched out around them, always just a hairsbreadth away, closing on thin air when they passed.

Thislen turned toward the High Way—only to find the Vaim had suddenly become an immovable wall. The spirits did not part before them. He barely stopped short of running into one of the ghost's chests. His skin went cold and he shuddered, quickly stepping backward.

"Not that way, then."

"Are they...herding us?" Mila asked faintly.

The gates of Perilee loomed ahead of them, large and sturdy. They stood four or five times a man's height. The wall around the keep itself was silvery gray in the moonlight, but the door was a dark black pit. It was closed. Thislen walked until he stood just before it. The Vaim moved out of his way.

He lifted his hand to the door and pushed.

Nothing.

"...come on, come on." He muttered, pulling his hand free from Mila's. He wrested the ring from the confines of his shirt and fumbled at the knotted fabric he had tied around it earlier.

"What is that?" she asked softly.

"Heirloom, that's all."

Mila pressed her back against the door beside him, flattening herself to the wood as if the shadows there would protect her from the Vaim. Her gaze roved over the watching, whispering crowd. Their heads twitched from side to side like curious hellhounds. Claw-like fingers twitched and relaxed. Every time the spirits moved they rustled like paper.

The knot was stuck, and it was too dark for Thislen to figure it out. "Damn it."

The Vaim pressed just a bit closer, the bubble of space around Thislen and Mila shrinking. *Are they getting tired of waiting?*

"Let's just go to the shop," she whispered. "We can hide there."

"It won't be safe. Be careful, don't trust them. I've seen what they...do."

A Vaim lurched forward, a hand outstretched toward Thislen. His stomach flip-flopped, and his heart leapt to his throat as he flung himself back against the door with an echoing *thump*. Apart from that one step, however, the creature did not move. Its fingers curled until a single shadowy digit pointed—right at Thislen's wounded shoulder.

A whispering hiss rose from the sea of specters at the gesture, flooding his ears like the dull and distant roar of a crowd. He went cold from head to toe, apart from a searing lance of fire where the Vaim's finger had pierced through his flesh. It was sudden. It was *painful*. Thislen clutched at it with a shout.

"Thislen!" Mila shouted, catching him as he sagged.

The Vaim's hand lowered. The pain faded. The specters around them stirred like leaves in a breeze. Their waiting had changed to *expecting*. Their whispers—he could almost make them out.

Open it, open it, open it.

Come, come deeper.

Come inside.

"They're...waiting for something." He gasped. It felt like he had swallowed a block of ice that chilled him straight through.

"What? Waiting for what?" Mila asked, helping him back to his feet. She watched the restless ghosts warily.

Thislen grit his teeth. It was strange. The more they urged him to come inside, the less he wanted to. It felt like the jaws of a trap waiting to close about him. The whispers had faded again, the indistinct rattle of the Vaim's words making no sense to his ears. It was like trying to listen to a merchant speaking a different language and only catching a single word here and there. *But I know the answer to Mila's question. I know the answer, and I don't think we should.*

"For us," he reluctantly said at last. "For us to go inside the castle."

Mila's hand found his once more, holding tight. They turned to face the ghostly throng.

"If we go inside, they'll kill us?" She asked, voice wavering.

"No, I don't think so." *But some things might be worse than death.*

Mila's slack-jawed fear was fading at last, her ever-strong sense of curiosity growing. Her brow furrowed and her mouth worked for a moment in the gloom. Her gaze was still intent on the creatures around them. "How...do you know?"

"The wound on my shoulder, it's—"

"From them, I remember."

Thislen smothered a flash of irritation at the interruption. *There are times and places to get angry about her habit of talking over people, and in a crowd of murderous ghosts isn't one of them. Besides, maybe it's normal for people to do that, and I'm just not used to it. I don't talk to people enough.* He took a deep breath.

"It is. And I think it did something to me. I think *they* did something to me." Thislen brought his hand up to the hidden injury, probing it with his fingers. "You can hear them, right?"

"Sort of. I can't make out what they're saying," Mila whispered.

"I heard them. Only for a moment. They...*want* us to go inside Perilee."

The Vaim stared, and Thislen and Mila stared back. The specters twitched and jerked as they wove in and out amongst one another, restlessly milling around them. The indistinct whispers rose and fell like waves upon the shore.

"If they want us to go inside, why don't we?" Mila asked softly at last.

Hostile red eyes jerked toward her in twos and threes, one after the other. The Vaim closest to the door put their hands upon the gates. Those further away slowly lifted talon-like fingers outstretched toward the door. Thislen and Mila stood in the center of a sea of supplicants. Some of the Vaim's outstretched hands were just over their heads. They couldn't see anything but the wood behind them.

Thislen felt a flash of sudden and desperate panic. He knew what they wanted, and he wasn't ready—he would never be ready—for things to change. *I want to leave this place. I don't want to try and fix it. I* can't *fix it, not alone.*

He recoiled from the wooden door, the Vaim scattering away from him with an angry hiss like oil in a hot pan. He caught Mila's hand in his own, towing her away from the door behind him.

"Thislen, wait!"

Thislen did not wait. He rounded on the spirits with a cold fire in his stomach, a pit of ice that sizzled and spat inside him. He advanced, and they gave way. So he lunged toward them, driving them back with angry murmurs. The massive crowd of the dead grew louder and more agitated with every step, weaving amongst one another in a dizzying dance. They reminded Thislen of hounds deciding if they would attack a bear. Despite every angry step, however, the bubble around him and Mila did not shrink. It grew.

As they stepped far enough away from the gate, the Vaim closed behind them like flowing water around a stone. Their dark forms disappeared in the shadows, leaving nothing visible but floating red eyes twisted into malicious glares. The whispers roiled around them like the angry drone of a hive of wasps.

Mila yanked hard on his arm, stopping Thislen in his tracks. Her grip was so tight on his that his fingers had gone numb. "Stop it! You're making them angry, Thislen!"

"They're making *me* angry!" he roared, swinging his arm toward the darkness. "Why don't you lot just finish us, then! I'm not going in there! Back off, leave us alone!" *They have the wrong man.* He refused to back down, meeting the angry stares of dead eyes with his own scowl.

"Stop shouting at them! You're going to get us killed!" Mila hissed.

"No! Go on, get! Go away! Leave us be!"

Mila whirled him around and slapped him. The shock of it froze Thislen in his tracks, eyes wide and a hand on his cheek. She was pale, and her expression was pinched and small. She trembled.

Oh.

In the sudden still silence of their prey, the Vaim closed the space around the pair, all stepping in together. They were close enough now that their living captives were well and truly trapped, and this time they did not retreat when Thislen leaned toward them. Their shadowy talons came out, tangling in clothing, tugging at cloaks and plucking at sleeves, gentle as a breeze. And yet every gesture was a threat, a promise of more insistence to come if the pair did not heed the silent commands of the monsters.

Thislen remembered the feel of all those hands plucking at him and pulling at him, trying to drag him back onto the island's shore. Each little brush of their ice-cold fingers on his skin and in his hair demanded something more of him. Each one wanted something he wasn't willing to give.

How long do we have before they drag us inside?

"Back off!" he growled, pushing away the cold wrist of one of the Vaim.

"Thislen, don't touch them!" Mila gasped.

"Well! *That's* new."

Despite the pressing issue of the angry specters that paced around them, pushing past whatever invisible boundary had protected them before, Thislen and Mila found their eyes drawn abruptly to the roof of a nearby shop that bordered the market square. The voice had come from one of three dark shapes silhouetted by the moon, dressed in browns and grays that would have rendered them invisible against the rooftop had they not sat at the peak of it.

One of the figures waved with a perfectly human hand. "Hello down there!" A bright tenor of a voice called. "Don't worry; we'll be right down before they get too agitated." His shadowy form vanished behind the roof's peak.

The second followed, a lean figure that moved more like a whip than a willow.

The third figure stood but did not descend. This shadow was tall and muscled but not broad in build. "Are you two alright?" This was the bright and soothing voice that had first spoken.

"We're...we're alright," Mila called back.

"Mila, stop it!" Thislen hissed, glancing back at her. "We don't know who these people are. We don't know *what* they are."

"They're people!"

"People can't survive on this island. Not with the Vaim."

Her eyes widened, and she looked back up at the rooftop warily. The shadow there did not move. Mila's wariness slowly melted away to another furrowed brow. "But we're surviving on it right now."

Thislen frowned. *She has a point, but I thought...* He shook his head. No, of course he and Mila weren't different or special. That meant there was something he didn't know.

Amongst the Vaim, a rustle and a parting ran through the gathered specters like wheat bending in the breeze. The spirits shifted. Two shadows pushed their way out of the crowd, seemingly unafraid of the Vaim as they gently parted them. Just as softly as mothers herding children, they eased the spirits away until there was once more a bubble of space around Thislen and Mila. Strangest of all was that the Vaim didn't see the pair, their burning red eyes still fixated on the captive thief and the displaced apothecary. It was like the strangers didn't exist.

They wore hoods, but pulled them away from their faces when they had finished nudging the Vaim away. A moment after that, one of the pair produced a small, softly glowing stone from a leather pouch on his belt and held it aloft. Their features were outlined in a pale yellow light, revealing that they were entirely, utterly, and completely—human.

They appeared to be twins, or at least closely related. The young man had ringlets of curly hair in a dark brown or light black. The woman behind him had hair of the same color pulled back into a bun, but identical wild ringlets had escaped here and there to hang free. They both had hazel eyes and the same up-turned nose. The most notable difference between them was in their expressions. The young man smiled gently, but the young woman's gaze was cold as ice.

Thislen couldn't tell what surprised him more—the Vaim's indifference to these people, or the fact they existed at all. On the island. In Astera. *At night.*

He slowly turned his gaze to the spirits that paced like eager hounds around the market square, watching their prey but moving no closer than the invisible barricade the strangers seemed to have erected around them all. *They really can't see them. How are they doing that?* Not a single baleful red eye ever fell to the pair that stood before him.

"Here, let's start with these. The Vaim will just get more and more agitated, and it's best to keep them calm," the young man said. He dug into a pocket, then held up his hand. Two beaten metal pendants dangled from fine chains clasped in his fist. They were embossed with tiny reliefs of Astera, with beams of light around the castle Perilee at the top. The soft yellow light made them gleam like gold, but they were made of some plainer metal.

Mila reached for them, but Thislen stopped her.

"Let me go first," he said, releasing her wrist to claim a pendant.

She huffed. "I don't need you to protect me from jewelry."

Thislen ignored that, pulling the chain over his head.

Nothing happened.

Patiently and with a broad and understanding smile, the young man mimed tucking the necklace into his clothes. Thislen did, ensuring his ring was hidden beneath his shirt as well. The cool metal of the pendant warmed against his chest, and quite suddenly, it *shocked* him.

"Ah—ow!" he yelped, already reaching for the chain. *Magic—like my ring.* His gaze snapped up, mouth open to yell at their apparent saviors for not warning him. Instead, he froze.

Beyond the pair of strangers, the Vaim had stopped looking at him entirely. Every single pair of red eyes in the milling throng of specters was fixed upon Mila and Mila alone. She hastily followed suit after nothing further happened to Thislen.

He heard the spark, like static electricity, followed by a gasp from Mila. Suddenly, the twisted and menacing shapes of the Vaim seemed lost, like a kite without a tether. The ghosts jerked and twitched, heads swiveling as they hunted for what they could no longer see. One by one, the creatures began to peel away with staggering, uneven steps, lurching into the streets. The crowd around them began to shrink. The Vaim joined their fellows in the distance, wandering the empty streets in an aimless parody of the daylight crowds.

"There. Much better, right?" the cheery young man said, thrusting a hand toward them. "My name is Aften. This is my sister, Tamsa."

Thislen looked down at the hand, but he made no move to take it. With a scoff, Tamsa folded her arms across her chest, staring him down.

"Oh, for goodness' sake!" Mila shouldered past him to clasp Aften's hand in her own. "It's nice to meet you. My name is Mila, and this is—"

"Don't." Thislen interrupted flatly. "We don't know who they are, remember? Or how they're alive. Or how they got ahold of *magic*." That was what the pendants and the glowing orb had to be. *No one has been able to make new magic in centuries. The only people with old magic are rich and powerful—or ancient. Which one are they?*

"You being overprotective is starting to get old," Mila huffed.

"How we're alive is simple enough. We're wearing the same pendants as you two," came the smooth interjection before Thislen could retort. The third shadow had slipped off the roof and now made his way toward them through the thinning crowd of ghosts. He pulled his hood down, revealing skin the color of walnut wood and close-cropped hair as dark as pitch. "My name is Darran."

Thislen frowned, stepping forward to put himself between Mila and the strangers. She frowned and elbowed him to one side, standing next to him instead.

The Vaim had finished wandering away, drifting around the abandoned city much like the residents did during the daylight hours, tending to whatever business and errands the dead had. The market square was almost empty—except for the five living people in front of the castle's gates.

"Don't worry. We're not here to hurt you. We'll explain about the Vaim, and the magic in the pendants. We'll even answer any questions you have. I just want to make certain you're alright first. Not hurt or anything, right?" Darran asked.

"We're fine," Thislen said, words short and curt.

Darran lifted his hands to placate the waspish Thislen.

"We *are* fine, and Thislen will stop being rude any moment now," Mila said, her own words clipped and crisp.

"I don't mind it. You'd be surprised how often people get angry when they're surprised." Aften said brightly, moving to sit on the empty counter of a nearby stall. He swung his feet. "Welcome to the Astera no one has ever told you Solfolk about." He spread his arms wide.

"I am not angry," Thislen groused.

"Solfolk?" Mila echoed, leaving Thislen's shadow.

"The people who live in the city during the day. You two are Solfolk," Tamsa said. Her voice was low and melodic, like the bubble of a kettle before it began to whistle. It was also dismissive and terse.

"Oh."

Darran gestured at the stalls and their locked chests of goods that sat behind the low wooden counters. "Why don't we sit down while we talk?"

Why don't we not? I just want out of here.

Mila was already halfway there, however, leaving him no choice but to follow. She sat on a worn wooden chest with a great iron padlock. Thislen perched on the other end of it. Darran sat beside Aften, who merely spun where he sat to face them with a broad grin. Tamsa leaned against the end of the stall, still watching the proceedings with a sour frown.

"First things first. We call ourselves the Nattfolk. We live on the island all the time, though it's rare that we come out during the day. We don't want to arouse suspicion. However, we also don't go out on those ships, either."

"All the time," Thislen scoffed. "No one can live on the island all the time. The Vaim kill everyone left on land." His hand chopped through the air with every word, as if it would hammer home the truth—despite the evidence that was quite literally before his very eyes.

If people could survive on the island at night, Percivan wouldn't have died. I wouldn't have been stabbed! My father would have come home! If there were a way for people to survive, then his life would have been drastically different. It went against everything he knew.

"No, they don't. They didn't kill *you*," Darran said. He was as calm as a still pond in the face of Thislen's rising ire. Thislen had a sneaking suspicion the man had had this conversation before.

"I've seen it up close. I watched them kill Percivan only a few days ago!"

"That was you?" Aften asked suddenly, feet stilling. He leaned forward. "In the rowboat? We saw it floating offshore after the Vaim got bored. We could tell someone was in it, but we couldn't get to you!"

Thislen shuddered, picturing these shadowy strangers watching him through the night. *What did they think when I let go of Percivan's hand? What did they think when they saw me asleep, as though nothing had happened?* Never mind he had spent that night sleeping fitfully, and only because he had been dizzy and exhausted and burning with fever. "Why didn't you stop them? Why didn't you help us?" he demanded.

"We don't *control* the Vaim," Tamsa said, "and we arrived after they had already gotten to him. From the shouting, we thought they had gotten to you, too. We thought you were dead."

Thislen went cold. "Well, I wasn't."

Aften nodded sagely. "They don't kill everyone. Just some people. Most of the time, we aren't aboveground before the sun goes down. It's difficult to get to the people the Vaim *do* go after when we're at a disadvantage."

"And how did you find us?" Mila asked curiously. "Astera is a large city."

"We follow the murmurs to the ones they spare. They watch and whisper and gather close. Never as many as there were for you two, though," Darran answered easily.

Spare? Thislen thought, his shoulder burning for a moment. *They think I got away, but a few days ago, the Vaim* did *want to kill me. They almost succeeded. What's changed?*

"So, you're saying the Vaim...don't kill everyone," Mila said, leaning forward intently. "What happens to those who have survived? We... Solfolk believe anyone on the island dies."

"Because we fake their deaths. All of them. After that's done, we give them a choice. The same choice we're about to give you," Darran said placidly.

"What choice?" Thislen asked, reluctantly rising to the bait.

"From the markings on your faces," Tamsa said, taking Aften's glowing stone and holding it up beside Thislen's cheek, "you two were sentenced to execution on the island. So you must be criminals. Are you?"

"You didn't answer my question."

"No, I didn't."

"Tamsa," Darran said, a sharp edge to the word. He looked Thislen over. "You have to understand, we're a society made up of those that Astera has cast aside. Our history begins with the remnants of the nobility who survived the kingdom's coup."

Which explains where they got magic from—old, powerful, wealthy families who pass their trinkets along. Thislen felt his hackles rising. Was this just another Ruling Council?

"We've grown through those who were abandoned or sentenced. We've been living here as long as the Vaim have, a few hundred years now. The thing that makes *our* people safe, the Nattfolk? It's the same thing that will make *you* safe: the lie that you've believed until now.

"The Solfolk think no one can survive on the island. We don't mind letting them think that. It keeps us protected. Our numbers aren't very large. We're descendants of criminals from generations back, noble lines that are thought to have died out, and those caught on the island by accident. All of them live with us," Darran said.

"Can't I just...go back?" Mila asked, voice wavering. Her hands were clasped tight on her lap.

Of course she wants to go home, Thislen thought, resisting the urge to put his arm about her shoulders. *Mila has a family who will mourn her.*

"No, I'm afraid not," Darran moved to kneel before Mila, meeting her gaze. "We Nattfolk have rules about this for a reason. Think about what would happen. If the Solfolk knew that only *some* people died on the island, they'd stop using it to execute people."

"Yeah, instead of leaving you to a fate like this, they'd just lop your head off," Aften said easily, popping the 'p' as he swung his hand like a headsman's axe.

Thislen shuddered. Mila stared at Aften with wide eyes in a pale face.

Darran let out a soft cough, lifting a hand to cover his mouth and the faintest of smiles. "Yes, exactly—that's one problem. Another is how many people would test to see if they were an exclusion; if they would be spared. We don't *know* why some are allowed to live. It would end more lives than it would save. How many Asterans would fall to the question of 'will I or won't I?'"

"And what about actual criminals? Those who earned their place here?" Thislen asked.

"Few and far between, we've found," Darran answered.

"You can tell. There's something about their eyes and the way the Vaim watch them," Tamsa said.

"Those who did something truly violent, we send to other places. Let them try and live their lives out somewhere else. Those who were trapped by accident, or who committed lesser crimes and were made examples of? We invite them to stay here with us." Darran smiled up at Mila.

"And that's the choice, isn't it?" Thislen asked.

Mila looked at him, clutching at the shawl tied around her shoulders.

"That's right," Aften's feet swung back and forth. "Depending on what your story is. You can stay on Astera with us Nattfolk and become one of us—or you can be escorted to a ship and seen to another shore."

Thislen felt his heart soar. *No coin needed; I can get off this damn rock once and for all!* It was everything he had wanted, and these Nattfolk had laid it square at his feet. His gaze met Mila's. It was freedom. It was safety! They could be free!

Except Mila's expression was solemn and grave, heavy as lead. This choice was not as easy for her; that was clear as day. Thislen's elation faded, and reality crept back in to tether him with tangled threads of duty once again.

She's right. I have to figure out Percivan's last request. She wants to be able to return to her family in peace. It's not just about me anymore. I owe them. He owed the sailor and his father, too—when else would he have such an opportunity to learn about the Vaim?

Still, he couldn't help but give a subtle shake of his head, a silent plea to Mila to say no, to let them go. Maybe he could live with the ghostly voices in his head if only he were somewhere else. Maybe they could *try*.

Mila drew herself upright, adjusting the shawl around her shoulders. "I would like to trust them, even if you don't. So, I'll make it easier and go first." She turned to the Nattfolk. "My story begins with a member of the Ruling Council."

Thislen sagged forward, burying his face in his hands. *She knows I won't just leave her with strangers. And why the hells not? What is wrong with leaving her behind?*

He knew the answer. Thislen did not want to add a pair of curious green eyes to the ghosts that haunted him.

Thislen listened as Mila recounted everything. *Everything.* Including how she had met him and what she knew of his sentencing as well as her own. The only thing she left out was his tie to Soren Bestant.

Well, at least she doesn't know *everything. Otherwise, I would have been in a different sort of trouble altogether,* he thought as her story drew to a close. He lifted his head, only to meet Tamsa's intent gaze. Something in Mila's tale had caught her attention, and she was regarding him with thinly veiled suspicion.

"You *are* injured, then?" Darran asked as the tale concluded, giving Thislen a worried look. "Your shoulder—"

"Is fine," Thislen said quickly. "It's been seen to."

"You're both perfectly innocent of all crimes and thus sentenced to death?" Tamsa asked, the Nattfolk's every word dripping with sarcasm.

"I never said I was innocent," Thislen said, regretting the words as soon as they left his lips. All three Nattfolk turned to stare at him intently.

Stupid!

"Then your sentence for the murder of Percivan Coppermund is true? And you kidnapped a woman?" Aften asked, eyes wide with giddy interest at the possibility of such intrigue.

"No, I tried to help Percivan get off the island, and the woman they said I kidnapped was taken when I was an infant; I couldn't have done it." He left out the fact the woman had been his mother, Elena. "I meant I was a thief before this, that's all."

The three Nattfolk had a quick and silent exchange, expressions changing as if they were holding an entire conversation that no one else could hear. Aften seemed eager, encouraging, and soothing. Tamsa just seemed angry. Darran collected both of their views with raised brows and soft nods, then turned back to the waiting Solfolk.

"Actually, if you can pick locks, then you would be quite an asset to us," Darran admitted.

Tamsa sighed. Loudly.

"So, they do get to choose?" Aften asked, feet swinging wildly with his growing excitement.

Darran nodded. "They do. Alright, Thislen. Mila. Stay…or go? The choice is yours."

"Let's discuss it, Mila," Thislen said quickly.

"No discussions we can't hear," Tamsa said smugly.

"Why? Are you afraid we'll run off?"

Darran gave a small, apologetic smile. "Yes, it's happened before. And I must warn you—if you try to run or escape after choosing to stay, we will escort you off the island ourselves. So, staying or going, you need to make your choice here and now."

Thislen burned at the ultimatum. His eyes narrowed, as if by squinting he could see the invisible threads of these strangers coiling out towards him, binding him all the tighter to Astera's shores.

I never wanted to know this island; I never wanted to get attached. But I could *stay. I could be a part of whatever community they have. I could grow into a dutiful member of their society.*

But what if this is just another broken system I can't fix? Can I become a tool in their hands? Can I trust these strangers? Will I have the chance to change my mind later if this doesn't work out?

Because I could leave. *I could start fresh somewhere else,* anywhere *else. I could sever every thread I have but Mila's and get her somewhere safe and far away. I could write to Olen when we arrive wherever and discharge my debt to him without any fear.*

All my secrets can leave this kingdom with me.

Go, a quiet part of his mind urged. His lips parted.

"Well, I'm staying."

Thislen choked, jerking around to stare at Mila at the words. He had almost forgotten that she, too, had a choice—and that he had known what that choice would be before she spoke. She would never leave her family behind.

If my father were still on this island, would I leave?

The worst thing about Mila's choice was that she had no idea what her decision meant to him. *Her* thread was already tied fast around him, binding him to her. Thislen cared if Mila were safe and happy. He cared if she was alone with strangers. Her choice took his away.

Mila stared steadily at the trio of Nattfolk, a gleam in her eyes and a lift to her chin that said she would not be swayed. Thislen felt the cold shock of her choice in his fingertips. There was a pit in his stomach as he turned back to the expectant gazes now fixated upon him.

You could still go. You could just leave her, part of himself whispered.

No. I can't.

"I'll stay," he said numbly.

What have I done?

Darran smiled, rising swiftly to his feet and clapping his hands together. "It's settled then. Welcome to the Nattfolk. We'll take you down to the Commons next. Aften will escort you both below, and Tamsa and I will handle faking your deaths."

"He means that he'll take a few chickens and spatter the blood everywhere so it looks like the Vaim tore you to shreds and didn't leave anything behind," Aften said, a note of dark glee in his voice.

Mila looked shocked. Thislen, however, recalled the words spoken earlier by Brother Restan. *"Sometimes the Vaim don't leave enough behind for us to perform the last rites."* Had those gruesome deaths with no bodies actually survived the menacing specters? Had they all been rescued by the Nattfolk?

"You'll have to excuse Aften," Darran interjected, pushing the younger man to his feet. "He's a born Nattfolk, and his father was, and his grandfather, and his great grandfather, too. Sometimes he forgets that all of this is more harrowing for you Solfolk than exciting. It's a change of pace for us."

"Oh. Right. I definitely did forget about that," Aften said, nose wrinkling. An awkward smile crossed his face, and he rubbed the back of his neck. "I'm sorry. I'll take you both somewhere you can rest. You're safe now, and you've got us to help you settle in. We'll teach you how everything works and have you in bed before dawn."

"Because now we're all *best* friends," Tamsa said dryly, walking away.

Darran gave the pair of Solfolk an apologetic smile and followed, leaving only Aften behind. Their guard and guardian stood, bouncing gently on the balls of his feet as he waited.

Thislen stood, turning to Mila. His voice dropped to a low murmur, back turned to the Nattfolk. "Are you sure you want to do this? If we stay with the Nattfolk, you don't get to see your father again."

"I know," she whispered back. "I have a condition for staying." She called after the retreating backs of Darran and Tamsa, almost out of sight.

Everyone froze.

What is she doing? We aren't in a position to negotiate—they made sure of that! Thislen thought, heart racing.

"What condition?" Tamsa called back, an edge to her voice.

"I want to know everything *you* know about the island and the Vaim." Mila glanced at Thislen. "That's what you wanted to know, wasn't it? For Percivan," she said, voice low enough now that only he could hear.

She's risking us both for that?

Still, Thislen glanced toward the darkness beyond the soft globe of yellow light cast by Aften's orb. Twitching creatures still lurched through the city streets like mad drunkards, their eyes distant pinpricks of hellfire. They trailed sharp talon fingers over the walls and shutters of windows of shops and homes as they passed. They gathered in small clusters of shadow. They seemed innocent enough, but Thislen knew better. It made the hair on the back of his neck stand up to remember how they caressed and welcomed their victims to the realm of death.

"And what makes you think you can make a demand like that?" Tamsa asked.

"The Vaim aren't even that interesting. Why do you want to know about them at all?" Aften held his globe aloft to study the nearest monster.

"Because for Thislen and I, everything we've known about them is a lie. And they still kill people! What people? Why? Doesn't any of it make you curious?" Mila asked.

"Not really," Darran said with a shrug. "That's just how it is."

"Mila has a point. They had Percivan and me cornered and they killed him—but not me. It makes *me* curious," Thislen said. "Everything I have ever thought to be true has been turned upside down. What was supposed to be the end of me *isn't*." The words fell from his lips so quickly they nearly tripped over one another.

"Yes, so excuse us for wanting to know why!" Mila stamped her foot on the ground.

Thislen felt the weight of all those questions settling onto his shoulders as if the City Guard were trying to bear him to the ground again. He gritted his teeth and looked up at the spires of Perilee with an almost accusatory glare.

All the answers are in there, and I don't know if I want them. He had a sneaking suspicion the Vaim needed him for something, and that it had something to do with their touching his blood.

As he turned back, Thislen noticed Mila was trembling very gently as she waited for the Nattfolk to respond. *She's upset,* he realized a heartbeat later. *Of course she is.* Her confident and strong facade was just that—a mask she wore. She was trying to adjust to a world she still couldn't see.

I have more practice facing the hells and coming out the other side. I've got to be more patient. One of us needs to be grounded.

"That seems like a lot of questions, and I'm afraid that even we don't have all the answers. We'll do what we can to help you find enough answers to satisfy you, I suppose. If you wish it. We've got a member of the Night Council who used to—"

Thislen cut Darran off as he whirled toward the Nattfolk, holding up a hand. "Wait, the *what* Council? You lot have a Council, too? Is it another group of corrupt, mismanaging, entitled, power-grubbing—"

"Hey!" Aften yelled plaintively.

Tamsa was across the distance between them in two great strides A hand dropped to her belt and closed around the hilt of a sheathed knife, nearly hidden amongst the gray and brown scarves tied around her hips. Thislen lifted his fists instinctively, bracing himself for a fight.

"Tamsa! Thislen! Knock it off, the both of you!" Darran snapped. There was a steel edge in his voice. He stepped between them with no hesitation, arms spread wide. "It's a valid question after what they've been through, Tamsa. Our Night Council is nothing like the Ruling Council, so far as I know, Thislen. You can even sit in on a few of their meetings and see for yourself if you'd like."

"What is *her* problem?" Thislen snapped, his initial question forgotten.

"Her father is the head of the Night Council; that's her problem," Darran said, pushing her a bit further back. "Walk it off, Tamsa."

Tamsa spat on the ground and whirled, storming away. Thislen scowled but dropped his fists. He, too, turned and walked a short way into the darkness to catch his breath. *If it's some kind of power-hungry cluster of thieves and cutthroats, this might be more dangerous than striking out on our own.*

Mila appeared at his side, laying a hand gingerly on his shoulder. "Are you alright?"

"I'm fine."

"Are you certain?"

Thislen didn't answer. Mila stood beside him for several moments with her arms folded across her chest, letting the silence settle around them. She was close enough that her shoulder brushed his. She stared up at the castle's distant spires. He followed her gaze, watching how the reflection of the stars and the moon gleamed on the glass high above the city.

"Why do I get the feeling you aren't being honest with me? About Perilee. About yourself. About everything."

A wash of guilt ran over Thislen in a wave that started hot, ended cold, and left him feeling strangely alone. *Alone is how I* should *be,* he thought, ignoring the ache in his heart. Yet he couldn't meet her gaze.

What would be the harm? What's the worst that would happen if I just gave up and trusted someone?

"Are you two just about ready?" Aften called from behind them.

"Ready for what, precisely?" Mila called, turning toward the globe of light behind them once more.

"To go to your new home, of course!" the affable young man said with a broad grin.

Home. Ha. Thislen scoffed quietly, glancing up at Perilee one last time before he turned away.

Mila took his hand, surprising him with the warm and familiar gesture. He looked down at their interlaced fingers, then back at the Nattfolk. Somehow, he was reassured. He couldn't quite figure out why.

"Yes, we're ready," she said firmly, her resolve strengthening his own. "Let's go and see what the ancestors have brought us now."

Aften tucked the glowing orb into its round leather pouch, plunging them all into silver-lit darkness. In the night, all five passed through a sea of dull red eyes that could not see them as they made their way home.

11

The entrance to what the Nattfolk called 'the Commons' was tucked away in a familiar graveyard near the castle's outer wall. It was the same graveyard where Thislen's father was buried, where he had fallen asleep just a few days ago—which led to him missing the last boats off the island. The quiet plot for the dead was also only a few streets away from the Ominir Apothecary, which Thislen hadn't realized until they walked through the great iron gate set in the low stone wall surrounding the grass and headstones.

Thislen was careful not to say anything. He refused to even look at the headstone as they passed. *They don't need to know.* Darran walked with them, leaving Tamsa at the gate into the graveyard. He closed it behind them all.

A single Vaim lurched between the headstones. They made their way deeper into the silent, shadowed yard where pale statues and obelisks loomed out of the gloom like the ghosts of other lands. The roughshod cobblestone path that wove between them met another that stretched from side to side, forming a 'T' intersection. The narrow upper path was lined with grand mausoleums, silent stone houses carved all over with heavy metal doors closed fast.

These housed the remains of the oldest of Astera's noble families, including a long unused one for the Royal Family Asteran that sat proudly at the head of the intersection. The small buildings on either side were emblazoned with their familial name above the door and decorated with carvings that spoke to ancient tales. One was covered with hounds and horses, a family of hunters. One was carved with elegant scrollwork and the fading remnants of gilt. Jewelers, Thislen presumed, or metalsmiths. Several were painted with fading frescos, the paint crackled and flecking off.

Once, these were the proudest families in Asteran history. Time had not been kind to them. Several no longer existed. Thislen could make out some familiar names, limned in moonlight. Barnweir. Artaith. Bestant. There were other names as well, unfamiliar ones that must have been lost to the coup that dethroned the last king of Astera.

It was to one of these long-abandoned stone buildings that they made their way. The name above the door read 'Sivivan,' though it was almost hidden by a tangle of wild ivy. The heavy metal doors swung open without the faintest creak from the hinges. The rust-clad lock, it seemed, was purely decorative.

The inside was painted in pitch black shadows only made darker by the moonlight behind them. A single great coffin carved of stone sat in the center of the floor. The walls were lined with empty stone cubicles and only a few had names carved into them. Thislen had expected it to be covered in a layer of dust, but it was spotless.

They were immersed in a darkness that pressed so close Thislen felt smothered. A heartbeat after the door closed and the shadows swallowed them, Aften pulled the softly glowing orb from its pouch again.

"Useful, isn't it?" he asked happily, holding it up and studying the shadows cast by his fingers on the walls.

"How did you get ahold of magic, anyway?" Mila asked quietly.

Aften shrugged. "It's from the age before magic disappeared from Astera. It's lasted a long time, passed down through my family. Every decade or so, it gets a little dimmer. At least that's what my father says. One day, it might go out. Then it will just be a pretty stone."

Darran walked around the far end of the coffin. His fingers traced over the carved filigree there. He pressed in. The hidden stone button slid home without a sound. The short top wall just before the Nattfolk swung open on a concealed hinge to reveal a door.

The entrance was slim and square, and all that was visible in the faint yellow light of the orb was a few worn stone stairs that stretched interminably down into nothingness. The tunnel was narrow. Thislen would be able to touch both of the rough stone walls with his arms outstretched.

He watched Aften with raised eyebrows as the Nattfolk crouched to slide through the relatively small entrance. He crawled, hunched over, down the steps until he could stand comfortably. The shadows cast by his fingers around the globe danced wildly over the walls. Once he was through and the light was steady, Aften called back to them.

"Alright! Come on down. Just watch that top step."

Thislen turned to Mila, a frown on his features. *I don't want to go down there.* He pictured the weight of the earth above him, smothering, choking. They had no idea what was at the bottom of the steps! What if this was all some elaborate trap?

Mila knelt beside the entrance to the tunnel. Though her hands were curled into small fists, she began to ease her legs through the opening.

Thislen grabbed her shoulder. "Mila—"

"Thislen, will you trust *me* this time?" Her gaze was steady, green eyes intent.

He stared. *She has...a plan?* Mila had never once asked her to trust him before this. Thislen slowly let go of her shoulder. *She trusted me first. She found the courage to turn Soren down and come with me. She braved Astera at night because I asked her to. She faced the Vaim.*

So why don't *I try trusting her? Once. See if it works.*

"Don't worry, Thislen. I'll go first." Mila awkwardly climbed down a few steps. She was shorter than Aften, though not by much, so she paused one step above their Nattfolk escort.

Thislen willed his shoulders to relax before he followed suit. The stone steps were very, very old. Despite being carved from the solid rock of the island, each step bowed slightly in the middle, worn away by the passage of countless feet. Thislen was a step below Aften and Mila before he could stand upright, facing the dark maw of the earth and whatever lay below them.

Once the three of them were down the stairs, Darran's head appeared at the small door. "Alright. Remember that new arrivals go straight to your father, Aften," he said firmly.

"I know." Aften said quickly.

"That's an order from your captain."

"I know, I said! I know."

"Don't get distracted."

"I don't *always* get distracted." Aften protested.

Darran laughed softly as he vanished from view. The coffin's small stone door closed behind them with a grinding sound. Mila's hand found

Thislen's with a gentle squeeze. He gave one back even as he debated pulling away. *Is she trying to reassure me, or does she need the reassurance?* he wondered.

Aften led the way down the carved stone stairs in silence. Their footsteps echoed off the rough-hewn walls around them, scrapes and taps that jumbled together and made it sound as if a small army were creeping through the belly of the earth beneath the city. The buttery yellow light from the glowing orb swayed and twisted, casting leaping shadows around them as they traveled down, down, down. The unchanging walls around them stretched on forever ahead and behind. Thislen glanced back once. All he could see were stairs marching up into the darkness. Looking ahead was much the same, but the stairs wound down. He wondered if they would ever reach the bottom.

A dull orange glow began to burn somewhere below them. Aften's orb was a softer light, and the closer they came to the bottom step of their descent, the more it was overwhelmed by the bright, flickering light of torches just out of sight. A murmur began to grow that rang faintly up the stairs. It reminded Thislen for an uncomfortable moment of the Vaim and their whispers. The smells of cooking meat and fresh bread reached their noses, a heady perfume that made his mouth water despite himself. He hadn't thought that buried beneath the earth, he would find the promise of warmth on his skin and food in his belly.

Aften tucked the orb back away into its pouch on his belt. With a broad smile and an out swept arm, the Nattfolk led the pair around a sharp left corner at the base of the stairway. A short tunnel led to the source of the chatter and light.

The walls of the tight passage opened up into a sweeping cavern split into two tiers. Its heavy stone ceiling was held up by equally large stone pillars that spanned the space. Tunnels and openings of various sizes and heights were carved into the walls as far as their eyes could see. Many were visible, their mouths open wide to hold stalls and shops, but just as many were blocked off with curtains made of brightly colored fabrics or obscured behind stands made of wood. Spindly rope bridges were suspended from the ceiling and crisscrossed the second level, meeting at platforms anchored to the pillars or the broad stone path of the upper level.

Every inch of the walls was a riot of color. The stone was painted with fanciful murals or draped with rich cloth hangings. Stalls had jewel-toned awnings, though there was no need for them below the ground. Everything was lit from above by lights dangling beneath the walkways or hung on great hooks from the ceiling. Low braziers of polished iron gave additional light. They warmed the cavern until it felt as balmy and brilliant as a bright spring day. The smoke that scented the air did not hang heavy, instead vanishing somewhere above.

And there were crowds! Far more people than Thislen had anticipated milled about the great open room. Men and women gathered in small clusters or tended to their various tasks. Children ran along the swaying bridges above or wove through the crowds below, playing games with sticks and stuffed cloth balls. The stalls that stood open in the middle of the cavern were filled with foodstuffs and surrounded by an assortment of tables, chairs, stools, and benches in a hapless mismatched jumble. Many of them were crowded with people eating and talking. Along the walls were stalls showcasing the wares of craftsmen. Menders worked alongside tailors and cobblers. Somewhere there was the faint rhythmic chime of a smithy. The second tier held more specialized services, tucked away in curtained alcoves with their signs painted on the walls. Healers, scribes, and a goldsmith, so far as Thislen could see.

People moved between the shops, getting food and drink. They ducked into curtained alcoves, chatted and jested, laughed, or worked on their wares. They all seemed to know one another. Considering there were, by Thislen's guess, more than a few hundred people, the familiarity surprised him.

What was less surprising was that their arrival garnered a wave of attention. Heads turned toward them, and conversation lulled before it took on new strength. The gossip of their presence spread like wildfire, hissing around the room like a breeze. At the same time, however, they were offered welcoming nods and waves of greeting. Some few smiled at their gap-jawed, slack faces. After a moment of observation, the residents of this hidden village turned away and let them be.

Aften waited politely for the pair to finish taking everything in, humming idly to himself with his hands tucked behind his back. Thislen was the first to close his mouth with a click of teeth, but it was Mila who broke their stunned silence.

"This is...incredible! Where are we? Below sea level?" Mila asked curiously, stepping out into the cavern and turning slowly to admire the paintings that trailed the walls.

Thislen followed, glancing at the fresco above the tunnel entrance. It was the same image as the magical pendants that hung around their neck

— Astera, with Perilee gleaming brightly at the top tier of the city. The paint was faded, chipped in places, but just as obviously had been restored before. He assumed it would be painted again and again, on and on into the years. It was the only painting of the city that he could see on any of the walls.

"Sort of. We're below the water, but we're also inland, beneath the foot of the Spine. Technically, I think we're somewhere underneath Perilee," Aften said, pointing toward the distant stone ceiling.

Thislen shuddered.

"Since the castle is the highest point of the city, being under it means we're safe enough from any flooding. They covered it in my history lessons once," the Nattfolk continued.

Thislen let out a low whistle. Despite all his earlier misgivings, there was a lightness in him now he couldn't quite explain. The Nattfolk were not a mass of murders and pickpockets, as he had assumed. They all seemed very normal. The soaring ceiling and the bright walls of the Commons helped him feel that the earth wouldn't swallow them forever. *Most important, the Ruling Council will never find me down here.*

"This is quite the setup. You said all these people are descended from the criminals, nobility, and lost?" he asked.

"The oldest families are descended from the lost nobility, yeah. They had to go into hiding after the coup of the Royal Family all those years ago. Criminals and accidentals followed afterward. Then they all stayed and had children, and their children had children. Sometimes there's no outsiders brought down for years. Sometimes we get two in one day, like you," Aften answered with a grin.

"What happens if a criminal does something against your rules, like steal?" Mila asked curiously, watching the milling crowds before them.

Aften gave a one-shouldered shrug. "We have an honor code down here more than rules. The people who can't keep to it end up on ships bound for other shores. We don't execute people down here. We just... send them away. There are a few merchant ships we work with. Well, that's not exactly true. There's one captain who knows about us. He used to be a Nattfolk himself. I don't think he tells his crew who or what they're transporting."

Thislen turned his head quickly, fixing on Aften like a hound that had caught a scent. "So you *can* choose to leave here for the daylight? Become a Solfolk again?" he asked.

Aften's brow creased into a frown. "I don't know if I was supposed to tell you that. In certain circumstances, I guess. He was raised as one of us, not rescued—and he got permission from the Night Council."

"Some rescue," Thislen sighed. Mila pinched him. "Ow!"

"What comes next?" she asked.

Aften laughed behind his hand at their exchange. He was still grinning when he lowered it to speak. "Easy! We go introduce you to my father, Councilman Rendyn Sivivan. Then you get a few suggestions of what to do around the Commons. Apart from picking locks, do either of you have any skills?" he asked as he turned to lead them through the throng of people. The flow of foot traffic parted before them and left them in a small bubble of space, as if the Nattfolk didn't want to crowd them too closely and spook them.

Is it out of respect or wariness?

"No, no special skills," Mila lied calmly. Thislen raised an eyebrow quizzically at her response when Aften wasn't looking. She clasped her hands together beneath her chin in a silent plea for his discretion. After a moment, he nodded.

What is she playing at? He wondered if he should have agreed to trust her.

They left the great central chamber of the Commons behind for a broad stone tunnel, shored up with wooden posts every few lengths like a mine shaft. Wooden doors were fitted into the walls, six on either side, at regular intervals. The tunnel ended in a wooden wall set with plain double doors. Lanterns glowed merrily on either side.

"This is the Council Chamber," Aften informed them proudly, gesturing at the unassuming doorway. "My father's the Head Councilman, so our family lives on the other side of this room. I don't know if they're meeting right now or not. Wait here, alright? Right here! Don't move!"

The Nattfolk was gone before they could say anything, disappearing behind the door and closing it quickly behind him. Thislen sighed, turning to pace down the corridor.

"Where are you going?" Mila asked, catching his arm before he'd gone more than two steps.

"Away. Nowhere. I'm just...I didn't ask to be rescued to this place—" he began.

"But you did. You agreed to stay."

He paused, staring at the smooth stone floor of the corridor. How could he explain to her that he couldn't leave her on her own? How could he tell her that even if he had gone on a ship, he would have had to return to Astera? Even if he never wanted to. How could he tell her about the spirits of Vern the sailor and Percivan Coppermund and his father, weighing on his soul? He couldn't explain all of it to her, not without telling her—

The door opened. "No meeting. Thank the ancestors. My father's just doing some paperwork. Come on in," Aften said, as bright as the noontide sun.

As small and slim as it had been, the chance to sneak away had passed. Mila towed him in her wake as she headed for the door, and Thislen was left with little choice but to follow along.

MILA WAS EXHAUSTED. She didn't think anyone had noticed yet, though it was difficult to tell with Thislen and his frowns. *Even if he did notice, he isn't the sort who would say anything.* She hoped it was because he trusted her to know her own limits and not because he didn't care. Her steps were a little slower, her boots scuffing on the stone more often. Her shoulders were hard to lift. Her eyes felt like they were weighed with lead, and she had to fight to hold them open. Her mind was filled with a cottony fog.

Even the majestic cavern of the Commons had only woken her for a few moments. Nothing could truly counter the fact that she hadn't been able to sleep since her sentencing.

The haze she was in kept the distant flutter of something dark just out of her reach, wrapping her in numbness like a down-filled blanket. Everything she had experienced in a single night remained politely in the back of her mind for her to examine later if she wished. For now, she had made a decision that led her and Thislen below the earth to present themselves to the nocturnal mirror of the Ruling Council.

I will not be cowed by this one.

Mila stepped through the door, pulling Thislen along behind her.

The Council Chamber of the Commons was just a wider portion of the broad stone tunnel that preceded it, hung with strings of lanterns on heavy wooden beams and from hooks in the stone above. A few candelabra glowed atop the large wooden table that had been polished to a gleam, which filled the bulk of the room. For such an elegant centerpiece, it kept ramshackle company. Benches and chairs of various sorts surrounded it on all sides, haphazardly tucked in or left askew a short distance away. An impressively large wooden chair stood at the far end of the table, just before the door that Mila now knew led to a living space. The only other door in this room was the one they had entered through.

There were no tapestries on the walls, nor any frescos. There were no decorations at all, in fact. Apart from the table, it was very utilitarian.

It looks stern, she thought to herself. As stern and uninviting as the lone figure seated in the carved wooden chair at the far side of the room.

Leaning over the head of the table was a man who was very clearly related to Aften and Tamsa. They had the same strong noses, dark and riotously curly hair, and hazel eyes. The man was taller and broader in the shoulder than his son. The only sign of age upon him was in the smoky gray streaks that ran through his hair. His clothing was as plain and serviceable as that of a farmer. Hunched over his work with a quill racing across the parchment in front of him, he looked entirely unremarkable.

"May I present my father, Councilman Rendyn Sivivan," Aften said, with a lift of his chin.

"And you, I gather," the councilman said flatly, "are Mila and Thislen. Aften gave me a rather hurried account of your rescue." He never looked up from the work in front of him. Rendyn reached over, pulling a book closer and scanning the pages.

"That's correct," Mila said hastily, not giving Thislen a chance to speak. She didn't know what he would say, but she *did* know that he could be rather abrasive. She worried that he would offend this leader of the underground. *If Thislen gets us put on a ship and sent far, far away because of his opinions on Councils, my entire plan will be ruined.* When she spoke, she made sure she was polite and calm. "We've decided we would like to stay and work, if you will have us. Both of us."

"Eager Solfolk. That's an oddity," Rendyn said, mostly to himself. He pulled over another piece of paper and made a note. "Aften."

"Yes?" The young man took a half-step forward.

"Their skills?"

"Thislen's got skills as a thief, he said. Mila said she hasn't got much of anything, really. I was thinking we could ask Darran if—"

"I did not ask you for your opinion. I asked for your report. Where are Darran and Tamsa?"

The interruption seemed to take the wind from Aften's sails, though his smile remained firm. "Up above. They're working on the deaths. Might have to find a pig to make it believable instead of a chicken since there are two of them."

"Then they'll return soon enough. Tell me, are you two tired?" He finally looked up from his papers to meet Mila's gaze, holding her fast. It was as if she were a mouse staring into the eyes of a serpent. That kind of gaze made it impossible to lie or look away unless you were released.

"I…I am a little tired, yes," she stammered. "I found it difficult to sleep before…" The words faltered and trailed off, the distant emotions she had tucked away threatening to break through like water from a dam.

Part of her was a little pleased to catch a glimpse of Thislen's frown easing into something that *almost* resembled concern at her admission. He turned to Rendyn and gave a single curt nod.

"I see. And you, Mila. You said you have no notable skills at all? What did you do all day?" he asked, setting his quill into the inkwell with the soft clink of metal on glass.

"I worked in a shop, is all. I can count alright, I suppose," she said, hoping her tongue did not trip over the half-truth.

"What sort of shop?"

"A florist."

It was technically true. There had been several afternoons she covered for Evelie and Ivan.

The thought of her neighbors made her eyes sting and her throat close. It made her think of her father, too. *They think I'm dead.* How broken were their hearts? How afraid were they tonight?

No, I can't think about that now. Not yet. She forced her mind away from those paths.

"Ah, I see. Thank you both for your honesty. We will discuss your possible roles among us tomorrow. It's getting early, and I will need to speak to Darran and Tamsa before we make any final decisions. You understand, of course." It was not a question. "Aften, take them to the Barracks and then return." Rendyn picked up his quill again, waving his free hand in dismissal as he bent back to his papers.

"Right away, sir!" Aften said brightly, giving his father a two-fingered salute. He turned to the pair. "You two will fit in just fine after a few days. Don't worry." He ushered them out of the room, silencing Thislen's protests before he could make them.

They walked back through the tunnel toward the Commons. Thislen offered Mila his hand as he passed. It surprised her. Usually, *she* was reaching for *him*. She caught up to him with the last of her flagging energy, lacing her fingers in his with a grateful smile. He drew her along as they followed Aften into the crowds of the cavern's market.

Cocooned in the chatter of the people around them, it was easier to speak to Thislen at last—without Aften noticing.

"I'm not going to stay here. I *know* that with your help, Thislen, we can find a way out of the city. We can still get to Barred Town on the other side of the island. As soon as it's safe. And as soon as I have my answers about the Vaim. What do you think?" Mila offered in a murmur as she wrapped herself around his arm.

He shot her a sideways glance, brows rising toward his dark hair, then looked dead ahead. "I could probably live happy in Barred Town. What will we do there?"

She sucked in a breath as she considered it. *What sort of life could I lead?* What life did she *want* to lead? How far could a restless spark inside her carry her when Astera was so small? All she truly knew was that this wasn't where she would stop. This wasn't where she was meant to be.

"We could be siblings or cousins," she mused. "We could run a pawn shop and see strange things every day."

"There're plenty of good places to set up a pawn shop. I can steal what we can't afford. We can make it all work, then write your family that we're safe. Ah— hush." He cut the conversation off, stifling any further plotting as they left the noisy Commons and passed into another, quieter, tunnel. This one ended a short distance ahead of them in a long low chamber.

Row after row of stone bunks had been hewn into the walls, each with a low stone lip and wide enough for a single person. Some were strung with curtains to offer privacy. Many had decorative items on the small stone shelves tucked along the back wall. More than half of the bunks did not have a straw pallet tucked into them, leaving them entirely bare.

"Welcome to the Barracks! Everyone lives here unless they're part of a family, and most of the children move out to these bunks over time. Families get proper living caverns. Space and privacy and all that."

"Most children move out?" Mila echoed. "Then, do you sleep here?"

"Oh, sometimes! Family of the Council Members aren't supposed to move out at all, but I like it better out here. My father wants Tamsa to succeed him, I think. They're a lot more alike." Aften's cheery exterior fractured, his smile faltering for a heartbeat or two.

Mila smiled softly at the young man. "I understand. Sometimes parents just want you to be something you're...not."

Mine wanted me to be safe, and near, and happy that way. Why couldn't she have done that?

Aften's smile returned, quieter than before and full of unspoken gratitude.

It was perhaps just after midnight, though it was hard for her to judge the time without the sky. The Barracks were mostly empty since it was the middle of the Nattfolk's day. A few people milled here and there, tidying up or tucking new purchases away in their private cubbies, from what Mila could see.

"Any empty bunk is yours for the claiming. I'll go get you guys the basics. Go on! Anywhere you like. I'll be right back." Aften said, gesturing at the hollows in the walls as he headed toward the back of the chamber.

The bunks ran four high, spaced out just enough for ladders to be carved directly into the walls beside them. Mila relinquished Thislen's arm, at last, to wander the small space, watching him from the corner of her eye as he assessed the options.

Thislen settled before she did. He picked a second-row bunk with an empty cubby above and below. Mila took the first-row bunk, perching on the cool stone.

"These are…quite nice," she managed. She didn't know why she was lying. It made her heart ache terribly to be down here. She longed for the colorful quilts tucked away on her ship, in her cabin, in her own bunk, somewhere in the ocean above them.

Father would be there. He'd hug me and kiss my forehead and scold me for being up so late.

A bitter, dry voice in the back of her mind spoke up. *Well, you wanted something different.*

Why had she *ever* longed for something different?

Aften returned, arms laden with two sleeping pallets, some curtains and string, plain blankets, and two sets of plain sleeping clothes. "Here you are. Let's get you all set up. You're tired, and it won't hurt to turn in early."

Thislen climbed down to help Aften set up their two small bunks, leaving Mila to hold their nightclothes and watch. She was grateful for them taking over. The haze she had wrapped herself in was wearing thin. It was all she could do to hold back the flood of her emotions. They were building up inside her, their tension like a pot that hadn't yet boiled.

They finished quickly enough. Aften bade them a simple goodnight and left as quickly as he had appeared in their lives.

Mila climbed into her cubby, pulling the curtains closed and changing into her sleeping clothes. It wasn't easy, but she couldn't imagine changing in front of strangers. She listened to the rustle of straw and cloth above her as Thislen settled in.

She lay down with a heavy sigh.

"Hey," Thislen called down.

Mila parted the curtain to peer up at him. He was hanging over the edge of his bunk, hair sticking out every which way.

"Don't worry, Mila. We'll sort all of this out."

"I'm not worried at all," she said, smiling as she pulled the curtain closed again.

They both knew she was lying.

12

"I'm sorry, we're what?" Thislen stared at the pile of mottled gray and brown clothing in his hands, brows raised.

"Joining our patrol," Darran repeated with a grin.

They can't be serious. This has to be some sort of trap.

"You're saying that you're willing to let us back out of this hole in the ground?" He began to pull on the dyed linens and leathers.

"Don't take that the wrong way; it's a very nice hole," Mila added behind the curtains of her own bunk below.

Thislen rolled his eyes with a scoff.

Aften beamed at Thislen as he rolled out of his bed and swung to the floor. "Absolutely willing! It'll be good fun. We'll teach you guys how to run the rooftops. The Vaim don't form up there for some reason. And we'll show you how we get ahold of the supplies we can't craft for ourselves."

"Let me guess," Mila called. "Does it involve stealing?"

"We prefer to call it repurposing," Aften said, waggling his eyebrows outrageously as Mila peered between the curtains of her bunk at him.

Darran laughed and gave Aften a gentle shove. "He's exaggerating. We only take one or two things from each place, so we don't leave much of an impact. We hope people think the things we've taken have been mislaid instead of stolen."

"And we don't take *everything*. Some of our residents might be criminal stock, but not *all* of us." Tamsa's every word was scathing and acidic.

"We mostly take scraps from the craftsmen, it's true," Darran agreed easily enough. "We work with a farmer who used to be a Nattfolk to get our vegetables and some livestock products—like meat and wool. It's the metals, really." He pulled a small roll of parchment from one of his pockets and studied it. "Ah, we need two spindles this time, and a few salves."

"Why us?" Mila asked, emerging from her bunk at last. "I mean, why me in particular, I suppose. I know why you would want Thislen."

Thislen wasn't entirely paying attention as he studied Mila in the plain leathers. There was a way she carried herself in her traveling clothes and in these clothes that he liked better than when she was in skirts. It was a lift to her chin and a squaring of her shoulders. The only thing that was off about the whole thing was the colors.

She looks like a shadow. She should be dressed like sunshine, he mused. More like she had above-ground, but with all the confidence she was discovering below.

But looking like a shadow is the whole point. Thislen shook his head and adjusted the dark hood around his neck, banishing the thought. He perched on the edge of Mila's bunk, gaze drifting to the rest of the Barracks while Darran and Aften explained things that didn't matter to him.

The Barracks were bustling at this early evening hour. There was a short line at the privies. Several people were changing out in the open, and several were shuffling off toward the Commons and the heady smells of breakfast. The occupants of the space were just as Aften had told them —young people who chatted and jested and played with no chaperones to guard them. No elders were peering in to ensure everyone behaved, and the atmosphere was bright and noisy.

Sort of a breath of fresh air after all the stilted manners of Astera during the day.

Wait, don't do that. Don't like them! Thislen scolded himself.

"We figured locking you up down here wasn't going to make you feel like one of us," Darran said easily, drawing his attention. "Scout work is a suitable transition. A little of this and a little of that."

Tamsa whirled from where she stood, several feet away. Her face was twisted in a scowl as she stalked toward them. "Darran, you weren't supposed to tell them that!" she spat.

"Why not?" Darran was as unflappable as ever, meeting Tamsa's fire with cool calm.

"Now they know we—" She cut herself off abruptly, glancing at the pair.

Thislen arched a brow. *So they don't trust us. Good. They shouldn't.*

"Don't...what?" Mila asked.

Darran cleared his throat. "Look, we know all of this is a surprise. We know you didn't expect to survive at all, much less have your entire life change because of it. We want to make this as easy as possible for all of us. That's all."

The Scout Captain was utterly sincere. Thislen could tell. He didn't look away from their eyes as he spoke. He felt one of those invisible threads wound around him tighten a bit. He believed Darran. He trusted him.

He *hated* that he did.

If I didn't like him, betraying him would be easier.

Mila bound her hair back with a small leather tie, shoulders rising in a shrug. "I wouldn't mind walking around in the open air, you're right. All this stone is a little...oppressive."

Thislen grimaced. Oppressive was an understatement. He had been trying to avoid thinking about the sheer weight of the earth above him, held aloft by—what, exactly? Nothing. He shuddered.

Thislen had spent his entire life sneaking aboard different ships to sleep on their decks in the open air at night and wandering the city streets by day. His hidden corner in Astera was beneath the crumbled roof of a Church of the Ancestors in the Gate Quarter, where the breeze could wander freely through the eaves. Sometimes being underneath a *roof* was almost too much to bear, let alone all of Astera.

The mass of stone pressed in around him, making it feel all the more difficult to move. Between the Commons itself and its welcoming occupants, Thislen wondered if he would ever be as free as he had been before.

Maybe not, but you also won't be alone anymore, part of him thought. *Isn't that worth it?*

He pressed the heel of his hand to his temple to push the thought from his mind, even as he fought down a pang in his chest. *No, with the threads of these people and their wants and needs tangled around me and with the weight of the earth above, I feel trapped. Not found.*

Not that I would ever tell them that, he mused. *They seem like they'd want to make me feel comfortable. They'd try and help. I can't afford that.*

Can I?

"Thislen?" Aften said. From the tone, he had said it before, and Thislen hadn't heard him.

Thislen looked up to find everyone staring at him. He dropped his hand from his head. "What?" he asked dumbly.

"Ready to go?" Aften asked, a slow grin curving up the corners of his mouth.

"Almost. How long did it take you to argue Rendyn around?" Thislen stretched as he stood.

Tamsa's ears turned red, and she scowled. "That's Councilman Rendyn to you!"

"That's *enough,* Tamsa. He's trying to get a rise out of you." Darran ushered her a few steps away, lowering his voice to speak to her.

Aften grimaced after them. "To be honest," he said lowly, "it took ages."

Satisfied, Thislen gestured for Aften to lead the way. With no further ado, the five of them headed toward the Commons and the winding shadowed staircase to the surface. Mila fell in beside him as they walked.

"What was on your mind?" she asked, voice soft and low.

"Threads," Thislen admitted.

"Threads?"

"It's something my father said." He explained as they began to climb the dark stone steps, guided by Aften's small glowing orb. "He used to say that every person you met was a single thread."

"And every time you get to know them better, their thread wraps tighter around you. Meet enough people, and those threads become ropes, and those ropes become nooses. The more of a hold people have on you, Thislen, the more likely you will do something stupid for them, like a puppet. You'll be pulled around by those threads, manipulated by them. Only accept the threads you want." Linden's voice echoed in his head.

Nothing good will come from telling Mila all of that.

"Weaving into a tapestry?" Mila guessed, smiling at him from the gloom.

That just confirmed his suspicions. *She thinks it was something sweet and innocent.* Thislen felt another pang in his chest. How could he explain that all of his father's lessons centered on staying hidden, unremarkable, and alone?

I wish I had been thinking something sweet. He *liked* Mila's company. He loved the idea of sneaking away with her and settling down in Barred Town and just living. No more running, no more worrying about being bound to others. He could have neighbors he knew. He could do the same thing every day and sleep in the same place every night.

I'm tired, he realized, steps slowing for a moment. *I'm so tired of hiding.*

"We have to wait when we get to the top," Darran said, shattering the comfortable silence between them. It made Mila jump beside him, her shadow leaping on the tunnel wall. Her shoulder brushed Thislen's.

"There's a bell down below," The scout captain continued, "that rings when the sun has set. Then the different crews can go aboveground. The farm crew will go outside of town to gather our purchased supplies and provisions. The water crew will go fetch fresh water from the parks in the Grand Quarter. They each have their own tunnel systems.

"And then there's us. We take care of our list and patrol the city itself. We're in charge of watching for new arrivals and making sure nothing strange is happening. It's usually pretty quiet, honestly. Halfway through the night, another crew takes over, and we come back below."

"Sounds like a really boring job," Thislen commented.

Tamsa barked out a laugh, surprising him. Her cheeks tinged faintly pink out of nowhere, and she cleared her throat. "Yeah, well. We're younger. All the boring jobs fall to us. Eventually, you age out. I'm going to inherit my father's seat. Darran will be in charge of the crews and managing their lists someday."

"...and Aften?" Mila asked after a moment.

Aften flashed Mila a broad grin. "Oh, I'll probably stick to this until I figure out something else I'm good at," he said airily.

Tamsa rolled her eyes.

What's going on there? Thislen wondered.

They reached the top of the stairway just as a great bell tolled somewhere below, reverberating off the stone around them. Aften tucked the orb away in its pouch, letting darkness settle around them.

Darran pulled a small lever on the wall. With the grind of stone on stone, gray light filtered into the staircase. The darkness had lightened only enough for Thislen to see the others around him as ink-black shadows in the gloom. He half expected them to turn and reveal glowing red eyes. The thought made him shudder.

Darran climbed out first. Mila followed after him. As Thislen crawled into the mausoleum, the scout captain opened the door, and red-orange light poured across the floor.

It was moments before sunset. The sky was pouring darkness down from above, but the lowest reaches still burned red and purple. Thislen stepped out into the open air like a man starved, soaking up the fading light and breathing deep the scent of salt brine on the air.

That had been one of the strangest parts, he realized. The earth below smelled stale and crisp, but the air up here felt *alive*. The breeze played over his face. He closed his eyes, feeling it tickle over his nose and stir his hair. He could feel the others nearby, but he ignored them.

Mila laughed. Thislen's eyes opened, and he watched her spin with her arms out, dancing in the graveyard. She stopped at his side, following his gaze to the setting sun.

"I never thought I would miss the sun," Thislen said softly.

"I never thought I'd have to." Mila's hand found his own.

Thislen's heart sank as the last of the light struggled to hold on to the sky. He knew it would lose. Darkness would settle in around them, and who knew when they would get to see the light again?

"It will be a good moon tonight," Aften said, stretching expansively.

Darran glanced up at the blue orb that hung low in the sky above Astera. "Good. That will give our two new recruits time to adjust to working without lights."

"Without lights?" Mila echoed. "But Aften has—"

"It's for emergencies only," Tamsa interrupted, "because we don't want Solfolk to know we exist, remember? What would they think out on their little toy boats if they saw lights bobbing around the city in the dark?"

"What she means," Darran said with infinite patience, "is that we use light very rarely and only when we aren't on the rooftops. They're for detail work, not general patrolling."

Aften slung an arm around Thislen's shoulders. "Don't worry, though! It's easier than you think. Your eyes will adjust."

Thislen shrugged the arm off, taking a pointed step away from the Nattfolk scout. "Alright. Let's get this over with. We're here. Walk us through what to do."

The last of the light was swallowed by the velvet cloak of nightfall, and their evening began in earnest. Thislen and Mila were led by the Nattfolk to the streets, where the Vaim had already appeared from the shadows. Unlike the last two times he saw the creatures, they did not so much as *look* at him now, let alone swarm.

The spirits wandered the streets like the ghosts they were, hands twitching and heads cocked as they lurched along. Their whispers were softer today, barely a sound on the breeze now that they weren't directed at their prey. In some twisted parody of the city during the day, the Vaim filled the city like Asterans did. They clustered together and wandered back and forth down the street like townsfolk on errands, though their hands were always empty. They leaned on the walls, watching one another pass. They took jerky, staggering walks through the parks side by side. The only true difference was that none of them went inside any of the buildings.

They made the hair on the back of Thislen's neck stand on end, stalking him or not. He did his best to ignore them as the Nattfolk did, reaching up to press the magical pendant against his skin and ensure it was still there.

Mila shied away from the Vaim every time one came too close. Her eyes were wide. She clutched at Thislen's sleeve, pinching his skin beneath the fabric until he winced, but he didn't stop her. He understood her unease all too well.

The Nattfolk had no fear of the Vaim. They wove their way around the shadows for the most part, but every now and again, they would reach a cluster that blocked the road. Without hesitation, the three scouts reached out and gently guided the Vaim aside with their bare hands, like the spirits were nothing more than unruly sheep. Thislen doubted he would be so brave as to touch them and risk drawing their attention. He did, however, begin to test his ability to pass near them unnoticed as they walked.

They found a low stone wall a few streets away from the graveyard and used it and a nearby crate to climb onto the rooftops. Thislen found it far too easy, a familiar gesture that somehow soothed him as the city walls fell away. It reminded him of climbing the thick vines that entangled the church he lived above. *Had* lived above.

Are my things still there? Can I go and get them?

A clatter behind him made his head turn. Mila was struggling to pull herself up. Thislen nearly bowled Aften over to help her, catching her wrist. Darran appeared at his side and took her other arm. The two of them hauled her up easily. Thislen gave her an encouraging nod as she found her feet, and she returned it with a weak smile.

Jumping from rooftop to rooftop wasn't difficult for the most part. Alleyways were narrow, and streets often had decorative arches somewhere that made convenient footpaths. Their way across the city's heights was full of minor detours taken to find easier ways across or around, but it was still more effective than weaving through the streets and dealing with Astera's shadowy nighttime occupants. Every leap brought with it a glimpse of dull red sparks in the black below and the impression of jumping over an endless, deadly void. Thislen quickly picked up the tricks of traveling the rooftops, especially with the little bits of advice called out softly in the night from the Nattfolk.

"Can't we just walk on the streets?" Mila was panting, hands on her knees to brace herself. She was the slowest member of their team.

"We try not to push our luck," Darran explained. "The Vaim may not see us, but we don't know how the magic in the pendants work. Someday it might weaken enough that we can't touch them anymore, the way the light in Aften's orb is weakening. Last night was plenty of chance for us. Now we'll be cautious for a moon or so. We can spend a few nights walking the streets after that."

"Better safe—" Tamsa began.

"Than ripped into shreds." Aften finished cheerily.

So they leapt across the gaps and walked the sloped, shingled rooftops of the city, weaving their way around chimney stacks. Darran pulled out their list as they reached the Guild Quarter at last, and they set to work. What they needed were handfuls of small bits and pieces. Two separate houses in the craftsmen's Quarter were visited, a single spindle taken from each. Four smithies lost a double fistful of metal from their scrap buckets of bent nails and broken tools, and a single iron bar apiece. One tanner lost a strange comb with no teeth that smelled rank and sour.

"They had to explain to me what it was and draw it on the list. Look," Aften said, showing the sketch of the strange instrument to Thislen with a grin that gleamed brightly even in the nighttime. "It's to help strip the hair from the hides and to rub the mixtures in that make it supple."

Thislen wrinkled his nose. The 'mixture,' he knew, contained urine and lye, amongst other things.

With the Guild Quarter goods finished, the scouts wound their way back upwards through the city. They dropped off the rooftops to duck into a few houses along the way, pinching sugar and salt a single spoonful at a time. A sheaf of parchment disappeared from a scribe's shop, though a few coins were tucked into his register book. They took several jars and bottles from other houses—though only one from each and already empty. It took them the better part of the evening to hunt down everything they needed and pack it away into the satchels that Aften and Tamsa carried slung over their backs.

Thislen proved himself useful early on by deftly picking locks on doors and flipping the latches open on windows using a dagger and a length of line he had taken from a fisherman's house.

Mila was very, very good at finding what they needed once they were inside. Her initial reservations were much relieved after she learned they never took more than one of anything from anyone, and never from a home that didn't have plenty to spare.

"And they just explain it all away?" she wondered aloud as they stepped into the night air once more, the bite of impending autumn setting in around them.

"They think they lost or misplaced them, we hope. Sometimes I'm sure they blame the Vaim. You know, just something that happens on a haunted island," Tamsa drawled, waving a hand languidly through the air.

They kept on through the list until the last few items. "These will be easy. It's just common medicinals, and we've got a usual place for this one. It's a shop run by someone who used to be one of us a few generations ago," Darran said as they dropped off the rooftops onto yet another street.

It was a quiet dead-end street, with a closed inn yard at the top, Thislen realized. There was a tailor, a potter, and a florist...

He froze. *No, no wait—*

Mila stood beside him, her expression slack-jawed and blank as she recognized the Ominir Apothecary. The Nattfolk turned toward the door. Her teeth clicked as she snapped her jaw closed, features twisting into something stern and challenging. Her chin was lifted, and her hands had balled into tight fists.

They wouldn't dare, Thislen hoped for their own sake. He sucked in a sharp breath as Darran pulled a key from his pocket. A key!

The Ominir's secret is that they have some tie to the Nattfolk? Is that what Soren Bestant learned? Maybe this tie is why Soren was after her in the first place! But no—if he knew about the Nattfolk, he wouldn't have sentenced us to the island. What does this mean? Thislen's mind raced.

"Stop *right* there!" Mila said, voice ringing out like a clarion bell. She planted her hands firmly on her hips.

Darran did stop. He turned wide-eyed toward Mila.

"You will not touch that door!"

"Mila—" Thislen tried to interrupt.

She held up a hand to stop him, storming across the cobbles toward the scout captain. "How long have you been robbing my father's shop? How many medicinals over the years? How many salves and tinctures and bundles of herbs? Are you why our lists sometimes don't match up? My father said he must have forgotten to mark things down, but it was *you*, wasn't it?" Her voice grew louder with every word until she was shouting. "You *stole* from us!"

"You're an Ominir?" Aften asked, eyes wide and voice hushed.

Darran's hands were up, brows raised so far Thislen half expected them to vanish into his hair or fly off his head entirely.

"You have no right to steal from my family! Give me that key. I won't stand for this." She insisted.

"Mila, we've—" Tamsa began, reaching gently for Mila. The soothing tone she used sounded strange coming from her lips.

Mila jerked her arm out of Tamsa's reach. "What? You're what? You've been stealing from my family for generations? Is that how you justify all of this? This is the way it's always been, and this is the way it will be? How many things were you going to take tonight?"

Thislen and Darran both began to wave their hands wildly, gesturing at Aften to remain silent— but they were far too late.

The chipper Nattfolk scout was looking down at the list in his hands. "Just six bottles of bruise salve and—"

"Six!" she said shrilly. "Six! Do you have any idea how long it takes to make a bottle of that salve? No, you don't, or you wouldn't be taking six bottles from one shop!"

"Mila—" Darran tried.

"No!" she said firmly. "My father is *grieving*; he won't have the energy to replace what you insist on stealing!" She stopped speaking abruptly, eyes filling with tears. Mila threw her hands up, fleeing the quiet street.

Tamsa started after her, but Thislen caught her arm. His steady dark-eyed gaze met her hazel one. "You have a key. It's an arrangement between agents of your Nattfolk. Am I right?"

"Yes," Tamsa said emphatically.

"How long ago?"

"I don't know. Generations?" She rolled her shoulder as Thislen released her arm.

"Let me explain it," Thislen said. He didn't wait for permission as he started away, though he noticed the look Tamsa exchanged with Darran and Aften from the corner of his eye. He ignored it, just as he ignored the fact the three Nattfolk headed for a stack of crates against the wall to climb onto the rooftops and follow after them.

Let them keep an eye on us. We'll be here until they relax enough for us to slip away, he thought sourly. Thislen broke into a jog and rounded the corner to follow Mila.

She was difficult to see, a darker shadow amongst the insubstantial bodies of the Vaim. She was threading her way through the crowds of spirits like they were regular townsfolk, her ire driving any hesitation from her mind. Her gaze was fixed on the cobbles beneath her feet. Her hands were curled into fists. Tears ran silently down her cheeks.

Thislen slowed as he caught up, walking beside her in silence for a while.

"Do you want me to tell you what's happening?" He asked at last, watching a Vaim they passed as it lifted a long-fingered hand to feel its dull, featureless face. They weren't far from the graveyard that would take them back to the Commons.

Mila stopped abruptly. Thislen didn't notice for a step or two. He stopped and glanced back as she wiped her cheeks and chin dry.

"What do you mean?"

"I mean, they had a key. They said the shop owner was a Nattfolk agent, like the ship captain they know and the farmer. Do you want to know about how they must have an arrangement with your father, and probably had one with *his* father, and most likely his father's father?" Thislen asked. "Because if you want to keep being angry and sad, I don't mind either way."

"I don't understand," she said, fingers slowly uncurling.

"You were distracted." He turned toward her. "Alright, as far as I can tell, you have some tie to the Nattfolk. Your father is part of providing them with what they need. That's why he defended the mistakes in your ledgers and didn't care about the discrepancies. That's probably also why the Nattfolk have a key."

"Does this have something to do with Soren, with why he wanted to marry me?" She asked slowly, her heart in her eyes.

Thislen sucked in a deep breath. He knew what answer she wanted, and he knew what answer was *honest.* They weren't the same answer. *She wants me to tell her that this is the only reason he ever noticed her.*

"I think he may have found out that you're a descendant of one of those old noble families, somehow tucked away and surviving all this time. I think Olen knows, but he didn't tell you. But I don't think Soren Bestant knew about the Nattfolk; otherwise, he would never have tried to execute us this way."

He must have wanted her for something else, something I don't know about yet. Every time he thought he found an answer, it just revealed more questions. It was going to drive him insane.

Mila stood with her head hung for several moments. Fresh tears dripped from her cheeks. Her hands were clasped so tightly that her fingers were white.

Thislen waited, tucking his hands into his armpits to keep them warm in the cool evening air. He was content to let her sort through her thoughts for as long as it took.

She looked up at last, lips parting—but she didn't speak. The color drained from her face. Her eyes grew wider and wider, fixated on something just past his shoulder.

Thislen whirled where he stood, finding himself in the shadow of a Vaim. It was growing, swelling up in size until it loomed over him, twice as large as it had been before—

And it was reaching for him.

13

Everything hung suspended for one perfectly still moment. The dark shadow of too-long fingers reaching toward Thislen's face was outlined against the dark blue of the night sky and barely silvered by the moonlight. The red eyes sparked and brightened in the Vaim's face, a glimmer of orange in the hungry heart of them. The whispering turned into a groan as the monstrously large Vaim lunged for its prey.

Thislen felt his heart slide down into his stomach as time flowed slowly around him. His breath caught in his chest. His pulse roared in his ears. *They said the pendants would hide us,* came the thought, followed by a sudden chill from head to toe as he realized it wasn't true. Outstretched talons cut across his vision in dark streaks. Beyond was the black pit of the Vaim's body.

There's no escape.

"Thislen!" Mila screamed, though she sounded impossibly far away. She grabbed onto his arm even as he thrust it back to push her away from the reaching specter. The Vaim nearby turned their heads one by one, fixating upon the pair. None of them moved any closer but the large one before them. Yet.

"Look out!" roared a voice from above as the reaching fingers began to close and Thislen fought down the wild scream that bubbled in his chest.

Aften threw himself from the nearest rooftop onto the Vaim, flattening the creature to the cobbles. He rolled smoothly to his feet just in front of Thislen. With a mighty shove, the Nattfolk sent them both stumbling into Mila.

"Run! Run, damn it! Go, go go *go go go*!"

The three of them turned and fled before the specter could rise, tearing down the streets at a dead run.

Three times. Three *times now! Why can't these bastards leave us alone!?* Thislen thought. He took the lead after only a few steps, flinging himself around corners and threading his way through the Goods Quarter as quickly as he could. Mila was right on his heels. Aften followed after them.

Hells, we're running away *from the graveyard!* he realized. The clatter of their passage echoed off the empty buildings around them, accompanied by a growing crescendo of ghostly murmurs. As they passed each Vaim, the specters turned to follow after them, lurching slowly along in their wake. There was no urgency to their hunt tonight. They knew, as Thislen did, that there would be more of them around every corner.

What do we do?

"Why are they following us?" Mila shrieked as they charged around another corner.

Thislen ducked under a shadowy arm. "You said they wouldn't!"

"Turn, Thislen! Left!" Aften shouted.

Thislen twisted to the left and turned into an alleyway, dodging a bin and leaping over a crate. He heard a clatter from behind and paused to glance back. Mila was righting herself against a wall. Her expression was pinched, her cheeks pale.

Aften was wild-eyed behind her. "There's a side gate in the castle wall." He pointed.

The alleyway they sheltered in cut across two streets, dead-ending at a tree-lined avenue at the base of the wall of Perilee. The wall was barely visible above the ink-dark masses of leaves in the night.

Thislen took off without another word. The three of them dashed across one street and back into the shelter of the alley with no interference, though they bore the scrutiny of the Vaim as they passed. A small cluster of dark shapes appeared at the mouth of the other alleyway before they could break free—more ghosts gathering at the end to block their way. They were trapped.

No. No, not like this, Thislen thought.

With a loud roar, he dropped his shoulder, ducked his head, and charged. Thislen barreled into the creatures at full tilt.

There was utter chaos for a moment as the young man and the spirits collapsed in a heap of tangled limbs. Cool skin was against his face, his arms, his hands. He felt the soft-and-solid give of bodies beneath him as they tumbled to the ground, the impact of something real and tangible. It drove the air from his lungs. He looked up into a pair of wide round eyes that were as red as low-burning coals, the air full of hissing around him.

A hand grabbed his arm and hauled him away from the heap. Aften shoved him forward again. They were through! The three of them ran on with Thislen flanked by Aften and Mila. The outer wall of the castle loomed above his left shoulder.

There was a gap in the trees that lined the wall ahead and a cobbled pathway to a small door. The promised side gate was real! Aften reached it first, slamming into the wood. He turned to Mila, catching her wrist and dragging her closer.

"Put your hand on it!" He insisted.

Mila hesitated. Aften did not. He lifted her arm and slapped her palm flat against the wood.

The lock clicked.

Thislen's eyes grew wide, his mind going absolutely blank as Aften pushed open the door and yanked him and Mila into the gardens of Perilee.

She is *of noble blood.* Old *noble blood!* The realization only spawned a thousand new questions in his mind, one louder than the rest. *Who is she?*

It may not have been him that the Vaim had been reaching for at all.

MILA FELL to the gravel as they were pulled inside, panting heavily as she stared at her hands. Her palms and one knee smarted, her chest was afire, and she found that core of heat pooling inside her stomach again, an ember that threatened to burst into flame.

What was *that? How did I do that?*

She looked up in time to watch Aften collapse onto the gravel beside her, kicking the gate just as the Vaim appeared at its mouth. It closed with a resounding *thud.*

Thislen collapsed onto his back beside her, limp as if he had fainted. For a moment, she feared he had until she realized he was gulping for air like a fish out of water. Aften groaned as he rolled onto his side, just as winded.

Mila studied her palms with a frown as she climbed to her feet, trying to calm herself. They were out of danger, though she didn't know how.

She had never been this close to Perilee in her life. The path they rested on led to the side of the castle, winding through beautiful, empty gardens. No Vaim wandered between the neatly trimmed hedges or the manicured flower beds. No one strode along the gravel or cobblestone paths. The gardens ended at the rocky cliff face of the Spine that the keep was built up against, laden with climbing vines. The spires of Perilee above them were outlined in liquid silver by the moon, but the bulk of the castle sat in shadows where the light didn't reach.

Crickets hummed, and frogs from the babbling fountains called their chirruping calls in the sudden calm, returning to their nightly symphony in the wake of the slamming gate. Thislen shifted behind her, draping his arm over his face with a groan. She could see the gleam of fresh blood from his shoulder on his clothes, dark and wet.

The heat inside of her flared right back to life at the sight. She rounded on Aften. "You said they wouldn't see us. You said these pendants would keep us safe!" Mila shouted. "What was *that?*"

"Which part?" Aften groaned.

"Why were they reaching for Thislen?" She demanded, folding her arms across her chest. She barely smothered the urge to stamp a foot. *I am getting my answers, and I am getting them* now.

The thief lowered his arm slowly at her words, a frown on his features. Mila stared. *Does he have a guess? Is it because he's a Bestant?*

"I…" Aften trailed off. He rolled slowly to his feet. "Mila, I don't think they *were*."

"Then who? There was only Thislen and me there. Who else could they have—" She stopped abruptly, sucking in a sharp breath of air. It felt as if she had been doused in cold water. "You aren't trying to tell me that they wanted *me*. Why would they be after *me*?"

Her mind leapt instinctively to the revelations of this evening. *Thislen said I might be part of some ancient noble bloodline, long since thought vanished. He said I have ties to the Nattfolk at some point in my family's past. I've been up here all night, and nothing happened until just now! That* can't *be it.*

What had changed?

Aften looked up at the wall behind them, then out over the gardens as he avoided her gaze. He didn't answer her question.

"How did we open the gate?" she pressed him, brow beetling down into a deep frown.

"Mila," Thislen called, holding up a hand. She took it, the thief's fingers closing around her wrist as she helped to haul him upright.

"Well," Aften said idly, rubbing the back of his neck and shifting his weight from one foot to the other, "I think it was unlocked."

He is absolutely, without a doubt, the worst liar I have ever met, she thought, a flush creeping up into her cheeks.

Thislen stretched and winced, gingerly feeling over his injured shoulder. "Aften knows more than he's letting on."

"I do not!"

"You do." Thislen leveled his dark gaze on the scout until Aften turned away.

Mila looked between them both. "I know he does. Aften, please. I need you to tell us what you know. You *did* promise me answers." She forced her shoulders to relax, trying to cool that molten core inside herself. She would win more of those answers with honeyed words than with sharp ones, she reminded herself. Earnestness and a gentle touch might get more out of the Nattfolk than anything else.

Mila touched his arm, and Aften's nonchalance broke. He hung his head.

"You know something about the Ominir line," Thislen said suddenly.

"What makes you think—" Aften began, poorly concealing his unease as he fiddled with the ties of the orb-pouch on his belt.

"It wasn't a question."

Mila looked between them both again. *Thislen's been thinking about this longer than I have. What does he know that I don't? Why hasn't he told me? And Aften knows something now, too? I asked for answers. Why is no one telling* me *about things that pertain to my life?*

"What do *you* know about my family line, Thislen?" She demanded.

He winced.

I knew *it.* She folded her arms over her chest again, a flush building in her cheeks. "What exactly is going on here?" Every word that fell from her lips was low and taut.

Thislen lifted his hands placatingly, giving a soft shrug of his shoulders. "All I know is that Soren wanted to marry you because, as he said, you were from one of the noblest bloodlines around. That information alone was enough to convince Olen to let me help you run away right then and there. I don't know what *he* knows." The thief gestured to Aften.

My own father kept secrets from me. The thought was bitter on her tongue. She trusted Olen more than anyone else in the world. It felt as if the very earth beneath her feet had changed to sand. *He kept life-changing secrets from me!* There was a dull ache inside her chest at the thought. Her eyes stung. Mila blinked rapidly, refusing to let the sting turn into anything else.

She turned to Aften, lips parting. Thislen raised his hand, forestalling any remark she might have made. *Wait,* the gesture said.

Aften paced back and forth, his fingers laced together. The pair watched him march to and fro, to and fro, with the gravel crunching under his boots. Mila huffed softly. Her patience was wearing thin.

"Alright, the thing is that no one outside of my family is supposed to know," Aften burst out a few steps later, whirling to face them. "*I'm* not even supposed to know. I only found out because I wanted to see what Tamsa was reading. I stole them. My father keeps the journals locked up in this big chest, but the key was under his mattress, and I found it years ago on accident, so I already knew how to open it. So I did!" The words tumbled over one another in his haste to confess.

"And?" Thislen asked.

"And they talk about a lot of things I don't really understand, I guess. It's just the early accounts of the Nattfolk and the building of the Commons, and something about staying safe. They even have records of when the Vaim began to appear. And then it goes into how they work, sort of, and I *know* that was where it said something about the Ominirs."

Mila's eyes widened. "Because we were there when they were building the Commons?" She asked hopefully. *Please don't say that I'm—*

"No, in connection with the Vaim, somehow," Aften admitted.

She felt hot and cold in turns, and the abrupt change made her feel dizzy. "I don't want anything to do with those nightmares!"

"Look, I might be remembering it wrong. There were a lot of them, and I read them ages ago. I just know that the Vaim were tied to the royal family and a bunch of the nobility, and the one name that kept popping up was Ominir, Ominir, Ominir. And you *did* open the gate! So there has to be some truth to it." Aften was desperate.

"You just said the door was unlocked!"

"I lied."

"He lied," Thislen confirmed, voice sharp and brows drawn sharply down. His face had a strange gray pallor, though it could have been the moonlight. "I can't *believe* you risked our lives on what you vaguely remember from journals you didn't even understand. You risked everything on what, the fact that Mila *might* be able to open the gate, according to her last name that you learned only *just* before?"

"We were running the wrong way. We couldn't get to the graveyard. What choice did I have?"

"You almost—" Thislen started, only to cut himself off.

Mila held up her hands. "Now, stop it. Stop! Clearly, this is going to take a little bit of time and talking to get through. Why don't we sit down somewhere?" She gestured to the nearby gardens. Placed here and there amongst the hedgerows were stone benches, half hidden in shadow.

"I am not about to sit down and discuss all of this like we're having tea," Thislen said sourly.

Aften had already fled toward the nearest seat. Mila began to follow the Nattfolk, but Thislen caught her arm and stopped her in her tracks.

"You're not the only person affected by all of this, Mila," He whispered. He paused as if he had more to say, but nothing further left his lips.

"I don't think you have any room to talk, Thislen," she hissed, "because you're not telling me how any of this affects *you*. You are being selfish right now. This is the most decent Nattfolk person we have met, and he is the only one offering us any answers. I *need* answers. My entire life has been upended because of questions I didn't know I had to ask. If we're going to survive in Barred Town, I need to know *my* secret. You already know yours." She pushed him off of her.

"Mila!" He followed.

"Where are Darran and Tamsa, Thislen? Do you think they'll let Aften tell us these things when they've caught up to us?" she demanded.

She was satisfied when he frowned. He stayed silent.

"We may not have a chance to learn this much again, so if you could kindly stop picking a fight with me, I would appreciate it." She marched on to the bench.

The jab had the intended effect. Thislen's rising ire cooled as quickly as it had begun. He swallowed whatever secrets had been on the tip of his tongue and followed after Mila in silence.

I just need my own answers right now. I can ask him for his later.

"Alright," Mila sighed as she settled on the bench beside Aften, "let's start at the beginning."

Aften ran his tongue over his lips. "How do they tell the Solfolk about the coup?"

"My father had me read a history book on it," Mila said, leaning forward.

"What did it say?"

"King Barleyn Asteran was a tyrant. People were dying of a plague that ran rampant throughout the kingdom. No one could work the fields, so those who weren't ill were starving. He did nothing to help," Mila recited.

Thislen's expression was hidden as he turned away from them, staring up at the spires of Perilee.

"The Vaim were peaceful spirits of our ancestors that walked among us. Watching their children die in droves pushed them into madness. They became dangerous and started attacking people. At that point, the Ruling Council had no choice but to stage the coup and save the kingdom. They killed or banished the nobility that remained loyal to the royal family, assassinated the royal line, and built the ships to protect us all."

Thislen snorted.

"What, what did I say?" Mila insisted.

"Nothing."

"Maybe he knows that isn't entirely true. I mean, according to what I read, you have everything out of order," Aften said.

Thislen glanced back at the scout. "What is the order you learned?"

"The famine and the plague came *after* the coup, and the Vaim came after the plague. They didn't exist before then."

Mila scoffed. "That makes no sense. Why would there have been a coup in the first place if everything bad happened *after*?"

Aften shrugged. "I don't really know. The Sivivan family, my family, is descended from one of the loyalist nobility. They only knew that they had to hide after the coup. Then they detailed how the wall was built around the Grim Quarter and how they changed its name to the Gate Quarter. Then came the plague, and the Vaim began appearing after that. They said the last of the royal family left the Nattfolk not long after that to try and solve the problem."

"What?" Thislen said quickly.

"The king's line still exists?" Mila asked, eyes wide.

"They disappeared centuries ago, so we don't know," Aften clarified.

"And the Vaim appeared *after*? After the coup, after the plague, you said. Why? And where exactly do the Ominir tie into all of this?"

"I'm not entirely sure!" Aften protested. "I just remember that they mentioned the Ominirs, and the Vaim, and..." He paused, looking up at the castle. "And someone going to Perilee."

All three of them stared at the elegantly carved walls of the castle, shadowed and massive, looming over them. Thislen shrank back as if the thought of going near the castle burned him.

Mila remembered what the thief had heard in the whispers the night they fled through the city. Time and again, she and Thislen were drawn toward Perilee. *Everything has changed. Everything I know has disappeared. Even my father doesn't feel like the man I knew. The only thing I have left is this castle.* That spark inside her that had insisted on leaving home in the first place now wanted only one thing: answers.

And they're in there.

She stood.

Thislen caught at her wrist, grip firm but not unkind. "Mila, please. I don't want to go in there."

"But that's where the *answers* are, Thislen. The answers to why all of this is happening —not just to me, but to the Nattfolk, to the entire kingdom! We have to look. We *have* to." She insisted, turning to them both. "We don't know what else we don't know."

Aften shook his head quickly. "No, I can't. We're not supposed to. We've always been instructed to steer clear of the castle. It's a rule. We're not even supposed to come *here,* to the gardens!"

Mila turned to Thislen, eyes fixed on the thief in a silent plea. She willed him to understand through the look alone. *I have to know.*

His usual stern expression softened just a bit around the edges. There was a flicker of something akin to understanding. "Just as far as the front door. We haven't got time to go inside. It's almost dawn. We'll have to make arrangements to do anything else later. Are we agreed?"

"Agreed!" Mila said, relief washing over her in a dizzying wave. She felt so light she imagined she would float away if she gave a good leap. A smile bloomed as she started forward, instinctively going to hug the thief.

She stopped herself just in time. *Wait, he might not like that.*

At the same time, Thislen stepped back at her approach, evading the embrace and starting across the grounds toward Perilee's heavy double doors.

"Wait," Aften pleaded, catching at Thislen's wrist. "I didn't agree. We *really* shouldn't go in there. I have a bad feeling about this. Please, please don't. The last time someone went to the castle, we were told the pendants stopped working for a while. Please, it's dangerous."

Thislen faltered.

No, we can't stop. We won't have a chance like this again, Mila thought.

She forged ahead of them both, marching toward the doors with her hands curled into fists at her side. "You promised me answers," she called over her shoulder. "After everything I've been through in the past three days, I feel like I might lose my mind if I don't get them. Are you saying I don't deserve at least that much?"

"Mila!" Aften called desperately, releasing the thief to follow after her. Thislen jogged to her side.

"Don't worry, Aften. We're not going inside. We're just looking. Right, Thislen?" Mila asked airily. It felt wrong to brush aside the Nattfolk's clear panic, but it was just as wrong to turn away from this—whatever this was. *I have no choice,* she told herself.

Thislen shook his head by her side, then groaned. His head fell back, and he stared up at the stars. "Ancestors, what am I doing?" he whispered.

"My father's going to be so angry," Aften said, chasing after them with his hands clasped together. "Please reconsider. Please, Mila, please? I'll let you read the journals."

"You said you couldn't even understand the journals. What if I can't understand them either? The answers might be *right* here. Look." She stopped in front of the massive wooden doors of Perilee's entrance, sweeping her arms open.

The great portal stood at three times a man's height and was just as wide. The thick wood was stained dark with age, plain and imposing and somehow regal in its simple, unadorned existence. The stone frame around the door had been carved, as had the walls around it, making it all the more noticeable. It was well-loved, polished enough to gleam faintly in the moonlight, and without a fleck of rust on the great metal hinges.

And it was closed fast.

"There, see. It's closed. Probably locked, too. Trying to keep the Vaim out, no doubt about it," Thislen said, breaking their silent contemplation of the doorway.

Mila wanted answers so badly that she was very, very willing to stay past dawn. *Consequences be damned, they're going to keep too close an eye on us after this to let me have another chance for ages.* She clapped her hands together, standing dead center before the great doors with her hands on her hips. Part of her hoped her stern expression alone might make them open before her. Her eyes scanned the carvings around the doorway like they might hold a clue, tracing over shadowy figures and coiling vines wrapped around the lintel.

Well, this worked once before...

Mila stepped forward and pushed on the doors.

They didn't budge. So she pushed harder. She pushed at the doors until her boots slipped and skidded on the cobbles, and then she pushed a bit more. It was no use. The doors didn't open.

Aften exhaled heavily, looking up at the windows of the castle. "They *do* lock it up. What a shame. I guess we had better leave now." His words were a bit too quick for Mila's liking. The scout was already starting to walk away.

Thislen turned to follow the Nattfolk. Mila's hand shot out, catching at his wrist.

"Please, Thislen. Before we go, *please* try to pick the lock?" She asked, pulling him over to the wooden door and laying his hand against the entrance. She pressed her hand over his, gaze intent.

He wasn't going to. He didn't want to. It was painted all over his face. In fact, he was starting to frown at her, that furrow in his brow dark as a thunderstorm.

A grinding sound came from the doors. They shifted beneath their hands, vibrating gently. Mila looked up quickly, realizing the bolts on the other side must have been sliding out of their holes. The wood beneath their combined hands shuddered.

It's opening!

She looked at Thislen. He was pale and clammy, his hand cold beneath hers. It looked as if he had swallowed an eel. Without waiting for him, Mila pushed against his hand.

The doors moved silently, swinging wide before them with hardly any effort. That wasn't nearly as surprising to Mila as the sudden flare of light as candles in great candelabra on either side of the door flared to life by themselves.

Thislen glanced over his shoulder. "I hope no one on the water can see the gate. It'll start rumors."

"Why did you do that?" Aften whined, twisting himself into knots behind them.

Mila leaned forward slowly, breath catching as she took in what she could see of the castle's foyer in the pools of flickering candlelight. She didn't breach the threshold—not yet, at least.

The entryway was lined with double doors, two on each side for a total of four. At the far end of the hall, two sweeping flights of stairs marched upward to a gallery level, curving like great arms protectively encircled around the largest and fifth doorway.

On that second level, ink-black pits stood on either end of the gallery, unlit corridors that led deeper to the palace's wings. They were still and empty, but Mila could swear something watched her.

A thick woolen rug in verdant blue lay like a road from the doorway to the great door between the staircases. *The throne room? Or a ballroom,* she guessed. Below the rug were pristine tiles made from some sort of polished stone, silvery and pale.

Tapestries with twisted crests of noble houses adorned the walls, vanishing into the shadows of the vaulted ceiling above. Paintings in great gilt frames sat high, their scenes difficult to make out in the poor lighting. A faint silver light glowed in the great round window above the entrance Mila stood underneath, but the moonlight didn't reach anything inside.

The air was cool, still, and smelled faintly of flowers and dust.

"There, Mila. You saw," Thislen said, voice hushed.

Her heart hammered in her chest. The hair on the back of her neck stood on end. A chill crept slowly over her skin, prickling as it went. *There's something in here...*

"Come on, let's go," Aften said.

"No, not yet."

Mila stepped into the foyer.

"Mila!" Thislen snapped, his hand darting toward her.

The calm around them shattered in an instant. Mila heard Thislen call her name. She felt his fingers curl around her wrist as she stepped into the castle. That was as far as she got. A massive *BANG* sounded behind them, followed by a rising babbling roar. The great gates in the outer wall flew wide, and the Vaim poured through in a pitch-black tidal wave, screeching.

Aften screamed. From the raw scrape in her throat, Mila knew she was screaming too, but she couldn't hear herself. She couldn't hear Thislen. Aften's shout was swallowed in the sudden sea of spirits that swept toward them. Mila tried to throw herself out of the doorway, but Thislen's grip was still vice-tight around her wrist. He was frozen solid, pale as a sheet beside her as the Vaim surged up the path. His fingers held so tight that his knuckles were white. Her wrist *hurt*. She was stuck.

"Thislen," she begged, sobbing as she tried to pry his fingers off or pull him along with her. Anything, *anything* was better than being trapped here.

The Vaim were upon them. It was seconds from the gate opening to being surrounded by the ghosts. Mere seconds. They were suddenly in the middle of a torrent of grasping fingers that scratched at Mila's skin. Pulling hands plucked at her clothes and hair, dragging her out of Perilee. She fell, but was caught by the flow of Vaim around her and pushed back onto her feet. The grip around her wrist broke free.

"Thislen!" She screamed, or thought she screamed, into the sea of whirling red eyes around her. Mila lifted her arms over her head, trying to protect her face. Burning crimson holes winked in and out of existence everywhere. She couldn't hear. She couldn't see. She couldn't breathe. She was jerked this way and that as taloned fingers caught on her clothes and tore them. The smoky hands of the Vaim seemed to pass her along from one to another in a whirlwind of pushing and shoving, a welter of shadows and candlelight.

And then, with another *BANG* and the *shhhhick* of the bolts sliding home in Perilee's door, the Vaim were gone.

Mila's entire body was wracked with uncontrollable tremors. Her pulse was loud in her ears, as were her harsh and ragged breaths. Her throat ached, and all the little scratches on her skin prickled and tingled as they rose as red welts. Slowly, she lowered her arms to stare in shock at the locked doors before her, an inch away from the tip of her nose. A few tears ran down her cheeks, though she didn't realize what they were until she wiped them away.

"Mila—" came a breathless voice from behind her.

She turned to face Aften, pale as the moon above and with his clothes torn as well. His hands and shoulders shook. His hair was a mess, and from the wisps in front of her eyes, Mila realized hers must be as well.

"I'm alright, Aften," She breathed, and then heaved a huge sigh of relief. "We're alright." She pressed her hand to her chest to soothe her racing heart.

"Mila," Aften repeated weakly, "...where's Thislen?"

14

Darran and Tamsa found them just as the sky was beginning to lighten in the east. Mila didn't pause. She flung herself at the doors again and again. She pushed at them, slammed her fists and hands against them, shouted wordlessly at them—the same as she had been doing since she realized the Vaim must have taken Thislen.

And that they must have taken him inside Perilee.

Aften sat slumped against the doors beside her, head buried in his hands.

"What did you do? What in the ancestor's names did you *do*?" Tamsa shouted as she ran up the keep's pathway.

"We have to go, now." Darran skidded to a stop beside Aften, pulling the scout to his feet without ceremony. Despite the stern furrow of Darran's brow, his eyes brimmed with relief. He caught at Mila's arm, his touch gentle. "We lost you when you all took off running, and we couldn't find you again until we heard the Vaim…*screaming*."

So what? Mila thought as she shrugged from Darran's grasp, turning helplessly back to the doors.

"I'm pretty sure the entire island heard the Vaim. And the sun is coming up. Darran's right; we have to *go*." Tamsa grabbed Mila's arm and yanked her away from the door.

"No! Thislen is in there; I can't leave him," Mila shouted, trying to twist free once again.

"I don't care," Tamsa said, shaking her until her teeth rattled.

Darran turned to Aften, brows rising toward his hair. "Thislen is…in there?"

Aften pulled away from Darran to push between Mila and Tamsa, much to Mila's relief. She rubbed her arms, certain she'd find bruises on them later. The rest of her felt…numb. No longer desperate, but stuck in a still, calm place.

Aften guided Mila a few steps away. His brows were drawn down, his frown set. *He's upset, too,* she realized. "We can't open the door, Mila. We tried for as long as we could. What we need to do now is go back to the Commons. We'll petition the Night Council; they'll help. If we get both scout patrols out here, we can find another way in tonight. Just a few hours from now! We'll find him."

Is he trying to convince me or himself? He sounded so earnest and hopeful…and desperate.

A flutter of panic beat its wings against the hard shell of her stupor, and she took a deep breath to push it away.

Does he really think the Night Council will help find one lost Solfolk? His father doesn't seem the sort to be charitable. Mila knew any lies Aften spoke were unintentional, born out of sheer hope he was right.

But I believe him. At least, I want *to.* Because the alternative to that was believing there would be no help. The Night Council might think the very same thing Mila was trying so hard to avoid thinking.

Thislen is dead.

She sucked in a sharp, deep breath, clasping her hands tightly in front of herself. "Alright."

Aften's expression was guilty as he turned away, and she felt panic threaten to overtake her once more. *Not now. Not yet.*

She wanted to believe that someone *would* help. Someone *had* to. What sort of world would they live in if no one would step up?

Aften turned away from Perilee and started down the broad path to the castle gates. They stood open from when the Vaim burst through them, leaving nothing between him and Astera. Darran fell in to walk beside him, close enough that their shoulders brushed a few times. Mila drifted after them, feeling like a wandering cloud. Everything was disconnected. She was untethered, and cold. Tamsa followed at the rear, no doubt to keep a close eye on her and make sure she didn't try to run.

The clangor of distant bells echoed over the shore as they reached the graveyard. The sun had just crested the horizon to the East. Darran closed the mausoleum door, banishing the first dazzling rays of sunlight and plunging them back into the gloom.

It's fitting. Like we're mourning. Aften entered the stairway first, offering Mila his hand to help her down. When she stood beside him, he didn't let go. Neither did she.

They shuffled down the long staircase in the dark and silence. The Commons, when they reached it, was almost empty at this hour. A few people sat around a brazier, conversing over their cups, but they were alone. The rest of the Nattfolk had sought their sleeping chambers or their bunks in the Barracks to rest. It was early, after all.

The four of them drew little attention as they wove between the quiet stalls and entered the tunnel leading to the Council's meeting hall. When they opened the door, it was to find no one was even there. The table was cleared of papers and ink.

Aften hesitated. He had a look Mila had seen before on the faces of some neighborhood children who had broken a window and didn't want to confess. Guilt, misery, a hint of fear. She felt an answering shiver of unease run down her spine.

Tamsa had no such hesitations. She crossed the Council Chamber quickly, disappearing into the family suite.

"Let's sit down," Darran said so quietly that the words didn't even echo off the stone.

The three of them found places to sit on the mismatched chairs and benches around the table. Aften picked the end of a bench, and Mila sat beside him. Darran sat beside Aften on a rickety stool that wobbled a bit as he settled. Darran gave Aften a reassuring smile, and belatedly extended the comforting expression to Mila.

"Don't worry," Darran said softly, "he can't get mad at you about something the Vaim did."

Aften scoffed. "You've met him. You know he can."

"Well, he won't be right."

"I don't know if that matters to him." Aften scrubbed his face with his hands, bracing himself.

The door opened and Rendyn swept into the room, pulling his vest on and tucking in his shirt as he came. He took in Mila's appearance at a glance, then his son's. Aften hunched where he sat, as if by making himself smaller, he would be safer.

Should I...be worried? Mila met Rendyn's gaze.

His eyes were steely, unforgiving, and cold as the depths of the sea.

...we are in so much trouble.

Rendyn said nothing to Aften or Mila. He turned to Tamsa, who was closing the door behind them. "Fetch the rest of the Council."

Tamsa nodded. She was across the room and out the next door in mere heartbeats.

"Aften," Rendyn said.

The scout looked up, hope dawning on his face like a sunrise.

"You will sit at the head of the table." There was no warmth to Rendyn's voice.

Aften's hope melted away. He looked like he had swallowed something cold and slimy as he stood. Reluctantly, he dragged himself to the top of the table and perched on the edge of the heavy wooden chair. He folded his hands on the table in front of him.

Mila frowned and slid down the bench to sit on his left. Darran moved around to sit on Aften's right side. *It looks and feels like Rendyn is setting Aften up to be interrogated. But we didn't do anything wrong!* A spark from that ember deep inside her flared to life, the anger helping beat back her fears and the overwhelming numbness.

We're all in this together. If he thinks he can blame his own son...

The door opened, then closed, then opened again. One by one, the members of the Nattfolk Council filed into the room. Many of them were still adjusting clothes they had clearly just put on. Four women and two men, all in some state of dishevelment, found their seats and turned concerned and curious glances onto Rendyn. None of them would look directly at Aften and Mila, ignoring the torn garments, wild hair, and scratched skin.

They're sneaking glances out of the corners of their eyes when they think no one will notice, though, Mila thought, catching one's gaze briefly.

The air in the chamber was so thick with tension that Mila half expected the ceiling to rumble with thunder and the lanterns to flicker like lightning.

Tamsa was the last to arrive, bolting the chamber door behind her and going straight to her father's side.

"Pardon me for being the first to speak, Rendyn, but what exactly is going on here?" One woman asked, adjusting the bonnet tied over her hair.

"Ami's right. It's early!" A man rapped the table sharply with his knuckles. "And why does your son look like he rolled through a bramble hedge?"

Another woman opened her mouth, but Rendyn's upraised hand forestalled whatever flurry of questions the Council wanted to ask. She closed her mouth without a word.

"Excuse me for interrupting you, Helena. Grayson, Ami, your questions are fair. This evening, we lost track of a Solfolk rescued just last night. It was Aften's responsibility to guard him."

Mila's head shot up. Aften flinched. *Guards? I thought this was a kindness, but they were just there as guards?* For a moment, she wondered if Thislen had known the Nattfolk didn't trust them. *Of course he did.* Mila was beginning to understand the thief's distrust of others.

"The poor young man was...misplaced, and on my son's watch."

A flare of anger rose in Mila's stomach, but before she could so much as move, Aften was on his feet. His cheeks were flushed with anger as he slammed his hands on the table. "First of all, it was Tamsa and Darran's responsibility too, and they lost track of me *and* the Solfolk. Why aren't they being interrogated? And second of all, Thislen isn't misplaced. The Vaim pulled him into Perilee!"

The table burst to life with conversation.

"Perilee?"

"But don't they have pendants?"

"The Vaim? The Vaim did what?"

Rendyn stood up from his heavy chair, waving a hand. The Council fell silent. "Why were you near Perilee to begin with? What did you do to end up separated from your patrol?"

"Why am I being questioned for what the ghosts did when Thislen's life is in danger? Why aren't you holding Tamsa responsible for any of this? Why should I be lectured for doing everything I could to save their lives? There were Vaim in the streets reaching for the Solfolk, even with the pendants on. We ran away! I knew the castle grounds would be safe." Aften's hands were balled into fists by his side, his jaw set as if he expected a physical fight instead of a spar of words.

There's so much I'm missing here, so much painful history between Aften and his father. What sort of life has Aften led? Mila wondered, stunned by the depth of the scout's fury.

"And you were wrong, weren't you?" Rendyn said firmly. He didn't look away from his son. He never raised his voice. He was *always* calm. Too calm. Perfectly calm.

Tamsa's expression hadn't flickered this entire time. Darran's lips were pursed and his gaze was on the table as he let Aften speak, a crease in his brow as he subtly nodded along with every word. Mila quietly clasped her hands on the tabletop to hold herself back as well. She only hoped they would hurry through these meaningless parts at the beginning and let her ask them for their help.

It was no one's fault, after all.

Except, maybe, hers. She had insisted on getting closer to the castle. She had insisted on finding answers after she opened the door.

"I wasn't wrong. The gardens were empty. I told them we ought to stay in the gardens, and we shouldn't go near the castle itself. I told them it might make the Vaim angry if we went any closer. The Vaim got angry *anyway*. And do you know *why*? Do any of you know why?" Aften asked, turning his gaze to the Council.

Rendyn's eyes narrowed. "Aften. Do *not*," he said, bare steel in his words.

"Because we used the old magicks to open the gate. And that gate opened because Mila is an Ominir, a line which has some kind of tie to the Vaim, and the castle, and the Nattfolk, *and* my own family!"

A murmur began amongst the Council's members. They leaned over to whisper to one another behind their hands.

"How do you know?" Helena demanded.

"Aften. Do. *Not.* Speak," Rendyn said, even more firmly than before.

Aften ignored him. He pointed across the table at the man. "Because my father has journals. He knows more about the ghosts than he's shared with *any* of you."

"AFTEN." His father roared, banging a fist on the table even as the Council burst into chaotic babbling.

"The time for secrets is long past, father, and I'm tired of you trying to keep them from everyone. Including me." Aften shouted over the noise.

Darran was staring at Aften, mouth slightly agape. Mila blinked. *He didn't know before tonight, either.*

Tamsa was shouting from the other side of the room, most of her words lost in the building chorus of the Council reverberating off the stone walls of the small chamber. She was looking directly at Aften.

"What is the meaning of this?" Grayson said.

"Rendyn, explain yourself!"

"What do you know?"

"What are these secrets? What aren't you telling us?"

"About the Vaim? We don't know something about the Vaim?"

"ENOUGH," Rendyn bellowed, and silence fell. The echoes faded away.

From the way everyone leaned back in their chairs, Mila guessed it was the first time they had seen Rendyn Sivivan truly angry, his calm facade cracked at last. His cheeks were red, his eyes narrowed, his face twisted into a deep scowl. He was panting faintly, hands curled into fists upon the table's surface as though he wished to smash it into a million pieces.

Mila's heart pounded faintly in her chest. Anger wasn't going to help her, wasn't going to help Thislen. *What did Aften just* do?

"Aften, you and Mila Ominir are to wait in your room while the Council and I discuss what you have said here. Darran, you are to forget every word. You are dismissed for the day, and your patrol will not go out tomorrow evening."

"But Sir—" Darran began.

"You will report to me tomorrow at the bell. You are dismissed."

"But Sir, Aften was only—"

"I said *you are dismissed.*"

Darran rose, his gaze lingering on the Councilman for a long, tense moment. As he turned to leave, he gave Aften's shoulder a squeeze. He gave the scout a subtle nod before he left the room.

"I believe I gave you your instructions, Aften. To. Your. Room," Rendyn said, standing aside to gesture at the closed door behind him.

Mila stood, ears ringing. She followed Aften as he slunk around the table, glaring at his boots with his shoulders hunched up towards his ears. The eyes of every Council member followed their progress. They passed Tamsa and her entitled smirk. Mila felt an extreme desire to push her over.

When they reached the door at the chamber's far end, Aften whirled suddenly, recoiling as he nearly ran into Mila. He hadn't realized she was behind him. He opened the door for her, ushering her gently inside before he turned back to those gathered around the table.

"When my father tries to tell you how I have lied and exaggerated, don't believe him. He won't want to show you the journals, but I think you should insist on seeing them. I think all of our leaders need to know."

"That is not your decision to make, Aften." Rendyn snapped.

"And why, exactly, is that a decision *you* made without us?" Ami asked.

The Council dissolved into overlapping questions once more as

Rendyn fixed his son with a glare that neared hate. A hand lifted, pointing imperiously at the door.

Aften slammed the door closed.

Mila wasn't certain what she felt or what was going to happen. There were things at play here she didn't understand, politics of a world she wasn't a part of. All that mattered to her was to get help, and they hadn't even let her ask for any yet. All she could do now was wait. She turned reluctantly away from the door.

The apartment she and Aften stood in had the air of something settled to it. It felt as if there hadn't been much of a change here in decades. A wooden couch stood with quilted cushions and blankets draped over the back, set before a fireplace carved into the stone wall. A desk sat in one corner beneath a painting of a window's view onto a meadow. The dining table was piled high with papers, and from the dust gathered on many of them, Mila guessed it always looked that way. The Sivivans did not use it to eat meals together. The kitchen was clean and tidy, standing beside a hearth fire that crackled softly in the otherwise silent space. The only other thing in the room was a sagging bookshelf, crammed full of books.

Four doors led off the main chamber, all of them standing open. One must have been Tamsa's neatly appointed bedroom, as plain and stern as the one beside it but with a smaller bed. The bath had a stone tub carved into the wall and a pump that sluiced water into it. The last had to be Aften's, a clutter of bits and bobs and books. Interesting things he had found aboveground had been affixed to the wall with nails and string. Feathers, dry leaves, bits of silk. What he couldn't hang up littered a small, crooked shelf. Seashells, a horseshoe nail, a few nice rocks. His bed was a nest of blankets and pillows.

Aften went to that bed and flopped onto it, staring blankly at the ceiling overhead.

Mila's mask slipped a bit. It was just them here, after all. Now she could afford to let the fear creep in like vines of ice and wrap around her heart.

"Aften?" She asked, perching at the foot of his bed.

"What?"

"We didn't get a chance to ask for the scouts. He said we weren't going to be patrolling tomorrow at all."

Aften dropped his gaze to Mila, his jaw gone slack.

Tell me there's a solution, she begged him silently. His expression remained blank and stunned, the gears turning.

"I can't do anything," he said with a sigh, pushing himself upright. "I can't sneak us out of here. The only way out is through the Council Chamber, and they might notice that, considering they're all…you know."

Mila felt herself wilt like a flower, burying her head in her hands. Tears threatened to choke her, rising from deep inside her chest. *I've failed him. After everything he's done for me, after every risk he took—I've let Thislen get dragged off and killed, and now I'm trapped!*

"I guess I can let you read the journals, though. The secret is already out. Your name is in them, too. We'll bring all of them in here and bolt my door so Tamsa can't stop us if she comes to check." His words were quick and desperate.

He's trying to distract me.

"Is that all we can do?" Mila asked, voice muffled and shoulders slumped.

"Until they decide to let us out of here, I guess," Aften said.

"…alright."

Together they went into Rendyn's room and pulled the worn wooden chest out from underneath the bed. It was heavy, but they managed to carry and drag it across to Aften's little den. He closed the door and pushed the bolt home through the hole carved into the stone for it. He turned up the light in the lantern hanging on the ceiling, and he and Mila piled into his bed.

Aften positioned the box before them, taking a deep breath before he opened it.

Mila wasn't entirely certain what she had expected, but she found herself disappointed anyway. Books were lined up, their spines pointed upward, and labeled with faded gilt lettering in simple numerals. He passed a handful to Mila and took a handful for himself. They felt like every other book she had ever seen, heavy and rectangular, and they certainly didn't seem like they would be full of answers.

In silence, they began to read.

The dull murmur of voices in the Council chamber just barely reached them. They grew heated and loud, faded to nothing, and grew loud. Over and over, the sound rose and fell as they debated. As they listened. As they spoke. They were informed, they argued, they questioned and learned.

Still, no one came for the pair of prisoners.

Aften and Mila took turns dozing and poring over the journals. Neither slept well. Mila was relieved to find the reading was a welcome distraction from the interminable waiting.

"Oh, here," Mila said, breaking their silence late in the day. She leaned forward, running a finger over the page as she read the neatly penned script. "*Willa Ominir says she believes her father has been caught up in something terrible. She believes the ghosts are angry with her and her family. We could not sway her opinion. She thinks if she were to leave the island, the specters might go as well. She left us in the night. We have not yet found her.*" She turned the pages backward a few times, brow furrowed. "But it doesn't say what she thinks her father did."

Why are they angry with us? If they were angry with me, why didn't they attack me on that first night on the island? This doesn't make sense.

"And it didn't work, either. Or maybe she never left the island at all? You're still here." Aften sat up to take the journal and skimmed through the passage himself.

"She must have tried, or they wouldn't have written it down." Mila picked up the next book, rifling through the pages.

Aften thumbed through more of the first. "*Willa has returned from the mainland with a husband. She is distraught at the news that her sacrifice did not save us. The ghosts, indeed, have not disappeared. We have overheard the townsfolk calling them 'Vaim.' They grow afraid as the sun sets. The Ruling Council has been building ships that the ghosts do not attack. The people are eager to leave Astera's shores each night. We saw a parchment on the notice board. It says the Vaim will soon turn on the populace if they do not figure out what the spirits want.*

"*Several have died each night. What do the spirits want? Will they turn on us here, below the ground? Willa has said she can protect us. Her husband is a smith. They plan to make us talismans,*" Aften read.

"So she did leave! And she returned. Keep reading, see if they say anything about Perilee," Mila said eagerly, moving to sit shoulder to shoulder with Aften as they read on.

It was there, on the very last page of the journal. They read it together in silence.

Willa has left her husband and children in a shop aboveground. She said she saw lights in the windows of the castle at night. She said it has been calling to her. No one remains on the island after dark anymore; she cannot be right. She said she saw her father's face in the window. We thought he had died during the coup. She insists she must see him.

We begged her not to go. She hasn't listened to us.

She hasn't come back.

"The way the candles lit up when the castle doors opened..." Mila mused.

"You don't think it's her, do you? Willa Ominir? Or maybe it's her father. Your great-great-great, however many greats-grandfather? If they're in there, wouldn't they have been waiting for you?"

Mila nodded slowly.

"Then why did the Vaim take Thislen instead?"

"He was standing right beside me, and he was holding my hand. They might have gotten confused because I moved, and he was still inside the doors," she said softly. Her hands shook, and her voice wavered. "It's my fault."

"Mila," Aften said reluctantly, "if the Vaim *were* waiting for you, they wouldn't need Thislen. They'll have killed him by now. What if we go to look, and there's nothing left to find?"

She felt a pang in her chest. Guilt and agony twisted together in equal measure inside of her. "There will at least be a body in the castle," she said firmly, blinking furiously to stop any tears from falling. *I won't mourn him before we find proof that he's gone.*

Mila turned to Aften, catching at his hands. "We have to look, Aften. We have to try. All of this, everything around us that's going wrong? The Vaim, the Nattfolk, the Solfolk, the corruption and injustice? If we can't find Thislen, we can at least find answers that might help us fix *those* problems. There's more than one reason to go."

Even if Thislen were the only real reason she wanted to.

There was growing steel in her voice. She could hear it. She could feel her shoulders squaring, her grasp tightening. *Please, believe me. Come with me. Help me!*

Aften returned her grasp, giving a firm nod. "I *promise* we'll try, Mila. If I have any say in it at all, we'll try," he vowed.

The door to the Sivivan apartment banged open. Footsteps marched straight to Aften's door. There was a rattle, then a bang as someone slammed their hand against the unmoving wood. Mila and Aften both jumped at the sound.

"I know you're in there, Aften. Open up. The Council wants to speak to you two," Tamsa said, as smug as ever.

That is it; *I am so sick of her!*

Before Mila could move, Aften was across the room. He flung the door open. "Why do you always have to be so mean about *everything*?" he shouted at his sister. "You aren't our father, and you never will be. It might be good for you if you stop *trying* to be. You're already heartless; you don't need to be an uncaring bastard, too."

Aften shoved past her, ignoring her red-faced sputtering.

She grabbed for his shoulder. "Hey!"

He shrugged it off without turning to face her. Aften said nothing, not a word, as he marched from their suite of rooms into the Council chamber.

Mila stood, clutching that last journal in both hands as she followed him. Tamsa swore as she realized the journals were littered all over Aften's bed and floor. She stayed behind. From the thumps and thuds behind her, Mila guessed Tamsa was packing the precious histories away again.

The Council looked exhausted. They leaned back in their seats or slumped forward over the table with dark circles under their dull eyes. *Who wore down who?* Mila wondered. It was silent as she and Aften made their way around to the foot of the table to stand side by side.

Rendyn was leaning back in his chair, fingers steepled before his chest. "The Council has come to a decision. In light of the new information they have been given, *without* our family's consent, they will be reading the journals of my forebears. So give it back, Mila Ominir."

Mila set the journal on the table and pushed it forward a few inches, lifting her chin.

"In exchange for access to these journals, they have given me full reign in handling your transgressions. Aften, you and Mila Ominir have riled up the ghosts. You have led to either the death of a new recruit in your care or the possible revelation of a secret that has been kept for generations: the existence of the Nattfolk."

"You think he ran away?" Aften asked. "That's ridiculous."

Without me? Mila wondered, a chill of fear running through her. She pushed it away. *No, I trust him. He wouldn't leave me here.*

"You are either guilty of murder, Aften, or you are guilty of treason."

"Treason!" Aften echoed numbly. His gaze roved around the table desperately, trying to catch the eyes of the Council members.

No one on the Council so much as glanced at him.

Mila felt her heart hammering in her chest.

Rendyn continued. "You were never suited for the work of sitting on the Council. I had thought to give you some freedom by allowing you to join the scouts. I was pleased to see you gain your health, and you seemed content. I decided to let you stay there. I had thought your newfound energy would do well with some laxity. However, I have found I cannot trust you with that freedom. You are lucky to be my son, else you would be sent off the island entirely. Instead, you will be reassigned to an apprenticeship of my choosing. You are to be supervised down here for the foreseeable future."

Lucky? He's—being imprisoned! Mila knew all too well how tight the bars of a cage could feel, even gilded. She had gone to desperate lengths to escape hers. How would Aften escape the oppressive weight of the island's stone?

Aften's hands curled into fists. A flush rose in his cheeks. "You can't—"

"I can," Rendyn said, finality in the two simple words. He leaned forward, folding his hands atop the table. "As for you, Mila Ominir. You are Solfolk. We have rescued you, and you were told when you came to us that there are only two options for Solfolk. You have proven that you do not fit well into our society. You have led to the loss of your companion and have proven that you do not care for our rules. You have put all of us at risk."

No.

"It is my decision that you will be sent off-island."

No!

Mila swayed, her knees buckling. Aften caught her elbow, holding her upright and staring at his father pleadingly.

"We will arrange for the next ship to take you away when it returns a few days from now. Until you have both been seen to and arrangements finalized, you will remain in my family suite. Mila, you may sleep in Tamsa's room."

"Father—" Aften began.

Tamsa reappeared, lips downturned and brow furrowed.

"Ah, Tamsa, arrange for a few volunteer guardsmen to ensure your brother and our guest remain here." Rendyn stood, chair scraping against the stone. "Now, it is quite early. I suggest we all retire and get what rest we can."

Rendyn Sivivan did not return to his family's chambers. He left through the door behind Aften and Mila, heading into the corridor that led to the Commons. Tamsa remained standing at the head of the table, her gaze on Aften and Mila as they held one another up. The rest of the Council members stood and filed out after their leader without a word. None of them would meet Mila's or Aften's eyes.

No one is going to help me, Mila realized numbly. *No, worse. No one is going to help Thislen.*

It felt as if everything in the world had tipped sideways. Nothing was certain. Nothing was stable. The ground beneath her feet might have been quicksand, ready to pull her down and smother her.

Everything has changed again. Everything keeps changing, faster than I can ever hope to keep up with. It had finally hit the point where there was nowhere to go but down. Down into her own thoughts, and the dark pit that formed in her stomach as she slid away into nothingness.

After everything Thislen tried to do to help me, I've failed to help him in return, and *I'm in danger. Alone.*

She was going to be alone.

Everything felt distant and slow as Tamsa stepped forward. She reached for her brother, her hard expression softening at the edges, but Aften jerked his shoulder away from her hand.

"Aften—"

"Don't you dare tell me that this was my fault. I will *never* forgive you," he said, acid dripping from every word.

"I never expected—"

"Don't do that. Don't give me some line about how this isn't what you wanted. You only wanted to prove you were better than me; it didn't matter how. Congratulations, Tamsa, you win."

"I wasn't trying to win!"

He held up a hand. "Just don't talk to me. I don't want anything to do with you."

"Mila, listen—" Tamsa began, lacing her fingers together and turning to the apothecary.

She wants someone to forgive her. Well, she shouldn't have done something that needed forgiveness.

"Please leave me alone," Mila said softly, but firmly. She met Tamsa's gaze. "We aren't friends, and I won't forgive you either."

"I just want to explain—"

"What's to explain?" she asked, feeling her lips stretch into a mad smile. "You were protecting your people, right? You must be so proud. Learn to live with your decisions, Tamsa. It's part of being a leader."

Mila didn't stay to listen to anything else. She felt like she was trying to walk through syrup, every step heavy and slow as she led the way into the Sivivan family suite. Aften followed her, silent and fuming as he ignored Tamsa trailing after him.

Once the Nattfolk scout was safely beside her, Mila very firmly closed the door in Tamsa's face.

They were alone. The fire in the hearth crackled, then let out a loud *pop*! The sound startled her, anchoring her back in her own skin.

If no one else will help Thislen or me, I'll have to do it myself. Her fingers curled slowly into fists until her nails dug into her palms. The pain gave her something to feel, something to focus on. Mila paced before the fire, her brow furrowed.

Aften sank onto the couch. His eyes followed her as she moved back and forth.

It's up to me now, but what can I do? Willa left the island. I could just go—but she came back, and Thislen needs me. The Vaim are tied to my family. They took Thislen instead. If Thislen is alive, I haven't got any time to spare.

"Are you *sure* there's no way out of these rooms?" She asked Aften, coming to a stop before him.

"I've lived here my entire life and never seen one. That door is the only way in or out." He sighed, gaze drifting to the flickering flames of the fire. "And now it's guarded. My own home is a prison cell."

Mila took a deep breath. It tasted like woodsmoke and stone. Her heart went out to Aften as she studied the sag of his shoulders and the fading spark in his eye. *I may be banished, but he's going to be held prisoner for the rest of his life, put on display as an eternal disappointment. Everyone he's ever known will see him fail every day. At least I'll be able to see the sky.*

She exhaled, sitting on the couch beside the scout. *I just want to go home.* Olen would know what to do. He'd wrap her up in his arms, and his whiskers would tickle her face while he told her all the answers.

But maybe now it's my turn to find the answers. It's not like I have a choice. Be banished, or fight back.

She smacked her fist against her palm. "There's nothing else for it. I'm going to fight my way out before everyone wakes up."

Aften glanced at her. "We. *We're* going to. There's nothing good left for me here. I'm not letting them lock me away for helping you and Thislen. I'm not letting them pretend they hate me for telling them something they needed to know."

"It was something everyone needed to know, Aften. Not just the Nattfolk, either. The Solfolk need to know it, too." She leaned her shoulder against his. "Thislen and I were planning to run away. After we find him, you can come with us. We'll cross Astera to Barred Town and set up a shop, and then we can share everything we know. Maybe if enough people ask questions, someone will find the answers."

"Alright," Aften said, pushing himself to his feet. He turned to the small kitchen, picking up the kettle and giving it a slight heft. "There's not much to arm ourselves with in here, I'm afraid."

"That's alright. We'll manage," Mila said, also standing.

"Are you planning to *fight* your way out?" came a familiar voice, slightly muffled.

Mila and Aften both looked around the room in surprise. A scraping sound above the dining table made them both turn their heads. Dust hissed down onto the piles of papers there. A crack appeared in the craggy ceiling, widening until a piece lifted up and vanished into darkness.

Darran's head appeared a moment later, upside down and grinning. "Why not go this way instead?" he asked Aften.

Aften's eyes were large and round. His surprise faded quickly into a broad grin. "You magnificent son of a blacksmith!" he crowed, abandoning the tea kettle and leaping across the room.

"Hey, not so loud. We have to get out of here. Now. Right now, while it's quiet and everyone's still asleep. We're not out of the woods yet," Darran said, lowering a hand.

Mila was the first to take it, not even hesitating as she climbed onto the table, crumpling papers beneath her boots. Darran hauled her into the small, dark tunnel above the suite. It was too small to stand in, leaving her awkwardly hunched in the shadows. Darran was much taller than her—he was forced to remain on his hands and knees.

The wooden cover to the secret doorway was propped against the wall behind the scout captain. It had been painted and carved to look like the stones of the ceiling. *Very clever,* Mila thought, *and of course it exists. Powerful people always plan for their escapes.*

"Then all we have to do is hide from the other scout patrols and hope they haven't figured out we're gone yet. And *then* we have to get to the castle without getting caught. And *then* we just have to get inside," Aften said as he was pulled up after Mila.

"What will happen to us if we're caught?" she asked, scooting back to make room for the Nattfolk scout.

Darran gave a grim smile. "Well, best case, we'll all be banished to the farthest place we can possibly be sent. With bags over our heads and not a single coin in our pockets."

Aften began to wrangle the hatch back toward the hole after finding his awkward footing in the small tunnel. Darran contorted to help him. The pair grunted as they wrestled with the heavy piece of wood.

"I guess," Aften panted as they got one end into place, "we had better avoid getting caught."

The hatch fell into place with a scrape and a thud, plunging them into darkness.

15

The tunnel was a nightmare. It was small and close, the weight of stone pressing in around Mila like the earth itself wanted to squeeze the air out of her lungs. Old filmy cobwebs brushed against her cheeks and hands until she felt sticky with them, despite Darran crawling through them first. She shuddered with the touch of each one, skin prickling. Darran had taken Aften's glowing orb with its steady light. As he held it in his hands and crawled along the tunnel, the shadows swung and danced in a way that left Mila faintly nauseated.

A lifetime later, they emerged in the back of a storeroom, behind a heavy shelf piled with blankets. *We must be near the Barracks,* she realized.

They were, as a peek through the door revealed. The curtains were drawn across many of the stone bunks, the soft rustle of blankets and the sound of someone snoring the only sign they were occupied. The room was dark, the lanterns barely pushing back the gloom.

Darran tucked the glowing orb back into the pouch on Aften's hip before they slipped out. Aften tip-toed across the open space, moving as silently as a shadow. Darran followed, picking at the thin white film of spiderwebs on his clothes as he went, shedding them in his wake.

Mila went last, hardly daring to breathe and with her fingers trembling. *Don't wake up, don't wake up,* she pleaded with the slumbering Nattfolk. No one did.

Still, she didn't dare breathe as they hurried across the empty, dim marketplace of the Commons to the staircase tunnel. There was no sign anyone had seen them. She felt the strangest urge to laugh building up inside of her, the tension winding her so tight she felt like a spring, coiled and ready to bounce off the painted stone walls.

I am not cut out for sneaking around. She was an apothecary. She worked in a shop, and that was all she wanted to do again. After all this was done, she'd put a counter between herself and the world and never leave.

I learned my lesson! Adventure is not all it's cracked up to be.

The darkness of the staircase enveloped them at last. With a heavy sigh of relief, Aften pulled out the orb again, and they began to lope up the stairs. The scouts took them two at a time. Mila began to lag, but she didn't dare stop. If they were caught now, she would never have another chance.

For Thislen's sake, for my *sake, I have to do this.*

It was sheer dumb luck that they didn't meet anyone during their escape. Mila found herself waiting, feeling like there was a target painted on her back between her shoulder blades, but no alarm was raised. No angry shouting Council members pursued them.

"Do they not know about the tunnel?" Mila whispered as they came to the top of the stairs and climbed out into the mausoleum.

"I don't think so," Darran answered with a wry grin. "Or at least they don't think *you* know about it. They'll figure it out before too long, though. Someone will probably bring you food, and then they'll know you aren't there."

Aften cracked open the door. Late afternoon sunlight poured in, rendering the soft glow of the magical orb obsolete. The Nattfolk both lifted their arms, shielding their eyes from the bright, warm light.

Mila, however, stepped right into it. She closed her eyes, savoring the play of warmth along her skin. *It feels like it's been a year since the last time I've seen the sun so high in the sky.* Had it truly only been a few days? It soaked into her torn, dusty, sticky clothing and warmed her from head to toe. *I never thought I would see full day again.*

She was glad to take the time to herself while Aften and Darran blinked and wiped at their streaming eyes and squinted at the open air. Darran let out a soft curse.

"Don't look directly at it," Mila suggested.

"I'm looking sort of *near* the light. I think it's working," Aften said brightly.

The hum of the city filled the air outside. Laugher, chatter, bells, and the clatter of a nearby cart floated to her ears. Mila felt the song of it all bringing her back to life. Her people. Her place. *I really am a Solfolk.* "Listen to them all. It's so nice to be back, to hear this again. It's *life,*" she breathed. She had never realized how quiet it was at night.

"We're going to have to time everything carefully, I think," Darran said. "You shouldn't be seen, and we don't exactly blend in."

Mila had to admit their gray and black leathers were very odd for Astera. The residents of the city dressed in bright colors lined with embroidery, no matter how simple. That didn't even account for the tears and scratches that covered her and Aften.

"Do you still have the key to my father's shop?"

"What? To the apothecary? Yes, I haven't exactly changed yet," Darran fished in his pocket, then held the iron key up to the light.

It's an exact duplicate of father's, she realized.

"Right. Well, I don't think we have much choice in showing ourselves. It's nearly time for everyone to leave for the night, but it's not yet so late that me popping in to grab something would attract too much attention. We're not far away from it here, nor are we too far away from—"

"Perilee's side gate!" Aften crowed. "You're right. We can take the alleyways again, and the Nattfolk patrols might not even see us because we don't usually travel—"

"At street level." Darran finished triumphantly.

The three of them exchanged elated grins. Mila wondered for a moment if they felt the same nauseating knots in the pits of their stomach as she did, despite all of their bravado. *Maybe it's just me.*

There was just so much that could go horribly wrong.

"We'll follow your lead, Mila. You're the Solfolk," Darran said, gesturing at the open door.

Mila felt a shiver run up her spine. The last time anyone had followed her, she'd gotten Thislen taken by the Vaim. *Am I going to get all of us into trouble? Again?*

No, she decided. She'd learned more during these trials than she had ever thought she would, and she would not put her friends at risk again. *What would Thislen do?*

He wouldn't hesitate. Mila stepped outside quickly, before her nerve could falter. The Nattfolk followed, closing the door to the mausoleum behind them. The graveyard was blessedly empty of mourners. Quietly, she led Darran and Aften to a side gate and onto an equally empty side street. No one was there to take note of their passing.

So far, so good.

Mila fussed with her hair and torn clothing, hoping she didn't stand out as much as she felt she did. She paused to adjust Aften's hair and straighten Darran's collar, then led the way toward the main thoroughfare.

They found themselves a small eddy in the stream of townsfolk just beginning their nightly migration to the docks. Darran and Aften gaped openly at the throng, slack-jawed and wide-eyed. *They probably never realized how many people truly lived in Astera,* she realized as they pressed close enough they were in danger of stepping on her boot heels. She took both of them by the hand and gave each a gentle squeeze.

"It's just like the Vaim, only these people will see you, and you can't shove them without getting cursed at," she said lowly as she led them through the crowd.

"And there are three times as many of them," Aften whispered back.

They threaded their way through a few streets and ducked into an alley not far from the quiet dead-end street that held the Ominir Apothecary. Darran drew them to a halt behind a stack of crates, kneeling down and peering through a gap between them.

"Let's wait for the crowd to thin out a little more," he said.

Mila and Aften settled in beside him. The wait wouldn't be long. The sun fell from the sky ever faster these days as the summer drew to a close and autumn enveloped Astera. Mila combed her fingers absently through her hair, working the tangles out while she watched the crowds and waited.

Is that—

Mila was on her feet abruptly, the crate beside her clattering. Aften caught it, swearing. "What the—"

But Mila's eyes were wide, fixated on a familiar tangle of bright red hair. Darran followed her gaze as he stood, putting a hand on her shoulder to hold her still. She was glad for that—the urge to run after Olen was so strong that her knees buckled.

They look so much older, she lamented. Olen leaned heavily on Evelie's arm, and she leaned just as heavily into him. Deep lines had been etched onto Olen's face. His shoulders slumped. Where once her father had been a bright, towering man, he now looked small and drawn. There was no new gray at his temples, but somehow the gray he did have stood out more.

Evelie, too, had aged overnight. Her steps were smaller, her fingers curled a bit like she'd never be able to unfurl them completely again. She had drawn her shawl tight around her shoulders and held it as though the slight breeze cut right through her.

They were followed by Ivan. Even Ivan, in all his gentle strength, seemed different. It was as if he bore a heavy weight, every step slow and purposeful as he carried the burden of his mother and her father both. He walked behind them with a basket over his arm, gaze on his feet. His hair wasn't neat and orderly, and his shirt was untucked at the back.

None of them smiled or jested with one another. None of them were even speaking at all.

Her heart broke.

"Mila, what is it?" Aften asked from down by her hip.

"My family," she breathed. "They don't know that I…"

Darran watched them beside her. "They don't know that you survived," he finished gently. There was a weight to his words, a bone-deep understanding.

"My father looks so unhappy." She clasped her hands in front of her, fighting the urge to run to him, to seek his arms and assure him she was alright. He would cry. Evelie would shriek. Ivan would laugh and catch her up in his arms in a hug so tight her ribs would creak.

And then what? Then she would be caught by Soren Bestant, or someone would spread a rumor, and then they would all be in trouble all over again, only worse.

"Look, Mila," Darran said, "Once we're through all this, I'll bring them to you myself. Another day, right? That's all we need. One more night, and we can all figure out what comes next. Together."

Mila nodded, unable to speak around the lump in her throat. Her eyes stung, but she blinked away any threatening tears. She craned around the boxes to keep her family in sight as long as she could, but too soon they rounded the corner and were gone. She swallowed once, then again.

"Well," she croaked, "if they've gone, we can go and hide in the shop."

"Do we need to?" Aften asked from the ground, brow knitted in concentration. "Why don't we just wait here? It will be easier on you than going home, and there will be a lull before the Sunset Bell rings down in the Commons where the streets are empty, right? They may not even know we're gone yet. They might not be in any rush."

Darran offered Aften his hand, hauling the scout up to his feet. "Did you just think of all that?" He asked, a brow raised.

Aften gave a cautious grin. "I do think *sometimes*, you know."

"Remarkable," the taller man said, a fond taunt in his dry tone.

"Besides, we don't want anyone who knows you to see you, right?" Aften turned to Mila.

Reluctantly Mila tore her gaze away from her home. "You have a point," she admitted. "And as much as I would love to go back, part of that is tied into how much everything around me has changed. I don't know if I would be able or willing to leave, and we can't take that risk. There will be time to stop by the apothecary after we get Thislen. Before we go to Barred Town."

Darran's eyebrows jumped upward. "Barred Town? So that's your plan. Not a bad one, either. We can decide there if we need to leave Astera, and take our time to do so. We haven't got a Nattfolk presence over there. After we start sleeping on a ship somewhere, they'll never be able to find us."

Aften's grin was quick this time, and bright as sunshine. "Clever, right? Mila thought it up."

"Actually, Thislen did," she corrected. Mila walked back through the narrow alley passage as the shadows grew long around them.

She led the way back along the same route they had run the night before, threading their way against the flow of the growing crowds until they reached another shadowed corner in a different alleyway. They nestled against the wall between a pair of rank-smelling bins, huddled in the lee of Perilee's outer wall with their sleeves held over their noses.

The sun sank. The streets emptied as the townsfolk filtered toward the docks. Bells clanged in the distance as the ships began to pull away from shore. *This is the strangest part of all of this,* Mila reflected. She had been on the island when it was full of people, when she had been one of those walking to the shore to leave for the night. She had been on the island when it was empty, and there were no ships at the docks as far as the eye could see. Now here she was, stuck in between.

She had never been on the island during the transition. Never had she watched the milling crowds pass by and leave nothing behind them. Never had she seen the streets left empty in the hushed moments after the throngs dispersed. It happened much faster than she thought it would. Noise died into quiet. The crowds were gone.

Darran sidled along the wall to the corner, peering subtly up and down the tree-lined avenue along the castle wall. "It's empty."

The three of them trotted down the street in single file, staying close to the trees in case they needed to duck behind them to hide from prying eyes. To Mila's relief, they made it to the side gate without encountering anyone.

Mila pressed her palm to the worn wood and felt the lock slide free with a faint *clunk*. She slipped into the perfumed garden beyond, followed by the Nattfolk. As soon as they were through, she pushed the door closed behind them.

Out of the corner of her eye, Mila saw figures in the distance. With a gasp, she dropped to the ground so fast she hit her chin. It hurt horribly as her teeth clacked together. She heard the sound of Darran and Aften following suit a heartbeat later. One of them cursed. She couldn't tell who.

Darran crawled through the gravel to the nearest hedge, levering himself up slowly to peer over the barrier. "The Royal Guard, it looks like. Maybe the last of the palace servants. They're closing the castle gates."

Aften let out an explosive sigh, rolling onto his back to stare at the darkening sky above them. "We got lucky with the timing on that one."

Red light bled into the darkness above them. Stars that had been dim specks in the sky began to brighten. The moon shone overhead, where it had hung even before the sun started to sink, heedless of the waning day.

A soft *boom* echoed over the grounds. Mila rose slowly to her feet, gingerly probing the abrasions on her chin. "I didn't realize they were the last to leave."

Aften laughed. "I didn't realize anyone ever went into the castle at all. Why do they do that?" he asked, stretching out where he lay.

"I didn't know that, either. It doesn't matter why they do or don't, though." Darran stood. "Enough of that. Let's get started."

Mila looked up as Perilee was swallowed by the gathering shadows, her heart rising in her chest. *Thislen is in there. He must be alright. He* has to *be.* Whatever else she did or did not know, she and Thislen were in this together—start to finish. *I don't know if I can do this alone.*

Aften clapped her on the shoulder as he passed, the first to head for the shuttered castle. "Let's look for side doors or something first; the front door didn't work out so well last night."

Darran snorted as he followed. "If you two are anything to judge by, that's an understatement."

Mila was about to drop her gaze and join the two Nattfolk when a glimmer in one of Perilee's windows caught her eye. She lifted a hand, stopping Darran in his tracks.

It looked like the flickering wink of a candle's flame in a corner window. Behind it, a shadow moved around in the room. It was slim, with a man's height. It moved to the glass, peering down at them. Whoever it was, they were too far away to make out, too distant to see any details. *Is it Thislen? Who else could it be?*

The three of them watched the figure in the window as it stepped back, vanishing. The faint and unsteady light disappeared as well. The shadows of the outer wall crept up the face of the castle, swallowing it in darkness and measuring the moments until sunset.

Mila hardly dared to breathe. *If it was Thislen, he'll come down. He'll meet us.*

Darran gently took her hand, towing her along in his wake.

They tried every entrance they came across on the ground floor, starting with the kitchen door and its windows. When that didn't work, they went around to the servant's quarters, the doors to the pleasure gardens, the door nearest the stables, and the barracks. None of them opened. No lights greeted them from within. The sun was gone, and the moon still rising by the time they rounded the front of the keep.

The grand front entrance was the only door left.

A soft creak met Mila's ears, startling her. Her gaze shot to the outer wall's massive gate, as if the shadowy Vaim would be coming through to drag them all away, but the gate remained closed. The whispering groan of the spirits rippled through the air over Astera, but none appeared on the grounds.

Candlelight flared to life, pouring out of the open doors of Perilee itself as they approached, painting the flagstones with warm golden light.

Mila felt as though a piece of ice had slid down her spine. "Thislen?" She cursed the faint waver in her voice.

"Is anyone else rethinking this plan?" Aften asked, voice hushed.

"I am. Somehow I doubt we'll be able to go back, though," Darran said.

They all stood frozen for a moment, staring at the welcoming doorway.

"Well, we got this far. What do we have to lose?" Darran's jest was hollow and wavering.

She answered him silently with a grim look. *Our lives?* She knew the Nattfolk were thinking the same thing.

Mila straightened her shoulders, taking a deep breath. "Let's go. It's the only way in, and we have to find Thislen. For Thislen," she said softly, holding up a closed fist. She was relieved that this time her words came out clear and strong.

"For answers," Aften said firmly, knocking his fist against hers.

"Together," Darran said, adding his own fist.

She was the first to move, leading Darran and Aften to stand before the open front doors of Perilee. Mila stared into the depths of the castle once more. The hair on the back of her neck prickled and stood up.

Nothing had changed. The entryway to the great keep was the same as it had been the day before. The rugs, the tapestries, and the paintings were all swallowed by shadows beyond the pools of candlelight. The sweeping stairways were huddled dark masses against the far back wall—inky blots of darkness deeper than the rest. The ceiling was lost in the gloom somewhere above them, giving the foyer a cavernous air. Nothing stirred in Perilee's depths.

Mila expected the Vaim to swarm them as soon as she stepped over the threshold. She braced herself for another whirlwind and eased a single foot inside. As her boots met the stone with the soft echo of her heel, *nothing* happened. The entire castle sighed and settled around her. A whisper of air floated past her, stirring her hair and setting the flames of the candles to dancing. When nothing else happened, she kept going. She stepped onto the plush blue rug and followed it forward.

Aften and Darran waited at the doorway, steeling themselves for the worst.

"It's fine. Come on, where should we start looking?" Mila called back to them.

More candles leapt to life in front of her, on either side of the staircases. Mila screamed, freezing where she stood with her hands clasped tight over her heart. It raced wildly beneath her fingers. There was a clatter of footsteps behind her as Darran and Aften ran to her side. To Mila's surprise, both of them now wielded short knives. *Of course they would be armed. Some scouts they would be otherwise.*

Darran had a grim frown on his features, though he was otherwise calm and composed. His eyes scanned everything around them, waiting for something to move.

Aften, too, looked in every direction, but more like a startled horse that was tossing its head. His movements were quick and jerky. His eyes were wide and wild.

She gestured for them to lower their weapons as her heart finally began to slow, taking a deep, steadying breath. "It's alright; it's just the candles."

"It's magic," Darran said flatly.

"So are your pendants and Aften's glowing orb."

Aften gave a nervous little laugh. "Yeah, but those are *old* magic, made hundreds of years ago. Magic's been fading ever since the coup. Most people can't even sense it anymore, let alone use it. This? This is...new magic. Strong magic. *Now* magic."

The air in the castle stirred around them again. It was cool. That was why Mila shivered, she told herself, and not for any other reason. *Whatever is in here won't harm us.* She hoped.

They resumed their wary walk, creeping along one slow step at a time like a herd of deer ready to bolt at the slightest sign of danger. Collectively, they froze as more candles flared to life ahead of them halfway up one of the staircases. When Mila went toward the double doors between the stairways, however, nothing happened. She laid her hand on the wood. They wouldn't open.

"I don't understand," she huffed, slapping her palm against the entrance. It reverberated, both in the foyer and beyond.

"It must be the throne room. Thislen wouldn't be in there. He'd be up where that...that person was," Darran said, pointing up the stairs.

"You mean the same way the lights want us to go?" Aften asked as he shifted his weight from foot to foot.

"Alright. Let's follow them, then," Mila said, starting to climb.

"What if we don't? What if we just left instead of going up the creepy stairs to find the creepy face in the window of the big, dark, creepy castle?" Aften asked.

A soft creak froze Mila in her tracks. All three heads swiveled to watch as the doors into the castle swung closed. There was a soft thud, and the great bolts built on the back of the doorway slid closed.

Ancestors, save us. We're trapped!

Mila swallowed. Her mouth had gone dry. "I don't think we have much choice," she whispered.

"This is not ideal," Darran said grimly.

They lapsed into silence. Mila fought the urge to run to the doorway and bang her fists upon the door. *I have to do what I came here for.* She was the first to turn and climb the carpeted stairs.

Lanterns burst to life before them every few feet, guiding them to the south wing of the palace and down long, echoing corridors. They passed tables with decorative vases and trinkets atop them. Suits of old armor glittered in the flickering light. Tapestries hung, woven with elegant and fanciful designs. They passed beautiful baskets of dried flowers that perfumed the air like incense, heavy and sweet. Between all these things were doors, all polished wood, and all closed.

"I can't take this anymore," Aften huffed, reaching for a handle.

"Don't, Aften!" Darran said, catching the scout's wrist.

"Why not? What if Thislen is behind one of these doors?"

"What if opening it summons the Vaim like we did last night?" Mila asked.

The scout jerked his hand back as if he had been burned, eyes wide. They did not stop to try any of the doors after that.

Down a long corridor, around a corner, a left there, and on they went. They followed the lights until they were led at last to a dead end. The passage terminated in a great stone wall with a massive tapestry hung upon it. There, in threads that seemed to breathe in the flickering light, was the image of the Vaim rising from beneath the castle, their too-long fingers outstretched over the whole city woven below. There were no doors nearby. They even checked behind the hanging.

"Nothing," Mila huffed. "We came all this way, following the silly magical lights, to find *nothing*? I'm going to look in the other wing." She turned to leave the way they had come, only for every lantern and candle behind them to snuff out all at once, plunging the corridor into inky darkness. The only lights remaining were the two lamps on either side of the great tapestry. Mila froze.

"We must be missing something," Darran said, a frown on his face.

Aften flung his arms wide. "Oh, look, a picture and a bunch of stone. There's nothing here, Darran. We just checked."

Darran rolled his eyes, vanishing behind the tapestry again. Mila peered around the edge to find the scout captain meticulously running his fingers over every inch of the wall. His brow was furrowed in concentration, but his eyes were closed.

A growing sense of unease was building around them. *It feels like we're running out of time.* What would happen next? Would the Vaim appear again, impatient and angry, and rip them to shreds?

"Mila, what if it has to be you?" Darran said at last.

"What?"

"The same way she opened the gate, you mean? Yes! Mila, try it. Try what Darran is doing." Aften pulled the heavy tapestry away from the wall, giving them space to work.

"Not every problem can be solved by having me touch a door or a wall, you know," she huffed, tracing her fingers over the stones.

The wall suddenly shifted beneath her palm with the rumble of rock against rock. Only a fraction, but it was enough that a shower of dust fell from the cracks of a hidden door. Mila coughed, covering her mouth and nose with a shirt sleeve. Her eyes watered. Darran and Aften coughed somewhere nearby as well.

The dust settled. Mila stared at the hidden entrance, lifting her hand. She pushed.

The door ground open before them, revealing a pale and wavering light that cast more shadows than it dispelled, and a room that she couldn't make out from where she stood.

Maybe I was wrong. Maybe I can *solve all of our problems by touching them.*

Mila stepped inside. One of the Nattfolk behind her inhaled sharply as she did.

Ancient chandeliers hung from the ceiling above, dripping thick cobwebs and covered in dust that made them look almost silver. They flared to life, one dancing flame at a time, hissing and spitting as the room filled with light.

The chamber must have been at the westernmost tip of the castle. Half of the great room had been carved into the stone of the Spine itself, its walls rough-hewn and uneven. The other half of the room was paneled in great glass windows at regular intervals. Through the grimy glass, Mila could just make out the cliff face of the mountain visible as a dark shadow on one side, and the glittering ocean with its soft stars of lanterns on ships below that.

The walls themselves were irregularly paneled with warped wood that looked ready to fall at the slightest touch, beautiful carvings, and crackling paintings worn beyond redemption. Everything was coated in a layer of dust so thick that every step Mila took kicked up a dancing cloud to choke the air.

The contents of the room were as strange as the build of it. Strong wooden tables stood everywhere, littered with jars bearing faded labels and grimy sides, vials covered in thick layers of dust, paper packets adorned with faded spidery script, and the spindly remains of plants long dead. A great bed sat rotting between two of the windows, the rich coverlets torn to tatters by vermin over the years. Feathers shifted fitfully in the draft of the open door, the last vestiges of pillows. A wardrobe lay open in a corner. The fine clothes within, long since faded and rotting, had fallen into heaps that poured out across the floor.

"Someone lived here," Mila said, looking over her shoulder at Aften and Darran. The Nattfolk had not yet set foot inside.

"Secretly, it looks like," Aften said.

"No one has been in here in ages," Darran said as he stepped cautiously over the threshold.

A growing light shone from a window set, impossibly, into the very stone of the mountain. Mila threaded her way through the worktables covered with parchment that looked thin enough to crumble away to dust and bottles with congealed and dried crusts coating their bottoms. The soft babble of running water met her ears as she got closer to the strange, wavering portal.

It's a waterfall, she realized in awe. The water ran over a massive piece of perfectly smooth glass, distorting what could be seen beyond. It fell into a small natural spring at the base of the window, a clear little pool full of darting white fish with no eyes.

It did not show the outside world, as she half-expected. Instead, it led into a small and pristine chamber. The walls were white as fresh-fallen snow, accented with gilded molding and carvings. A great canopied bed and two nightstands stood proudly, as if on display for anyone peering through. The whole room was brilliantly lit by a golden chandelier. Its candles didn't show a single drip of wax, like they weren't really burning. There was no need to decorate this room of stately elegance with baubles and paintings. It was breathtaking in its apparent simplicity.

A dark-haired figure lay atop the covers of the canopied bed, dressed in an opulent silk-trimmed tunic and a fine linen shirt. It was difficult to distinguish the features through the water, but Mila would have recognized Thislen anywhere. His eyes were closed, and he wasn't moving. For a moment, she feared the worst. She held her breath until she saw his.

His chest rose, then fell.

"It's Thislen!" She shouted, reaching out to bang upon the glass. Water spattered over her arm and soaked her sleeve, pittering onto the stone around the little spring. "Thislen. Thislen, it's us. Wake up!"

Darran appeared at her elbow with a clatter of boots, feeling over the walls nearby. "There must be another switch or something, or a key—"

"I'll look for the key," Aften called. Mila heard rummaging and clattering as the scout began to comb the worktables.

Mila craned to see more of the golden room, but there was no visible entrance or exit anywhere. She banged on the glass once more. "Darran, he isn't waking up."

She whirled. Aften sorted hastily through the heaps of parchment on the worktables. He moved jars and beakers out of the way, wiping cobwebs and dust off on his pants as he went. The tops of wooden boxes were flung back, and the contents quickly sorted through.

"Anything?" Mila nearly begged.

"Nothing! There's just notes and letters and journal entries and empty bottles. I don't see a key at all."

She turned back to the glass, lifting her arm.

"Do not bang upon the window again. I would thank you not to break it. It was very costly, and it is very old."

Mila froze. Slowly, she scanned the room for the source of the strange, deep voice. The half-rotted bedding on the decrepit bed didn't move. The great wardrobe doors didn't open any further. The scattered worktables did not show any sign of being touched. No hidden doors opened. Even Darran and Aften didn't stir.

There was no sign of *anyone,* yet the voice that had spoken didn't belong to her or the Nattfolk. Aften and Darran looked reluctant to even breathe, let alone speak.

"Lower your arm. You look foolish. And look, you've gotten water everywhere."

Mila's arm fell.

"Thank you." The room's dusty haze began to condense. Dust and cobwebs and some of the candles' golden glow pulled together, coalescing into the figure of a man. Unlike the Vaim, his shell was hazy and indistinct at the edges, like smoke that might vanish in a good breeze. His eyes were golden orange, bright with an ancient fury. That wasn't the only difference. Unlike the specters, he had distinct features and perfectly normal hands and fingers. He was dressed, too, if it could be called that. A floating robe hid his legs and undulated slowly around him. Cobwebs had gathered and twisted to form the rough idea of ornate trim and sashes in fashions long abandoned.

And the biggest difference of all between this shade and the Vaim, of course, was that he spoke.

"Who—" Mila began, faltering as soon as she spoke.

"Look what you've done. You've made a dreadful mess of all my things, and I can't clean it up." The spirit said. He strode toward her, but every step carried him further than possible. It was more of a glide, though his robe moved as if his hidden legs had set the fabric to billowing. His entire being ended in such an indistinct cloud that it was hard to tell.

Mila hastily backpedaled into Darran. He caught her elbow as her foot slipped, keeping her from toppling into the small spring.

"Are you Willa Ominir's father?" Aften asked from across the room. His eyes were wide enough the white showed all the way around, and his voice cracked—but his tone was polite and calm.

"Hm?" The ghost stopped his advance, turning to the scout. "Ah, what a clever one you are. Yes. I am Ninian Ominir. I am the personal magician and head alchemist to the Royal Court." He bowed, deep and low.

"Ominir?" Mila echoed faintly. It felt as if the blood had rushed up to her head and was racing around with her thoughts. She felt dizzy. "A magician?"

"There's no such thing as magicians, not in Astera," Darran whispered beside her.

"Yes, Ominir. As I said. One of you must also be an Ominir to open the door to my chambers. Is it you, clever one?" Ninian asked, drifting slowly across the floor toward Aften like a cloud scudding across the sky.

The scout hastily lifted his hands. "No! No, sir. My name is Aften Sivivan."

"Sivivan, eh? Good family. If I recall, you were driven underground a long, long time ago. You have no need for the pendant you're wearing, you know. Willa's work, yes?" He raised a finger, pointing toward Aften's chest.

Aften's eyes widened, but he could only let out a soft squeak in response.

"She always was talented with spell craft. This one, though. I can feel *his* pendant working quite hard." The magician turned, fixing a glowing orange eye on Darran.

"Darran, sir. Descended from the Coppermunds."

Mila startled, glancing up at the scout captain.

"How so?" Ninian asked, holding unnaturally still, like a cat waiting to pounce.

"Their great-grandfather sired my grandfather, sir. A bastard sentenced to death for trying to claim his inheritance."

Ninian gave a smug smirk as he floated toward Darran and Mila. "The Coppermunds were considered new blood in my time. I have a secret for you, though. The daughters that married into the name were from Barnweir stock. Your blood is even older than you know, and it. Is. Angry." He reached out, hazy finger an inch from Darran's cheek.

The captain's eyebrows shot upwards, lips parting for a moment. Before he could say anything else, however, the spirit dropped its finger to point at Mila.

"Which leaves you, my dear girl. Are you my granddaughter?"

Do I want to be the granddaughter of a ghost?

The flickering orange eyes fell upon her. Mila felt as if Ninian could see into her very soul. She stood on her own, facing the man with her hands by her side. She was sticky with cobwebs, grimy from the tunnels, and wet from the spring's water—all things she was suddenly keenly aware of. She was also, somehow, related to this spirit. And to magic.

"My name is Mila Ominir, apothecary. And you are my great-great-"

"I do not hold with the many greats that will come before you finish. Let us simply call one another Grandfather and Granddaughter. We are that, in a way, are we not?" He swept his arms wide, taking in the great expanse of the ruined chamber. "Welcome, my dear, to what should have been your home."

My home? Perilee? Mila wondered, looking around. The decrepit room was not inspiring—and there were more important things to discuss. "What did you do to Thislen?"

"Thislen? The young man who rests beyond the glass?" Ninian asked, drifting over to peer through the window. "The Vaim brought him to me. He was afraid at first. He shouted at me for some time. After some rest, we spoke. I healed his wounds and cleared the last of the Vaim's poison from his veins. I could not let him leave, however. Not while there were still so many questions to be asked."

"Questions?" Darran echoed. "Thislen was asking questions?"

"No, Master Coppermund. I was asking questions—of you." The golden eyes fell to Mila once more. She felt a knee buckle as she fought the urge to step back.

There's something wrong with his eyes.

"What about *our* questions?" Aften asked, leaving the dusty worktables behind to join his friends.

"What about them?"

"We need answers," Mila said firmly.

"As you wish."

He said nothing further. Ninian floated before her, hands folded across his chest as he waited expectantly, expression smooth as stone.

Her mind raced. "What…turned you into a spirit?" She asked at last.

He smiled, a hazy and indistinct thing full of obvious amusement. "Ah, so you do have some brains in you, after all. Well done, my dear. A good question. As for what turned me into a spirit, the answer is quite simple.

"I did."

16

Excuse me?" Mila said, manners filling the blank space that rang in her mind.

"I turned *myself* into a spirit, and the souls of many others as well," Ninian said, floating across the room to peer out a window. In the silver moonlight, he nearly vanished.

"The souls of others—do you mean the Vaim?" Aften asked weakly.

"Clever again, young Lord Sivivan. Yes, I do. It took every ounce of magical power in the kingdom to cast my spell. It still pulls from those ancient sources. The Vaim, as you call them, are the spirits of long-dead Asterans."

Darran stepped away from Mila, sinking onto a wooden stool that creaked alarmingly beneath his weight. "You mean we don't go to our ancestors? We turn into those murderous—"

"Not at all." Ninian interrupted. "All of the souls in your streets are as old as I am. A few hundred years by now, if I recall. The souls of the recently departed are free to travel to the stars. I am not here to help *them*."

"Help them?" Mila echoed, "How does keeping them alive and forcing them to murder others *help* them?"

Ninian sighed, a cloud of dust leaving his lips. He turned away from the window and wafted back towards them. "I fear what you know of our island's history may be false. Willa told me long ago the tales they were trying to sell. I can only imagine what they tell you now. Sit. I will make everything clear."

Mila delicately moved papers and jars, clearing a space on the corner of the table near Darran's stool. She hopped up to perch there while Aften settled on the dusty floor with his legs crossed.

Once they were suitably arranged, Ninian glided before them and lifted his hands. A rush of air and a tingle lifted the hairs on Mila's arms. The ember inside her stirred faintly, as if it recognized what was happening. Dust flew off the tables around them, drawn suddenly inward to the specter, solidifying him before their eyes. Just as quickly as he formed, however, his haze spread out once more. It swallowed them entirely. Sparks of light flickered in the dust, bursting slowly into blooms of color. It plunged them into something that felt like a different world, reminding Mila of a scene in a mummer's play.

"In my day, the kingdom of Astera was ruled by a young King named Barleyn Asteran. The cities of Barred Town and Astera herself were crowded, full of so many people that there were not enough houses to keep them all. King Barleyn created an initiative to build new villages on either side of the Spine, which would have taken valuable farmland to make more homes for his people."

The island of Astera appeared before them in miniature, in a sea of silver-blue dust. Buildings began to grow in small farming communities and fishing hamlets, expanding into new towns.

"All the nobility disagreed with his plan—for different reasons, of course, but the consensus was the same. Some wanted to ensure the farmland was not taken. Some wanted to build new cities on the slopes of the Spine, taking only game land. Some wanted to build nothing new and renovate the city itself. But there was one faction," Ninian said, voice rumbling like thunder around them, "that decided the true problem was the *people*."

Dark figures surged out of the cloud around the seated trio, making Mila jump. She caught at Darran's hand, holding it tight. Several of the shadowy forms stood in the center, facing out toward the rest.

"They split from their fellows. While many touted ideas of expansion through treaty or conflict, and others offered programs to support those who chose to leave Astera for better shores, or any other number of ideas, this faction knew what they wanted. They told no one. Instead, they manipulated everyone else around them, and the very island itself.

"Merchants and traders and farmers were offered great wealth in exchange for their food stores. While the nobility and King Barleyn argued about the best way to sustain life on the island, the small faction robbed the people blind. King Barleyn and his court found that 'eventually' had become 'now.' *Now* they did not have enough to sustain the people. *Now* people were going to starve. *Now* their worst nightmares were coming true."

Heaps of shadowy sacks and crates began to pile up in a mountain around them, protected from the rest by the shadowy figures in the center of the haze. A sea of tiny people appeared around them, hands outstretched. The air was filled with whispered pleas and groans.

Mila drew her feet up onto the table with a shiver. Aften hastily climbed beside her as the tiny figures crawled over his legs and feet. The little people began to thin before her eyes.

"The people were starving, desperate. An answer was needed. King Barleyn decided we would expand Astera to the nearby mainland. Our island is isolated, but a sliver of the continent to the southeast could have been negotiated to us or won in a small war. It would have been enough to save us, to build a port town that we controlled."

All the dark figures, those in the center and around the edge, began to clap—but no sound reached Mila's ears.

"That is when this manipulative faction of nobles came to me." Ninian's voice darkened once more, the magician's words echoing impossibly loud off the chamber's stone. He appeared once more, hands folded neatly. The dark people stepped toward him, offering a hefty coin purse.

"They offered me their unending patronage in exchange for a single small vial—an alchemical to be used against our enemies. One soldier, they said, sneaking into the camp and poisoning the meals of the opposing army. They told me it could save the lives of thousands of our people and turn the war to come in our favor. We were so small a kingdom. Any fighting would have been catastrophic to our way of life." He reached out a shadowy hand, taking the coin. "So I agreed."

The dark figures and their heaps of goods vanished. Instead, glittering worktables rose all around them, full of vials and jars that bubbled over flames, piles of plants, and other, stranger things. "You must understand. I thought I was doing what was right for our people when I designed a toxin that could not even be traced as such. It took the form of a plague, a sign of the ancestor's scorn. The Ravan kingdom to the south believes strongly in such portents from their gods. I had designed for them a sign, so they might surrender to us. I thought myself so clever. So wise."

Ninian bowed his head, even as he lifted a roll of leather with several small stoppered bottles inside. He coiled it closed, fastening its ties and holding it out. The shadowy figures appeared around him and took their prize.

"The war never came," he said, the shadows falling away from him. The dust settled around them slowly. "First, they staged the coup. King Barleyn died. His son, Yewen, barely escaped. They said it was Ravans who had caught wind of the war. Few believed them. Leaderless, Astera floundered. That faction began its manipulations again. They convinced the others that renovating the city was necessary. They began by building a great stone wall around the poorest homes of our city and renaming it the Gate Quarter."

Half-heartedly, the dust built a small wall that ran through the room.

"The vulnerable lived there. The nobles of that faction took their ill-gotten food stores and poisoned them—then gave them away. They *gave* them freely to the poorest and hungriest first. To the needy, the desperate. It was *relief*. And as the apparent plague swept through our kingdom, those nobles took seats of power—to *save* us, they said." Ninian's lips coiled in disgust as the flickering light of the candles sputtered to life above them once more.

"The Ruling Council…murdered Asterans?" Mila asked, numb from head to toe.

"They did, and we Ominir? We helped, my dear."

Nausea rolled over her. Mila wrapped her arms tight around herself. She felt as if she couldn't draw in a breath. *My family helped murder innocent people?*

"So they got rid of the king because he wouldn't agree to poison his own people? That's awful!" Aften said, incensed.

"And his most loyal followers. The last dregs of once-great noble families were forced to flee into the hills and eventually into the tunnels they dug beneath our fair city. Your family, Aften Sivivan, is one of the oldest noble houses in Astera's history. You were the third, I believe, to be given noble title after the founding."

Aften's eyes widened.

"But the Vaim—" Darran began.

"Ah, yes." Ninian interrupted, lifting a hand. "I told you that was my doing. After I realized what the newly formed Ruling Council had done, I was angry. I found out what they had planned next, as well. Either I would be *their* mage, lauded as their greatest ally and loyal to their every whim—or it would be revealed that it was my toxin that killed our people. They would say it was at the late King Barleyn's orders. I would be slain as a convenient scapegoat.

"I could not let them do that, of course. To me, to my family, or to the Asterans. The truth would not be buried with me, not if I could help it. I vowed to set it right with every ounce of my power—and all the power in our kingdom.

"The Vaim are the result of my curse."

Mila started, knocking a jar off the table. It shattered on the stone floor. Aften jumped at the sound.

"Curse?" Darran asked blankly.

The ghost of Ninian Ominir rose several inches off the floor, his arms spread wide. The cobweb sleeves and hem of his robe fluttered wildly around him as the air swirled. The candlelight flickered and swayed madly above them. Jars and bottles rattled. Dust fell off the tables with a hiss.

Ninian's voice reverberated like the bone-deep toll of a bell. "Let those who have been wronged rise to find their justice and their peace. Let those who wronged them die by tooth and claw and rending hand. Let those who failed their people suffer until every drop of their blood is wiped from this kingdom's shores. Let those who descend from them find no welcome here. Let them be Asteran no more."

Aften stood abruptly as the magician's ghost sank back to the floor, hands curled into fists. "The Vaim are the spirits of the poor that were murdered all that time ago—and they're bound to *your* revenge!"

Darran remained seated, his face ashen. "They murder the descendants of that noble faction that paid you. They murder the descendants of the original Ruling Council."

Silence settled around them all for several moments. The realization of it all sank into Mila's skin slowly. It burned within her. *The Vaim are my family's warped creation, my family's responsibility. We twisted Astera into the nightmare it is today. We changed the life of* everyone *on this island.*

For what? Revenge? We've murdered as many people over hundreds of years as the Ruling Council killed in one fell blow!

She was on her feet, pacing back and forth. She didn't know when she had stood. Her mind churned. "It's up to us to do something. Curses can be broken, can't they?" She turned to her grandfather.

He gave a soft smile, hazy and indistinct, and nodded once.

"How do we break the curse?" she asked hastily.

"There are three ways to do it. I tried to make it...easier." Ninian said placidly. "First, we get our revenge upon those who wronged the spirits of our people."

"But after all these years, the people dying aren't just members of those families," Aften shouted. "They'd kill Darran, who hasn't done anything!"

"Three hundred years ago, they had bastard children," Mila continued. "Those bastards had children, and *their* children had children—and all the while, the Ruling Council kept making more bastards. You might end up killing hundreds or *thousands* of people!"

"Yes, that is something that I realized some time ago," Ninian mused. "I had not thought they would be clever enough to leave the island each night. My mistake was not realizing that I could only bind a few at a time. The Vaim killed two on their first night. It took me moons to summon enough for the task. I couldn't get the Ruling Council all at once. They caught on before I had finished and took to their ships."

"The Vaim in the water—who are *they*?" Aften asked suddenly.

"The Ruling Council ordered the Gate Quarter closed to contain the plague—and fired canons at the poor who tried to row around their wall. Those who died in the water haunt it."

"All this time..." Mila pressed her fingers to her temples.

"I had anticipated a much shorter-lived affair. However, once a curse is cast..."

"You have to break it." Darran rose from the stool.

Aften groaned, dragging a hand down his face. "Why does magic have to be so complicated?"

"So that it cannot be misused," Ninian answered.

"What's the second way?" Darran asked.

"For the descendants of the Royal Family to be anointed with my blood and reclaim their throne. I trust the progeny of King Barleyn to rule Astera wisely and would go quietly into the night. I am the last of his loyal subjects left alive."

"Alive?" Darran said blandly.

"In one sense of the word," Ninian agreed with a soft laugh.

"The rumor about the descendant of the king that escaped..." Aften mused.

"Yes, the Royal Family had one survivor," Ninian said, lifting a single finger into the air.

"And he stayed with the Nattfolk for a while, underground."

"But the journals said the descendant vanished and was never seen or heard from again." Aften groaned.

Ninian gave a sad smile. "It was our crown prince who escaped, Prince Yewen." He sighed. "They hunted for him a long time. They hid his existence from the people, squashing all hope. They tried to hide me, too, when I would not tell them how to break my curse. They built the wall to hide my chambers."

The magician began to laugh, a deep laugh with a manic edge that raised the hair on Mila's arms. "The fools. The dead do not forget or forgive! The curse demanded my life; now all that I have *left* to tether me to this earth is my revenge!"

Mila shuddered as the half-maddened spirit cackled. She sucked in a deep breath. "And the third?" She asked loudly, interrupting his deranged mirth.

Ninian sobered at once, meeting her gaze. "My clever granddaughter. The third option is to ensure it can never happen again. Our island is getting crowded—in a decade, they may hurt our people once more. I want the rest of my poison back. The leader of the Ruling Council has it. He always has."

"They still have it?" Aften's voice cracked.

"Yes, and I will not let them use it. Not if I or any of my descendants may prevent it," Ninian said. His orange eyes bored into Mila's.

She gasped, hand flying to her lips. Her mouth went dry, and she swayed where she stood. *All the answers—they were right here.* "I'm insurance. Soren wanted to merge his family line with mine. With yours, Grandfather!"

Darran caught her elbow, lowering her onto the stool, worry lines etched into his brow. "What do you mean?"

"The nobleman that wanted to marry me, he wanted to tie our bloodlines together as...as some sort of protection. To end the separation of my line from the Ruling Council's. Why would his family ever try to break the curse? He said I was of the noblest of families—he meant because of my ties to *you*!" She looked at Ninian. "The Ruling Council *knows*. They know what the Vaim are. They know what they did."

The depth of their lies and corruption was stunning. It left Mila reeling.

"They do," Ninian confirmed. "They pass the secret along to whoever takes a seat upon the Council. *Only* when they have taken their seat. Anyone who does not swear to keep the secret is murdered. Any they deem unworthy of ever hearing it dies conveniently before they can take their place. Like the young man that Thislen and I discussed," He drifted over to the window and its waterfall, peering through it to study the sleeping thief.

"Percivan Coppermund," Mila breathed, eyes wide.

"And their leader has the poison?" Aften repeated, rubbing his head and squinting at the floor.

"Which one is their leader, Mila?" Darran asked.

"Lord Soren Bestant, I think. The man who wanted to marry me," she whispered.

Ninian turned his attention to his granddaughter, a brow raised.

"Well, do you know where to find him? Do you know where he might hide something?" Aften asked.

"On his ship, probably. Thislen's been there. Thislen knows more than any of us about where it is and how to get aboard, and how to take something without getting caught." She rose from the stool, joining the spirit beside the shimmering glass. "We need him, Grandfather. Please."

Ninian studied her closely. "He is important to you." It wasn't a question.

"Yes. He's my friend, and a protector. He's better at solving problems than anyone else I know." Her chin lifted. "He's the reason I'm here, and the whole reason I'm not married off to Soren Bestant right now."

He stared at her in silence for an impossibly long time. The only sound in the room was the soft chime of the water as it poured down into the pool.

What is he thinking? What does he see? She wondered.

"You would do well to take good care of your friends, Granddaughter. They are all more important than you realize." He said slowly, and lifted his hand.

Beyond the glass, Thislen jerked awake as if he had just left a bad dream. He rolled to his feet instinctively, freezing as his boots landed on the floor. Mila watched his head turn, taking in the ornate room. She watched him feel over the fine clothes he had been dressed in. His awe was clear. At last, he turned toward the glass.

At the sight of Mila, all the tension ran out of his shoulders and he grinned.

Mila's heart lifted at the sight, and she found she was smiling back. Every ounce of weight she had carried on her shoulders was gone. She could have flown.

One of the wooden panels of the wall swung open within the room. Thislen stepped through it without hesitation. Stone ground against stone and another hidden door opened. The thief emerged a heartbeat later.

"Mila. Aften, Darran. You came." He sighed, smile wide. His relief dripped from every word.

A moment after he finished speaking, Mila threw herself across the room. She flung her arms around his neck, hugging him tightly.

He caught himself so they wouldn't fall, returning her embrace tightly. "*Ouch,* Mila. Why—why are you all wet? What did I miss?"

THISLEN KNEW EXACTLY what he had missed. He remembered the Vaim and their clutching hands dragging him up the stairs like eager pups taking their owner a prize. He remembered the stone door opening and the spirits disappearing behind him. He remembered Ninian appearing before him.

"Ah, I had not thought to see one of your kind alive on this island," Ninian had said.

The same tale Mila was recounting to him now was the same tale he had been told—only his version contained more detail.

"So we have to break the curse. We can help *every* Asteran, Thislen. My family made a mistake. Please, you'll help me fix it, won't you?"

Thislen's mind went to Percivan Coppermund. *"Find Soren, he's—"* The voice in his head called.

He was naming his murderer. Percivan Coppermund had been lured to his death by the Ruling Council just for being too kind to keep their dark secret. Vern the sailor had died keeping Thislen's, two spirits that only existed because they had been murdered.

Where Mila had seen a way to help all the people of the kingdom, Thislen had seen only more corruption revealed. The Ruling Council couldn't get away with this. He understood Ninian and his curse better than he thought he would. Thislen wanted revenge against his cousin. It burned within him, a small flame that threatened to grow large and wild if he let it out of his control. *The least I owe Percivan is closure. I'll see Soren Bestant pay for his crimes, one way or another, and be done with it.*

"Of course I'll help. We can't leave things like this," he said grimly.

"What about you?" Aften asked, clapping Thislen on the shoulder.

"What do you mean?"

"What happened after the Vaim took you at the door?"

Thislen studied the concerned and eager faces of his companions and weighed his options. Did they want to know the truth? He could spare them, tell them only the barest details of what happened, of what was discussed—or he could add to the secrets revealed in the dusty workroom of the dead magician.

Am I ready? Is this the right time?

Was there ever a right time? Hoping there was, Thislen tucked his secrets away once more. "The Vaim dragged me up here. Tore my clothes up. I was a mess. Worse than you lot look right now, if you can believe that."

Mila tucked a cobweb-sticky strand of hair out of her face with a soft scoff. "I doubt that."

He shrugged. "Everything went black after Ninian came out. When I woke up, I was on the floor out here. Ninian apologized to me and offered to talk. We talked about what he was, and I told him all about you." Thislen met Mila's bright green eyes.

"You talked about me?"

"Not exactly," Ninian interjected. "Only that my family line was still going strong and was alive, and was helping the Nattfolk get by. The best I could have wished for my lineage."

"I told him that Olen wasn't telling me everything, and neither of us could figure out exactly what it was your father was keeping secret. Then he told me I should rest. Next thing I know, I woke up in that fancy room, dressed nice as you pleased and smelling like flowers—and you were here."

Mila huffed softly, slugging him lightly in the shoulder. "I was worried sick that you were dead, and here you were getting baths and napping. It isn't fair."

Thislen gave a rueful smile. "Didn't mean to worry you. Ninian wouldn't let me out again, and I'm pretty sure the sleeping was because of a spell or something." He glanced to the side, only to find the space empty. His brow furrowed as he cast about the rest of the room.

"Hey—" Aften said, following Thislen's gaze. "Ninian's gone!"

Though the lights still flickered above them, the dust and haze had settled. There was no sign of life or undeath in the room besides the four companions.

"He just…left?" Mila murmured.

"I did not." Ninian's words came as an indistinct whisper floating all around them. "However, it is time for you to do so. Goodbye for now, Granddaughter." The stone door that led to the rest of Perilee swung open as his voice faded away.

The candles flickered, their flames growing smaller and smaller until they at last winked out. The only light that remained poured out of the gold and white room beyond the waterfall's window, spilling across the floor. Thislen stared at that room for several moments before he turned to leave. The others followed.

As he strode down the corridor, Thislen rolled up his fine shirt's sleeves. His new clothes were old-fashioned, but not out of style. He was glad they were at least practical to move in. The lanterns in the corridor flared to life before them as they traveled the carpeted hallways and faded when they had passed. He did his best to ignore the tapestries and paintings on the walls, not daring to look into the expectant faces of figures long dead or forgotten.

"What's our plan, Thislen?" Mila asked near his shoulder.

His steps slowed. He felt his pulse flutter in his neck. *Wait, when did I become the one in charge?* "You're asking me?" He lifted a hand to point toward Darran, only for Mila to interrupt him with a heavy sigh.

"You're right. This is my family's problem. I should take some responsibility. It's my job to fix it." Her brow furrowed in thought.

That wasn't what I meant, but I'm not going to argue. It might be good for Mila, he reflected, to take control of her own life.

He dropped his hand back to his side. Mila led the way toward the grand staircase that would take them out of Perilee. Thislen found himself walking shoulder to shoulder with Darran. Aften was on the other side of the scout captain.

"Nice clothes," Darran said quietly.

"Uh. Thanks." Thislen ran his thumb down the embroidered trim of his tunic. The fine fabric caught on his rough fingertips.

Down the stairs they went, their footsteps echoing as they reached the polished stone floor of the foyer. The once-closed entrance of Perilee now stood open to the gardens and the stars beyond. As they headed for the open air, Thislen felt the looming double doors of the throne room behind him like eyes boring into the space between his shoulder blades. He refused to look back at them, though it made his skin crawl. The air in the castle was heavy with expectation.

Leave me alone, he urged. The feeling vanished.

As they passed out of Perilee, it was as if a weight had been lifted off his shoulders. He breathed deeply of the salt-sweet air of Astera.

Mila whirled abruptly before them, coming to a stop and planting her hands on her hips. It startled Thislen. *Exactly how long was I asleep?* Mila Ominir was covered in dirt and grime. Her clothes were a torn and dusty mess. She was no longer a demure young woman, tucking her hair behind her ears or politely smiling at Soren in her shop. She was no longer clinging to Thislen's hand for support. He saw in a glance that she was different. *Maybe learning her family's secret has somehow put steel in her spine.*

"Alright, here's the plan," Mila said firmly. "Well, it's more of an idea, but we can figure out the details together. Thislen, you know which ship belongs to the Bestants. We'll just sneak on board and search the ship when it's quiet."

"The ships are hardly ever quiet, and it's almost impossible to get on board," Thislen pointed out. "I did it alright when it was just me on my own, but there's *four* of us. During the day, there's housekeepers to tend to the ship. At night, there're sailors and staff on hand. The sailors stay awake all night. Every one of those people would notice four new faces."

Her expression fell. "Then they'd notice if we tried to disguise ourselves *as* staff." She sighed, pacing back and forth on the cobblestones before the castle, deep in thought.

Thislen grimaced. *This is going to be suicide, all of us going at once—but she's determined. If we're to have half a chance, I need to help.*

"The best way onto the ships is to swim to them. Aften, Darran, do the pendants keep the Vaim in the water from coming after us?"

"No," Darran said heavily.

"I wish we could ask Ninian why not," Aften said.

"Want to go back in there and try?" Darran asked, turning toward the darkened castle.

The front doors swung shut with a dull *thud*.

"If we can't swim at night, it just means our window of opportunity is smaller." Thislen interrupted before they could go try to open the doors again. "The best time would be right after dawn. The ship pulls in, the docks get crowded. If we're quiet about it and we duck behind a pile of crates or something to hide what we're doing, no one will even notice us slipping into the water. Staff and provisioners and noble families will all be milling around, and we'll be inconsequential."

"And once we're in the water, we can swim around to the far side of the ship. No one will see us there." Mila suggested, her pacing coming to a stop.

"Exactly," Thislen said.

Mila began to gesture animatedly as she caught on to his plan. "We get in the ship, find a good place to hide, and then wait. Late at night, everyone below-decks will be asleep even if the sailors aren't. We'll have plenty of time to search uninterrupted. So we just hold out until evening, and then—"

"We find the vials!" Aften cheered.

"We bring them back to Ninian," Thislen said.

"And that will break the curse." Darran finished firmly.

Mila came to a stop once more. The four of them looked at one another. Thislen watched Aften's grin grow and spread to Darran, then Mila. His was the only solemn face of the bunch.

"This isn't a game," he reminded them. "Remember that if we fail, our lives are forfeit."

Mila's smile vanished. "Then we had better not fail," she said grimly.

"Let's go then," Darran said, glancing up at the sky. "It's only an hour or two before dawn. We spent a lot more time here than I thought."

"Magic," Aften said with a shudder.

"Could be," Darran agreed.

Aften shuddered again.

They slipped back into the streets by using Perilee's side gate. Slowly they wove their way through the alleyways of Astera, alert for any sign of Nattfolk pursuit. They didn't know if Mila and Aften's escape had been noticed yet. Thislen was furious when they explained in whispers what the Night Council had done.

They also avoided the milling Vaim, afraid the creatures might stir and follow them down the streets like large and vengeful hounds once more. It made it difficult to travel, but not impossible.

At last they reached the bridges that led to the Grand Quarter. Darran took the lead, crouching and running along in the shadowed lee of the low stone walls. The broad avenues were bereft of the Vaim milling about. Instead, crowds four or five deep were gathered around some of the gates of the great estates, expectant red eyes fixated on the empty abodes as if they could sense where their murderers lived.

Maybe they can, Thislen realized. A shiver arced through him like lightning. Perhaps that was how they had known of his Bestant blood.

They threaded their way through the broad avenues in the deep shadows of the trees that lined them, making good time to the docks on the eastern edge of the island. They arrived well before dawn's light.

"Wait here," Thislen said. He trotted toward the corner of the wall that led to the Bestant estate and the vessels behind it, taking stock of their options. The wood planks of the dock were neatly stacked with crates at regular intervals, no doubt full of goods for replenishing the nobles' ships when they came ashore. None of the heaps of goods was large enough to hide all four of them at once.

After looping the dock and the back of the Bestant estate twice, Thislen was forced to concede the best hiding place was behind the hedges that lined the estate's back wall. A bit of prodding revealed a place where the shrubbery had died from a lack of light, leaving a small, hidden hollow.

Thislen was quick to lead his companions to their safe haven. Once the four of them had pushed their way into the bush, it was uncomfortably crowded. Darran's knees were pressed against Thislen's, and Mila's elbow dug sharply into his side. They wriggled and twisted until they were all as comfortable as they could get, muttering soft curses the entire time.

"Ow, that's my foot!"

"Hells, whose elbow is that?"

"What is this? Oh, it's a rock."

"Ouch! Will you please watch your shoulder? That was my eye."

At last they stilled. *We're safe,* Thislen thought with a sigh, head tipping back against the wall behind him, *we're all safe—for now.*

"My clothing should be good enough to fool people into thinking I am a nobleman, a rich merchant, or a seneschal. They'll think you belong with me. New hires for one of the ships, maybe," he whispered.

"Then we can sneak into the water," Mila said, pleased with herself and her plan.

"Are you sure this will work?" Aften asked from somewhere behind Darran.

"It should. I've done it before. Just before Mila and I were captured."

"Is that how you got caught?" Darran asked dryly.

"No."

They lapsed into silence, waiting for the dawn. Thislen couldn't help but look down the row of his companions—no, his *friends*—and feel a knot forming in the pit of his stomach.

When did I become responsible for this many people?

MILA'S FOOT WAS ASLEEP. The sky was lightening and the tedious wait was coming to an end, but it would still be some time before they moved. And when they *did,* her foot would be asleep. She worried that limping might draw attention to them, but she couldn't stick her foot out of the hedges and wiggle life into her toes when they were supposed to be hiding! Could she? What if she did, and she and her companions got caught?

Some heroes we would be. Who would rescue us then?

But she had found Thislen. While it hadn't been the daring rescue she had anticipated and feared, she had still braved the unknown to do it. Now she was faced with an actual rescue on a much larger scale.

I have a chance to save the life of every resident of Astera and all the Asteran people to come. She had never mattered this much before. In a few days' time, she had gone from entirely unremarkable to the descendant of a mad magician who could break a curse. Yet if she failed, no one would ever know.

If I succeed, I can explain the truth to the whole kingdom. Would they understand? Would they blame *her* for her greatest grandfather's curse?

His *curse*! The Vaim were on the island solely for the revenge of Ninian Ominir. *Even if he thinks he is helping those murdered, is he really?* The hundreds of years of deaths and the fear of an entire kingdom for generations were squarely on the magician's shoulders. The entire underground city of the Nattfolk only existed because of the Ruling Council's callousness and one man's choice to avenge the dead.

Yet no one ever asked the Vaim if they wanted to be avenged. No wonder they always seem so angry.

There was time yet before the sun rose in earnest, and she couldn't take it any longer. Mila eased her foot out of the hedges. At Thislen's curious glance, she gave a sheepish smile.

"I'm just stretching."

He nodded.

Nothing more was said. The sky lightened. They heard the clangor of the first bells on the water. Dawn had arrived at last, and the ships would be making their way back to their berths. Mila grimaced. It hadn't been long enough. Her entire leg was still tingling as she pulled her foot back in.

Something caught around her ankle in a vice-like grip. She gasped, picturing the talon-like fingers of the Vaim. *But it's dawn!*

The unseen hand pulled.

Mila kicked, covering her mouth with a hand to smother the urge to scream. She grabbed Thislen's arm.

He looked at her a moment before she was yanked forward.

Darran and Thislen caught her arms and hauled her back into the shelter of the hedge, pulling her assailant in as well. Tamsa fell into the bush with a snarl. "I knew I'd find you," She spat, nearly nose to nose with Mila. She reached for the apothecary's hair.

Aften flung his arms around his sister without hesitation, toppling them both. They wrestled in the dirt, grunting and growling. Darran and Thislen made room and helped pin Tamsa down. Mila wrangled the Nattfolk's feet.

When everything stilled, the four of them sat perched upon the trapped Tamsa. They were all panting heavily. *Ancestors, what if someone heard us?* Mila thought, heart pounding in her chest.

"What do you think you're doing?" Tamsa seethed, beating her fists against what she could reach of Aften's legs. "You're about to break the oldest law we have, Aften. And how *dare* you drag Darran into this mess just because you—"

Aften slapped a hand over Tamsa's mouth, giving Darran a wild-eyed look.

"No one dragged me into this, Tamsa. You don't understand what we're doing." Darran said, ignoring whatever secret Aften had just hidden.

She jerked her head away, glaring up at her brother. "I know *exactly* what you're doing. You're running away to the Solfolk, which is forbidden. I demand you all come home with me right this instant. You're all going to be banished from Astera, do you realize that? Father can't protect you from this, Aften! You're so selfish; you've torn our family apart."

Mila's heart went out to the scout as Aften flinched. His expression crumpled, though he turned away quickly to hide it from them. Darran touched Aften's shoulder.

Heat rose in Mila's cheeks. "Aften did *nothing* wrong. We are not trying to rejoin the Solfolk, Tamsa; we're trying to get rid of the Vaim!"

Tamsa scoffed. "Right, because that's possible."

"It is," Darran said, steel in his voice. "You need to learn to listen to others if you want to lead, and you can start by listening to me. I joined them willingly. After everything you learned in those journals, I'm surprised you aren't joining us, too. We've found a way to save the

Nattfolk and the Solfolk alike from any more suffering. We have a chance to help the entire kingdom. Tamsa, we can stop hiding!"

Tamsa scowled. "We don't *want* to get rid of the Vaim. They're our security. They keep the Nattfolk safe. All those deemed too dangerous by the Ruling Council are spared by us, saved by us. Our entire society is protected from those bastards by the ghosts you want to get rid of. You're the ones in the wrong."

"You don't have to be a separate society," Mila said, voice rising. "You can't ask countless people to be at risk and live in fear their entire lives just because it's convenient for you."

"Shut up, Solfolk."

The clamoring bells were closer now. Somewhere just beyond the screen of leaves, the first ships were coming in to dock.

There's no more time to argue with her, Mila realized. "I have a proposal, a compromise," she said.

All eyes turned to her. Their scrutiny made her falter. Tamsa's dismissive roll of her eyes was bad enough, but the hope in Darran and Aften's eyes was somehow worse. Thislen watched her with a calm and calculating gaze.

He hasn't said a word this whole time. What is he watching for? Is he waiting to see if I might fail? How many more times could she falter and have him there to pick her up? Here she was, once more gambling with their lives.

"Tamsa, give us today to do what we came here to do. Come tonight, we'll explain everything. All of it, I swear. If we fail, you can take us back to the Nattfolk, and we can leave our fate in the hands of your father and the Night Council."

If they failed, however, she knew they wouldn't make it back to shore.

Thislen's brows rose. Still, he said nothing. Not a word. Unease settled between her shoulders, but she kept her chin lifted and her expression calm. The thief turned away from her, his shoulders taut and squared.

He doesn't think she'll agree to let us try. He has a point.

Tamsa scoffed. "Do I even have a choice? What are you doing here anyway? What's your foolish, stupid plan?"

"Shh," Darran hissed, covering her mouth gently with a hand.

Voices had begun to sound beyond the hedgerow. Mila shifted until she could see through the leaves. In the early morning light, night servants were pouring off the ships to tend to what chores they had to do before the daylight servants arrived. Mila watched some of them jog toward the homes of the nobles they served. Others carried things off the galleons. Some began to load goods *onto* the ships from the heaped crates on the docks.

The nobility did not yet appear. *Most likely, they're all still abed or just now waking up.* Perhaps they were just rising, waiting for baths to be drawn, hair to be styled, or fanciful clothes to be laid out. None of them would be seen for some time yet.

"Is this the sort of crowd you wanted, Thislen?" She whispered.

The thief studied the milling throng. "Not just yet. We have to wait for the first servants to come back. That's how we know it won't be suspicious. They'll think we've arrived from some other ship."

Tamsa began to struggle once more, thrashing beneath them. Mila held on grimly to her ankles. Aften let out a sudden quiet curse before he pinned his sister's arms down by her sides. "She punched me in the nose! Is it bleeding?"

"Let me see." Darran leaned over. "No, you're alright."

"Doesn't feel like it," Aften groaned.

"We can't risk her causing a scene, Mila," Thislen whispered.

"Someone will have to stay here with her, then."

"I'll do it," Aften said. "We have some things we need to talk about anyway."

Mila knew the conversation would *not* be a pleasant, loving one.

"There," Thislen said sharply.

The first carriages were arriving from the houses of the nobility to take them in comfort back to their own estates. The clop of hooves on the cobblestones mingled with the murmur of the crowds. The light was growing stronger.

"It's time, right?" Mila whispered urgently.

"Yes." Thislen said.

"Stop this right now," Tamsa spat quietly from the ground. "Whatever idiotic plan you have, you're wrong. You can't have it both ways. You can't go out during the day without exposing us. You're risking the life of every Nattfolk, and for what? Revenge against some petty nobleman?"

A nervous laugh bubbled in Mila's chest. She smothered it with a snort. "In a way, this *is* about revenge."

Just not mine. Everything that had come before learning who her family was and what they had done seemed so inconsequential. It wasn't *her* revenge that drove her, but rather stopping Ninian Ominir's.

I'm not even angry at Soren, she realized, *not really. He's just one in a long line of terrible Bestants. What chance did he have? No, I don't mind that I was set on this path.*

I...like it here with the Nattfolk. Well, with Thislen and Darran and Aften.

Every day was a new adventure where no one tried to coddle her and protect her and keep her tucked away safe. She felt more like herself than she ever had when she worked in the shop. All that was missing was her family.

We can get them as soon as we're done here.

"Mila," Thislen said, low and urgent.

"Right. Let's go," she said firmly, fighting the sudden knot in her stomach as she climbed out of the hedge.

Thislen was the next on his feet, dusting off his fine tunic and pushing a hand through his dark hair. Darran followed, falling into step beside Mila as she let Thislen take the lead. Aften was left sitting squarely on Tamsa's back, holding her arms pinned down.

"Right, you lot, keep up. Come along. Have to get you cleaned and dressed if you expect to work here," Thislen said. His tone surprised Mila, sending a shiver down her spine. He spoke with a cultured tone that sounded just like Soren or Avasten or Garridan, pulling it on with the ease of a mask. The thief snapped his fingers in their direction. "I say, pay attention."

Darran had been gawking left and right, very convincingly playing the dazed commoner. *Or perhaps he isn't play-acting at all,* she realized. He started when he was snapped at, turning his attention to Thislen.

"What? Oh. Yes, sir. Sorry, sir."

"Now, were you listening when I described your duties?" Thislen asked a moment before they were swallowed by the milling crowd.

The chatter around them negated the need to speak any further. Mila felt as if she could breathe again. Somehow being one in a crowd seemed safer to her, as though she were entirely anonymous. She was back to being just one woman in Astera, nothing more, and she couldn't hope for more than that.

Mila followed Thislen as they wove through the mass of people, traveling along the dock beyond the first ship. Darran was a half a pace ahead of her. Thislen showed no sign of stopping even though the side of the hull read *'Bestant Belle.'*

Instead, he led them a short way down the dock. They ducked behind a stack of crates, and Thislen gestured for Mila and Darran to quickly climb into the water. Darran went first, and Mila followed, lowering herself into the waves to avoid making a splash. It was frigid, and her clothes clung uncomfortably to her arms and legs. Thislen joined them a moment later, heedless of his finery.

He led them beneath the pier a few lengths. With a deep breath, the thief sank beneath the water's surface. Mila could just make out the shape of him swimming around the bow of the *Belle*. Darran followed. Mila did her best, but she did have to surface once to catch her breath. No surprised shouts met her ears, no one calling out.

In the lee of the ship, Thislen was treading water and holding onto the massive anchor chain. "Swim down to the other end. I'll get the window open to the great room and find a rope," he whispered.

He moved like a squirrel, up the chain and across the decorative carvings of the ship. Mila couldn't help but cast around, waiting for someone to notice him. No one did. Their luck was holding.

Maybe the island itself wants the curse broken. Maybe our ancestors do.

She swam slowly along the length of the ship with Darran behind her. The rope fell in front of her face, startling her. Though her hands were numb with cold, she held on tight and let Thislen haul her up to the window ledge.

Mila lay panting on the plush rug of the great room, staring up at the unlit lanterns of the ceiling as she tried to catch her breath. Thislen braced himself as Darran climbed up the rope next.

"We made it," Darran panted, shivering.

"We did. Now we should hide somewhere dry," Thislen said.

"But it'd be in here, wouldn't it?" Mila sat up, looking at the bookshelves along the walls, the heavy ornate desk in the corner, and the delicate bar tucked beside the door. "Thislen, where would you hide a...a safe or something?"

Thislen looked around the room. "In here? Behind..." He glanced at the painting above the bar. "Behind a painting, under a rug, in the desk itself."

Mila stood, hurrying over to the painting and giving it a pull. It didn't come off the wall—but it did swing.

A safe.

"Thislen, open it!" She whispered urgently. *Please let the vials be in there. Please let it be this easy.*

Thislen passed Darran the rope, and the Nattfolk began to coil it up as the thief crossed the room, pulling tools out of the pouch on his belt.

Darran swore suddenly, tugged forward. He leaned back instinctively, and a moment later, Tamsa's head appeared at the window. "Stop right there!" she shouted.

Mila felt her heart stop in her chest. "Tamsa?"

Tamsa tumbled through the window, crossing the room and grabbing Mila by the wrist so hard it hurt.

"Get off me," Mila said urgently.

"No! I'm not going to let you rob them; you're going to get us all in trouble."

"I lost my grip," Aften panted, his head appearing at the window as well. He pulled the end of the rope up with him as he slung a leg into the room. "I'm sorry." Water was making the blood from his nose run all over his face and shirt front.

"Let's go. *Now,*" Tamsa insisted.

She wasn't bothering to be quiet. *Our plan,* my *plan—*

Thislen scowled and turned back toward the safe.

"Stop that!" Tamsa shouted.

"Get her!" Aften lunged from the window with Darran was hot on his heels. Mila backpedaled out of the way— right as the door opened. She bumped into someone. She whirled, hands raised to cover the mouth of the servant or sailor she was sure they had alerted.

Only it wasn't a servant. It was Soren.

"Well, excuse you," he said, grabbing her wrists and yanking her to one side. A few sailors hurried in after him, separating the brawling trio of Nattfolk on the floor. Thislen dropped his tools and turned toward the window to run, but he was tackled before he had gone two steps.

Mila twisted in Soren's grasp even as her heart sank to the ground. She felt the icy chill of the seawater in her clothes fall to her bones. Her plan had failed.

"Leaving so soon, Mila?" Soren whispered hotly in her ear.

Every inch of her skin crawled. Instinctively she twisted a hand free to punch the smug Lord Bestant right in the nose. Soren let go with a squawk of pain, hands flying to his face. A sailor grabbed Mila's arms instead, twisting them behind her back.

With a hand over his nose and his eyes watering madly, Soren glowered at her. "I will be very interested to hear how you are alive, Mila Ominir. Take them all to Ship Artaith," he commanded.

There was no hope now.

They were caught.

17

Ship Artaith was only a few ships up the dock from the *Bestant Belle.* As they reached the open air, Mila was shrouded in a cloak and guided along, stumbling every third step.

They don't want anyone to see me.

She tripped going up the gangplank of their new prison. For a heart-stopping moment, she pictured herself tumbling into the sea. Could she get the cloak off her head? Could she swim away? The guard that held her hands behind her back caught her with a yank and set her to rights with a wrench of her shoulder. She grimaced, biting back a yelp. Her arm throbbed as she made it onto the broad deck.

She caught only glimpses of the others from beneath the shelter of the cloak. Aften struggled wildly against two guardsmen who carried him lifted between them, thrashing like a fish in a net. Darran trudged along behind Aften, his guard on his heels. The scout captain's eyes darted this way and that, hunting for any exit—and finding none. Thislen had been knocked unconscious and was now being carried up the gangplank over the shoulder of one guard, groaning as he came around. His fingers twitched and curled slowly into fists.

Tamsa walked between her two guards with her head lifted like a queen. Every inch of her demeanor was icy and self-righteous as her eyes met Mila's. The "I told you so" radiated out from her smug, angry gaze like a beacon.

The nerve, when she's the one who got us caught! Mila flushed as that ember in her stomach stirred to life.

"What's all this, then?" Garridan asked from somewhere nearby.

"I'm certain Soren will tell us," Avasten said.

"I will. Can we use your guest suite, Garridan?" Soren said, following behind his sailors. He held a handkerchief up to his nose, dabbing away blood as bruises bloomed rapidly beneath his eyes. Mila took a grim pleasure in the damage to his pretty face.

The young Lord Artaith took command as his sailors quietly drew up the gangplank. "You lot, take them below. Put them in the big one." Garridan turned away from his captives to sweep an arm toward the cabin set upon the foredeck. Avasten and Soren headed that way, their host on their heels.

"Soren," Mila snarled, lunging toward him. The cloak fell to the deck. Her guard wrenched her back around, and Mila struggled to twist free. "Soren!"

"We'll talk later, Mila," Soren called without turning toward her.

The ember flared to life, growing into a hot molten core that heated her cheeks and fingertips. *Ancestors, if I could just reach him, I would smack him again!*

"Never," she spat. "I know what you did, you bastard. I know what your family did. How *dare* you do that to Percivan Coppermund? How *dare* you hide the secret of all those murders? You're the reason that the Vaim—"

Soren was across the deck so quickly she didn't even see him move. He slapped her full and hard across the face with a loud, crisp report. For a stunned moment, Mila felt nothing. Then, it began to burn.

"You will be silent," he hissed, leaning in. He grabbed her chin, forcing her to look at him. "You will not say another word until I *tell* you to. Then, you will sing, my little canary. I have so many questions for you now."

Though her eyes were watering, she refused to let a single tear fall. Soren leaned in toward her, his gaze dropping to her lips. Mila spat in his face. He jerked away with a disgusted growl, wiping the spittle off with the blood-spattered handkerchief.

"Take them below. Uncivilized spawn," Soren hissed. He walked away, toward Garridan and Avasten.

"Boorish prick!" Mila shouted at his back as her guard yanked her away. It felt *amazing* to vent her frustrations on their source—even if her circumstances were dire.

She was led, wrangled, and pushed down a narrow staircase that led below-decks, then shoved along a short, narrow corridor lined with doors. It was strange; there was no sign of opulence. The doors no doubt led to cabins, but the locks were in the corridor.

Cells. It's all cells, she realized.

At the end of the corridor was a cabin door that bore no lock at all. Mila was forced through it, stumbling into a single large chamber. The ship's ribs pulled inward at the sides only a little, but the ceiling was wider than the polished floor below. Glass-sided lanterns hung from heavy iron hooks in the beams. Narrow portholes let in the morning light at regular intervals. It would have been bright and inviting if it hadn't been for the iron bars that divided the space. A single door was set into the iron wall. Behind them, along the walls and fastened to the floor, were chains and heavy metal cuffs. All of the iron was pristinely polished, unlike *The Brig*'s damp and rusty cells. That didn't stop Mila from feeling a deep unease growing inside her.

The other half of the room, the half that was not a cell, bore a few tables and three different types of wooden chair, all bolted to the floors. Each chair had cuffs affixed on the back, on the sides, and on the arms. There were neatly rolled tubes of leather on the tables, the sort that often held workman's tools.

Somehow, I doubt they hold anything that would be used for honest craftsmanship.

The wood of the tables, chairs, and floor were well-polished, but there was a strange sickly red-brown staining to them all. It was mottled and inconsistent, grouped only around the furniture.

Mila felt herself go cold from the inside out at the dawning realization of what she was seeing. She recoiled against her guard as the man pushed her across the floor.

They're going to torture us, she thought, testing how it felt in her mind. Her unease grew wings and fluttered through her chest. She couldn't feel the tips of her fingers or her nose. *I won't last a single moment; I know it.*

Mila tried to summon the image of stone to her spine. People were depending on her. Not just her companions, but her father, the Nattfolk, and all of Astera. They only had a chance to break the curse if she were strong. *You have to try harder than you've ever tried,* she lectured herself. They were going to try and break them all, and all she could do was try not to shatter.

They were searched briefly, one by one. Mila was first. When they found no weapons on her, they flung her into the cell. She stumbled over the chains on the floor with a rattle, falling hard onto her hands and knees. They didn't take anything else from her.

Aften was quickly relieved of three knives and his glowing orb, which the guards observed with much interest. He was shoved in after her, though he caught himself quickly and flung himself at the door as it closed. The scout rattled the bars of the door. "Let us out, you bastards."

The cell door was opened again. Three guards bullied Aften back into a corner while Thislen was thrown unceremoniously onto the floor like a sack of flour. He groaned as he landed, rolling sluggishly onto his back. Mila crawled across the floor to his side, gingerly feeling the swelling lump on his head, probing it with her fingertips.

Tamsa was divested of a sling, a pouch of pebbles, and a knife. Mila only really noticed her in the cell when she stumbled into them and fell, landing beside the apothecary with an indignant yelp. Mila scowled and shoved the Nattfolk away from her.

Darran was last, stripped of his knives and a small keyring before he was pushed just inside the door. The guards that had been harassing Aften retreated. The Nattfolk scouts were not willing to be closed in without a fight. They struggled against the guards, shoving and swearing. It took an age for the men to get the cell closed and locked.

"Ugh!" Aften shouted, banging his hands against the door. "Assholes."

One guard laughed as he and his fellows left the room, abandoning the five companions to the soft creak of wood and the smell of soap and metal. No one spoke, though the air was heavy with panted breath.

Thislen reached up, fingers wrapped around something about his neck. He pulled it free with a sharp tug as he sat up, tucking it away in his boot.

Aften rattled the cell door again. It didn't budge.

We're trapped. We have to try and figure out what to do. There has to be something we can do. Mila thought, over and over. She couldn't see any way out, but that didn't stop her from wracking her brain.

Aften rounded on Tamsa, the fury of a hurricane in his eyes. "This is all *your* fault, Tamsa, you selfish witch."

"I was trying to save us all."

"No, you were trying to be *right*," Aften spat, "and to be Father's proper little shadow. Well, congratulations! You're going to kill us all, condemn the entire kingdom to an unending curse, *and* get our people killed. You *did* it! Aren't you *proud?*"

"Shut up, Aften," Darran said hastily from beside the bars. He was scanning the ceiling, the walls, the floors. "Don't say another word. We have to try and protect everything we know."

"We wouldn't have to if she—"

"I know." The captain turned to Aften, clasping his shoulder and cupping his cheek to draw the scout's attention. "I know," Darran repeated firmly. "She's wrong, and we're all going to suffer for her ignorance. Do you know what else I know? Nothing you say to her right now will change where we are."

He dropped his hands as Aften's shoulders sagged. The scout quietly dropped his forehead against Darran's shoulder.

"I wasn't trying to get us locked up. I meant to stop you from doing something stupid in the first place. How was I to know *her*," Tamsa turned a glare onto Mila, "stupid noble suitor would be there?"

Mila took a deep breath, looking up at the ceiling of the cell as if she might find some stray patience floating about. *Darran is right. Arguing with her won't help us now.*

"Whatever you *intended*, Tamsa, you're the reason we're trapped. Take your measure of the blame. Darran has a point; we can't change what happened. But if I were *you*? I would stop speaking. You are not among friends."

Tamsa opened her mouth, but Mila fixed the Nattfolk with a steady glower. Her gaze did not waver. Tamsa slowly closed her mouth. She turned to Darran and her brother, her silent gaze seeking even a flicker of care or forgiveness in their eyes. Darran's features were hard and unforgiving. Aften wouldn't even lift his head. Not a single ounce of pity was given to her.

With a huff, Tamsa gathered herself and retreated to a sloped corner of the cabin cell in silence.

Thislen opened his eyes, struggling to sit up. He grimaced as he felt over the lump on his head, taking in their surroundings for several moments. Mila couldn't read his expression. Was he resigned? Afraid? Did he have a plan? *I wish he would just open his mouth and speak.*

"The knot on your head will go down soon enough," Mila said, "but you should try not to sleep for a day or so."

"Where are they?" was all Thislen said in answer.

"Not here." Darran pulled Aften to sit near the thief and Mila, forming a small huddle as far away from Tamsa as they could.

Thislen met Mila's gaze for only a heartbeat before he tore his gaze away. His shoulders were taut beneath her hand. A shadow in his eyes made the fluttering in Mila's chest all the stronger.

He knows something I don't know. Still! He still *has secrets.* A flash of heat rose in her cheeks. Mila thought they had left the last of the secrets behind in Ninian's chambers, but she was wrong. The urge to shake Thislen grew stronger every second until she lifted her hands to his shoulders, turning him toward her. "Thislen—"

The door flew open with a *BANG*, startling them all. Mila hastily drew her hands back. Soren swanned in with Avasten in his shadow. Two personal guardsmen in Artaith livery followed, each carrying a cushioned chair. They set them near the table and a restraint-laden chair in the center of the room before retreating to flank the door.

Garridan stepped into the room last. He had changed out of his opulent clothing in favor of something a craftsman might wear. A plain brown shirt, a vest, and an oiled leather apron.

Avasten was the first to sink into a chair, propping his cheek on his hand as he leaned back. His every move had the air of someone about to watch a show they knew would disappoint them.

Soren smoothed his fine tunic before he sat, crossing a leg and lounging indolently like a young king upon a throne. He had cleaned himself up and set his nose, but the bruises under his eyes had turned a dark purple that was impossible to hide.

"The interesting thing about Astera's most noble families," he said as he laced his fingers together, "is that each one has a specialty they pass down. They're secrets, of course, for the most part. We so rarely get to discuss them. Take the Artaith family, for example. Centuries of work have gone into learning how to torture the enemies of the Ruling Council. He rarely gets to share that knowledge. You wouldn't mind if he shared it with you, would you?"

No one in the cell spoke. They didn't even move. Mila felt the flitter inside her return.

"Shall we begin, then, Garridan?" Soren asked airily.

"As you wish," the stocky torturer agreed. He went to the row of leather rolls, picking one and setting it on the table without opening it. Mila found herself grateful for that small mercy. The trembling in her chest already felt like it was building to a scream, and she wasn't certain she would have been able to hold it in if she had seen the contents.

"Who shall we start with, Soren?" Garridan asked, looking them over with his arms folded across his chest as he leaned casually against his workbench.

Like he's choosing a head of cabbage at the market.

Soren's gaze was predatory as he observed their captives, but his tone was as dismissive as someone debating which bottle of wine to serve with his supper. "Mila has little value to me; leave her for now. Hm, I suppose my cousin and I have our own unfinished business to attend to, don't we?"

Thislen bared his teeth. The Nattfolk turned to stare at him in numb surprise.

That's right. They didn't know, Mila realized. *We didn't tell them.*

"As you wish, cousin. You can wait. That leaves the three strangers. How *exciting* to have something new to play with." Soren leaned forward.

Instinctively, Darran put an arm up across Aften's chest, angling himself between their captors and the scout. The movement drew the attention of the gathered lords. Avasten leaned forward, steepling his fingers in sudden interest.

"Ah, there we go." Soren said smugly. "The brunet, Garridan."

"No!" Darran shouted as the guards left their posts beside the door and approached the cell.

Mila didn't remember getting to her feet, but she and the others were all standing as the guards opened the cell. Even Tamsa flung herself at the men in Aften's defense. Mila found herself in a confusing welter of limbs and sounds, lashing out with her elbows and feet. There was shoving, punching, shouting. She heard the sharp crack of someone getting slapped. The air flew out of her lungs as she was punched in the stomach. She staggered and fell to her hands and knees, coughing and gasping and fighting the urge to vomit as she fought for air. Feet flew around her and fists above, and then suddenly, the cluster of bodies broke apart.

The door to the cell clanged closed. Aften struggled wildly between the two guardsmen, writhing like he was possessed by one of the Vaim as he fought every inch of the way to the chair. They wrestled him into place and pinned him down while he snarled like a caged animal.

Calm as a mountain meadow, Garridan fastened the cuffs of the chair around Aften's neck, wrists, and ankles, securing him in place.

Mila flung herself at the bars of the cell, Thislen and Darran on either side. Tamsa, too was at the bars in her own corner. All of them were shouting. Her throat felt raw with how loud she was.

"Leave him alone!"

"Aften. Aften, hold on."

"Let him go, you bastards."

"He's not even part of this!"

They clamored and protested even as the guards stepped away. Garridan unrolled his tools. The lordling took his time, tracing his fingers over the selection of tiny saws, strange needled pinwheels, hooks, wires, and knives. Lovingly, he selected a filleting knife that had been polished to a gleam. It was small, delicate, and from how little he had to press it to the tip of his thumb before it drew blood? Sharp.

"I suggest you all *shut up*," he barked, "or I'll have no choice but to hurt him *before* I ask any questions."

The silence was immediate from everyone except Tamsa.

"Don't hurt him. If you swear not to hurt him, I'll tell you anything you want to know. Everything! *Everything* I know. Please, don't hurt my brother," she begged, clutching at the bars.

Garridan's brows shot up, but he stopped turning the small knife over in his hands.

Avasten let out a soft chuckle. "Oh, that *is* interesting."

"Tamsa, don't!" Aften shouted, glowering at her from the chair. His hands twisted and turned in the cuffs.

For a heartbeat, Mila felt numb at Tamsa's words. A cottony haze filled her head. *I must have misheard her. No one could be so stupid.*

But no, Tamsa had offered every single secret they had for nothing. *Why? To prove that she's not a horrible sister? To try and win Aften back, she's willing to sell out her entire people?* Heat rose through her, incinerating the downy feeling in a sudden flash of anger.

Mila launched herself across the cell with a shriek. "You absolute *bitch*!" She screamed so loudly that it scraped its way out of her throat.

They tumbled into the wall with a rattle of chains and a solid *thud*, then fell to the floor. Mila wrestled her way on top of Tamsa, grabbing her hair and clothes to pin her down. Tamsa pushed at her face, shouting something—but the apothecary wasn't listening. Not anymore. She punched Tamsa again and again and again.

Hands were suddenly all over her, tearing her away from the Nattfolk. Mila screamed wordlessly, kicking and lashing out at Garridan on one side and a guard on the other. Thislen and Darran fought with the second guard, trying to escape the corner they were pinned in. Mila was dragged out of the cell. She flung her feet and elbows and head indiscriminately as they went.

"Just throw her in a private cell for now," Soren shouted over the chaos. "I can deal with her later."

The second guard slammed the bars closed. Thislen and Darran rattled the door, shouting her name. Aften struggled in the restraints of the chair. Tamsa groaned on the floor, head lolling from one side to the other as she regained her wits.

The last thing Mila saw before the door was closed between them was the thief's pale face, their eyes locking together. His lips moved, but she didn't hear a word.

I'm out of ideas, Thislen realized. Mila had been dragged from the room. He could hear the faint hammering of a door somewhere, letting him know she was unharmed and angry—for now.

When Garridan and the guard had returned, they solved the problem of infighting once and for all. He, Aften, and Darran had been wrestled just far enough apart from one another that they could not touch and fastened to the walls and floors. Thislen was leaned against the gentle slope of the ship's side, the metal edges of his restraints biting into the flesh of his wrists.

Tamsa, the traitor, was now sitting in a cushioned chair obtained by the guards. She was unrestrained. A cool, damp cloth was pressed to her nose. One of her eyes was blossoming in a vivid purple bruise, and her lip was split and swollen.

Garridan was tending to her as gently and kindly as his noble heritage might wish. As if he weren't a part of his family's dark trade. Soren and Avasten sat nearby, looking on with feigned concern and *tsking* softly over her injuries as Tamsa felt them all over. It was feigned, Thislen knew, because these lords had no souls. *They don't care about anyone. Don't fall for it, Tamsa. You still have time to change your damn mind! Fool.*

Thislen closed his eyes. Things couldn't get any worse. *Here I am, captive again. Worse, Mila is captive again. Worst? Darran and Aften have been dragged into all of this mess.* He was out of options and out of time. And ideas.

"Are you feeling well enough to speak to us now?" Garridan asked softly. Thislen opened his eyes to see the lordling's hand outstretched for the cloth.

Tamsa passed it over, casting an uneasy glance at the three men chained up in the cell.

Good. Be afraid, Tamsa. Be very afraid of what I will do to you if I can get my hands on you, Thislen thought, hoping the threat read clear on his face.

Garridan dampened the cloth and passed it back to her. "Don't worry. You have our word as noblemen of Astera—we won't harm your brother. We'll put the two of you somewhere safe after you help us understand. Help us clear all of this up, yes? Let's start with something easy. What is your name, miss?"

She ran her tongue over her lip before she answered. "Tamsa."

"What are their names?" Garridan asked, gesturing toward the cell.

"My brother's name is Aften. The tall, dark one is Darran. The other is Thislen. Is he a Bestant?"

"A bastard," Avasten corrected, rubbing his chin as he studied Thislen quietly from across the room. "Just a bastard."

"Miss Tamsa, how do you know all of them? Well, aside from Aften," Garridan asked with a smile. He knelt before her chair.

Tamsa's lips twitched, but she did not relax. "Darran lives with us. He has for years and years now. Thislen…he came to us a few days ago."

"And you let him onto your ship for the night? The girl, too?"

Thislen held his breath.

Tamsa nodded. "Yes, sir. My Lord, I mean. We're just fisherfolk. We live right outside the city, and we usually berth there. We had been in town getting supplies. We were nearly late leaving the island because we bought two big crates of salt and it took us ages to get them back to the docks. They came running up at sunset, begging us for our help."

There wasn't a flicker in her expression as she lied. She kept an earnest, wary look on her face the entire time. *She's a damn good actor,* Thislen thought. *I almost buy it, and I was there. Let's hope* they *do.*

"Did you see the markings painted on their faces?"

"Yes, my Lord."

"How did they convince you to let them aboard?"

"They said they were falsely accused. They said they got married in secret and made some powerful nobles angry. The way they talked about it, I thought the girl, Mila, was a noblewoman. She was the worst. She kept clinging to Darran and Aften, sobbing and wailing for them to let her on the ship." Bitterness crept into Tamsa's voice.

Darran sat up with a rattle of chains, lips parting, but Thislen raised a few fingers and shot the scout captain a warning glance. The Nattfolk lapsed into silence, slumping back against the wall. When he looked at Tamsa through the bars, he caught the sidelong glance of Avasten. Their quiet exchange had not gone unnoticed.

"You must understand, my Lords, Aften has a soft heart. We didn't know the truth. We still don't," Tamsa pleaded.

"They lied to you," Garridan agreed soothingly. "They tricked you. It was cruel. What did they do next?"

"We took them to our home. They stayed with us for a few days and paid us with pendant necklaces. We'd never seen anything so nice before. They told us they knew how to get more and convinced Darran and Aften to follow their plan. They said you were evil, undeserving. They said we should rob you and then run away with the wealth. *He* said he knew how to rob you." She pointed at Thislen.

He lifted his chin, gaze hard. *Lying about Mila and me won't save the Nattfolk, no matter how hard you try.*

"Pendants? May I see yours?" Garridan asked, holding out his hand.

Tamsa pulled her beaten metal pendant and gave it to the lordling without protest. Garridan tipped it this way and that in his hand, studying it beneath the lantern's light. He gestured at the guards. The two men crossed to the cell without a word and opened the door.

Aften was red in the face, trembling as he tried to contain his fury. He growled when the guards approached.

He doesn't understand. She has *to give it over, or else her delicate lie will fall to pieces around her,* Thislen mused. He hadn't given her enough credit, it seemed. It was a clever tale.

Quietly, he gave the Nattfolk scouts a subtle gesture. Aften caught it. He jerked his head back and glowered but made no other move as a guard took his pendant. Darran sat perfectly still.

Thislen did his best to lean away from the men as they fished his pendant from underneath his fine linen shirt. He was glad his first instinct upon waking up had been to pull his ring from around his neck and tuck it into his boot. If they had found that, everything would be much worse for all of them.

No time to waste. I may not know her plan, but I need to play along with my role in the tale.

"Stop it. Leave me alone," He snapped, chains rattling as he tried to catch all the pendants. "Those are mine by rights."

"What rights?" Garridan asked heartlessly. "Bring them to me."

Thislen surged to his feet. The cuffs caught at his wrists, making him stumble and fall to his knees as they bit into his skin. "Those are mine! Give them back!"

The guardsmen closed the cell and deposited their stolen goods into Garridan's waiting hand. The affable-looking torturer gave Thislen a broad smile. "I'm afraid not. Whatever you stole is mine, now."

He passed the pendants to Soren Bestant. The golden-haired noble lounged in his chair, turning the charms over one by one. "What interesting crests," he murmured, studying the markings etched upon them intently. "These look quite old."

"They're nothing," Thislen shouted.

"Silence, cousin."

Garridan cleared his throat. "Now, Tamsa. You were caught on Soren's ship, in his cabin..." He trailed off expectantly.

"I never wanted to do this, I swear. I was against it from the start," she said hastily, leaning forward. She clutched the forgotten cloth in her hands. "Aften is young and stupid. I was trying to stop him. He's easily swayed. He didn't know any better. Please, my Lords. Please have mercy on us."

"I am *not*. Shut up, Tamsa."

"Quiet!" Garridan snapped, shooting a glare at Aften. "Your sister is trying to save your life. I suggest you let her."

Soren cleared his throat delicately, holding one of the pendants up to the light. "Pardon me for interrupting, Garridan. It seems I have a few questions for the young lady." He was calm. Too calm.

Does he know?

"Tell me, Miss Tamsa, what did Mila mean when she began to talk about the Vaim? Up on the deck."

Thislen froze. *Tamsa doesn't know about the curse, not unless Aften told her. If she has a tell, they'll know when she's being honest.* The truth could ruin everything.

Tamsa faltered, lifting a hand to the bruising by her eye for a moment at the mention of Mila. Her shoulders slumped. "I'm sorry, my Lord. I don't really know."

Soren let out a thoughtful hum. "I find I believe you, my dear. In fact, I find I believe that none of you poor fisherfolk knew anything about the ghosts. Did *you* tell Mila about the Vaim, Thislen?"

Thislen lifted his chin, gaze steady and intent. *Believe whatever you want. I am not afraid of you any longer,* he thought.

The remarkable thing was he meant it. He had spent his entire life running and hiding from people whose powerful existence hinged on one secret and a few vials hidden away somewhere. All it would take to break their hold on Astera was a blow in the right place, and that power would crumble away. There was nothing left to fear except dying before they succeeded. *I won't let that happen. I don't know how yet, but I won't.*

"That answers my last few questions." Soren didn't look away from Thislen as he spoke. He rose from his chair, pocketing the pendants. He tucked his hands behind his back as he crossed to stand before the bars of the cell.

Ancestors, let our lies have worked, Thislen prayed.

"Put Mila Ominir back on the island tonight. Without the help of kind-hearted people, she will cease to be my problem. Fasten her to the stocks outside the Justica to ensure she does not escape this time."

Thislen narrowed his eyes.

"Are you certain, Soren?" Avasten asked, studying his nails.

"If I cannot own her family line, I will end it. Besides, I think we have something much more interesting to deal with."

Thislen did his best not to look relieved. *They don't realize you can survive on the island at night. The Vaim won't harm her. She'll be found by the Nattfolk.* His heart rose, and then plummeted. *She'll be found by the Nattfolk and shipped so far away that she'll never see Astera again.*

His chest went cold. His frown deepened.

Soren Bestant's smug smile grew as he watched the muted reaction. "Now, we of the Ruling Council are men of our words. Tamsa and her dear brother are to be spared for their help. We understand they meant no harm. However, to ensure they have *thoroughly* learned their lesson, tie that one out, too." He pointed imperiously at Darran.

"What? No!" Tamsa shouted, rising from her seat. Garridan's hand on her shoulder pushed her abruptly back down.

"No, don't touch him. Darran!" Aften shouted, straining at his bonds. His voice cracked.

Darran stared slack-jawed at Thislen as the guards came in and unfastened him. They hauled him to his feet.

"But Thislen, I'll die," he breathed, eyes wide and face ashen.

The bottom of Thislen's stomach dropped away. Darran's drawn, pinched face and wide dark eyes—would they join the ghosts that haunted him?

"Find Soren!"

"Why?"

"But Thislen—I'll die."

He sagged back against the wall. *What have I done?* What had Tamsa done? She had orchestrated a beautiful lie that had gotten the pendants taken away without revealing what they were, making her tale utterly believable. In telling Darran to let that happen and *helping* Tamsa with her lies, Thislen had condemned him.

No, not again.

"Let it be a lesson to you and your brother both, Tamsa," Soren said over their protests, "that you should not trust strangers or criminals. Put Tamsa back in the cell. We'll ensure their story is the same come dawn tomorrow before we decide what to do with them."

Dawn. Come dawn, it would already be too late for Mila. It would be too late for Darran. Come dawn, there would be another person dead. Another ghost would haunt Thislen forever.

I could have stopped it all.

He turned a fierce scowl onto Soren. The Lord Bestant had not stopped smiling the entire time he played his cruel and twisted games with his new toys.

"I believe we will have a most interesting day together, Thislen. You and I have so much to discuss," Soren said, wrapping his fingers around the bars.

"I doubt it," Thislen spat.

"You misunderstand me, cousin. You won't have a choice."

18

Mila spent hours in an overwhelmingly empty cabin. No bars, no windows, and no bunk filled the small space. She beat on the door until her hands were sore, until her arms were tired, until she had shouted herself hoarse.

This is all Tamsa's fault. We had half a chance, and she ruined it.

That didn't help her escape. It didn't help her or her friends. She had brought nothing but pain and disappointment since the day she left her shop. *I never should have left home. What was I thinking? That adventure would be worth it? That nothing bad could happen to me? Astera is a rotten apple, all glitter on the surface and worms underneath.*

Mila slid down the wall, sitting in dazed silence until she heard the lock click. The guards came in, each grabbing an arm and dragging her unceremoniously up the stairs to the deck. They emerged into late afternoon sunlight that stung her eyes. While her eyes adjusted, more men swarmed her.

Mila shouted and struggled as her hands were wrestled behind her back and tied fast. Then the guards picked her up, catching her kicking feet and hobbling them together. The rope was rough against her wrists and too tight around her ankles. They chafed as she twisted and strained against her bonds.

When they set her down, she stumbled and fell to her knees. It took all her balance to keep from toppling all the way forward. The guards moved away, leaving her facing another bound figure. His features were slack, his face ashen, his eyes blank.

"Darran—" She gasped, struggling to find her feet. Despite the crowd of guardsmen and lords around her, she was determined to get to his side.

For, of course, there were lords amongst the guardsmen. Soren and Avasten were there. Garridan, no doubt, was below. *Ancestors, please protect Thislen and Aften.*

Avasten Barnweir stepped between her and the scout captain as Mila got close, stopping her with a hand on her shoulder as he knelt before her. "I would appreciate it if you would wait a moment, Mila. We haven't brought the rowboat around yet."

"Rowboat?" Mila echoed numbly, staring at the redhead. Her gaze drifted to the sea that surrounded them. Ship Artaith was already out on the water. Not more than a few ship lengths away, the bulk of *The Brig* sat at its berth. The dome of the Justica rose behind it. The sun was just lowering toward the horizon, daylight bleeding away steadily in the red-streaked sky. "Wait, you're going to—"

"We are," Avasten interrupted with a small, cold smile.

"But you can't!" *The Nattfolk will ship me off, or worse.*

"I assure you that we can. Your fate has already been decided, Mila. Why, we even left the docks early. All for the pleasure and honor of escorting you to the stocks beside the Justica."

"I never stood trial for this. You said if I survived a night on Astera—"

"But you did *not* survive a night upon the island, did you?" Soren stood just behind Darran, his arms folded over his chest. "You snuck off of it, taking advantage of others. Quite slippery of you, Mila. Quite clever. I admit that I underestimated you."

What is he talking about? I never...

Avasten reached out, long soft fingers pushing a lock of hair behind her ear.

Mila pulled her head away from his hands with a scoff. "I didn't do anything for *you* to think I'm clever. I did what I had to do to survive."

"As you wish," Soren said dismissively.

"If you survive another evening on the island by some miracle, Mila Ominir, I look forward to the pleasure of presiding over your execution myself," Avasten murmured.

Mila believed him. The tip of her tongue went dry and her mind raced, searching for a clever retort to mask her growing dread.

"Avasten, you boor. There's no need for that. She won't survive." Soren pulled Mila to her feet, sliding his arm around her waist and pulling her close. "Shame you made the wrong choice, Mila. We could have had such fun."

Disgusting, disrespectful monster!

Then she had an idea. She leaned forward, tucking her face against Soren's neck. He sucked in a small breath and held it, as if in awe. "Changed your mind, have you?" he murmured, clearly pleased.

Mila bit the join between his shoulder and neck savagely. Soren shouted, shoving her bodily away and sending her careening to the deck. Guardsmen swarmed them, hauling Mila away between two of them before she could turn on anyone else. Lord Bestant was left clutching at his neck in shock, checking for bleeding.

"You think me meek and helpless? I have news for you, Soren Bestant. I will *never* be weak again. If I survive this night, it will be with the sole goal of ruining your entire life, no matter *what* you do with the rest of mine!" Mila shouted, voice cracking.

Never had she been so close to understanding her greatest grandfather's need for revenge. The ember within her was a pool of molten lava, threatening now to erupt at the slightest provocation. Part of her yearned for him to press the issue, to push her over the precipice. What was on the other side?

Lord Soren's cheeks grew bright and red. It spread to his ears and down the length of his neck, vanishing beneath his ruffled collar. His hands were shaking. "You insolent bitch," he hissed between clenched teeth. "Take her out of my sight this instant!"

"To the rowboat, gentlemen, if you please." Avasten took Soren's arm, guiding him toward the cabin on the foredeck.

They don't even plan to stay and watch their handiwork this time? Ha! Good. Run away, you cowards. Run away from me.

She struggled against the guardsmen even though she knew there was no escape. There was nowhere to go, no way to swim or fight her way out. Darran was towed along after her, blank as a piece of paper and still as could be. His eyes were hollow and empty. He hadn't said a word.

A rowboat bobbed below the ship at the bottom of a swaying rope ladder. An Artaith guardsman was already waiting at the prow of the small vessel, his legs drawn in.

"How do you expect me to climb down that when you've trussed me like a deer?" Mila said.

The guards pushed her off the side of the ship.

For a sickening moment, her stomach was left behind. A scream was torn from her lips as she watched the deck fly away above her. She squeezed her eyes closed, bracing for impact with the frigid water—but it never came. Instead, she hit the bottom of the rowboat with a *splash* and a *thud,* the air driven from her lungs.

The guard on the prow pulled her toward him. Dazed, she did not resist.

A moment later, another shout rent the air. Darran landed beside her, the boat rocking wildly from the impact. Before either of them had fully regained their wits, they were lashed to the bottom of the rowboat shoulder to shoulder. Two more guards climbed down the wobbling rope ladder. They put the oars into the water and began to pull them across the waves.

Her arms were pinned beneath her, slowly going numb and tingly. Her legs were uncomfortably cramped. She couldn't move. None of that was as pressing as the fact they were running out of time; *she* was running out of time.

"Darran," she whispered, voice low and urgent. She tried not to move her lips. "Darran, what's going on? What's happened?"

He wheezed softly, trying to adjust his own contorted position. His dark eyes were wide, and his pulse was racing in his neck. "They're going to leave us to the Vaim. Your pendant—did they take your pendant?"

"No. No, why?" Mila went cold from more than the chill prickle of sea spray that spattered over them as they crested a shallow wave. "Did they take yours?"

Darran nodded. His jaw trembled. "I'll be alright."

Liar. Ninian said you needed yours.

"You don't have to be alright. I'll get my pendant to you. Somehow." She promised.

He gave her a small smile that stretched his face the wrong way, a smile he didn't believe. He knew the same thing she did.

He's going to die, and there's nothing we can do.

In the distance, the call of ships' bells began to sound over the water as the residents of Astera loaded aboard for the evening. It was the second time Mila had been rowed to shore this way, and this time was all the worse. Despite the first trip being shrouded in uncertainty, despite not knowing if she could trust Thislen or his outlandish claims, the first trip had come to an end with them alive and together.

This time, Thislen wasn't here to help her. She didn't know where he was and in what state. She didn't know what had become of Aften, either. She didn't know what tale Tamsa had told.

She wouldn't have a chance to ask Darran and find out. Even if the Nattfolk saved her, they wouldn't arrive in time to save Darran. She would watch him die in front of her, and then she would be banished from her only home.

I wouldn't be surprised if they blamed me for Darran's death and for Aften and Tamsa's capture. Rendyn already hated me. I'll be gone, and Thislen and Aften will be trapped with those...those monsters.

Part of her wished she had never followed that small voice inside that told her to leave home. If she had never given in to it, would she be happier? If she had learned to live as Soren's bride, would she be all right?

No, that isn't what I want. Not now, not anymore. I want to help my island, and I want to save the people of my homeland. I can do it, too. I just have to survive. Let the Nattfolk send me away; I'll come back as soon as I can.

The Nattfolk didn't murder people, they had said, but she wondered if they might make an exception. After all, she'd been personally responsible for the end of the Sivivan lineage after hundreds of years. Had that ever happened before? It *was* her fault that Aften and Darran were in trouble. It was *her* plan that had put all of them here.

Mila knew with a growing, resounding certainty that she was no leader. Her attempts to be one had failed. Her feeble bid to save the residents of Astera, none of whom had *asked* her to save them, would vanish with her. Who was to say if she would actually have that second chance?

Who was to say she deserved one?

The shore loomed before them. Quietly, she lay her head against Darran's shoulder. "I'm sorry."

"Don't be. It isn't your fault. I'm glad we tried." Despite the encouragement in his words, every one fell from his lips like lead. "If this is how I go, at least I can be glad of that. We tried, for Astera. For Aften." His voice cracked when he said the scout's name.

Mila felt a lump start in her throat as the rowboat pulled up to a dock near the base of the Justica with a *clunk*. "Can you imagine what it would have been like? The future we wanted for our home?"

He gave a soft, sad laugh. "Not at all." They were silent for a moment before he spoke again. "I wish I had told him."

Mila didn't have to ask what Darran had to tell. It had been clear to her for some time the two had feelings for one another—feelings neither had confessed yet. Her eyes stung.

The guards pulled them from the bottom of the rowboat. Mila did not struggle. It was her burden to bear witness to Darran's end for her foolishness.

The square before the Justica was empty, the people having left for their ships and safety perhaps moments earlier. The air was still heavy with the scent of meat pies and sugared pastries. The guards marched their captives across the cobbles to the stocks that stood on one side of this small market.

Great wooden poles had been placed on their end in the island's stone long ago. Cuffs made of split wooden planks had been affixed to the tops by great chains that could be pulled and adjusted and locked in place. It was to these that Darran and Mila were fastened, the biting ropes exchanged for the rough edge of the weathered wood.

The guards didn't bother to shorten the chains, though they did ensure that neither captive could free their wrists. In silence, the strange men in their colorful livery turned away, leaving Mila and Darran to the sinking sun.

Mila didn't even wait for them to leave the square before she began to writhe and twist. She worked the pendant awkwardly from around her neck, nearly choking herself with the edge of the wooden cuffs as she pulled it free. It was awkward to shuffle toward Darran with the chain clasped in one hand. Her ankles were still hobbled. So were his.

What was the point of this indignity? To make things easier for the Vaim? Those cruel bastards.

"Darran! Come over here. Put your head down."

He strained, leaning his full weight against his chains to put his head as close to her as possible. She twisted, pulling against the cuffs to try and reach him—but she couldn't.

"Throw it!" he pleaded desperately.

Mila did. There was a *clink* and the soft hiss of the chain as the pendant fell to the cobblestones at Darran's feet. He tried to shift his foot out to pull it closer, but the ropes around his ankles prevented him from doing more than nudging it. Mila watched with rising horror.

He stilled, a small and broken smile on his face. "Well. There's not much more that we can do, is there?"

A breeze cold and heavy blew through the empty square, redolent with the smell of salt.

Darran inhaled deeply. "I just want to say...we've only known one another a few days, but I've never met anyone who just takes things in stride as easily as you do. I've never met anyone so determined to see things fixed around here, to see things be different. My father used to tell me you have to be flexible to survive but always on the move toward the next horizon. I never understood what he meant until you showed up."

The lump was back in her throat. Her eyes stung. Mila tipped her head toward the sky, blinking rapidly. *I will not cry for him while he still lives,* she vowed. Inky darkness was spreading overhead.

"When they find me, is there anything you want me to pass on?" she asked, voice cracking.

"Tell my mother I wanted to change the world. Tell her I thought it was worth it. Tell her I love her. And if you ever see Aften again, tell him—"

"Ho! Here, over here!"

A clatter sounded in an alleyway nearby. Darran fell silent, and Mila jumped. Quickly, she looked to the west—but there was still orange in the sky. *Foolish girl, the Vaim can't talk,* she chided. But if the sun hadn't set yet, and it wasn't the ghosts, then who...?

A shadow separated itself from the darkness of a nearby alley. "It's Darran." It was the same voice as before.

Darran nearly went limp with relief, staggering with a rattle of the chains holding him fast. "Trevon! Hurry, they took my pendant."

"What? Where?" Trevon was at their side in moments, dressed in the mottled gray and brown clothing of the Nattfolk scouts.

"On the ground, here."

Ancestors be praised, he's saved! We're saved!

Trevon stooped to scoop the pendant off the ground right as the last of the sunlight vanished. A groan echoed through the streets. The hunched and malformed shapes of the Vaim began to drag themselves out of the shadowy recesses of the city. Darran went rigid, tensing from head to toe. Mila strained at her bonds, meeting the red eyes of the specters as they burst into being all around her, feeling her breath catch in her throat.

They won't hurt me. It didn't make her feel any better.

Trevon flung the chain over Darran's head and shoved the pendant down his shirt. A Vaim lurched toward him. Darran shouted, squeezing his eyes shut.

Mila heard a soft whistle of air, though nothing stirred around her. She felt a strange tingle in Darran's direction. The Vaim stopped their advance. Instead, the specters turned to coil around the Nattfolk like serpents, their burning eyes fixed on Mila.

No matter how much she told herself they would not harm her, Mila's heart still hammered beneath her ribs like it would run away without her given half a chance.

More Nattfolk scouts appeared, working their way through the shadowy specter's ranks. They cut the ropes from Darran's ankles and picked the lock that held his cuffs in place. They spoke together so quietly that Mila couldn't hear them over the rising murmur of the ghosts.

The Vaim circled Mila like curious hounds, lifting and lowering their shadowy hands inches away from her arms, her face, her hair. Each time they reached out, they got closer and closer. She could almost understand their whispers now. They were expectant and hopeful. Did she find it? Did she save them? When they found out she didn't have the vials, what would happen? Would they grow angry? Were they angry with Ninian? *Would* they hurt her?

Mila heard the chain rattle as the cuffs fell away from Darran's wrists. She twisted to offer her own out—but the Nattfolk were leaving.

"Hey!" Darran shouted. "Where are you going? We have to help Mila."

Trevon, the captain of this second patrol, turned to give Mila a once over. His brow was creased. His teeth worried at his lower lip for a moment. "Rendyn said only to find your patrol. He said to leave the Solfolk out of it. We already had to come aboveground during the day to find you. They even pulled a patrol out of retirement. We had to break all our rules to find you lot, and we still haven't found Aften or Tamsa. If we bring back the Solfolk girl and *not* his children—"

"Her name is Mila," Darran said hotly. "You're a damn fool if you think you should leave behind the only hope we have of actually saving Rendyn's precious daughter. We need her."

"She isn't *our* hope. I don't even know her. Come on, Darran, we have to go."

Mila felt as if she were sinking into a deep pool of water. She couldn't bring herself to inhale, afraid she might drown if she did. Voices sounded further and further away, wavering in her ears until she could hardly tell where the Vaim's whispers ended, and the discussion of her fate began. She was staring into a sea of dark, indistinct bodies and flickering red eyes, catching only glimpses of the scouts beyond the crowd of the dead.

They're going to leave me. She would spend the entire night tied to this post. The Vaim may or may not murder her or drag her away to her grandfather's ghost, or she would be discovered here come morning light. When she was found still alive, she would be killed by Soren Bestant. *There's no way he'd let me go again, not after all of this.*

I tried so hard to get away from him. I chose death countless times. All of it was for nothing! Come dawn, I will have lost everything.

A tear rolled down her cheek. With a gasp, she drew in a sharp breath. It shattered the illusion around her, driving every whisper and the trailing talon fingers along her arms and cheeks into sharp focus. The pressure in her chest swelled into a single scream.

"Wait!"

Darran had not left her. The Nattfolk scouts stood just beyond him, all five startled into sudden silence at her outburst.

"I *can* help. I know where Aften and Tamsa are, and more important—I know Lord Soren Bestant and his cronies. I know how to live during the day. I can help you all."

"Help us all. Right," one scout scoffed.

"I can stop the Vaim."

Trevon snorted, waving a hand dismissively. "No one can stop the ghosts."

"She can," Darran said firmly, emphatically. "And if we don't take her with us, we'll never get to Tamsa and Aften on time. They're going to be tortured. Tamsa lied during their first interrogation; they don't yet know about the Nattfolk—but how long will that last? How long do we have to waste? Mila already has answers that can help us. Let her help!"

The scouts murmured amongst one another, each watching Trevon, waiting for him to decide.

Darran's voice wavered. "They're my scouts. All of them. Even her. I'm responsible for all of this."

"We're not going to debate this, Darran," Trevon insisted. He marched over, grabbing Darran by the arm.

Darran jerked free with a wordless shout, storming over to Mila's side. "You don't get it. I'm not leaving her. Go on, then, get out of here! We don't need you. I'm helping Aften."

Long fingers ran through Mila's hair. She jerked around to stare at the Vaim withdrawing its clawed hand. They were crowding closer, pressing her against Darran's back. "Darran," she gasped.

"Give me a pendant for Mila, Trevon."

"No. I'm under orders."

"Give it to me!" Darran bellowed. He pushed through the sea of Vaim to resume his argument with the older scout captain, the two of them vanishing behind a forest of dark arms. The spirits crowded all the closer, plucking at her clothes and her hair, tracing the tips of their fingers down her cheeks. They hissed softly amongst themselves.

Where? Where, girl? Where is it? Give it to us. Show it to us. Take it to him, we'll take you to him...

A scream escaped Mila as the Vaim grasped her wrists, cool fingers firm against her skin. They pulled, pressure mounting until it hurt. *They're going to break my hands or tear them off!* She screamed again.

Darran appeared, shouldering the Vaim aside. He bore a knife in one hand and a pendant in the other. Wordlessly, he flung the cord over her neck. The talisman warmed quickly against her skin.

The Vaim went strangely still. The ones holding her let go in muted surprise. Their heads swiveled on their long, crooked necks as she vanished abruptly from their sight. It was only then Mila realized she was trembling like a sail in a storm.

The scout captain bent to cut the rope around her ankles.

"Darran, even if we take her back to the Commons, *you* will have to convince Rendyn that she can help. He's already going to be furious with you, too." Trevon lectured, stepping out from behind the milling ghosts as they drifted away.

"I don't care," Darran snapped.

"I'll plead my own case," Mila said. Her voice sounded shrill and high in her ears. She wondered if she looked as lightheaded as she felt, if her face was pale as snow. She ran her tongue over her lips, but both were dry. "I'll speak to him. Please, take me back to the Commons. All I want is to help. All I want is to fix this."

Darran held out his hand insistently, staring Trevon dead in the eyes. The staring contest between the two captains went on for what felt like an age. It ended as abruptly as it began. With a snort, the older Nattfolk slapped a set of lockpicks into Darran's waiting hand.

"This is probably the worst idea I've ever had," Trevon muttered.

The cuffs fell away with a clatter and a rattle. Mila drew her hands against her chest, rubbing life back into her wrists one at a time. She turned to look at the little dock they had been marched down. Beyond, out on the water, lay the glittering portholes of ships at berth. They were glimmers of light, of hope, in a sea of shadow.

"Let's get going," Trevon said.

"Just a moment," Mila said softly. She stepped away, walking to the end of the dock and stopping just at the water's edge. The sea slapped against the posts, sloshing quietly beneath her. Darran had followed. She could feel him standing just behind her.

"Aften is out there," he said quietly at last.

Mila took his hand in hers. It was rough and calloused, and she was grateful as his fingers curled around hers. Her hand was small and cold, and she was glad of the warmth. "Thislen is out there, too."

"Tell me you have a plan, Solfolk."

I didn't want to take this chance again, not this soon—but I have no choice. So many lives hinge on me, on my ability to convince everyone that I know what I'm doing.

I could go home. I could just slip away right now, go and hide and wait for dawn. I could just go home, and my father and I could leave Astera. We can take Evelie. We can take Ivan.

But if I leave, the Vaim will haunt these people forever. Won't that haunt me*?*

"I'm beginning to think of one," she said at last. "It's time for some changes around here, though. Starting with me."

Darran glanced at her, brow furrowing. "What do you mean?"

The molten core inside of her warmed her slowly from head to toe. Her heart beat steadily, becoming the sounding call of a war drum as she stared at the ships and imagined the smug, too-calm face of Soren Bestant.

"We can't leave things this way. We know what the Vaim are now, and we know how to stop them. We know where the vials are, too. Do you know what my father used to say to me, Darran?"

Darran shook his head.

"One person. It only takes one person to change the world." Mila looked at the Nattfolk beside her. "We have two. We're well on our way to being an army."

"An army!" The scout captain let out a short, bitter laugh.

Mila nodded firmly, turning back toward the water. "I know we can change minds. I know we can do this. And I know something else."

"What?"

After everything she had been through, one thing was abundantly clear.

"I can't be a Solfolk anymore."

The time for secrets had passed. Mila had a lot of preparation to do and plans to lay. It was time to stop hiding from everyone in Astera and start trying to help them. For *his* sake. A newfound fire burned in Mila's eyes and soul, straightening her spine. First things first.

I have to get on that boat.

END OF PART ONE

ACKNOWLEDGEMENTS

This story began a long time ago, with an outline looked over by Misty, and a lot of support from TWT - The Writing Tribe. Notably from Venessa, Sean, and Rachel. Extra thanks to Rachel Brune, for helping me shape it up for submission.

Thanks to Falstaff and John for picking it up, and to Claire and Lucienne for telling me that, based on this book, I had something going for me.

And credit where credit is due! Thank you, Kara and Liz, for reading the book long before it was decent, and reading it again once it was. Thank you Kyla for your help with the map, and Gretchen with the cover pitch.

Thanks to Dillion for always making sure I eat at least once a day when I'm on deadlines, and for being one of the best human beings I know.

And I know I'm forgetting a thousand people and a thousand things, so thank you to them and those!

ABOUT THE AUTHOR

October K Santerelli hails from the Rocky Mountains of Colorado, where he lives with his two dogs. He loves palm trees and the snow. Often he can be found traveling the country to speak at conventions to readers and writers alike, especially those who are LGBTQ+ like him. He also does work as an LGBTQ+ sensitivity reader.

FRIENDS OF FALSTAFF

Thank You to All our Falstaff Books Patrons, who get extra digital content each month! To be featured here and see what other great rewards we offer, go to www.patreon.com/falstaffbooks.

PATRONS

Dino Hicks
John Hooks
John Kilgallon
Larissa Lichty
Travis & Casey Schilling
Staci-Leigh Santore
Sheryl R. Hayes
Scott Norris
Samuel Montgomery-Blinn
Junkle

Made in the USA
Columbia, SC
17 March 2023